NICHOLAS caught up with her, catching her by the arm in order to swing her around against him. Crimson took a sharp breath of surprise as he pushed her urgently back against the wall. His hands stayed on her shoulders, the palms pressing just above her breasts.

"How could I resist the setting," he murmured, bringing his face close to hers. "Doesn't it bring to mind Madame's staircase at Saint-Cloud when you first aroused such passion in me?" he inquired sardonically.

Crimson tried to push him away. "Don't speak to me of your—your passion!" she spat at him. "Let me go!"

He was laughing now, mocking her. "Oh, my dear, how can you keep denying yourself—and me! Come, we both know you want me to make love to you."

And before she could stop him, his mouth was upon hers, mastering her until she surrendered to the desire she could not defy. : . .

CRIMSON GLORY

by

Theresa Conway

FAWCETT GOLD MEDAL • NEW YORK

FOR RON

with all my heart

CRIMSON GLORY

© 1979 Theresa Conway

All rights reserved

Published by Fawcett Gold Medal Books, a unit of CBS
Publications, the Consumer Publishing Division of CBS Inc.

ISBN: 0-449-14112-8

Printed in the United States of America

10 9 8 7 6 5 4 3 2 1

PROLOGUE:
1650

The wind was driving the hard-falling rain in sheets against the sides of the coach, as it sped along the badly rutted country road that connected Oxford with London. The force of the thunderstorm was not unusual in England for June, but to the sobbing woman in the coach, it seemed only one more burden to be borne on this terrible night.

The man who was sitting opposite the woman looked at her without compassion—with, in fact, very little interest. His long, narrow face—framed in the collar-length brown hair, which was suspiciously long in these days of Oliver Cromwell's Roundheads—was lined with a deep frown of thoughtfulness.

When the woman let out a short scream at some distant thunder, the man drew his handkerchief from his cuff and presented it beneath her nose. She took it carefully in her fingers, as though afraid of touching him.

"Stop your blabbering, Deborah," he finally put in soberly. "We'll be in Oxford in another hour, providing this damnable rain does not impede us any more than it already has. For God's sake, woman, you act as though Cromwell himself, the old bastard, were hard on our heels with the entire cavalry!"

"Oh, James, I'm so frightened! I knew we should never have gone to London! I knew it. It was nearly the death of both of us. Cromwell's spies are everywhere, and he'll be informed now that you're a secret supporter of the king. They'll follow us to Oxford and arrest you! My God, and the baby due so soon!"

The man's dark features seemed to contract in brief pain and anger. "Don't yelp about that little bastard in your belly, Deborah," he said through clenched teeth. "God knows I would never have married you, had I but known that someone else's seed had already been well sown and was bearing fruit!"

The woman looked up contritely and tried to stop the sniveling that so irritated her husband. "I—I'm sorry, James. I know that you were sorely vexed when you—"

"Vexed!" He laughed in amazement. "Your choice of words astounds me, madam! Let us say 'enraged, furious,' to come more to the point! How could you have run to me and begged me to marry you for protection against the Roundheads, knowing all the time that some unlikely fool had already gotten you with child? It defies all sense of decency!"

His features took on a decidedly injured air as he glanced quickly beneath the oilskin curtain to look out the window. Deborah looked at her husband with an expression of mingled fear and exasperation. She moistened her lips with her tongue and dabbed at her eyes with the handkerchief.

"He wasn't a Roundhead," she said quietly after a moment.

He looked at her and she felt the weight of his stare like a heavy iron.

"It wasn't one of Cromwell's men, even though—even though they tried to take me when Father was arrested. It was a friend of my father's, a loyal supporter of the king. It was—"

"Silence! I don't care to hear your confession now, madam!" he said with a swiftness that belied his studied indifference of a moment before. "Whoever he was, he should not have been allowed to go unpunished. And the worst punishment I can think of for him would be to marry you!"

6

His cruel remark smote her like a blow and she pressed her hand to her eyes to stop the ready flow of tears. "James, I thought you would protect me. I thought you would understand more than anyone else. You and I had grown up together, and I think our fathers both wished for the marriage between us. I cannot help a mistake that I had already made. I was frightened then, too."

"You are always frightened of something," he cut in sarcastically.

"I *was!* He was handsome, one of the king's Cavaliers, and so ready to comfort me when I needed it. Things suddenly became different between us, and before I really knew—"

"He had skewered you like the strumpet you are!" her husband finished for her in mocking tones. "Well, that is all very interesting, Deborah, but I'm afraid I don't really care to know all the details of the affair."

"Oh, James, why can't you believe me when I say that I did not know that I was with child when I begged you to marry me? Do you think I would have brought such shame to you of my own will?"

"And when you found out, madam?" he asked her slyly. "When you found out, why then did you not do something about it?"

She looked at him with bewildered eyes. "What would I have been able to do?"

"There are ways of ridding oneself of an unwanted child while it is still in the womb. All women must know of such things."

He heard her indrawn breath of pain. "James! How could you even suggest such horror! It would be an awful sin against God to murder my unborn child. You know that it is against our faith!"

"Pah! Our faith! What has the Pope done to protect his faithful Catholics, who starve and go homeless because of a rabid dog that dares to sit on England's throne?" He snorted in disgust. "I should have divorced you on the day you came and told me."

"Why didn't you?" she asked dully. "You say you no

longer hold to your faith. It would not have been hard for you to obtain a release, under the circumstances."

He shrugged. "There was hardly time to worry about our personal problems when so much else was at stake. These secret meetings are becoming more and more dangerous. I, for one, would like to see them discontinued. Old Cromwell won't live forever, and his son is nothing but a milksop who'll be easy to overthrow. The king will be back on the throne soon enough without us risking our necks in his service while he dances and rides to the hunt with those damned Dutch!"

Lady Deborah Haviland fell silent, realizing that it would only further anger her husband should she attempt to explain her feelings to him. She thought of the man who had taken her virginity that fair September morning, the man who had loved her with passion and tenderness, and then had gone away to the war to be killed. His name hardly mattered. It would not conjure up the man himself. If only it could!

Lord, he had been a handsome soldier, with his glossy blond hair and the bright, tender eyes that flashed like green emeralds at the height of his passion. He had loved her as a man should love a woman—with fire and spirit, and afterwards, he had been nothing but tenderness. She had been at fault as much as he, she knew that. But so many things had conspired to bring about the event—her father's arrest for treason, the war so close at hand, her terror and her need for comfort. She swallowed the sob that welled so painfully in her throat, and she crushed the handkerchief to her lips.

Why had she ever turned to Lord James Haviland, she wondered not for the first time in her marriage. Of course, they had been neighbors all their lives and it had been more or less understood that they would be married someday. But even then, Deborah had been aware of his deceits, his immense vanity and pride. Why had she thought that he would be the right one to protect her?

That he had actually married her had been a curious thing. Perhaps his remembered oath to his dead father had prompted him to do it. Perhaps it had been the promise of

8

her rich dowry, as soon as her father was cleared of the charges. But her father had not been cleared. He had been put to death for treason, and all his lands forfeited to Cromwell. It must have been a blow to James, realizing that he had married a penniless woman, the daughter of an avowed enemy of the Lord Protector.

They had retired to a modest country home near Oxford, close enough to London to continue their underground activities with the faction that still served the king. And then, four months after their marriage, she had shown him her distended belly, proof that he could not possibly be the father of the fruit of her advanced pregnancy. He had not come near her bed since, as though fearing to contract some deadly disease. She had not been sorry for that, for his embraces were hard and insensitive, and she had already tasted those of a sweeter love.

A sudden jolting of the coach brought her out of her thoughts, and she glanced quickly to her husband in that fraction of time before the coach overturned in a deep pothole.

"James!"

The coach lay tilted on its side in the mire, the rain still beating heavily against its upturned side. Flung against the side lying against the ground, Deborah could not get her breath for a moment, and she struggled against her husband's weight, which was inadvertently crushing her.

James recovered himself at last and moved off of her so that she could breathe easier. He yelled for the driver to open the door so that they could climb out, but there was no answer above the pelting rain.

"God's blood! Where is that cursed driver?" he muttered between his teeth, attempting to gain a footing on the leather seat in order to hoist himself to the door. It took him ten minutes to throw open the door, thereby letting in the rain that drenched the huddled body of his wife.

He poked his head out and could barely see the body of the driver lying in the road. It looked as though the driver's neck might have been broken when he had been thrown from the vehicle, and James let out another curse, turning his head to look for lights in the distance.

"I can see a light off the road, perhaps a mile away," he called down to his wife, who had begun to groan softly. "I'll get out and give you a hand up. You'll have to pull yourself out, for I can't right the coach by myself, and it looks as though the driver is dead."

He pulled his cloak tightly around him, and, pushing with his hands against the side of the coach, managed to wriggle out of the door in order to kneel next to the aperture and thrust his hand in to clasp his wife's.

"Give me your hand!" he shouted to her roughly, when her fingers touched his palm and then slid off again.

"James, I—I think I've hurt myself. I have an awful pain in my side and I don't think—"

"Dammit, woman! The babe's more than three weeks away. You're all right, if you'll give me your hand. I'll have to leave you here otherwise to get help."

She obeyed through the mist of pain that was quickly descending on her. She feared being left alone more than injuring herself further as she forced herself to stand and climb slowly out of the coach. Once outside in the pelting rain, she had to clench her teeth to keep from screaming as the knifelike pain shot through her back, crippling her for a moment, so that she stood in the mud, unable to move.

"Thank God, the horses haven't all bolted," James muttered and went to unhitch them. It took him the better part of an hour to free them from the tangle of harness and reins. He was cursing when he finished, completely drenched, his hair hanging stringily about his face.

"You'll have to ride bareback, Deborah," he said to her, leading the horses over.

"I—I don't think I can manage to ride alone, James," she said faintly, her teeth chattering.

Her hair hung in rattails down her back, for she had lost her hat in the coach and had forgotten to bring it up with her. Angrily, he took off his own and put it on her head, noting with a certain grimness the way in which the jaunty feather was now lying wet and bedraggled across the shallow brim.

"Come on then. You have to ride behind me." He hoisted her up on the back of the horse and heard her moan sharply as she settled on it. "Hold onto my waist," he said, swinging up and urging the horse forward.

The horse shied at the sound of crackling thunder and reared up, nearly unseating both of them. Swearing horribly, James tried to calm it and finally was forced to walk the animal around the ruts and holes in the road, making the mile seem agonizingly far.

When they finally reached the light, they saw it was coming from a sturdy farmhouse on the outskirts of one of the numerous villages which dotted the countryside around London. Thankfully, James slid from the horse and led it to the door of the house, banging on the wood with his fist.

"Ho, there! We are two travelers in need of some shelter," James called out.

After a moment, a stout man came to the door, holding a candle, his plump wife peering around his shoulder, her eyes settling on the forlorn figure still on the horse with a start of disbelief.

"Lud, Sam, 'tis a poor woman and her husband. We must let them in!"

The man nodded and opened the door wider, while James went to lift Deborah off the horse. She nearly fell into his arms and, with surprise, James saw the pool of blood which ran down the horse's sides and was quickly washed away by the rain. He carried her half-fainting form inside, where it was dry and blessedly warm.

"My wife has been injured. Our coach overturned in the road," James explained, his mind still numb with shock at the sight of his wife, whose skirt was completely drenched with blood.

Her face was devoid of color and her lips looked blue in the wavering light. He laid her gently on a cot by the fire after taking off her cloak. The yeoman's wife bustled about, bringing water to boil on the fire and producing

11

clean cloths from a cupboard in the corner. She called to one of the wide-eyed children who had retreated to the loft above, and a girl, older than the others, detached herself and scampered back down the ladder.

"Annie, you watch the water while I undress the lady. Glory be, but she looks as though she's about to bring that babe into the world," she added under her breath, catching sight for the first time of the bulging belly.

She peeled off the sodden clothes and wrapped her in warm blankets, but they did not seem to lessen the trembling of her body. The wife shook her head, muttered a hurried prayer to God, and spread the blood-spattered thighs in order to see how far the birthing had come.

James, watching her with a distinct nausea, threw himself into a seat and absently accepted a mug of hot cider from the farmer. He watched as the woman pressed on his wife's stomach and put her ear to listen for the heartbeat of the child.

" 'Tis clear she'll not be able to sit in the birthing chair for this one," she muttered to herself, casting an eye toward one corner at a stout oaken chair fashioned with a large hole in the seat; in it, she, herself, had given healthy birth to all five of her children. "She'll not be able to rise from this bed for many days, that is to say, if she lives at all," she added.

Annie drew water from the kettle and filled a pewter jug with it. Then, according to her mother's instructions, she poured a little into a shallow basin and mixed it with ale so that it made up a lukewarm liquid. She fetched a knife from the cupboard drawer and a piece of rope, about which she wound a clean cloth.

"Put it in her mouth," her mother instructed, nodding to the moaning woman. "Bite down on it, mistress, when you feel a pain," she said soothingly.

Deborah hardly heard her, but bit down into the cloth instinctively, bearing down at the same time, feeling the birth pains growing more and more urgent. The babe wanted to be born. This would not be too difficult, she told herself.

Her eyes opened and saw the farmer's wife leaning over

her, laying warm cloths over her belly. She turned her head to look for James, and saw him sitting at the table, his face frozen in disbelief. She wished he would come to her and hold her hand, stroke her hair. But no, James was not like that. *He* would have done it—the father of this child. She remembered how he had stroked her unbound hair, spreading it over the grass and murmuring, "My crimson glory. . . . "

Deborah felt the pain, severe again, then receding, then ripping through her whole body. She felt as though she was lying in a pool of warmth and knew that she bled. She had seen the blood on the skirt that the woman had taken off her. Her chemise had looked as though it were dyed red. So much blood! Would the baby be strangled by it?

She continued to push, her teeth clearing the cloth and biting into the rope itself. Her hand reached out instinctively for James, but he did not see the gesture. The girl, who could not have been more than twelve, slipped her own hard little palm into hers and pressed gently. Deborah looked at her and wished she could smile at her, thank her in some way, but the rope was in her mouth and she could not speak. If they took the rope away, she would scream and scream with the pain.

"Ah, here it comes," breathed the farmer's wife.

Deborah pushed with what little strength she had left, and that last push seemed to take everything with it. She lay back against the cot, drained, feeling as though her chest were going to cave in. She could hear the slow, thick thudding of her own heart, and then a high wail, thin and uncertain. The babe!

The girl took the rope from her mouth and rubbed her aching jaws with her fingers. " 'Tis a girl, mistress, a tiny one."

"Let me see her," Deborah whispered tiredly. She felt suddenly overcome with exhaustion.

The woman was cutting the cord with a quick snap of the knife and then hurried the baby over to the basin, to bathe it in the warm liquid she had prepared. The baby continued to emit breathy little gasps that sounded as though at any moment they would cease altogether.

"She's a mite little, my lord, but not so bad as I feared. When was the birthdate to be?"

James did not answer. He was staring at the baby with a bleak look.

"Three m-more weeks," Deborah managed, suddenly afraid of James' expression.

The woman gave the baby to her daughter to wrap in blankets, and went back to Deborah. Deborah heard the gasp of dismay and knew that she still bled too much. The bedclothes felt sticky and wet all around her thighs and hips and seemed to be creeping up as high as her waist.

"Oh, mistress, you've suffered a terrible injury in your accident. I—I must find some way of binding you," the woman murmured, more to herself than to Deborah.

The farmwife began to knead at the stomach, knowing the afterbirth must come next, but knowing also that as long as it took her to massage the abdomen, it would also bring the flow of blood coming.

Deborah felt another jarring wrench somewhere inside her and saw the woman emptying the contents of the cloth into an earthen pot. She reached for a fresh cloth to position under her, but Deborah could see by her expression that it was hopeless. She would bloody all the poor woman's clean cloths before the night was through. Was she really going to die?

"Let me see her," she said a second time.

The girl brought the swaddled infant over to her. It seemed to be breathing normally now and its face was pink and round, the eyes screwed tightly shut. It was small, but so had Deborah been. She smiled, glad that her little girl would live. Something must survive from the sweetness of that night with the king's Cavalier. It was such a shame, though, to have to leave her so soon after bringing her into the world.

"Let me hold her," she whispered to Annie, who bent low to hear.

The baby was settled in her arms which could not quite find the strength to clasp it close. Somewhere below, she could hear the woman's hands tearing more cloths to bind between her legs, but she could feel nothing, no more

14

pain, nothing. She was numb to the waist, a numbness that seemed to be creeping upward with alarming rapidity.

Deborah craned her neck with an effort to kiss the moist little head on which a mist of red fuzz could be seen. *This child is her mother's image,* she thought. *Her mother's hair. Her crimson glory.*

"My lady—I cannot—I cannot—" the farmer's wife was saying.

"It's all right," Deborah murmured softly and gazed once more at her child.

"Is there a name you would wish for the child, mistress?" the girl called Annie was saying, pressing a corner of her apron to her eyes.

Deborah smiled, but she was not seeing the girl's anxious face. She saw the handsome face of her beloved as he looked tenderly into her eyes and stroked her hair.

"My crimson glory—" Deborah murmured softly, and her arms relaxed around the sleeping infant as her eyes closed.

PART ONE:
Exile in France

1

"Make a wish, my lamb, and then blow all of your candles out! You must blow hard, as hard as you can," the young woman admonished her ten-year-old charge, whose birthday the two of them were celebrating quietly in the maidservant's quarters in the attic.

"Oh, but Annie, do you think I will blow them all out?" inquired the little girl, pushing from her cheeks her abundant hair, hair that had darkened considerably from the downy crimson of her birth and was now a deep, smooth auburn.

"How can you ask me such a thing!" the maid sighed, feigning surprise. "You've got more breath in your little body than anyone I know. You never stop chattering and running about, until it makes me lose my breath just to watch you!"

The little girl giggled at the thought and her bright aquamarine eyes glanced up at the other girl with sudden adoration. "Oh, Annie, you do love me as much as I love you, don't you?" she whispered, and for a moment the childishly grinning mouth trembled uncertainly.

Struck by the wistful beauty in the child's face, Annie reached over to enfold the girl in her arms. "Oh, my precious lamb, of course I love you. More than my life, I love you."

"More than that stableboy I saw you kissing last night

in the courtyard?" the girl pressed, happily snuggled to her bosom.

Annie gave a start of surprise. "Crimson! Were you watching from your bedroom window?"

Crimson pouted for a moment, then sighed. "Yes, I was, but only for a little time. I—I suppose Jacques is nice enough," she conceded.

Annie burst into laughter. "I like Jacques, Crimson. He has been very kind to me, here in France where I am truly a foreigner. But I don't want you looking out your bedroom window on any more nights. You should have been asleep!"

"All right." The answer was reluctant, but after another quick hug from Annie, the girl laughed again and turned her attention back to the study of the glowing candles on the sugarcake, made especially for her by the cook, Margot, who had thereby risked a scolding from her mistress, the Marquise d'Onges.

"Now, my curious baggage, will you or will you not make that wish?"

Crimson drew a deep breath and shut her eyes tightly, then opened them and blew out the candles in one puff. She clapped her hands, her eyes shining and looked to Annie again.

"Shall I get my wish now?" she demanded. "Can I tell you what I wished for?"

Annie laughed. "If you tell me, it might not come true."

The girl tossed her head. "Then I will tell you anyway, for I know it will never happen. I wished that you were my mother, my real mother, Annie."

"You're a dear child, Crimson," Annie murmured, touched. She kissed her on the cheek and then brought out the small package she had been hiding in the folds of her skirt. "Happy birthday," she added.

Crimson squealed in delight and turned the small parcel over and over, trying to guess what was inside, fingering the plain brown wrapping and rubbing her nail over the red and white ribbon. Finally, unable to bear it any longer, she tore at the wrappings and opened the box inside.

"Oh, Annie, it is beautiful!" she exclaimed, holding up

the small, wooden figure of a little girl holding a flower basket. It had been painted in bold colors that delighted the child's eyes.

Annie watched the light on the girl's face, and thought that to be able to please the child, it had been worth the extra work she had done for the marquise. It would have been too much to ask for the child's own father to remember her birthday. He was away for the most part, with the exiled English court, or in Paris, attending the deposed English queen, Henrietta-Marie, at her small and rather impoverished court in the city. Crimson was lucky if she saw him once a month when, as part of his duty, he called on his cousin Violette d'Onges, who was in temporary exile from the king's court, as she had been a supporter of the Prince d'Conde in his bid for the throne during the recently ended civil war in France. Because she was in exile (childless, widowed for six years), she had accepted the guardianship of her cousin's motherless child, demanding that James try to speak to King Louis in her behalf.

The country chateau of the Marquise d'Onges was situated on the Loire River in the city of Orleans, some hundred miles from Paris. Annie could still remember her first glimpse of the building that had seemed a fairy palace and a welcome haven, after years of existing in posting houses and inns as she struggled to keep up with Lord James Haviland and the exiled court of Charles II.

The sight of the peaceful chateau had helped to wipe out the horror of Crimson's birthnight, when the Roundhead soldiers had come upon the farmhouse in the small hours before dawn. They had come looking for Lord James Haviland and his wife, Deborah, with orders from Parliament to arrest the pair of them and any others who would offer them aid.

At the sound of their knocking, Annie's mother had directed her to take the baby to the back and hide in the vegetable garden outside the house. Annie could remember the smell of the freshly tilled earth in her nostrils as she watched the small troop of soldiers force their way into the house.

She could hear the short scream of her mother, then the clang of steel and her father's loud bellowing. The Roundheads had not waited for any explanations. They searched the house, missing the carefully hidden cellar door which stood between the planks under the kitchen table, and where Annie's father had hidden the hunted man. But the soldiers had already seen the overturned carriage in the muddy road, the lifeless body of the woman they were seeking, and evidence of the birth of a child.

Enraged, thinking their prey had escaped them, and goaded by the unpleasant weather through which they had been marching all night, the soldiers had taken out their fury on the farm's inhabitants. The children had all been killed immediately, as they were all too young to afford the soldiers any other kind of pleasure, but Annie's mother had been raped repeatedly and her father put to the torture, his feet put over the kitchen fire to roast slowly and agonizingly, until they had tired of the sport and had hanged him from the loft rafters.

When they set fire to the house itself, Annie had waited, more dead than alive, hoping for some sign of life from within before the house went up in flames. Suddenly, a crouching figure had emerged from the back door, stooped and coughing, weaving towards her in the grotesque light of the pyre. The soldiers had already mounted and were leaving in the opposite direction, back to London, and so the man had escaped their notice.

"You escaped?" The hoarse voice had nearly frightened her out of her wits, but she could see his charred, black face, and nodded.

"The babe too," she had whispered back.

The man had laughed mirthlessly. "Ah, the little bastard has survived, eh?" He had shrugged. " 'Tis too bad you did not let the soldiers have it. Perhaps they would have spared one of your own sisters, and at the same time, rid me of the unwanted little vermin."

Annie had held the baby closer to her thin breast, determined to protect it now at all costs. " 'Tis too bad my father did not let the soldiers have you, my lord, for then
22

my whole family would have been spared," she retorted and had taken a step backward at the anger in his face.

"Don't remind me of the blood on my hands, child!" he had cried out. For a moment, he had stood looking at the girl and the infant, then shrugged. "Come with me. I won't hurt either of you. What is your name?"

His voice was only tired now and Annie dared to hope. "Annie, my lord."

"Annie, you will have to serve as nursemaid for now. Come, we must find some horses somewhere and make all speed to Oxford before they think of setting my house afire. I'll need money for the journey."

"Where are we going, my lord?" Annie questioned, her sturdy, young legs following him easily.

"To France."

Annie, sitting in her room, felt a shiver run through her at the memory of that night, when, as a trusting child, she had put her faith in a stranger, a man for whom her entire family had been butchered. Once in France, it had been, at times, nearly too much to bear, with never a permanent home or any idea where they would get enough food for the child as well as themselves. They had traveled from France to Holland to Belgium, with Haviland forever petitioning the young king for money. But Charles II hardly had enough to meet his own expenses, and there had never been enough to go around. Annie had worked, hiring herself out for various odd jobs in whichever city they were staying, coming home weary and disheartened at the baby's fussing. It had been like a miracle when Lord Haviland had informed her that he had found a permanent lodging for them with his cousin.

The first thing Annie had seen to at the Chateau d'Onges was Crimson's baptism, for although Annie had always called the child by the name that her mother had formed before she died, there had never been any formal christening. So the seven-year-old girl had been christened Mary Deborah Crimson Haviland in the little Catholic chapel at the chateau. In the three years that they had spent at the Chateau d'Onges, Crimson had grown rapidly, speaking French fluently and saved from being totally ignorant of her native tongue by the efforts of the maidservant, Annie.

"Annie, don't you want some cake? You're daydreaming!" came Crimson's clear voice, bringing the other girl back to the present.

"Of course, I want some cake, ragamuffin. Do you think I'll leave it all for you to eat and to grow fat on?"

"Fat and dreary as old Margot!" Crimson laughed, licking cake from her fingers after Annie had cut it in half.

"Crimson, don't be unkind. Besides, it was Margot who made this cake for you," Annie reprimanded her.

Crimson shrugged her shoulders. "Well, I thank her for that," she began, "but it is funny to watch her stuff herself at table. 'Tis no wonder that she had no husband of her own." The little girl was silent for a moment, thinking. "I wonder if madame la marquise will think to try and find me a husband when I grow up?"

"I think that will be up to your father," Annie said thoughtfully.

"Oh, Papa doesn't care about me enough to find me a husband, Annie. And even if he did, he would probably find me some nasty old Englishman, who would be just like him, to marry me! Ugh, I would much rather marry a Frenchman."

"You have quite a while to decide whom you want to marry, Crimson." Annie laughed at the serious expression on the other's face.

The aquamarine eyes gave her a look that mingled anxiety with a certain curiosity. "But what about you, Annie? Will you be married someday?"

"I expect so, my lamb."

"Soon?" the girl pressed.

"That depends. No one has asked me yet," Annie answered her, smoothing back the hair from her forehead.

"But you are so pretty, Annie," Crimson sighed. "Surely, it will not be too much longer."

"Goodness! Are you trying to get rid of me?" the older girl laughed.

"Oh, no! I shall miss you if you would have to leave

me. It would be very nice if you would marry Jacques, if you must marry anyone."

Annie colored. She was wondering how to answer her charge, when a soft tapping at the door was followed by the entrance of one of the houseboys, poking his straw-colored thatch around the wood and grinning at the two of them. "M'sieu Haviland has just arrived and wishes his daughter to be brought downstairs to the drawing room," he said, winking at Annie.

Annie did not return the wink, but hurried Crimson downstairs, knowing that a delay might put the little girl in her father's bad graces. There were sticky cake smears on her dress, and her hair should have been combed, but Annie was not going to take the time to do that now. When they arrived at the door of the sitting room, they saw the Marquise d'Onges and Haviland seated, talking with considerable animation.

At sight of the two of them, Haviland signaled to Annie to bring in the child. Crimson stepped in hesitantly, not used to being called by her father into his presence. She took a chair near the marquise, who patted Crimson's gleaming hair with an absent hand.

"The king has been returned to his throne!" James Haviland cried out in obvious excitement. "King Charles II has been gloriously acclaimed throughout all of England!" His eyes, dark with excitement, gazed at the child, then his servant. "This means I am free to return to the land of my birth, no doubt, to be rewarded for my faithful service by the return of all my lands!"

"Are you not glad for your papa?" the marquise prompted the little girl.

"Oh, yes, madame," Crimson said dutifully. "But I always thought that the king of France, Louis XIV, was king of the whole world."

The marquise smiled ironically. "Ah, no, my child, not yet. King Louis is a most powerful man, but he does not yet have the whole world in his grasp." She looked up to see Haviland frowning in irritation.

"Does the child have no inkling of her own background, madame?" he asked.

"That was only within your power to give her, James, and you have chosen not to do so. I'm afraid you have a little Frenchwoman for a daughter."

A strange smile filtered across the man's face, then disappeared. "Of course, then, you understand why I have decided not to take her with me this time. There are many things that I will have to see settled before I can send for her. I hope, dear cousin, that I can prevail upon your generosity to shelter her for a time until I can return for her?"

The marquise hesitated visibly, her eyes flickering over the head of the little girl. "But, James, I am hoping to have duties of my own soon enough," she said. "You did say you were able to intercede in my behalf with the king through the graces of Henrietta-Marie?"

Haviland cleared his throat. "Actually, Cousin, I was only able to talk with her daughter, the Princess Henriette-Anne, who has promised to catch the king's ear to plead your cause."

"The princess? But, James, she is only seventeen, a mere child! I fail to see how you have helped my cause."

"She has some influence, I believe," James interposed hastily. "There is talk that she will marry the king's brother, Philippe."

"The king's brother! That travesty of a man!" Violette laughed without humor. "If she is so blind that she cannot see he will never make her a fitting husband, then I can hardly believe she is smart enough to catch the king's ear."

"She is smarter than many people guess," Haviland murmured, lowering his eyes to disguise the disdainful expression on his face.

The marquise tapped her fingers on the arm of the chair fitfully, then sighed. "All right, James. I will agree to house your daughter for as long as you require, with the idea that I will soon be installed in my rightful place among the king's court. I will be waiting most anxiously for a summons from the young princess."

"You have my word on it, Cousin," James said. Then, noting Annie standing quietly behind Crimson's chair, he went on. "There is no need for my servant to remain here.

26

The child is old enough to do without her, and I daresay I may need her services in England."

"Good. My money cannot feed everyone," Violette grumbled absently.

Annie whitened. "But, my lord, Crimson is only ten years old and I—"

"Annie, you'll not raise your voice to me in front of our kind benefactress," Haviland returned, his voice syrupy smooth. "You'll come with me, girl, or be dismissed."

Annie's expression was pained, then resigned. "As you wish, my lord." She dared not look at Crimson.

"You cannot take her away, Papa! You cannot!" Crimson burst out, trembling at the thought of losing her best friend in the world. "She loves me! She will marry Jacques and—"

James Haviland looked at the child with distaste, and his voice was cutting. "She'll do as I say, or you'll not see her again!"

Crimson began to cry loudly, causing the marquise to put a hand to her head in distressed exasperation. "Please, James, could you have your servant take the child to her room? She's in no condition to be coherent now."

Haviland nodded, and controlled himself with an effort. He gave a curt order to Annie, who bowed her head and led a sobbing Crimson out of the room. "There is nothing more to say, Cousin. My servant and I shall leave in the morning."

2

For a long time, Crimson was sure that Annie would come back and take her to England to live with her. She painstakingly endeavored to learn all her letters so that she could write her own correspondence to London, hoping against hope that she would receive some reply. But none came. Of course, the maid had not been taught to read or write, so it was doubtful if she ever knew what the girl's letters contained, but Crimson continued sending them faithfully.

An occasional letter would come to the marquise from James Haviland, explaining in vague terms why he could not come this year to take his daughter back to England. When Crimson was fifteen, she learned that Annie had died of the terrible plague that had scourged London that summer of 1665. She wept bitterly and cursed her father for taking the maid to that awful city. Secretly, she wished that he had died, then, horrified at her own thoughts, she hastily did penance.

The marquise had never said anything about the fact that Haviland had not sent for his daughter, and Crimson had not pressed the question, for she was beginning to hope that he would never send for her. She had no wish to leave France for a land that had first taken her mother, and then her best friend.

True to his prediction, Haviland had been able to persuade Henriette-Anne, or Madame—as she was now called as wife to Monsieur, the king's brother—to send a summons to the chateau of the marquise, inviting her to wait upon her at Saint-Cloud, the permanent residence of Philippe d'Orleans. Violette had been ecstatic at the news and had promptly left Crimson to her own devices at the chateau while she herself was reinstalled at court. The marquise was a good deal in Paris with the court now, because of social obligations and Louis' penchant for keeping a close eye on all of his nobles, especially those who had participated on the wrong side during the Civil War, or Fronde. To remain in one's country estates for more than a month at a time was to signal veritable disgrace and exile.

Because of these increasingly long absences, Crimson was finally sent to the Convent of St. Mary's at Tours, in the autumn of her fifteenth year. Although Crimson found some peace in the quiet countryside and the daily routine of the convent, she received with pleasure the news that she would soon be leaving the nuns.

At seventeen, she had begun to feel that life held much, much more than was to be found within the stone walls of St. Mary's. She had learned much with the sisters, but had never felt any real kindred spirit with them, and knew that she would not miss her convent days.

The cause of her coming home was enough to make any young girl leave the routineness of the convent behind. Violette d'Onges had been able to secure a small post for Crimson with the retinue of Madame herself. Crimson could not realize the enormity of this feat because, as yet, she was unaware of the difficulty in obtaining even as small a post as hers. Such positions were much in demand, especially those that could put one under the very eye of the king. Posts were bartered at cards, fought over in duels and bought for outrageous sums of money by those at court, in their determined scramble to be among those elite who could claim the favor of the king.

It had only been luck that had enabled the marquise to land the position of third lady-in-waiting in Madame's closet. Luck, and a careful stressing of the fact that Crimson was English, her mother having been a martyr to the English king's cause. Third lady-in-waiting meant simply that Crimson truly waited on the second lady-in-waiting, who must serve the whims of the lady-in-waiting to Madame. There would not be much contact with the princess, but it was more than enough to have a post that would enable her to be free both of the marquise's dubious generosity and her father's chance command to return home to London.

It was with a lightened spirit that Crimson arrived at the palace of Saint-Cloud on the thirtieth of June, unmindful of the shabbiness of the coach she had been forced to hire for lack of suitable funds. The driver, who had an irritating habit of spitting before answering a question, fumbled with her light baggage and carried it grudgingly to the doorway at the back of the palace, which served as the servants' entrance.

She was ushered by a young chambermaid to a small apartment on the topmost floor, and instructed to wait there until the marquise was able to speak with her. Disconsolately, Crimson gazed around the small room, which was really more like a cubicle, taking in the pristine whiteness of the sheets which covered a narrow bed resembling that which she had slept on at the convent. The other furniture was minimal and Crimson had a sudden longing for the large, comfortable room she had had at the Chateau d'Onges. She seated herself on the bed to await her cousin's pleasure.

Nearly two hours later, the marquise entered, puffing distractedly. The two relatives exchanged formal greetings while Violette eyed the younger girl speculatively, sniffing at the simple gray-striped convent uniform which Crimson had been obliged to wear for lack of anything grander. The youthful curves were outlined in a pleasing enough light, but the color did nothing for the blooming complexion or the wealth of deep auburn hair which was so striking with the brilliant gray-green of the eyes.

"I hope you have used your education at the convent to best advantage, Crimson," the marquise said briefly.

"Yes, madame. I am most grateful for your indul-

30

gence," Crimson said dutifully. "And I thank you for your efforts on my behalf, here at Saint-Cloud."

The marquise seemed pleased by the girl's soft voice and obedient tones. She noted the perfection of delicate features, which hardly resembled those of her cousin James at all. For a moment, there was a slight strain as the older woman realized the potential of the young girl in front of her. The brows, the same shade as Crimson's hair, arched delicately over wide-set eyes that shone with an aquamarine tint as provocative as it was unusual. Her fine-drawn mouth curved up at both corners, accentuating the single dimple in her right cheek.

"Have you refreshed yourself, child?" she asked, brushing aside the moment of strain.

"I—I haven't eaten since this morning, madame," Crimson replied, embarrassed to admit that she had not had enough money to buy a meal along the route.

"Come with me to the kitchens, then, and we will see about getting you something to eat. You can't expect to fulfill your position adequately if you are not nourished, Crimson," Violette scolded, taking her full skirts in both hands and leading Crimson back down the stairs and to the kitchens of Saint-Cloud.

Once having eaten her fill at the large, wooden table in the huge kitchen, Crimson sat opposite the marquise and listened to her instructions.

"Your first responsibility is always to Madame, of course," Violette began, "but you must take care not to step on anyone's toes when you are carrying out your duties. You will be immediately under Jocelyn du Mont, who, in turn, secures her orders from Madame's lady-in-waiting, Marie Aubergne. There are certain times when you will be required to make yourself available, and other times when there will be no need for you to be there. These you will have to acquaint yourself with as soon as you can. Jocelyn is pleasant enough and will most likely be patient with you the first week or so. Are you a quick learner?"

Crimson bit her lip. "I think so, madame."

"Good. Your apprenticeship cannot last too long, for

31

Madame requires that all her household run as smoothly as clockwork. You must find yourself a most accomplished courtesan as soon as possible."

"I shall certainly try very hard, madame," Crimson said quickly, feeling a strong need to defend herself under her cousin's speculative eye. "Will you always be with Madame?"

"Much of the time, although I do receive personal invitations to the court at Paris that may keep me for several days. There is only one thing that you must be especially wary of, and that is not to flirt with the king."

"Flirt with the king? I? I can hardly see when the time—"

"Oh, you are pretty enough to catch the rover's eye. He is getting tired of Louise de la Valliere and has been sampling many of the ladies at court for the last year or two. King Louis has a weak side when it comes to beautiful women. He and Madame were once lovers, it has been rumored, but Queen Anne put a stop to that, forcing Madame to use one of her ladies-in-waiting as a shield to allay the queen's suspicions. Unfortunately, she chose Louise and found her nose completely out of joint when the king established la Valliere as his mistress."

"I see," Crimson murmured as Violette stopped, as though awaiting her comments.

The marquise rose from her chair and beckoned to Crimson to follow her. "Come. I will introduce you to Jocelyn du Mont, who will see to obtaining suitable clothes for you." The marquise stopped on the stairway and turned to gaze at the other girl. "I have secured you this post in the hope that you would never do anything to discredit me for having done you such a favor, child. After all, your father left no written wishes as to what was to become of you while in my care."

Crimson stiffened. "You remind me of my duty, madame," she said carefully. "Has there not been any word from my father?"

"Nothing, since the news of the Great Fire in London last year. Of course, we know that it ravaged a large portion of the city, clearing out great sections of the rotten, infested slums. I heard reports this past January that certain areas were still smoldering! It was a tragic happening so soon after the Plague, but from all I have heard, only the slums and other lower sections of London were affected. The houses of the aristocracy have, for the most part, escaped destruction. I'm sure your father is well and that he is—merely waiting for the right time to have you presented to him."

The right time! How Crimson hoped that that time would never come! She often wondered if her father had actually forgotten her existence. If only it were so! She would infinitely prefer being part of Madame's household, even in her present menial position, than to have to return to the unloving care of her father in a city that was now foreign to her.

"I suppose I should write to him?" she asked, biting her lower lip.

"I have already done so, informing him of my efforts in your behalf."

"Then you will relay his answer to me as soon as you receive it?"

She nodded. "But I am already sure of his answer."

3

Crimson settled in to life at Saint-Cloud with the quick enthusiasm of her age. As her cousin had said, Jocelyn was, indeed, very agreeable and patient with her, and Crimson was extremely grateful for her much-needed lessons. In her room at night, when all of her duties had been taken care of, Crimson would pore over the written notes that she had made during the day, acquainting herself with the hierarchy of the court, the lineage of the royal family and the tastes and preferences of her employer. There was a lot to learn, and her head would fairly spin after an exhausting day followed by late hours in her room. Sometimes she would find it hard just to drag herself from her bed in the morning, and she marveled at the fresh faces and animated conversation of the other ladies in the antechamber. Jocelyn assured Crimson that her tiredness was temporary, and that soon she would grow used to the rigorous schedule at the palace. Ladies, especially at the court of Louis XIV, were expected not to feel the cold or the heat, the effects of a late night in the arms of a lover, or too much indulgence in wine and cards. They must always appear fresh and composed, otherwise the king would think them sickly, and the king disliked anyone who had a predisposition towards ill health. So there was nothing one could do but bear up under the daily routine, and hope to catch up on one's sleep the following night.

Crimson had already made one trip to Paris and had wound up with a head cold the very next day. She couldn't be sure if it had been due to the horrible smells of the city or to the difference in the city air. To be sure, Paris had hardly lived up to her expectations. The streets were terribly dirty, with wide channels cut down their centers to wash away the debris and sewage of the inhabitants, but most of these were clogged and backed up so that she wondered how the townspeople could walk through them so nonchalantly.

The air was filled with bilious clouds of smoke from the soap factories, which only added to the soot and dirt already in the air, causing immediate congestion to the lungs of everyone who had not yet become used to it. Crimson had been obliged to keep her handkerchief to her mouth when traveling out of doors, and she wondered if she would ever get used to the pollution. Needless to say, she was not looking forward to the time when she would be obliged, as part of Madame's retinue, to apply to the king's court at the Louvre. She could understand why the king was choosing to take his court more and more frequently to his newly remodeled palace of Versailles.

There had been no reply to the marquise's letter to her father in London, so nothing else had been said between the two women, and Crimson assumed that she would be more or less on her own, until the time came for her to take a husband. She accepted this fact philosophically, realizing that, as a young, unmarried woman, there would be frequent attacks on her virtue as well as her reputation. At least a husband provided some protection against unwanted suitors.

The thing most galling to Crimson was the relative inactivity of her position at Saint-Cloud. She had, as yet, to be presented before Madame. She tried to fill her idle hours in reading for her own pleasure from the expansive palace library, and in taking walks within a few yards from the palace, since she was not yet familiar enough with the surrounding landscape to venture too far away. Even had she felt secure, taking the air was not generally a thing one did for pleasure at the palace since everyone was busy with his or her own tasks, and Crimson did not want to be singled out for laziness.

As she dressed in her room for an evening's entertainment one night, she reflected on the uselessness of her position. But she was determined not to succumb to low spirits tonight, for, finally, she was to be presented to Madame. There was nothing else to do, but put on a brave façade.

"Enchanted, mademoiselle." The Comte du Mont was bending over her hand, his lips brushing it delicately.

The words drifted over to Crimson in a cloud of strong cologne, and she looked at the dark-haired young man who was Jocelyn's brother. He was slightly built, incongruous beside the plump bulk of the young lady he was escorting this evening. His clothes were as splendid as the feathers of a peacock, with the buttercup-yellow suit trimmed lavishly in point-de-Venice lace that flowed from his wrists to cover almost the whole of his hand. The hands themselves were white and well-formed, as though they might do well to belong to a musician or an artist.

When she realized that she was staring at the comte too long, Crimson curtseyed swiftly, hearing his nervous little cough. "Jocelyn has told me so much about you," she murmured inanely.

He smiled and nodded to her, then walked on into the room, waving his handkerchief in the air as though to make sure everyone received a liberal dose of his cologne scent.

Crimson turned and waved to Jocelyn, who had been watching their small repartee with an anxious look. The latter smiled back at her and returned to her own conversation with others of Madame's retinue. Meanwhile, Crimson stepped unobstrusively away, in order to lose herself among the greenery of potted plants that lined one wall. She hoped to be able to observe these courtiers, a truly remarkable breed, as she judged from the specimens assembled here tonight, without having herself observed. After all, she would hate to make any mistakes on this night of her own debut.

She glanced with varying degrees of excitement at the beautiful faces, the sparkling jewels, the richness of fine clothes. One of the new arrivals seemed to be carrying a fortune in diamonds upon his person. Crimson thought such a show a bit ostentatious and wondered if he were anyone important. A lady walked by, her gown cut to reveal almost the whole of her bosom, which was plumped and powdered to perfection.

"Everyone is so handsome," Crimson murmured to herself, gazing down at her own gown of turquoise silk with a sigh.

A small group of ladies had moved closer to her observation post and she felt suddenly embarrassed, as one of them spied her among the greenery and gazed steadily at her. Feeling as though she must make herself known, Crimson abandoned her relative safety and curtseyed swiftly in front of the young woman. To her relief, Jocelyn came hurrying over to make introductions.

"Madame, may I present a new arrival to your suite? Mademoiselle Crimson Haviland, daughter of Lord James Haviland of England."

Crimson turned her attention to the petite young woman of possibly twenty-three or twenty-four years, who had an elfin air about her and large blue eyes which continued to gaze at her with some curiosity. The brown hair was elaborately curled about her small face and a ruby diadem was fixed between the curls on her forehead. She was dressed magnificently, but there was no hint of haughtiness about the childish mouth and expressive, intelligent eyes.

"Madame, I am honored to be presented to you," Crimson said, curtseying once more. She felt the nervousness begin to steal over her and forced herself to remain stiff, her hands clenched into fists within the folds of her skirt. If she made a fool out of herself now, she would never be able to face these people again.

"You are English, my dear?" the princess asked delightedly.

"I am English because of my parents' heritage, Madame," she answered, "but I truly consider myself a Frenchwoman, as this is the only country I have ever really known."

"Oh, how can you say such a thing! England is a wonderful country and her king—" She smiled with sudden embarrassment at her outbreak. "Forgive me, my dear, but I can never forget that I am also Henriette of England, sister of her king, Charles II. I am very proud of that."

Crimson did not know what to say, or even if a comment was required. She would never get through the evening without making at least a hundred mistakes, she told herself, and she had no one familiar with the court to guide her, except for Jocelyn, who was busy with her own duties.

"You may accompany me to the garden, mademoiselle. I am in need of fresh air."

Crimson checked her surprise that the princess would single out a stranger to take the air with her, but the hidden sneers among some of the other women made her wonder if, perhaps, the English princess was not well liked among her own peers. She followed the other woman, a step behind her until they reached the terrace where the moist summer air wafted over them.

"You say you have been in France since your birth, mademoiselle? When was that? I am intensely interested in anything to do with that country which I have not seen in many years. My brother is dearer to me than my own husband," she ended with a sarcastic twist to her lips.

"I was born in the year 1650, Madame," Crimson answered, finding suddenly that she liked this rather serious, straightforward young woman, no matter if Madame was pitied, despised or disliked by her court. "My mother died at my birth. I know that she and my father were fleeing Cromwell's soldiers on the night I was born and that the farm where they had taken refuge was put to the torch for harboring them. Only my father and one of the children survived, and they brought me to France."

"Cromwell was a devil!" Madame hissed with hatred, cursing the man who had sent her own father to his death. She recovered herself quickly. "But what of your father?"

"I have not seen him for seven years, Madame. He returned to England on the occasion of the king's Restoration, and has been busy with his own affairs." She could not meet the princess' probing eyes.

Madame was shrewder than she looked and did not press the subject. Instead, she broke off a small twig from a nearby tree and studied it absently. "How I wish I could return to England again and visit my brother. If only I had the freedom to do so. He has so many sorrows, so many burdens to bear for his subjects."

As do all kings, Crimson thought, but kept silent as the princess continued.

"He has written me that the Great Fire was almost a blessing, as it rid London of the major part of its slums," Madame went on. "A new city is to be built on the old one, a city more modern and more glorious than even our Louis could imagine." Another soft hint of sarcasm.

"Madame, you sound so lonesome," Crimson burst out, touched by the sadness in the other woman's voice.

"If you only knew what I wouldn't do—" The wife of the king's brother seemed suddenly to realize to whom she was talking. "I think it would be wise if we return now to the others," she said with sudden authority.

The two women arrived inside to the start of the first dance of the evening. Crimson was about to excuse herself, but the princess stopped her with a hand.

"But, Madame, surely people will be looking for you to dance now. Your husband—"

"My husband does not care to dance," Madame said almost savagely. "I'm not even sure if he has deigned to attend tonight." She scanned the room and then nodded. "Ah, yes, I see him over there on the settee, surrounded, of course, by his fawning favorites." She sighed with a wealth of emotion.

Crimson followed her nod and saw a little man, dressed in pink satin trimmed with scarlet ribbons, holding court in a small alcove. There were three young men hovering about him, all dressed magnificently, and she noticed the man in peacock blue with the wealth of diamonds she had noted before among them. He quipped some joke in the prince's ear, to which Monsieur laughed shrilly, waving his handkerchief in front of his face with feminine grace. Crimson watched his actions curiously.

"See the tall, handsome man with him," Madame was half-whispering to her, "the one with the face of an angel, they say. That is the Chevalier de Lorraine." Hatred trembled in her voice as she spoke his name. "See how he shows off his diamonds in such vulgar display. The one in white is the Comte Dornet, and the one in green has only just arrived at Saint-Cloud. His name is Nicholas Brentwood, Earl of Dorset, and it makes me sad that an Englishman could practice the art of Italian love. The idea disgusts me. If there was a way to rid him from my court, I would gladly do it."

"Pardon, Madame, I'm afraid I don't understand," Crimson said helplessly, wondering what in the world she was talking about.

"You mean you have never heard of that peculiar brand of affection between men, which we here in France choose to credit to the Italians?" Madame tittered suddenly, but her laughter was devoid of cheer.

"I know very little of any love, Madame," Crimson returned hurriedly, her cheeks pinkening as she began to sense the implication in the princess' words.

"Of course, of course, my dear. How cruel of me to be so blasé in your knowledge of the excesses of some of the people of the court, and especially those that seem to surround my husband. You know, I have heard some describe Saint-Cloud as 'the sewer.' I myself think it is aptly put, but if it comes to the attention of Monsieur, he simply laughs and thinks it all a good joke." She shook her head.

Crimson bit her lip, wondering at receiving such confidences from the wife of the king's brother. She was sure that Henriette would regret her candid observances to a stranger, and one never knew about the caprice of the mighty. In her embarrassment, she might have Crimson banished from court. Crimson swallowed nervously.

"You have my permission to withdraw, my dear," the princess was saying, to Crimson's extreme relief. "You did not tell me, though, what post you hold in my household. I have not seen you before today, have I?"

"No, Madame. I am third lady-in-waiting, behind Jocelyn du Mont. I will not be much in your company."

"Ah, but it has been most refreshing to be able to talk with a person of your intelligence and innocence, mademoiselle. Then too, you are English, a race of which I am especially fond. There are so many here who hate me because I am not as stupid and dull as they would like me to be. I believe I will ask the king to grant you leave to ascend to one of my ladies-in-waiting. I would have you near me, mademoiselle, for I may have need of you in the future."

Crimson carefully kept her mouth from dropping open. "I would be extremely honored, Madame," she breathed, and for the moment, did not think about the last words of the princess.

40

4

Crimson awaited the king's pleasure in the large antechamber, where several others cooled their heels during the long wait to seek audience with His Majesty. Her heart seemed to alternately pound in her throat and stop completely when the door was opened and the majordomo announced the next person in. Her eyes whisked back and forth about the room, fastening on trivial things, while her fingers twisted themselves in the emerald green of her gown. She wished desperately for a hand mirror in order to check her appearance once more, hoping her coiffure was not too simple for such an occasion. She had coiled her hair on the back of her head, allowing two lovelocks to escape on either side, to frame her face and help give her pale cheeks some added color. Instead of arranging small curls on her forehead, she had swept her hair to either side, in soft wings that nearly met the arch of her brows. Jocelyn had helped her to pick out the gown she wore; its green satin bodice, cut deeply across the bosom, was relieved by a froth of lace about the cleavage and at her elbows. The matching skirt was drawn back on either side by darker velvet bows, which clasped the material in order to show the cream silk underskirt to best advantage.

"May I sit beside you, mademoiselle?"

The strong, deep voice startled her, and Crimson

looked up to see a young man, dressed entirely in sky-blue, bowing over her hand. Something about the man seemed familiar, but she was in such a state now that any distant memory escaped her entirely. She nodded briefly.

"Of course," she answered, moving down a little on the bench.

"May I present myself? Nicholas Brentwood, Earl of Dorset, at your disposal, mademoiselle."

Crimson turned her head, remembering the name now as one of those linked with Monsieur's crowd. Hadn't Madame said that he was English? She thought he must be for she could detect a barely discernible accent in his French. Her voice was cool as she answered him.

"Crimson Haviland, sir."

"Oh, I already know your name, mademoiselle."

Her eyes widened. "How is it that you should know that?" she questioned him, feeling as though she might be affronted at his knowledge.

His laugh was in a high, falsetto voice, which she had heard Monsieur use repeatedly, and which grated on her ears annoyingly. "Why, you are one of my fellow English, mademoiselle. I try to make it my business to know my countrymen in a strange land. Don't you think it wise?" He made his inquiry before pulling out a lace handkerchief and delicately patting his forehead, as though wiping away a few beads of sweat.

"This land is not strange to me, monsieur," she answered him, slightly repelled by the remembrance of her conversation with Madame, when this man had first come to her attention. "I hardly think we have much in common."

He sighed elaborately and shrugged. "Perhaps not, mademoiselle. But, doubtless, we shall see each other often, as we both will be residing at Saint-Cloud."

"Then, what business brings you to Paris, monsieur?" she asked in some curiosity, her eyes straying to the slender, long-fingered hands, which did not seem as delicate without the handkerchief in their grasp.

He faced her fully for the first time and she could see the deep blue of his eyes sizing her up, as though aware of

42

her impertinence in asking such a question. They were so dark as to be nearly indigo, and she thought that she had never seen eyes so utterly blue before.

"The king has requested me to attend him, mademoiselle. I have no idea why, unless he might wish to discuss English fashion or the like." He sniffed delicately and turned away his blue gaze before continuing, "And your business with the king, mademoiselle, as long as we have decided upon such personal conversation?"

Crimson would have liked to retort something uncivil, but realized that she had displayed a most unladylike curiosity in his own business. "Madame had requested that I attach myself to her household as her personal lady-in-waiting. As I did not—have the means—to secure the post on my own, Madame most kindly offered to pay for the position herself, but asked that I apply to the king for his approval."

"How fortunate for you, mademoiselle!" the man said quickly. "Indeed, Madame must have a special liking for you!" His carefully powdered face revealed nothing of his feelings, whether he was truly delighted for her, or merely being sarcastic.

"I hardly think that is your concern, monsieur," Crimson said hurriedly, wishing he would stop sniffing so affectedly. Truly, she thought, he did not in the least seem to belong with those other fops from the cut of his physique. He was much taller than Madame's husband and broader of shoulder, although she recalled that the Chevalier de Lorraine seemed an extremely fit sportsman also.

"Forgive me, mademoiselle," he responded automatically with a bored air.

They were both silent then, as the Englishman calmly surveyed the room. Crimson watched him covertly out of the corner of her eye, noting the full periwig that he wore, which was so light it was nearly a silver-blond in color. It curled down to his shoulders, brushing over the silk knots there. In profile, his nose was slender and aquiline, beneath which grew a thin moustache, a dark shade of blond that matched his eyebrows. His firm lips were molded over

43

strong, white teeth, which just now held a lozenge that he was sucking distractedly.

"Mademoiselle, I request that you not stare so at me," he said now in a lower voice, which held a curious note of warning in it.

Dismayed at her own lack of propriety, Crimson hastily averted her head. "I'm sorry," she murmured, hoping the blush was not too discernible in her cheeks. "I did not realize that I was doing it." She opened her unused fan and began swishing it heatedly over her face.

"You're blowing my hair." The voice came again, amused this time.

Angry now, Crimson snapped the fan shut so quickly that it broke. She felt like crying, but managed to stem the flow of tears, at the same time wondering how she would explain the damage to Jocelyn, from whom she had borrowed it. She was about to stand up and depart this odious man, when the majordomo came through the doorway once more and announced her name.

Nervous, Crimson wetted her lips, all thoughts of Nicholas Brentwood banished from her brain. She was going to see the king! As she moved with unconscious grace past those who still waited, she tried to remember everything she must do and say. But Jocelyn's advice, all her instructions were wasted at this hour, for Crimson was too aware of her own trembling nervousness as the door was opened for her and she entered the large room, at one end of which she could see the figure of the king, seated at his desk.

She immediately dropped into a curtsey, remaining there more to get her bearings than to impress the young man before her. His voice came to her across the room, imperious, yet gentle, and she took heart.

"Please, come forward, mademoiselle."

Crimson stood and walked towards the desk, keeping her eyes carefully at a place somewhere in the middle of the king's chest. When she stood before him with only the desk separating them, she curtseyed once more.

"Sire, I—" She stopped, not knowing what to say, and the king, sensing her reticence, interrupted her.

"Mademoiselle Haviland, is it not? Madame has already sent me a short note, stating your business with me. You should be honored that she would take so much trouble in assuring you a post within her retinue. Your family is in England?"

"My father lives in London, sire. I have lived with my cousin, Marquise d'Onges, for several years." Crimson had not straightened yet.

Quickly, the king gave her permission to rise. He looked at the fair, young maiden before him with the eyes of a connoisseur and was pleased with her. His face, however, gave nothing away.

"You have been happy at Saint-Cloud, mademoiselle?" the king continued, rising abruptly from his chair to stand closer to her.

Crimson nodded. "Yes, sire. I—I have no wish to return to my father and he—" Her eyes went to those of the king. "He does not bother himself with my well-being, here in France."

"You are lucky to have such a sponsor as Madame," the king said, brushing aside the girl's last words. "I think I cannot but do otherwise than to set my complete approval upon her choice. You shall certainly be a lovely jewel among her ladies, mademoiselle." With the courtesy he showed to all women, King Louis bowed over the trembling hand, which he captured easily.

"Thank you, sire," Crimson breathed, surprised that the interview was over, and that it had all gone so easily. She waited for the king to release her hand.

"I think, mademoiselle, that I shall expressly request that Madame show herself at Versailles next week. You will accompany her, of course."

"Thank you, sire," Crimson said again. When he released her hand, she curtseyed once more, backing away as gracefully as she was able to the door.

When she had once more passed into the antechamber, she felt as though a great burden had been magically lifted from her shoulders. The interview had gone easily, despite her anxiety, and the king had agreed to Madame's choice for lady-in-waiting as though it had been his own. Indeed, he had seemed most kind and gracious, hardly the king, during their private audience. With a light heart, she hurried out of the anteroom into the hall outside.

The great corridors of the Louvre were shadowed in the dimming twilight as servants hurried to get all the candles lit before complete darkness. Crimson hurried down the corridor, passing courtiers and servants, each going about his own business with no more than a brief glance at the lone young woman. She wished she had thought to keep the coach that had brought her here, but had let the driver go, knowing that she could get another coach to take her back to Saint-Cloud. She had not realized, though, that she would be obliged to wait so long before the king would see her.

She turned a corner and heard the sound of music and laughter from the gaming rooms. Inside were splendidly clad men and women gambling ferociously against each other. Crimson had heard that the king did not approve of gambling, but was always ready to make good the losses of his favorites. She watched the gala group for a few moments, amazed upon hearing the high amounts of money that were called out loudly by the participants. A servant passed her to light the candles in an alcove next to her, and she was reminded that she had best hurry in order to hail a coach to take her back to the palace.

As she lifted her full skirts to walk more quickly down the hall, she heard footsteps behind her, and then a familiar voice hailing her.

"Mademoiselle, please wait!"

Crimson turned in some annoyance to perceive the tall figure of the Earl of Dorset striding purposefully towards her. "Yes, monsieur?" she inquired impatiently.

He stopped before her and pressed his handkerchief to his mouth as though to calm his breathing. "I just thought that, perhaps, you would like to share my coach with me, mademoiselle, if you have not already secured one for the ride back to Saint-Cloud. The hour grows late, and you are alone, are you not?"

Crimson did not like to readily admit that she was

46

alone, but the man seemed to be able to read her face so easily. Could he see the slight feeling of anxiety there at the prospect of sharing a vehicle with this man who, from all reports, was as perverted in his passions as Madame's husband?

"Yes, I am alone, monsieur, but I feel sure that I will be able to hail a coach at the front of the palace. I'm sure that you may have other—duties that will oblige you to make haste to Saint-Cloud. Monsieur will be awaiting you?" She was careful to keep the sarcasm from her words, but couldn't help watching the man's face closely to see what his reaction would be.

The dark blue eyes narrowed slightly, and the smile that shaped the firm lips could not be called cheerful. "Monsieur does not hold the leash around my neck, mademoiselle."

Crimson blushed and couldn't help feeling ashamed of her words. "I'm sorry, monsieur. I meant no harm."

The aura of masculine virility seemed to leap out to her from this man, and Crimson felt her heart beat faster as he came to stand closer to her. But in the next instant, the image was gone, replaced by the arrogant, insufferable courtier again as he laughed shortly. "Come, mademoiselle. You simply must share my coach now. I insist. Madame would never forgive me if she found out that I had left one of her ladies-in-waiting stranded in Paris." He bowed and offered her his arm.

With a sigh of resignation, Crimson took it, placing her hand softly on the rippling satin, aware with a slight tremor of the hard muscles beneath. As they continued down the corridor, she tried to think of something pleasant to say, but this man seemed to have the strangest effect on her so that she could think of nothing. When they arrived outside in the heavy air, Brentwood called to a waiting servant who immediately went in search of his coach.

"The night is unpleasantly warm," Crimson said to break the sudden silence.

"Very uncomfortable," he agreed absently. "Let us hope there will be a breeze once the coach gets started."

47

It did not take long for the coachman to bring up a large blue and silver coach drawn by four milk-white horses, which pranced temperamentally as though eager to be off on the open road. Brentwood assisted her into the coach and seated himself opposite her. Her full skirts covered most of the seat, and the hem fell over his calves as he sat with his arms folded in front of him, waiting for the coachman to start the team of horses.

"You have a splendid coach, monsieur," Crimson murmured.

"Thank you. I am especially proud of the horses, as they were a present to me."

A present? From whom, Crimson wondered. From Monsieur, perhaps? She forced the thought out of her head. Why must she continually think such terrible thoughts of this man who had shown nothing but kindness to her, really?

The coach was jostled as the horses brought it through the streets of Paris, which were slippery after an early afternoon shower, causing the sewers to overflow. Crimson would be glad when they reached the gates of the city and were on the open road. From there it would not be too long a distance before they arrived at Saint-Cloud.

"Have you been in France long, monsieur?" Crimson asked, feeling uncomfortable in the silence.

"Only a few months."

"You are on a vacation from England then?" she wondered.

She sensed his sharpened gaze on her and drew back towards the seat. Perhaps this man did not enjoy trivial conversation, she thought, or perhaps his reasons for being here were not things he liked to discuss with a young lady who was, after all, a stranger.

After a thorough silence, she heard him say, "Business mixed with pleasure, mademoiselle. I suppose you could say a vacation."

They sat quietly until they were at the gates of Paris. Crimson kept her hands carefully folded in her lap, her eyes on the lace of her skirt while she hoped for the ride

48

to be over soon. Goodness, if all courtiers were this hard for her to talk to, she would most certainly not retain her position very long. Ladies-in-waiting to Madame were expected to be charming, knowledgeable and witty—things in which she had not been educated as yet.

When they were out of Paris, Brentwood seemed to relax a little, and he stretched his legs, striking her ankle with the toe of his shoe.

"Forgive me, mademoiselle. Did I hurt you?" he asked solicitously.

"No, monsieur," Crimson murmured hastily. She reached down to rub at the ankle for a moment, unconsciously affording him a generous view of her bosom as she leaned over.

"Tell me," he said unexpectedly. "Why are you not in England with your father instead of here in France?"

She looked up in surprise. "I have not seen my father for many years, monsieur. He lives as a bachelor in London. Needless to say, my presence in his household would be—uncomfortable for him. I suppose that one day he will marry again and then, who knows?"

"But you do not mind being separated from him?"

"We were not close, monsieur," she answered almost defiantly. "I have been able to take care of myself very well without him."

"Of course, of course, but you were a child then with older people to guide you. Now, you are a young woman who lives at Saint-Cloud as lady-in-waiting to Madame. It is well known, mademoiselle, that the atmosphere at Saint-Cloud is not kind to young girls of virtue, like yourself. It is said that degradations abound at the palace of Monsieur."

"You sound as though you are warning me, monsieur," Crimson said, her brows slanting upward. "I can assure you I can take care of myself."

"Can you?" His smile seemed to grow ominously close to her and Crimson leaned back in the seat. Her eyes closed involuntarily as she felt his hands reach for her and settle on her shoulders, bringing her back to him so that he could bend her easily in the crook of his arm.

His mouth, smelling pleasantly from the cinnamon lozenge he had had earlier, came closer to hers and touched the corner of her lips with tantalizing slowness. It moved down to her jaw, then back to imprison her mouth with a sudden quick greed. Crimson felt somehow like a trapped bird as his mouth pressed with more and more urgency against hers, seeking to open it. When he succeeded, she felt his breath mingling with hers in an intimacy that half-shocked and half-delighted her.

When he let her go, she opened her eyes to see a burning look in those blue depths that frightened her instinctively. Her own hand had come up to clasp his shoulder, and she took it away as though the thought of it there was suddenly too much to bear. She was aware in the suddenness of the moment of the strength of his arms holding her, the unspoken question that lingered somewhere in his eyes and her own wildly beating heart.

"*Can* you take care of yourself, Crimson Haviland?" he asked her again with evident sarcasm.

She took a deep breath and struggled out of his arms and back to her seat. She could not speak from the tightness in her throat and looked away from him, horrified at the sudden, unexplainable tears that threatened to spill from beneath her lowered lashes. Accurately divining her predicament, he handed her his handkerchief.

"Why—why did you do that?" she asked him.

He shrugged. "To make a point, mademoiselle. You do not belong at Saint-Cloud."

"And I suppose *you* do?" she inquired angrily. "I suppose you are used to such degradation, as you call it!"

"Yes," he answered. "I am used to it, mademoiselle."

She glanced at him quickly, wondering if he were making fun of her again, but the look in his eyes was serious and sad and angry at the same time. He did not seem to be teasing her and she wondered at the strange contrasts in this man.

"Why do you stay?" she inquired softly now.

He shrugged and his previous expression was gone, replaced easily by the mask of the foppish courtier. "You must not question me too closely," he chided her, "else you may regret knowing the answer."

Crimson would have liked to continue the conversation, but he motioned her to silence and they continued the rest of the journey in quiet.

5

A week later, Crimson had settled in to her new job, although there was still much she had to learn. She enjoyed being around her mistress, for the king's sister-in-law was both witty and intelligent, two attributes which Crimson admired greatly. Her own duties were varied—from handing Madame her fan for the evening to reading to her from Madame's favorite works. She had a good deal of time on her hands, as none of her jobs was very strenuous, and she took advantage of these free periods to explore the gardens of Saint-Cloud, which Madame had had done over in the English style.

In was during one of these walks that she came unexpectedly on Monsieur and three of his cronies, which included the Chevalier de Lorraine. As she was still afraid of the husband of her mistress, she quickly lost herself behind a tumble of shrubbery, glad that the English style of gardens held to a sort of calculated disarray instead of the formality that the French loved. She had in mind to wait quietly there until Monsieur returned to the palace.

"So, you liked my little gift last night?" Monsieur was saying in his falsetto voice to the Chevalier.

"The boy was young and inexperienced, but he promises to make a delightful pupil," the Chevalier returned, laying an arm affectionately around his prince's shoulders.

"Ah, my pet, do not make me jealous," Monsieur continued. "I only sought to provide you with amusement while I carried out my—duty—with—"

"Don't speak her name," the Chevalier cut in quickly. "That woman tries everything to break us apart. She hates me with a passion I find distressing in a female." The Chevalier's beautiful mouth curled disdainfully.

The Comte Dornet, who was also in the group, tapped the Chevalier playfully on the shoulder. "Come now, you know all her entreaties to the king have had no results. I daresay the king grows bored with her continual demands."

"Perhaps my brother has better things on his mind," Monsieur interjected, gazing up at the Chevalier with devoted eyes. "Like his latest conquest—Madame de Montespan. Vulgar woman, really."

The Chevalier relaxed at the turn in conversation. "Have you seen the breasts on that one?" he asked coarsely. "Nearly fit for milking! Her curves are too opulent to be in good taste. At least La Vallière was thin and—"

"La Vallière's days are numbered," Monsieur cut in. "Let my brother have his cow. She will keep his mind off our little games here at Saint-Cloud."

The men laughed and Monsieur brushed a disarrayed curl into place on his shoulder.

"What do you think of the Englishman, Brentwood?" the fourth man said abruptly as the others were about to walk back. "I must say he's a handsome devil, but he ignores most of my overtures. I don't understand him."

Monsieur tittered. "Nicholas is most intelligent. I believe he would rather wait for bigger game, François. He is most attentive to me." He looked up to check the Chevalier's reaction.

As he hoped, it was angry. "Brentwood is an Englishman and not to be trusted. I have seen his eyes following your wife as often as they follow you, Philippe," he said to the king's brother. "I am not at all sure that he is one of us, but what he hopes to gain is beyond me."

"Oh, the usual trifles, no doubt," Monsieur put in. "Well, he is a handsome lad, and I wouldn't mind making it worth his while if he decides to accept my invitation one evening. If, as you say, he pays court to my wife also, the victory would be all the sweeter, don't you think? To steal a lover from dear Henriette—how original!"

The men laughed together and retired from the gardens towards the palace, the Chevalier and Monsieur linked arm in arm.

Crimson breathed a sigh of relief when they were gone. What they would have done if they had known she was eavesdropping, she wouldn't care to find out. "Degradation," Brentwood had called it. Surely the activities of these men could be called something much worse. How dared Monsieur ridicule his own wife before such men who were her enemies?

She walked from behind the shrubbery and followed one of the paths towards the edge of the garden grounds. Looking back at the palace of Saint-Cloud, she thought how magical it looked in the pinkening glow of twilight, with the evening mist beginning to rise softly around it as though to shroud it in mystery. Surely, it was one of the most beautiful of the French palaces. Why must it be given over to men and women who cared nothing for its beauty, who were only interested in such perverse pleasures as could hatch from their wicked minds? Crimson could begin to see what Brentwood had meant when he told her that this was, perhaps, not the place for her.

As though her thoughts had the power to conjure up the man himself, she saw a tall figure coming towards her on the path. As he came closer, she could easily make out the silver-blond wig and dark-blue eyes of Nicholas Brentwood.

"Good afternoon, mademoiselle," he said, and his eyes betrayed for a moment his surprise at seeing her. "What brings you this far out into the gardens?"

Crimson glanced at him with a raised eyebrow. "I am normally in the habit of taking walks in the garden, M'sieu Brentwood. You seem to have ventured even farther, though. What delights do the woods hold that would tempt you to get your shoes muddied?"

As she eyed him impudently, a movement caught her attention, and she could see a small, slender figure running out from the woods towards the palace. Her surprise was complete when she thought she recognized Madame's sea-green dress, the one she had helped her lace this very morning. She checked her involuntary movement towards the woman and glanced up at the man before her.

"An assignation, monsieur?" she questioned him.

He bowed. "You have guessed it, mademoiselle. I'm afraid that I am not without blemish in my private life, and have succumbed to one of the fair ladies of this court."

"Certainly, monsieur, you could have picked less audaciously?" She pressed him further.

His eyebrows went up. "What do you mean?"

"I doubt that Madame would want to have her love affairs aired in public, monsieur. You would have to be more careful if you are to continue." Crimson felt the anger within her in some surprise. What did she care where Madame found solace from the indifference of her own husband?

"You refer to the king's sister-in-law, mademoiselle. I must caution you to be more careful." His voice was devoid now of the playful falsetto that he had used earlier, and there was a hard, steel note that had crept in to warn her off.

"I would not do anything that might harm Madame, of course," Crimson returned defiantly, "but I fail to see what she finds so attractive in one of her own husband's playfellows!" She blushed at her own words and noticed the man's tightened jaw and narrowed eyes.

"You seem well up on things, Mistress Haviland. In other circumstances, I could be flattered at your interest in my business."

"Oh! You *are* insufferable! As Monsieur said just a moment ago, I suppose you are hoping for some trifles that would satisfy even a most jaded courtier like yourself!"

He caught her arm, and despite her brave words, Crimson felt a faint prickling of fear at the back of her neck. His blue eyes were blazing into hers, and she wished that she could disappear into the all-shrouding mist that was enveloping this sloping end of the gardens with startling quickness.

"What are you spouting, wench? What's this about Monsieur? Tell me, or I'll give you a bruised arm for your inquisitiveness!"

Crimson swallowed and realized that she would not be able to free herself unless she obeyed him. "A little earlier, as I was walking down this way, I nearly ran into Monsieur and the Chevalier de Lorraine and two others. They were talking about—" She hesitated, hoping he would not press her for details.

"What did they say about me?" he asked her pointedly.

"One of them said that you—that you had ignored his innuendos and that he didn't understand why. Monsieur said that he thought you were waiting on his pleasure and that you would be happy with whatever trinkets the affair might bring to you. The Chevalier said that you seemed to be paying court to Madame at the same time, and Monsieur thought it would be very—diverting to steal a—a—lover away from his own wife." She hung her head in shame, feeling her cheeks scarlet from embarrassment. Oh, why didn't he just let her go!

"That pompous façade of a man!" Brentwood said between his teeth.

"Please let me go now," Crimson pleaded, feeling the mist, close and sticky about her clothes and face. "Madame may be looking for me."

He pushed her back against a tree trunk and held her there, his face so close that she could feel his breath fanning her cheek. His expression was brutal, and there was no mercy in those indigo eyes.

"Listen to me, Crimson Haviland. You'll not breathe a word of our conversation today, or of even seeing me out here. If anything of this reaches the ears of Monsieur or anyone else in this stinking hole, you'll pay dearly for it! Do you understand!"

"Y—yes, yes," she breathed, desperate now to get away from him.

He released his bruising grip on her slowly. Crimson rushed away from him down the path, brushing her gown carelessly against the wet moisture on the shrubbery. She must get back to the palace, back to the safety of Madame's apartments that seemed like a haven in the blackness that surrounded her.

Once inside the palace, Crimson stood for a moment with her hands pressed tightly to her temples as though to blot out her fears. She took a deep breath and made her way to the princess' apartments, hoping to change her gown quickly before Madame would see her. Such was not to be the case, for Madame had been calling for her and one of the other ladies saw her in the corridor and hastened her to her mistress.

"Crimson, I—what happened to your gown, my dear!" Madame had already removed the sea-green gown she had been wearing earlier and was clad in a dressing robe while one of the servants did her hair.

"I was out too late in the mist, Madame. I had taken a walk in the gardens."

Madame's knowing eyes grew sharper in her small face. "In the gardens?"

"Yes, Madame. I have only just returned from them. Pray forgive me while I take a moment to change my gown." Crimson's eyes did not leave those of the princess and there was a slight challenge in her tone.

Madame hesitated, then nodded. "Of course, Crimson. And when you return, I would have you tell me if your sojourn in the garden was eventful."

The other ladies tittered knowingly, for hadn't all of them conducted assignations in the gardens, which lent themselves so romantically to a sensual interlude with a man?

"Hardly eventful, Madame. I was alone the whole time and dozed off on a bench before a servant came to awaken me."

56

Madame relaxed and laughed softly. "Ah, Crimson, I shall have to speak to your young man for you. I do not want any of my ladies to be ill-treated by their swains."

"Thank you, Madame, but I doubt that I shall see the young man again after the way he has embarrassed me today."

"Perhaps that is the best idea, Crimson. In that case, I shall not interfere."

Crimson curtseyed quickly and went off to her own room, which she shared with two of the other ladies-in-waiting, to change her dress.

6

Versailles was just really coming to King Louis' attention in 1667. He made plans and had many drawn up by his master builders to enlarge and glorify the original structure, which had housed his father during his hunting expeditions to the countryside surrounding it. For now, the palace still retained much of the flavor of a fairyland castle, with its pink and white architecture.

Crimson was bumped and jostled in the coach, which was carrying them down the deeply rutted road through the forest that still surrounded the chateau on three sides. She looked out the window and exclaimed in delight at the sight of the rosy glow of the buildings in the morning sun.

"Madame, it is so much more—breathable here than in

Paris!" she said to her mistress, who smiled with slight condescension at the girl.

"Wait until we have arrived, Crimson, before you make judgments. The king has so many builders and workers employed to carry out his plans for the chateau that there leaves little enough room to be comfortable. The corridors are still too narrow, and there are hardly enough apartments to go around. Some of the noblemen will be obliged to stay in compartments in the attic, separated in many cases by boards or cloth to retain the minimum of privacy."

"There will only be enough room in Madame's apartments for two or three ladies-in-waiting," Marie Aubergne returned with haughtiness. "No doubt, you shall find yourself in one of the attic compartments."

Madame smiled to soften the other girl's words. "I'm afraid Marie is right, Crimson, for I did promise that she and Madame du Roure would attend me on my next visit to Versailles. But I shall speak to the king about giving me a little more room as soon as possible."

Crimson was silent, aware of Marie's dislike for her. She looked once more out the window and saw Monsieur's red-striped coach ahead of them on the road, the horses dragging it at breakneck speed through the forest. She knew that, with him, rode the Chevalier de Lorraine and Nicholas Brentwood, and she hoped she would not be obliged to see any of them during their short stay at Versailles.

The king had expressed his wish to do some hunting and hoped to remain in the country no more than three days, after which time he would retire to Fontainebleau until Christmas. Courtiers were allowed to accompany the king to Versailles only through written invitations, and no one would dare to come uninvited to the chateau unless he wished to risk disgrace.

The coach was slowing now and would soon come to a halt in the small park in front of the chateau. Crimson brushed her bodice to straighten the bows at her breast and patted the curls of her hair into some semblance of order after the windy ride in the coach. She followed Madame, with beating heart, up the marble steps and into the wide receiving room of Versailles. Madame followed a liveried servant to her apartments on the first floor and instructed her ladies-in-waiting to freshen the clothes she had brought in her trunk.

Monsieur stuck his nose through the half-open door. "I see you have settled in, Madame," he said briefly, before laying a hand on the Chevalier's shoulder and following him to the apartments set aside for his use.

Madame had not had time to do more than curtsey to her husband, and Crimson could see the look of hatred that passed over her face as he left with his mignon. However, the princess said nothing, and as soon as her things were unpacked, she told Crimson to run along to find her own room upstairs.

Taking her chambermaid with her, and a lackey who shouldered her own trunk, Crimson made her way slowly upstairs to the attic above where a milling throng of courtiers, nobles and servants mingled freely in their attempts to find their rooms, bring up their wardrobes and get dressed in time for an appearance before the king. Crimson pushed her way with difficulty through the narrow hallway and gazed about her distractedly for something with her own name on it. A servant bowed before her and asked her name, which Crimson gave him thankfully, for it took him only a moment to locate the small cubicle that had been assigned to her.

Inside there was barely enough room for herself and her servant, and she found herself pressed up against the narrow bed while the lackey set her trunk in a corner. She, at least, was lucky enough to have been given one of the windows and hurriedly instructed her maid to open it.

"Mademoiselle, how will I be able to dress you?" wailed Gisette, staring about the room in despair.

"We shall have to make do," Crimson snapped back, unwilling to admit that it would be sheer torture for the next three days.

At least her neighbors on either side seemed quiet enough, for there were only rough partitions separating them. Or perhaps they hadn't arrived yet. At any rate, she couldn't worry overmuch about privacy now, for she must hurry and change from her traveling clothes to a gown for this evening. Resigned, Gisette was laying out her underthings on the bed, while Crimson rummaged through her trunk to pick something suitable. The pink and white patterned gown on top was the only one that had escaped being completely wrinkled, and she told Gisette to take it down to the kitchens to press it.

"Excuse me."

Crimson looked up to see a young man, half in and half out of her doorway. He was smiling at her engagingly. "I was pushed in by someone in a deuced hurry," he explained, righting himself to bow before her. "This place is worse than the Pont Neuf, is it not, mademoiselle?"

"At least, let us hope we need not worry about getting our pockets picked in the palace of the king," Crimson returned, deciding not to take offense at the warm, young man.

"I don't believe I know you, mademoiselle. The Marquis de la Valliere, at your disposal."

The king's favorite's brother! Crimson curtseyed. "Crimson Haviland, monsieur."

"Good Lord! I *thought* you were English. How delightful! I hope to see more of you, mademoiselle." And with that, he was hurrying down the corridor to find his room.

He was replaced quickly by another man and Crimson drew back in alarm as she recognized the features of Nicholas Brentwood.

"I thought I recognized your voice, mademoiselle. I am next to you, on your right," he said, bowing.

For all his polite courtesy, their meeting in the garden that one afternoon could have been imagined. He was dressed already in a suit of olive green broadcloth, detailed with gold thread at the lapels and buttonholes.

"How do you find your quarters?" he inquired further, as she remained silently watching him.

She shrugged. "I can hardly grace them with the name. And yourself?"

"The nights promise to be most interesting, mademoiselle. I shall do my best not to listen to any private company you might decide to entertain, and I should hope you would grant me the same favor."

Crimson started at his boldness. "I shall most likely be required to wait upon Madame throughout the late hours, monsieur, so I doubt that I shall be here to disturb your privacy," she returned stiffly.

He smiled mockingly, then bowed and was out the door, leaving her feeling affronted and irritated that he seemed always to get the best of her in their conversation together.

When her maid returned with the pressed gown, Crimson hurried into fresh undergarments and sprinkled perfume lavishly about her person, for there was no space in which to bathe and she did not know where to go for water. She was dressed fairly quickly and hurried down to Madame's apartments.

When she arrived, she found that Madame had already gone to the king and she had left word that Crimson was to attend her in the Main Salon later in the evening after supper. Crimson looked around hopelessly, realizing that she had quite a deal of time to kill before the hour of supper. Speaking of supper, she was famished at this moment, for she had eaten very little for breakfast, and the hour was close unto noon.

Once more out in the corridor, she moved aimlessly about looking for someone who seemed to know what they were doing. She was relieved to spy the Marquis de la Vallière in a small anteroom with a group of ladies and gentlemen, and caught his attention with a wave of her hand.

"Mademoiselle Haviland, how pleasant to see you again so soon."

"Oh, monsieur, I do hope you can help me out. I am nearly starving and haven't the slightest notion of where to turn."

He smiled. "Come with me. There are tables laid out in another room. All the people have been in there stuffing themselves since I came down."

He took her arm and led her to a room that looked to be only half-finished, for one wall was papered in silver and gilt and the other three were in various stages of being painted. Tables were set out between the rolls of paper and old plaster, upon which food of all types had been set, mostly cold. Crimson took a plate from one of the tables and filled it with cold pigeon pie and baked turnips, carefully dusting off a swarm of flies before taking some cooled caramel nougat. She ate ravenously, seated next to the marquis in an adjoining room, where several others were also eating.

The marquis brought her two glasses of wine, after which she felt marvelously fit again and thanked him profusely. She told him she was attached to Madame's retinue and asked if she would see him again tonight at the entertainments the king had planned.

He shrugged ruefully. "Alas, mademoiselle, I would be only too happy to escort you, but I have already promised Madame d'Effate the evening. But I will see you tomorrow morning at the hunt?"

She laughed. "I have never hunted in my life, monsieur, and doubt seriously how well I shall look on a horse."

"But you must attend, mademoiselle, or the king will be displeased. He expects everyone invited to the hunt to participate." His chest swelled with unconcealed pride. "My sister will be wearing a rust-colored habit. You will recognize her easily, for she will be at the head of the hunters all day. She is a most excellent horsewoman."

"I shall be looking forward to seeing her then, monsieur," Crimson responded, touched by the young man's devotion to his sister, who, many said, would soon be ousted from her position in favor of a woman who wore better under the strain of being the king's mistress. It was rumored that La Valliere was pregnant again, and that after each pregnancy, she grew less lovely in the king's eyes. Crimson could feel a twinge of pity for her.

After the marquis had left her, Crimson headed for Madame's suite, hoping to be able to relax for a while before the evening, but she found her cousin waiting for her in the corridor.

"Marquise, I did not know you would be here," she said, surprised.

62

Violette d'Onges shrugged. "Oh, the king has invited me before, but I had to send a special request this time, for I had to see you."

Crimson ushered her into an alcove where they could talk without being in the mainstream of people. Her cousin looked tired from the day's traveling, and Crimson had decided to invite her to use her bedroom in the attic, when Violette broke in hurriedly.

"Your father has written me, Crimson. He wants you to come to London."

"My father!" Crimson stared at the older woman, flabbergasted.

"Yes, I only received his letter yesterday and when I found you had accompanied Madame to Versailles I followed you out here. I knew you would want to know about it as soon as possible. You will have to make your arrangements with Madame, of course."

"But—but he cannot ask me to come to England when he knows that I am lady-in-waiting to Her Royal Highness. Why would he do such a thing?"

"Perhaps he does not know it. I don't know why he wants you to come now, Crimson, after all these years, but there was some urgency in his letter. I gathered he was hoping that you could make the crossing over the Channel before Christmas."

"Oh, I will *not* go, I tell you! He cannot force me to go. I will apply to Madame and beg her to keep me here in France. It would be like journeying to some foreign country! I cannot do it!"

"Crimson, you've got to obey your father. You're only seventeen, and he is still your legal guardian." Violette spread her hands wide in a gesture of futility. "There is really nothing you can do about it, my dear."

"Oh, I must tell Madame. She may know of something!" Crimson said, on the verge of tears.

Here she was at Versailles! She promptly forgot the uncomfortable lodgings she had been assigned and the cold food and crowded rooms. She was near the king! She would see him tonight with all the other great and noble courtiers that flocked around him like plants 'round the

63

sun. The spell could not be broken now after only a taste of such glory!

"I'm sorry," Violette was saying with sympathy. She patted her shoulder and walked away, presumably to continue on to Paris.

Crimson did not even register the fact that she had gone. She felt too miserable to care about anyone else now. She would have to wait until tonight when she would be able to catch a private moment with the princess. Surely Madame would not want her to leave!

Unfortunately, Crimson had miscalculated the depth of her mistress' love for her native country and her brother. Instead of feeling sorry for Crimson's "misfortune," Madame was as excited for her as though Crimson had just been handed the keys to the kingdom. Crimson was nonplussed as she watched Madame walk about the room, enumerating the joys of English life, the grandeur of her brother's court, the poignancy of an English winter.

"Oh, I am envious of you, my dear," the princess sighed, finally dropping into a chair. "How I wish I could accompany you, Crimson!" Her blue eyes sparkled. "I shall make you an official ambassadress from me to my brother. Charles will receive you with open arms and more gifts than you can imagine. You will be feted at court! How lucky you are, Crimson!"

"But, Madame, I—"

"Oh, don't worry about your post here. I daresay it will be hard to find someone as sweet and considerate as yourself, my dear, but it shall simply have to be done. I suppose Madame Louvois would be only too happy to accept."

As the princess was undressed, Crimson suddenly realized how little she had meant to her mistress. She had thought that Madame would at least be a trifle chagrined at losing her services, but here she was, already replacing her with someone else. Ah, the thoughtlessness of the mighty!

7

The days at Versailles had passed too quickly for Crimson, eager to drink in as much of the court as was possible in the few weeks she had left to remain in France. Madame had arranged for her to leave from Calais on November first, before the icy winter winds and gales would make it dangerous to cross the Channel. Crimson miserably hoped her ship would sink to the bottom of the ocean with her aboard. She was in such low spirits that Madame excused her from her duties for a few days when they returned to Saint-Cloud, fearful that Crimson had caught some fever.

After four days of the inactivity that was causing her greater hardship than her thoughts of England, Crimson decided to appear before the princess to resume her duties. It was as she was climbing the stairs to the chambers of her mistress that she nearly bumped into Nicholas Brentwood. His hands were immediately around her waist to steady her.

Angrily, she drew away from him. "What are you doing on this staircase, monsieur?" she inquired loftily. "This is only for Madame's personal household's use."

"I have just come from Madame's rooms, mademoiselle, and her husband had requested entrance, so she asked me to leave this way." His blue eyes lazily touched on her

65

hair, her throat, her bosom, before returning to meet her gaze. "You seem upset, Mistress Haviland."

"Oh, don't talk to me!" she burst out suddenly. "I hate anything English!"

"Then you must hate yourself," he replied with amusement, catching the hand that had flown up to slap his face. He grasped it steadily in his own so that she could not continue up the staircase.

"Let me go! What I do is none of your concern!" she flung at him, growing angrier by the minute.

"Calm yourself, mademoiselle. You cannot appear before the princess in such a state. She would most certainly think the fevers had laid hold of you." He was laughing at her and Crimson itched to scratch him.

"Shut up and release me, or I shall tell everyone of your secret meetings with Her Highness!"

Immediately, a hand was placed over her mouth and she was pushed back roughly against the cold stone of the wall behind her. His expression was no longer amused and the hand was crushing her mouth brutally. Crimson struggled for a moment, but he was leaning against her, pressing her back into the stones.

"If I really thought you would do such a thing, mademoiselle, I'm afraid I would have to arrange for you to have a small accident. You know nothing of what is going on between the princess and me. Take care that you do not try to spread lies in order to get back at me. Need I remind you that poison is widely used these days, among the mightiest at court, to get rid of a troublesome witness to some wrongdoing? Even those who may be innocent are done away with on a whim." He paused and searched her face. "Do you understand?"

She nodded, petrified at the strength in this man. How could she ever have thought he was one of Monsieur's gang? There was something strange about this man. He was not what he seemed to be, or what he tried to make others think he was. What was it that he wanted? And why would the princess be intriguing with him? It would be too dangerous for her to consort openly with an Englishman.

66

They both started at the sound of heels on the stone steps of the staircase, and Crimson stared at her captor in alarm.

"Damn!" he cursed under his breath. "It must be Monsieur!"

Quickly, he took his hand away from her mouth, only to replace it with his lips, which began kissing her roughly while his hands held hers at her sides. Crimson felt the warmth of his body even through their clothes, in contrast to the coldness of the wall behind her. She was stiff in his embrace until his hands came up to her bodice to cup her breasts beneath the thin stuff of silk. At the sound of a slight cough, they sprang apart to see Monsieur on the stairway, watching them with detached cynicism.

"Nicholas! You here, with one of my wife's ladies! Really, how uncivilized!"

Brentwood bowed swiftly before the little man who would have reached only to his shoulder if they had been standing on the same level. Monsieur was pursing his lips, gazing with disdain at the fluttering bosom of the girl.

"Monsieur, I did not know you were there," Brentwood replied easily.

"Obviously," the other man returned drily. "Well, I suppose it is as the Chevalier thought, Nicholas. You do not feel inclined to share our games with us, as I had thought earlier. You were teasing me, weren't you?" The red lips smiled in what was supposed to be a flirtatious grin.

"Monsieur, I certainly did not want to mislead you. I value your friendship above all else, but cannot bring myself to leave the young ladies alone."

"If you value my friendship, monsieur, you would do well not to be seen so often in my wife's company," the little man reproved him with a sigh. "And is it true, that you have been noticed talking most earnestly with the English ambassador?" The rather vacant brown eyes became probing.

Crimson stole a quick glance at the Englishman and did not see him waver at the prince's question.

"Yes, I did talk with Montagu yesterday in order to

renew an old acquaintance. If I may remind you, Monsieur, Montagu has been invited to Saint-Cloud for the entire week, and many people have been seen talking with him."

"You may not remind me of anything, Nicholas! He was invited here by my wife, against my express wishes! I would sooner not see the fool and be constantly reminded by his presence that I am married to his master's sister. Would that I had married a Frenchwoman instead!" He turned to the trembling girl. "You are lucky, mademoiselle, that you will soon be leaving our shores. My friends and I have taken a dislike to you." He turned his nose up as though her scent were most foul in his nostrils. "You, too, Nicholas, may find yourself overstaying your welcome," he warned in a high voice that revealed his agitation.

Then, without saying anything else, the man left them on the staircase, obviously to go in search of his paramour, in order that he might be comforted by him.

"That pompous bastard!" Brentwood hissed when the sound of his heels had died away. "How I would like to show him the tip of my sword!"

"For heaven's sake, monsieur!" Crimson pleaded with him. "You nearly had us both put in extreme danger. Whatever possessed you to—"

"Mademoiselle, the sight of your sweet, ripe lips made me blind to any danger and I—"

"Oh, do be quiet!" Crimson said, her anger returning. "Don't act the gentleman with me. I know you well enough now not to be fooled by your charade!"

He drew closer to her. "How good it is when a woman puts a man at his ease," he sighed mockingly. "I agree, my gentlemanly act is nothing else but a mask. How I would love to show you just what I would really like to do with you, mademoiselle." His blue eyes leered at her sardonically. "But the time is not now, nor the place this not-so-private staircase. Another time, mademoiselle." He bowed and hurried down the stairs, leaving her with no one upon whom to vent her indignation.

The weeks of autumn passed too quickly for Crimson,

but after Monsieur's words to her on the staircase, she could not help but realize that she was no longer welcomed at Saint-Cloud. It would be useless now to plead her case to the princess, in hopes that Crimson would be allowed to remain in France. At least, she told herself, she would not have to put up with Brentwood's presence much longer, for he now was in the habit of coming to Madame's rooms nearly every night. At his approach, the ladies-in-waiting were asked to leave, and Crimson wondered if Madame had taken this infuriating man as her lover. He was risking his neck, meeting the princess like this, but the thought did not seem to bother him. Well, he would soon find out that one did not come and go as one pleased at Saint-Cloud without Monsieur finding out about it soon enough—and taking steps to stop it.

October was drawing to a close, and Crimson would be leaving tomorrow in order to take the coach to Calais, where she would spend the night at an inn before continuing to England by ship. She had said her good-byes to those at Saint-Cloud whom she had come to know in these short months. There had been no tears on either side because all of the ladies were aware of Crimson's fall from grace in the eyes of Monsieur, and they did not want to endanger their own positions by being too friendly with her.

Only Madame seemed oblivious to her husband's glowering looks, as she made every attempt to make Crimson's departure a happy one. She gave her two or three gowns, which, she assured her, would be the envy of every woman at the English court. A few personal tokens were added to Crimson's luggage, with a letter to Madame's brother, which would be Crimson's introduction to court. Madame instructed her endlessly to assure Charles that she was well and happy at Saint-Cloud, for she had no wish to be the cause of damaged relations between the two countries.

"Who knows? Perhaps we shall see each other soon in London, Crimson?" she said wistfully as the last of her luggage was packed up that evening.

Crimson nodded without conviction, and couldn't help the lump that came to her throat at the thought of leaving

69

this proud, brave princess alone in a palace whose occupants hated her, for the most part, because they couldn't understand her.

Madame had excused her from her duties that night, so that Crimson could get some rest before her journey the next day, but Crimson could not stay in her room with the noise of the entertainment downstairs, and she escaped to the coolness of the gardens, wrapping a light shawl about her shoulders to ward off the misty chill. How much colder would the English nights be, she wondered.

There were many people in the gardens that evening despite the coolness of the temperature, and Crimson skirted them wearily, not wishing to see their closed looks turned towards her. She walked out to the edge of the garden gazing absently at the forest beyond, remembering that night she had seen Madame with Nicholas Brentwood.

"So, you're leaving tomorrow?"

It was as though he had stepped out of her memories. Crimson could see his face only dimly in the deepening shadows, but she would have known him had he said nothing to her.

"Yes," she said quietly, wondering at the quickening of her heartbeat.

"You must be sad to leave all of this." Mockery heavy in his tones now.

She laughed nervously. "I'm not sure anymore. I suppose I should be glad my father called me home. He could be saving me from Monsieur's vindictiveness and thrusting me into the refuge of King Charles' court."

"Do not let yourself be fooled, little one. There are as many intrigues and petty jealousies in London as there are in Paris. At least, you will have Madame's introduction, which should land you into the arms of her brother with little inconvenience."

She looked up at him in surprise. "What do you mean?"

His laugh was cynical. "Everyone knows that Charles is extremely partial to a beautiful woman. To have one sent to him like a Christmas present from his sister will make
70

his conscience completely at ease, despite your obvious youth."

She drew herself up a little. "Perhaps you overestimate your king, Lord Dorset, for I have very little intention of ingratiating myself to him once I arrive in London."

He shrugged. "Oh, it is hard enough for hardened courtesans to resist the king's charm, my dear. It will not be hard for him to bowl you over."

"You sound as though you speak from personal experience," she said in a huff.

"I do. My sister was one of his earlier conquests."

"Oh, I didn't know that you had family in England."

"She died in the Great Plague, along with my mother."

"I'm sorry." Crimson twisted her fingers nervously in her skirt, feeling with a part of her as though she should walk inside and get away from the power this man seemed to hold over her senses, while at the same time wanting to stay with him, to lean on him during this last night at Saint-Cloud.

"I suppose this will be good-bye between us," she went on carefully.

He said nothing, and she knew he was watching her with keen eyes, waiting for her reaction. They stood together for another moment as though each was sending out invisible feelers, trying to gauge the other's emotions.

"Crimson—" His arms went around her suddenly, crushing her against his lean, hard body. His mouth swooped down out of the darkness and fastened on her own, drawing the sweetness like a sigh from her lips.

Crimson did not question her own response, whether it was loneliness or sadness or some primitive need that drew her to this virile man who had been the first to ever kiss her. Her arms went up and around his neck and she pressed herself closer to him in a gesture that was half-defiant, half-eager. Their kiss was long and intense, making her lose track of where she was. Then, he was lowering her onto the ground, the coolness of the grass jarring her back to reality.

"No, no," she protested feebly. "Not here."

"There is nowhere else for us," he answered her, kiss-

71

ing her eyes, her cheeks, her temples. "I want you now, Crimson. I can feel how willing you are."

"But this—this isn't right," she said, struggling to keep command of herself. "You shouldn't do this. You—"

"It will be all right, Crimson, I promise you. I won't hurt you, little girl."

He began kissing her again, smothering any further protests, while his hands began to untie the laces of her bodice. Crimson sought to escape him, but his mouth was too demanding, his hands too sure, and she knew with a sudden sense of panic that she was lost. Soon he had opened her bodice and pulled down the silk of her chemise in order to capture her trembling, young breasts. The chill made the tips spring upward against his palms as he fondled them slowly and expertly.

She was shaking now, whether from the cool air or the enormity of what was about to happen to her. She shouldn't be here, she shouldn't be here with this man. Why should he be the first to awaken her girlish senses? They would not see each other again, and certainly they were not in love with each other.

"I don't want—" she began as soon as her mouth was free.

He was trailing warm kisses down her throat to her breasts, and she gasped as his lips took possession of one of those pink tips which seemed to be the very centers of her entire being at this moment. Despite the coolness, she suddenly felt as though she were on fire. His hands were pulling her skirt down, pushing it past her hips so that he could caress her flesh with artful, burning strokes.

Her breath was coming fast and a wave of swift emotion rolled over her, leaving her feeling devastated by its force. She wanted this man to make love to her, she thought incredulously. What did anything else matter against the strength of that terrible need? Sighing, she gave herself up to him.

He knew, instinctively, the moment of her capitulation and the ease of his victory puzzled him. But he did not let it worry him for long, for his own desire was urging him

72

onward. Soon her skirt lay discarded in the wet grass and he had pushed her petticoats around her waist.

Crimson lay back, letting the warm feeling cover her like a blanket. She felt his hands stroking her breasts, her hips and thighs and she could not help the low moan of pleasure that escaped her. She did not know when he had removed his own breeches, but very soon his naked flesh was warm against her own. She shuddered at the shock of contact.

She could hear his breathing, strong and quick now, matching the hard thudding of his heart against her breast as he lay on top of her. He kissed her again, long and slowly, holding her head between his hands. Crimson moved against him instinctively, hardly aware of what she was doing.

His hands moved from her head, downward to her hips, caressing them artfully as his knee slipped between her legs to open them. Crimson panicked again at this invasion of her most private place and tensed her knees to keep her thighs close together. Once more she shook her head, denying the need that was sweeping over her faster and faster now.

"No, no," she whispered. "Please—"

But it was too late. He could not stop the flow of passion that drove him onward. He must taste the hidden secrets of this woman—he must. With practiced experience, he forced her knees apart.

The gesture seemed brutal to Crimson, who had been lulled into a sense of security by the softness of his previous caresses. Her thighs ached from their tenseness, and the pressure of his legs holding them apart made them cramp painfully. Seeking to alleviate the pain, she arched her knees in a reflex gesture, bringing her heels down to dig into the soft earth.

"That's a good girl," he murmured, nibbling her ear.

Realizing then that she had only aided him in his triumph, she would have brought her knees down again, but he had hooked his arms around them, to hold them up while he readied himself to deflower her. Crimson became fearful as the full realization of what she was doing completely dawned on her. Thoughts that had been suppressed in the back of her mind came unbidden now to the surface. What if he hurt her, what if she would no longer be able to find a husband after this defilement, what if she became pregnant? The last thought made her struggle in earnest against him, but it was useless, for she was in his power now, drawn tautly in his grasp, open to his onslaught.

With a patience that was lost on her, he pressed himself to the core of her womanliness. She shuddered, feeling a tingling within her at his touch. Something hot and probing was moving towards her, something that stopped for an instant, poised to strike, and then did so with a swiftness that made the breath catch in her throat. Crimson felt as though she had been split in two and lay back, gasping, twisting her body to escape this thing that seemed to want to impale her.

He waited until her struggles lessened, then drove in once again, making her moan a little from the pain. A great pressure was building as his attacks increased in urgency, and then something broke, like a dam bursting inside of her, and he slid in abruptly, making her whimper softly at the hurt that was like no other she had ever experienced.

But the hurt did not last long, for as his movements continued, slow and gentle, it ceased to be more than a tiny ache that was soon lost in an expanding wave of pleasure that broke over her. Her hands reached up for him and her arms wound themselves about his neck to bring his mouth down to her once more.

She was drifting along on the tide of gentle passion that lay between them. Crimson opened her eyes wide, gazing up at the star-filled sky that seemed to twinkle through the thin veil of mist that had descended on the gardens. The only sounds in her ears were the comforting chirps of crickets, her own sighs, and her lover's steady, deep breathing.

And then, his breathing changed, grew more erratic as his movements, too, became more urgent, less gentle. Instinctively, Crimson tensed again, not knowing what lay

74

behind these changes. Her tenseness made it more painful again and she bit her lip to keep in the cry that threatened to escape her. He was almost oblivious of her now, it seemed. His eyes were closed, his hands sought her breasts in a reflex motion.

Suddenly, something inside of her seemed to let go and Crimson lifted her hips to meet him. She was moving with him, with his rhythm and her breath was short and quick, tearing through her lungs as she sought some pinnacle of shared feeling she could not name. Half-sobbing, she flung her body against his, and then everything seemed to shatter as an indescribable feeling surged through her, making her whole body tingle and vibrate.

His movements slowed, became gentle again, then stopped, as they lay, panting together, beads of sweat dotting their faces and bodies. His kiss was deep, searching and Crimson lay back weakly and let him have his way. Finally, he rolled away from her and propped his head on his hand to gaze down into her face. Her eyes opened slowly as she felt his burning look on her.

"Oh," she sucked in her breath, feeling the chill of the night air, hearing the sounds of the distant palace entertainment, staring at this stranger whom she had let make love to her without a struggle. And the realization made her afraid. "What have you done to me?" she sobbed.

The thoughtful look changed subtly on his lean face, narrowing the jawline and tightening the mouth. "I have made you a woman, Crimson," he said quietly with a trace of contemptuousness.

"But—but I don't want—didn't want you to—" She was beginning to cry childishly, reaching for her skirt as she pushed her petticoats over her exposed legs.

"It's a little too late for second thoughts," he replied sarcastically. "The damage has been done, my sweet, and I must say, I thought you willing enough."

"But you tricked me!" she accused him, standing in order to pull on her skirt. At the sight of its grass stains and wetness, she began to cry in earnest. "This should never have happened. Oh, why didn't you leave me alone?"

Disgusted, Brentwood rose and put his own clothing into order again. He watched her dispassionately as she fastened her bodice with shaking fingers, then brushed her hands aside and tied the lacings himself. She was silent, valiantly trying to stifle her tears, as he finished dressing her.

"Hurry up now and get to your room, my charming little companion of the evening," he admonished insolently. "I'm sure you will want to erase all traces of our time together."

"That is impossible and you know it!" she said, sniffing a little. "You—you should have been gentleman enough —when you found out that I was—"

"I doubt that you would have hated me any less if I would have stopped at the most crucial moment," he said, laughing a little. "At least you will no longer be encumbered with your virginity, madamoiselle, when you arrive in England. The king will, no doubt, be pleased."

"The king! Oh, shut up with your filthy thoughts!" she snapped at him, trying to find her slippers. "I should never have trusted you! If only I hadn't felt so sad and lonely tonight, I—"

"Why must a woman always think of an excuse after she has enjoyed herself with a man?" Brentwood sighed mockingly. "Can't you admit, Crimson, that you enjoyed it?"

She stopped and blinked at him, her angry retort stuck in her throat. He laughed at her discomfiture, and recovering herself, she flew at him to rake his face with her nails. He caught her hands easily and pressed her against him, reaching down to kiss her with hard, masterful lips. When he released her, she was trembling and would not meet his amused gaze.

"At least you lost it on French soil," he said lazily. "That should bring you some comfort when you think back on it."

"But it was with a damn Englishman!" she returned, slipping into her shoes and walking towards the palace. She had gone a few steps away from him when his voice detained her.

76

"Crimson!"

She turned curiously, wondering if, perhaps, he had decided to make her an apology.

"You won't forget me, will you, my darling?" The voice was mocking with laughter held just below the surface.

Anger flooded through her and she stamped her foot. "I shall do my best!" she retorted and turned away with a hurried pace, the tears in her eyes blinding the lights of the palace to her.

PART TWO:
Marriage in England

8

Lord James Haviland gazed about the glittering ballroom, noting any absences from the card tables and nodding to acquaintances as he caught their eyes. The betting was extremely heavy tonight, and Haviland flexed his fingers as though to feel the shape and texture of the cards in his hands. He would have to win big tonight if he was going to recoup even a portion of what he had lost the night before. Curse his luck! The cards seemed to be going against him with alarming habitualness. Hadn't he already gotten himself into an extremely dangerous situation with that young Gardner fellow?

Dangerous was not the word, Haviland admitted grimly to himself, casting a quick eye about as though searching for the fellow. A thin film of sweat clung to his forehead as he pondered on the amount of money he had lost to him over the past three months. He should never have continued playing with the man, but something had driven him to try to erase the smug, arrogant smile from the courtier's face.

Gardner's luck was phenomenal! If Haviland had been a more clever man, he might have tried to convince the court that Gardner's luck owed much to his ability to cheat at whist and cribbage, but Sir Reginald had too many friends among the noblemen and his influence was too great for Haviland to attempt any such tactics.

Somehow, he must find a way to pay back the other man without digging himself in deeper with his already clamoring creditors. He had gone over his assets with his solicitor, a discouraging pastime, and then had remembered that he still had an unmarried daughter who had been recently appointed as lady-in-waiting to King Louis' sister-in-law, King Charles' own beloved sister! The possibilities had become more intriguing, when Haviland had learned that Sir Reginald Gardner was only recently widowed of his second wife and looking around discreetly for a third lady to fill the post.

Gardner's treatment of his previous wives was not a thing one boasted of, but there were very few women in these times who were treated lovingly, or even fairly, by their husbands. Only those women who could wheedle themselves into the good graces of a powerful man at Court, like that beautifully decadent Barbara Palmer, Countess of Castlemaine, mistress of the king for over seven years now, had very little to worry about as far as indifferent husbands went.

Haviland actually licked his lips, thinking of the handsome bitch who, some were whispering, was soon going to lose her exclusive post as *maîtresse en titre* to the king, because of her stormy rages and incessant demands for money and jewels. Oh, but if that woman needed someone to comfort her in her distress, Haviland knew he would only be too glad to aid her. He half-closed his eyes, picturing the vibrant red hair spread on the pristine whiteness of his bedsheets, the magnificent body, rumored to be well-schooled in the more erotic forms of love—

"Haviland?"

James Haviland opened his eyes to the reality of the gaming room and turned automatically, the smile quickly becoming stuck involuntarily to his face when he perceived the figure of Sir Reginald Gardner staring at him with some amusement.

"I swear, my lord, you were standing there smiling to yourself as though concocting a most diabolical scheme. Do you think you might let me in on your secret?"

82

Haviland laughed distantly. "Hardly worth the trouble, sir, as I was only thinking of trifles."

The two men bowed to each other, and then Haviland took the liberty of locking an arm about the younger man's, drawing him to a private alcove.

"I should like some conversation with you, Sir Reginald, if you have a moment," Haviland explained, feeling the slight tug on his arm as Gardner attempted to release himself from his grasp. "It is of some importance, I assure you."

"Ah, Haviland, if it is about the money you owe me—" began Sir Reginald abruptly, "I would rather not discuss that here or now. My solicitors will come 'round to speak with you about making payment." There was a slight emphasis on *solicitors,* and Sir Reginald finally succeeded in releasing his arm.

Haviland swallowed and felt light perspiration on his upper lip. "Sir Reginald, forgive me for insisting, but I would very much like to discuss this with you now. I am, as you must be well aware, on short funds these days, and to be quite honest with you—it would be somewhat of a deprivation to me to attempt to pay the whole of the amount I owe you in one lump."

Sir Reginald brushed a stray lock of brown hair back from his shoulder, patting it absently into place in the periwig that he wore so rakishly. His whole manner indicated dismissal of the subject, but Haviland pressed on, inviting him to sit for a moment on the bench in the alcove.

"Only for a moment, please," Sir Reginald insisted, "for I have a young woman hot to win back from me tonight what she lost to me last week. Her payment, should she lose, will be a warm night in my bed—no doubt easier for her to dispense with than her precious coin." He sniggered at the implication, and Haviland tried to smile in return.

"Women—we have many at court who are devoted to the cards," Haviland said finally, wondering how to broach the subject of marriage to his daughter. "I suppose, Sir Reginald, that such women would hold little charm for you in your selection of a new wife?"

Sir Reginald shrugged and looked at him with a bored

air. "My selection of a wife is hardly your concern, Haviland. I presume you did not wish to speak to me about such things, but about your own passion for gambling."

"On the contrary," Haviland went on quickly, "I can sympathize with your hesitation in such a delicate matter as chosing the proper woman to share your name with you. As you can see, I have never remarried myself, due to lack of women I deemed eligible to carry on in my dead wife's place." He paused for a suitable moment, finding it impossible even to recollect Deborah's face in his mind. Then in a brisker tone: "But I believe I might have a solution to both your problem and mine, Sir Reginald, if you are willing to trust in me for another moment."

Gardner glanced at Haviland with a mixture of boredom and curiosity. "Good God, man, I'm not sure I've been following you *so far!* What you could possibly have in mind, I haven't the slightest idea." He looked out into the crowd as though trying to find someone to rescue him, then returned to stare at Haviland. "But please go on," he said with strained politeness.

"Sir, I have a daughter of marriageable age, only seventeen, she is—and very beautiful." Haviland prayed that she was beautiful, cursing himself that he had not thought to ask Violette about Crimson's looks in any of his letters. "She has never been married, and, in fact, has lived most of her years with my cousin in Orleans."

"How delightful," Gardner returned with little enthusiasm.

Eagerly now, Haviland pressed forward. "She was only this year accepted in the household of the king's sister, Madame of France, to be her lady-in-waiting and has, I am informed, done all her tasks well as befits a maid-of-honor to royalty."

Gardner's dark eyes had lightened at this latter news, and Haviland could sense the small vein of interest that had suddenly taken hold of him.

"I have only recently required that she return home to stay with me and, although it nearly broke her heart to leave France, she has complied like a dutiful daughter. No doubt, she will come bearing many fine gifts from her mistress as well as a personal recommendation to the king. You recall when Madame sent Frances Stuart over to England, Sir Reginald?"

Sir Reginald did remember. It was perhaps five years ago that Madame had sent a young lady-in-waiting of hers to her brother's court, and Charles had quickly become enamored of her. He had become nearly a slave to her every whim, only hoping for the ultimate gift from her which she would not bestow because of her supposed loyalty to her new mistress, Queen Catherine, Charles' wife. The king had tried all his wiles on this young beauty, but to no avail and, when she had eloped this spring with her cousin, the king had been hard hit, swearing that she and her husband would never be allowed in court circles again. Ah, yes, and with Castlemaine's influence waning, the king was ripe for a new woman to control his easygoing life. A personal recommendation from his beloved sister, whom he referred to as "Minette," was all that was needed to insure Haviland's daughter a good chance at such a position.

Gardner glanced warily at the older man, wondering how much he could trust him. The man owed him upwards of a thousand pounds, and his financial dealings were already in need of urgent solving. Would he be willing to barter his own flesh and blood in order to erase the slate? Gardner smiled to himself. He knew Haviland too well. Of course, he would be willing to sell his daughter. Haviland was interested only in himself.

And the girl, herself, how much would she be told? Gardner frowned, wondering how biddable she would prove. If she were successful in influencing the king, there would be no end to favors and grants that she could obtain for her husband, who would, of course, not stand in the way of the king's sexual happiness. The thought that he could give over his own wife to another man's desires did not bother Gardner in the least. God knew, there were plenty of women to be had and any man who was stupid enough to prove jealous of his wife's infidelities was made a laughing-stock among the courtiers. Hadn't the king himself proclaimed this the "age of cuckoldry"?

"I must say, my lord, that your idea intrigues me,"

Gardner finally said after the long moment of thoughtfulness.

Haviland breathed an inward sigh of relief. Of course, he knew he would be able to count on Sir Reginald's greed. "Then, might I suggest that we wait for a few weeks until my daughter arrives from France to continue our discussion of our—debts?" he inquired softly.

Gardner nodded in acknowledgment. "I would like to be presented to your daughter immediately upon her arrival in London, my lord." He stood up then and bowed.

Haviland watched him saunter over to one of the tables, where he touched a young woman on the shoulder, whispering something in her ear that sent a defiant laugh from her reddened lips.

9

Crimson stood impatiently on the dock at Portsmouth, awaiting the arrival of her father or his messenger. She was not in a particularly good mood, especially as the trip across the Channel had not been a good one for her. This late in the year, the passage was rough and the waves choppy with strong winds shifting the ship dangerously to either side. She had been seasick several times during the voyage, and had found herself actually relieved to see the shores of England, a sight she would never have believed would bring her any joy.

As she stood with her serving woman, a young lady who

would be transported back to France on the next ship out, Crimson thrust her fingers firmly into the large muff supported by a string of gold lace around her neck. The November air was chilly and smelled of moisture, tickling her throat and nose. She turned at the sound of carriage wheels, thankful that someone had come at last for her.

A large vehicle, smartly driven by a liveried coachman and drawn by six matched bays, careened around a corner and stopped several feet from her. She watched as the door was opened and a middle-aged gentleman stepped out, his eyes immediately alighting on her without hesitation. Crimson recognized Lord James Haviland easily enough from memory, although now his face was more deeply lined, his dark hair streaked liberally with silver. She was a little saddened that there was no lightness in her step as she walked to meet him, no gladness within her breast at the sight of her own father, whom she had not seen for seven years.

"Ah, Crimson!" The forced joy was too evident in the man's tone to escape even Crimson's naïve ears. "I hope the voyage went well enough?"

She shrugged, and they stopped before coming close enough to touch. "As well as could be expected, I suppose," she answered lamely.

After a moment's hesitation, Haviland placed an arm about her shoulders and drew her into a quick embrace. "Come then, and we'll be off to the inn. Lodgings have been secured for both of us, as I was not sure if you would be fit enough to travel on to London today. I'm sure you would like to rest and have a good supper, and then a night's sleep before you arrive in the city."

Crimson nodded and followed her father to the coach, where he helped her inside and then paid her serving woman, who would be leaving shortly.

Inside the coach, the talk was trivial, Crimson noting the coldness of the weather, Haviland remarking on how much she had grown in the last seven years. Once they had arrived at the inn, Crimson felt a lightening just to be out of the confinement in the coach. She went straight to

87

her appointed room, assuring her father that she would meet him in the dining room for a light supper.

"Dear God!" she murmured to herself once in her own room. "Why did he have to bring me back here?"

The answer escaped her for the moment and she could do nothing but lie down on the bed as he had suggested to relax for an hour or two before supper. She could not sleep, however, and rolled restlessly between the sheets, feeling terribly homesick for France already. She missed Madame and the other ladies, the sweet mistiness of Saint-Cloud, the glory of basking near the light of the king of France himself. She would never admit that she might miss a certain Englishman who had made her a woman on the night before her departure from France, but his visage passed several times in her mind and the remembrance only made her more determined to hate everything in this new country of hers.

When the maid knocked to help her to dress for the evening, Crimson felt hardly in the mood for supper, but allowed herself to be dressed listlessly and followed the maid downstairs to the large dining room that was filled already with diverse people.

"Crimson, you look marvelously fresh, daughter," Haviland said gallantly, after she had seated herself opposite him at the oaken table.

"Thank you," she answered demurely, hesitant at calling him "Father." "I am glad you decided to stay the night at the inn. I'm sure I couldn't have borne up under the journey to London today."

"Good, good. And now, I must insist that you order from our host something to please your appetite. Their kidney pie is excellent here, and their roast pheasant something bordering on a delicacy."

Crimson ordered listlessly, her mouth watering for the French meats and side dishes she had become accustomed to after all these years. The sight of the kidney pie, in fact, nearly made her stomach roll over and she shook her head, as though to rid herself of the strange moment of queasiness. But in spite of her famished air upon arrival in

88

the ordinary, she soon found that eating more than a third of the pie was out of the question.

Shoving the uneaten portion to the side, Crimson folded her hands on the table and leaned slightly toward the man opposite her. "If you please, my lord, I would like to know why you sent for me."

Haviland's head came up from contemplation of his own meal, and surveyed the young girl reflectively, causing Crimson to blush slightly under his scrutiny. He smiled and took his eyes away from her.

"Crimson, my dear, I am your father and I only want the best for you. Trust me as to your future, my daughter, and I can assure you that I will provide for you most adequately."

"But you have not answered my question," she persisted, not willing to be fobbed off.

He shrugged. "It was not by choice that I left you in France, if you will recall," he began tentatively. "The king had just been restored to the throne and my own lands as well as those belonging to your mother's family would have been snatched up by some loyal follower, if I hadn't been here myself to insure that I was treated fairly."

"I understand that," Crimson put in quietly, remembering that day when her only confidante had been taken from her, to die far away from her of some horrid disease.

"It took me a long time to build up my image as a courtier, to feel welcomed by the king, to remain in his good graces. 'Tis not an easy thing, Crimson, to live this life in London. There are always those who might be more grasping than you, less concerned with the dictates of morality or decency." He paused delicately, allowing the girl to think about his words.

"Paris is much like that," she said finally. "Madame used to tell me that one needed to be minus a soul in order to be truly happy at court."

"Ah, yes, Madame is very wise then," Haviland returned, brightening at the reminder that this girl who was acclaimed as his daughter was friends with the sister of King Charles.

"But you still have not said what plans you have for

me," Crimson continued, determined to press home to the point.

Haviland looked down carefully, studying his polished fingernails with an absorbed air, before continuing. "To be honest, Crimson, I am in some trouble."

Crimson breathed inwardly, realizing that, unconsciously, these were the very words she had expected to hear. And what sort of price was she to pay for the mistakes of her father?

"I have always had a passion for cards. Gambling, if you must," he went on, still not looking at her. "My luck has been all bad for some time now, and I'm ashamed to tell you how much I have lost at the tables." He glanced up from beneath narrowed lids to gauge her expression. He was satisfied to see the air of concern about her face. "In short, my dear, I am having difficulty settling with my creditors."

"But surely, you have other assets you can rely on," Crimson interrupted quickly. "Your lands, jewels—"

He waved his hands in the air as though to dismiss her words as mere nonsense. "Not enough," he said. "There is one particular creditor who will take nothing but coin to settle our debts. His name is Sir Reginald Gardner, one of the brightest stars at court."

"Surely, this Sir Reginald is an honorable man. He—"

"Honorable, yes. Patient, no. He wishes to settle with me immediately. You, my dear, will have an opportunity to meet with him soon when he presents himself at our home. He has expressed a wish to see you, Crimson."

Crimson flushed. "Why ever for? What have I to do with your business with each other?"

Haviland shrugged. "I was hoping, my dear, that the sight of your lovely face and superb figure might cause my creditor to forget his financial troubles with me, at least until I am able to come up with the money."

Crimson pressed her hands together and looked away from the brilliant gaze he was bestowing upon her. "So I am to lure his mind away from more mundane details of his visit?" she questioned, a trifle bitterly.

Haviland snorted. "You have only to appear on the
90

threshold to do that, my dearest daughter. Please don't think me a terrible ogre to use you in this way. I hardly thought you would take it amiss of me to want to introduce you to the most influential people at court. It will be to your benefit, too, my dear."

"I don't care about your English court!" Crimson returned heatedly. "I only wish that you had left me in France, where I belong!"

Haviland noted the trembling hands and flushed face of the girl and decided to cut the conversation off for the evening. Time enough to get her used to the idea of marriage with Sir Reginald after she had met him. After all, what could she do if he decided upon the marriage? Nothing. She was only seventeen, clearly not old enough to make her own decisions in such matters. Everyone at court would look upon the marriage as being most advantageous to the girl—public opinion would certainly be on his side. The king would do naught but give his blessing.

He almost smiled to himself, but sobered as she excused herself from the table to go to her room. God, but she had turned out lovely, he thought objectively. He could see the likeness to Deborah, or at least tried to assure himself that he could. Naturally, there was nothing in her of him. How could there be?

He downed his tankard and prepared to retire himself. His own sweet daughter. He wondered, cynically, if Deborah was turning over in her grave.

Traveling was somewhat difficult through the muddy roads that led to London. Several times, Crimson and Haviland were forced to get out of the vehicle so the footmen could deliver it from the squelching mud that caused wheels to sink up to the axles.

Despite Haviland's hopes that they could reach London by late nightfall, it was clearly impossible, as twilight settled over the English countryside and they were forced to seek shelter for the night at a wayside inn.

It was still difficult for Crimson to think of this man who was almost a stranger to her as her father and she had, with his tacit agreement, taken to calling him "my lord." It suited her better, and she wondered if she would ever feel comfortable with him.

As the carriage had taken them over the roads that led away from the coast of England, she had found herself thinking more and more of France, Paris and Madame—all the things that she had loved from the time she was a little girl. With a sinking heart, she had a premonition that she would not see any of them again.

10

London Bridge was jammed with every imaginable vehicle, from hackney coaches and peasants' carts to splendidly equipped carriages carrying the gentry to visit Whitehall Palace. Crimson took a curious glimpse from behind the sheltering curtain at the window of her carriage, noting the mass of humanity that walked or rode across the bridge in a continuous stream. Along the sides of the bridge were shops, houses and buildings of all sizes, built dangerously close to one another and leaning forward like pot-bellied, old merchants.

"It reminds me a little of the Pont Neuf," she murmured to Haviland.

"Ah, yes, and just as dangerous. London Bridge is seething with people at all times during the day and night. Among their lot walk a number of cutthroats, pickpockets and villains who are the curse of the large cities. It is so —even in Paris?" he inquired with smooth sarcasm.

Crimson glanced at him and shrugged. "As you say, my lord, it is the curse of the big cities."

"From here, one used to be able to see the tall spires of St. Paul's, but after the fire last year, I'm afraid the once-magnificent building is nothing but ruins."

Crimson did not comment, but occupied herself with gazing out at the throng of people, interested in spite of herself in these countrymen of hers that she had for so long denied. What difference, really, from the townspeople of Paris? They were both a melting pot of varied species of human beings from the beggars to the courtiers, all living in some kind of strange, hostile harmony within the confines of the city gates. All that differed was their language, really. She sighed. Much as she regretted it, she knew that she would get used to London with a great deal more ease than she had first thought. Madame would be proud of her.

The way across the bridge had become so packed that, for a moment, the coach was unable to move and Crimson glanced at her father out of the corner of her eye, to see him tapping impatiently against his knee, an expression of frustration written on his lean face.

"Curse these vagabonds who clog the traffic here!" he muttered.

"I feel a little sorry for them, my lord, in this cold atmosphere. I can see that many of them are not suitably clothed for the weather. Your king did not do overmuch for the common folk when he was returned to his throne?"

Haviland detected the faint sarcasm in her words and smiled. "No more than Louis XIV in all his magnificence has done for the poor of France, my dear. Kings seldom concern themselves with those people who cannot directly pay tribute to them. These poor will no doubt always go on as they have for the past centuries. No king or dictator or commonwealth is going to change their lot."

Finally, the driver was able to clear a lane ahead in order for the horses to pass through and the carriage was off the bridge and onto the cobbled London streets. Off to the east, Crimson could make out a tall stone building, surrounded by smaller, squatter edifices, and she pointed them out to Haviland.

"The tall building is the Tower, where prisoners of state are secured. There is also, within the Tower grounds, a zoo and a mint which are open to the public. I shall have to take you there one day, my dear," he remarked.

They drove past tumbled ruins, which, Haviland informed her, were those of St. Paul's Cathedral, and then on past the Temple, where lay students were admitted, and Lincoln's Inn, where many of the gentry passed entertaining afternoons, to the Strand, where stood some of the most magnificent homes of the nobles. They turned down the Strand onto St. Martin's Lane, and very soon stopped in front of a house that was nearly as imposing as those they had already seen.

"Here we are, my dear. Home at last."

"Home," Crimson repeated dully, gazing up at the brick facade with little excitement.

Haviland escorted her inside and up to her rooms, which, he assured her, had only recently been redecorated, he hoped to her own tastes. Crimson politely assured him that they would do fine, and after his departure, promptly fell into a storm of tears. She only just finished wiping the last traces from her cheeks when her luggage was brought up, accompanied by a ponderous maid whose sullen face bespoke her distaste of this "French foreigner."

When her gowns had been put in their proper places and Crimson had changed from her traveling clothes, she ventured outside her room to go downstairs in search of her father. She must have the opportunity to pick out a more suitable personal maid if she was expected to tolerate living here.

The drawing room was slightly ajar and she knocked softly.

"Who is it?" Her father's voice was impatient at being disturbed.

"Crimson, my lord. May I have a moment to speak with you?"

The door was opened, and a feminine laugh, devoid of any real warmth, came out to greet her with the essence of

94

strong perfume. Two dark eyes, set in a face as smooth and white as marble and haloed by dark curls, moved over her curiously.

"So this is your daughter, James?" The voice seemed not to belong to the owner. It was deep and quick, and Crimson instinctively slipped away from the beringed hand that sought to draw her inside the room by her shoulder.

"Crimson, I thought you would be resting until dinner, my dear," Haviland hurriedly rejoined, coming over to bring her into the room. "Let me introduce you to Lady Philippa Belgrade, wife to Lord Brent Belgrade. They are our neighbors, Crimson."

The woman tittered. "Actually, you won't be seeing much of my husband, Crimson, since he is always away fighting, usually in Ireland. The king thinks him a wonderful soldier, an opinion which my husband shares enthusiastically."

Crimson curtseyed swiftly, her eyes avoiding the woman's, sensing that her intrusion had somehow been ill-timed. "Forgive me, my lord, I was hoping to speak with you about a maid for my person. I'm afraid—"

"Of course, my dear. Tomorrow, you and Philippa can go shopping, see the city, whatever you want. We were only just discussing our plans for you."

"Yes, Crimson. I certainly want you to feel towards me as you would a very good friend. Your father and my husband are quite close." Philippa looked at the younger girl as though challenging her to think anything to the contrary.

Crimson hurriedly excused herself and withdrew from the room. The idea that her father might have a mistress did not concern her in the least. He was not a married man, after all, and the lady seemed not to care whether she herself was married or not.

The next day, Philippa arrived early to take Crimson through the city. Phillipa was dressed quite modishly in a long, fur-lined cape that enveloped her entirely from the chill outside. Crimson felt secure in her own dark green velvet cloak, with its attached hood lined in silver fox,

95

which had been a present from Madame. The green velvet ribbon that hung around her neck and was attached to a matching fox muff caused an "Oh" of feminine delight to escape from her companion's lips.

"How adorable!" Philippa sighed longingly. "I swear, we English can never quite seem to keep up with the French in fashion. I simply must have a cloak copied from that pattern, my dear, if you don't mind. I should be the envy of everyone at court."

"Of course," Crimson murmured, settling her hood over her deep auburn tresses, which had been dressed in gleaming coils at the back and sides of her head. She had had to do the hairstyle herself, as the maid at her disposal had no idea how to fix a lady's hair properly. Crimson hoped to find a more suitable maid today, and pulled on her gloves with a decided air as she followed Phillipa outside to her awaiting carriage.

The day was chilly and overcast with a promise of freezing rain or snow in the air. One's breath left in a cloud of vapor to hang in the still air like white smoke. Huddling herself into a corner of the carriage seat, Crimson rubbed her hands inside the muff to keep them warm.

"Lord, it is cold today," Philippa muttered distractedly, pulling the shades down over the windows to keep out the coldness. "My poor feet will be frozen with walking about on a day like today!" She buried them deeply into the lap blanket that protected both women against the chill air within the coach.

"I suppose we could make this another day—" Crimson began hesitantly.

"No, no, of course not, my dear. No doubt my nose will be red and dripping by the time we return to your father's house, but we shan't have any better weather if we wait 'til tomorrow."

Crimson shrugged to herself. "I suppose the most important thing is to engage a new maid for me. The one my father has there now is fit only for the kitchens. She would be much happier basting a fat capon than dressing me for a winter outing."

Philippa laughed smugly. "I warrant you'll not find a
96

maid that will suit you, my dear, having been used to those in France. Good domestics are extremely hard to come by this year in London, but I will take you to a place that has them for hire and, perhaps, we will be lucky enough to find someone to your likes." She turned to the younger girl with narrowed eyes. "Good gracious, I do hope you're not going to be impossible to please, Crimson."

"I'm not impossible, Philippa," Crimson smiled back in the same vein, "just exacting."

The conversation remained a series of parries and thrusts on the part of the two women, until the coach reached London Bridge, which was, despite the cold, extremely crowded and nearly impossible to navigate. The coach made its slow way through the people until the driver stopped in front of a tall, wooden building which boasted a new coat of paint. The sign above the door depicted a maid's dust cap, and Crimson concluded that they had arrived at the domestics' hiring house.

They descended the carriage steps carefully and made their way inside the building, which already held two or three other clients who seemed to be patiently awaiting the appearance of the owner.

"Lady Philippa! Good morning."

Philippa turned to see a tall, fair-haired man in his mid-thirties bowing gallantly towards her. She curtseyed swiftly and drew Crimson to a seat close to the gentleman.

"Oh Philip, how nice to see you! What brings you out on such a cold morning as this, my lord?" she asked coyly, taking a moment to throw back the hood of her cloak and loosen her scarf to expose the long white throat.

"I was about to ask you the same question, Philippa," the gentleman returned, eyeing Crimson with the air of a connoisseur.

Philippa preened. "We're looking for a maidservant for my young friend here. She has just arrived from France, Philip, and finds too much fault with our English servants." She laughed softly. "May I present Crimson Haviland, daughter of Lord James Haviland, and only recently lady-in-waiting to Madame of France. Crimson, this is Philip Stanhope, Lord Chesterfield."

Crimson bowed her head in acknowledgment and felt her hand taken and held by the man in a clasp of undeniable firmness. His lips bent to place a kiss on her wrist and she felt color come to her cheeks.

"Your servant, mistress," he said, making the words sound almost like a caress.

"You are very kind, sir," Crimson returned, looking at Philippa's laughing eyes with a touch of bewilderment.

He released her hand and began to ask her questions of France and the Court, insisting on details of Madame's own welfare. He seemed extremely worldly to Crimson, and his wit sometimes escaped her, so that she found herself blushing more than she liked, and was relieved when his servant was brought in, a stout-looking footman, and he was forced to take his leave.

After he had gone, Philippa turned to her with a mischievous look on her face. "You seemed terribly nervous around dear Philip, my dear," she observed quickly. "Why so?"

Crimson shook her head. "He kept looking at me as though he—" She stopped and, to her annoyance, blushed again.

Crimson shook her head. "He kept looking at as though he—" She stopped and, to her annoyance, blushed again.

Philippa laughed. "Oh, Crimson, Philip is very good at doing that to women, even the more experienced ones, so please don't be embarrassed. If you must know, he was the one who had first honors with the king's own mistress! Yes, he actually deflowered our beloved Castlemaine and won her undying love as a young girl. Much good it has done either of them. She's too mighty, now, to give him more than an embrace in a corridor of Whitehall, and he's too greedy to keep a love alive for one woman alone. 'Tis said that he even had the temerity to seduce the king's own sister, Madame, before she was married to King Louis' brother! It all sounds delicious, I must say. You wouldn't believe all the scandal that's been linked with him since he gave up on Lady Castlemaine. Decidedly, he's one of the better-looking men at Court and always seems to have someone new on his arm, curse his luck!"

"Is he married?"

"Gad, yes, to a cat of a woman if I do say so myself!

Lady Elizabeth Butler she was before they married, and you'd still think her a single woman by the way she carries on with the duke."

"The duke?"

"The Duke of York, James, the king's brother! Oh, the gossip that has flown about all of them—it's simply too juicy to spill out here, my dear." Phillipa leaned forward in her eagerness. "Gossip is the lifeline of the court, Crimson. Those who don't indulge get gossiped about anyway, so one has to listen just to see if one might get mentioned in the same breath as some exciting scandal!"

"Would that be a great honor?" Crimson asked curiously.

"Of course! You have not arrived, my dear, until you are the subject of someone's gossip!"

Crimson nodded helplessly. "I see."

A large, benevolent-looking gentleman was bowing low before them, and Phillipa cut short her discourse to outline the kind of maidservant that Crimson was looking for. The man frowned, scratched his head, then turned on his heel with a rejoinder that he would be back directly with someone he thought might do.

"We shall just have to hope for the best," Philippa whispered to Crimson.

"He seemed pretty confident," the latter returned.

"Oh be careful of that," Philippa warned. "His confidence might make you think the girl is exactly what you wish, when she may very well be a terrible maid. Joseph is very good at selling his merchandise."

Joseph returned with a small, dark-haired girl who seemed to be very close to Crimson's own age. She had a slightly challenging air about her that seemed somewhat amiss in a servant, and Crimson had strong reservations about accepting her at first glance, but, to her surprise, Philippa seemed satisfied with her after a few probing questions.

"She'll do very well, I think," Philippa announced.

"But how do you know—" Crimson began.

"Look at her own hair," Philippa whispered. "She must

99

do it herself, and it lies perfectly. Her clothes are neat and clean. What more do you require?"

"I suppose you're right," Crimson affirmed finally, sighing a little as she realized the extent of her ignorance in such matters. It seemed that, in spite of her desire not to have to rely on her father's mistress for help, she undoubtedly would soon wind up indebted to her.

11

Two days later, Crimson received her summons to the Royal Presence. She had sent the king the letter from Madame, delivering her into his hands, and had been hoping for a quick response. It seemed her hopes were to be fulfilled and she found her hand shaking slightly as she gazed at the thick, dark handwriting on the sheet of notepaper which had been signed simply "Charles, Rex."

Glancing over at her from the breakfast table, Haviland noticed the look of trepidation about her features and smiled secretly to himself as he wiped his mouth with a napkin.

"Good news, Crimson?"

She looked up quickly and nodded. "The king wishes to see me today, this afternoon."

Haviland's brows shot up in mock surprise. "Really? Well, it seems he is most anxious to get a look at England's newest French import." He laughed softly at the girl's puzzled expression. "Just teasing, my dear. Actually, I'm sure the king wishes news of his sister. I'm sure you have much to converse with him about Madame and her life in France."

"I will certainly tell him all that I can," she replied modestly, folding the letter and tucking it inside her sleeve.

"Ah, Crimson," Haviland went on expansively, "this is just the beginning for you. No doubt, the king will wish you to remain close to him when he lays eyes on you, as much for your connection with Madame as for your own beauty, my dear. Your place at court will most assuredly be properly placed and you will have no need to worry about anything. You have only to be nice to the king, my dear, and he will see to all your needs."

"My needs are not many," Crimson replied, glancing at the man, with a hint of suspicion on her face. "I was under the impression that you yourself would be able to provide the bulk of them."

Haviland sighed. "Ah, I could not give you a tenth of what the king, should he be so disposed, could entice you with."

"Oh, yes, I remember our conversation about your gambling debts, my lord," Crimson replied stiffly. "Surely, your—friend—is overdue in expressing his compliments upon my arrival in England?"

Haviland shrugged. "Don't worry, my dear, Sir Reginald is a most busy man and will, I'm sure, approach you himself when he feels the time is right. No doubt, you will see him at Court today."

"I was under the impression that Sir Reginald was most anxious to tidy up those gambling debts," Crimson pressed.

"It seemed so to me," Haviland replied nonchalantly, "but I daresay he is a decent enough man to allow me some time with my own daughter."

Haviland stood quickly as Crimson rose from the table to go to her room. Surreptitiously, he pulled the chair out for her and, in doing so, brushed her shoulder slightly with his. He noted her immediately pulling away from him, but said nothing, engrossed for the moment in the porcelain perfection of the cheek that was turned towards him.

"You—remind me very much of your dear mother," he said stiffly, as Crimson made to leave the room.

She turned at his words and eyed him sharply. "That is the first time you have spoken of my mother since I have arrived in England," she said, an accusing note in her voice.

Haviland cleared his throat. How easily the lie came to his lips! "That is because the memory, even now, is still too painful to dwell on, my dear," he murmured, glancing at her from beneath lowered eyelids.

Crimson said no more, but hurried to her rooms to prepare herself for the appointment with the king. Beth, her new maid, who had adjusted surprisingly well to her situation in the Haviland household, had already laid out her day wear, but Crimson quickly told her of the upcoming event and the need for a gown more suitable in which to be presented to the king of England.

"Of course, mistress. One of your French gowns?" the maid asked, dutifully taking away the other dress.

"Yes, I'm sure that the king would be most pleased to see me in one of those gowns which his sister so dotes on. I daresay, he will expect it."

Beth went to the armoire and passed an experienced hand over the lovely silks and velvets that hung there. Her catlike eyes gleamed with a touch of greed as her hand brushed over a long fur cloak of softest sable. She collected herself quickly, though, and with a darting look at her mistress, selected the wine-red velvet gown with the under-petticoat of pure cloth of silver.

"This would look beautiful on you, I think," she murmured.

Crimson nodded. "Very good, Beth. You do have an eye for colors," she went on absently, seating herself at the dressing table so that the maid could take down the coiffure Crimson had hastily pinned up this morning.

Beth unpinned the long tresses of gleaming auburn that felt like heavy silk as they slipped through her work-roughened fingers, and couldn't help marveling privately at their thickness and shine. No lice had ever found a home there, she reckoned to herself as she brushed thoughtfully.

Because of the cold weather, Crimson simply sponged her body with perfumed water, then dressed in a heavy silk shift embroidered with blue forget-me-nots, which the princess had included in her many gifts. Her round, tight breasts rose high beneath the low neckline, a pearly sheen making them seem almost carved from white marble. She smoothed the shift over her slender midriff and pressed slightly at her belly, pleased by its flatness.

Beth powdered Crimson's shoulders and arms and tinted her lips with rouge. The cold would cause enough color in her cheeks, and her eyebrows were dark enough not to warrant any penciling.

Crimson suddenly giggled. "I wonder if I dare wear one of those black beauty patches which are all the rage in Paris? Would it scandalize the ladies of the Court, do you think, Beth?"

Beth frowned and her mouth hardened. "I hardly think 'twould, mistress," she answered. "But since it is the first visit you've made—"

"Ah, yes, I suppose I should try to be conservative," Crimson agreed, setting aside the tiny gold box which held numerous black velvet patches shaped like half-moons, stars and hearts.

When her hair had been done to perfection with one long lovelock dangling alluringly over her shoulder, she proceeded to the gown itself. It was breathtaking with the richness of its wine-colored velvet complementing the creaminess of her skin. The front part of the skirt was drawn away on either side and fastened with silver bows to allow viewing of the exquisite silver petticoat underneath. A wealth of silver lace cascaded from the elbow-length sleeves and was repeated around the low neckline. An artificial silver rose was tucked behind one ear and, with the addition of earrings and several bracelets, her ensemble was complete.

She twirled a little in front of the cheval mirror. "What do you think, Beth? Am I worthy to be received by a

103

king?" Her tone was playful, with no hint of the irony that might have been there had she been less naïve.

"Truly worthy, mistress," Beth replied thoughtfully.

Crimson laughed and picked up the gilt fan while Beth laid the sable cloak around her mistress' shoulders with loving hands.

"Don't wait up for me, Beth," Crimson called back gaily as she left the room. "I may decide to dance all night."

Crimson's exuberance was due mainly to her realization that she was going to meet, not only the king of England, but the beloved brother of her former mistress, a woman whom she had come to like and admire. If Charles were anything like his sister, she had no doubts that her settling in to English life would be a lot less painful than she had at first thought. A vague misgiving settled somewhere in the back of her mind. What was it? Something someone had said about Charles and his women— She brushed the unwelcome thought aside and concentrated on the excitement of going to court. She hoped with all her might that Whitehall would live up to Madame's glowing reports. Certainly, it would be much nicer to be admitted to the gaiety of court life, rather than remain in St. Martin's Lane with her father and his arch mistress.

She was pulling on her gloves and settling the hood of her cloak over her head when Philippa herself came in, her eyes lighting up at sight of the splendid magnificence of her finery.

"Oh, Crimson, you do have a look about you in those clothes! Where are you off to now, my dear? Need some company?"

Crimson shook her head and smiled. "No, Philippa. Today I am on my own. I have an appointment with the king!"

"The king! My dear, how marvelous, how utterly exciting for you! I'm sure you will carry off the day with flying colors." Philippa moved to pat her hand in maternal fashion. "You just be careful, Crimson."

"Careful, Philippa?" she returned with raised brows. "I hardly see—"

104

"Oh, just a little advice which you should heed, my dear. You wouldn't want to step on anyone's toes." She gave her a look which Crimson thought must mean something, but Crimson failed utterly at interpreting it.

"Well, thank you for the advice, Phillipa," she said lamely, "but I'm sure everything will turn out for the best."

Phillipa shrugged, kissed her on the cheek and watched her go outside into the waiting carriage. There was an expression of mixed anxiety and worldiness on Phillipa's features, which irritated Crimson for some reason, but she determinedly shrugged aside the feeling, not wanting Phillipa's notions to upset her arrival at court.

The coach made its slow progress through the narrow, twisting streets of London to King Street, where it entered the Whitehall buildings through a gateway. Once inside, the driver took her to what seemed to be a main entrance and Crimson quitted the carriage to enter the old stone walls.

Upon inquiring within of a cold-faced footman, Crimson was told that she would have to proceed to the Stone Gallery in the very center of Whitehall. Bewildered, but determined not to become flustered, Crimson went on through the long corridors, passing several people, some obviously courtiers, others common folk who gawked incongruously at the splendid wall hangings and paintings, some stopping in one of the corners to relieve themselves against the walls. Crimson hurried past them, wishing she had brought Phillipa along with her now.

She was outside once more and walking despairingly towards another set of buildings when she heard a gentleman's voice calling. Partially relieved and a little anxious, she turned around to see a young man hurrying towards her.

"Mistress, wait a moment please," he called, halting her progress.

When he had caught up with her, puffing a little in the cold, she could see that he was perhaps in his mid-twenties, with light brown hair and handsome eyes which were, just now, roving over her with practiced finesse.

"You must be Crimson Haviland," he said with an air of surety that amazed her.

"Yes, I am, but—"

"Pardon me, mistress. I am George Hamilton, personally attached to King Charles and ordered by him to escort you through Whitehall. I had expected you at the King Street Gate a few minutes after you arrived, and was told by one of the footmen that there had been a young lady inquiring the way within. 'Beautiful young lady,' he said. And how right he was, mistress."

Crimson blushed at the compliment and lowered her lashes. "Thank you, sir. To be sure, I am glad that you found me, for I was just thinking that I would be terribly late for my appointment and the king might not take kindly to me."

Hamilton laughed. "I can assure you, mistress, the king can do nothing else but take kindly to you. His biggest weakness is redheaded women."

Crimson's head came up sharply, but the face was nothing more than kind and the eyes sparkled mischievously at the air of challenge about her.

"Have I said something to offend, Mistress Haviland?" he asked, taking her arm possessively and tucking it within his elbow.

"Not that I know of," she replied with spice, and fell into step beside him.

They walked through a large park and into another building which opened on one side into a large theater.

"The Cockpit," Hamilton explained. "Just beyond is the long Stone Gallery."

"And the king will be there?"

He shook his head. "He will be awaiting you in his own apartments, mistress. You are very honored." He allowed his free hand to come across and press hers that was tucked in his arm. "I daresay you will make your mark at court. I do hope you will remember one who rescued you in your hour of need?"

"Oh, most assuredly," Crimson laughed.

He was delighted. "You laugh like an innocent, mistress. I must confess, already I am itching to lay licentious hands on you." He leaned closer to her and Crimson could feel his breath fanning her cheek.

"Sir, you give me cause for much confusion," she returned, not willing to engage in a tête-à-tête with this young man when she had too much else on her mind. She cast him an artless look from her aquamarine eyes; she hoped it would satisfy him with a vague promise, as she had seen the other ladies-in-waiting do at Madame's court.

Hamilton, though, seemed suddenly inspired by her look and he would have drawn her into a secluded alcove had it not been already occupied. Crimson cast an embarrassed glance at the couple ardently embracing and was surprised to see the man she had met at the servants' hiring quarters, Lord Chesterfield, and a pretty courtesan. Chesterfield's eyes caught hers briefly and lit with recognition that caused a smile to shape his mouth before he turned back to his pleasures.

The little interruption seemed, though, to bring Hamilton to his senses and he hurried his charge into a long gallery upon which hung various portraits and tapestries. A throng of people walked up and down the corridor, exchanging news and gossip, forming little groups here and there.

"The London Bridge of Whitehall," Hamilton whispered. "No doubt, some of them are talking about you."

At the thought, Crimson grew uneasy and shied away from eye contact with the many people who looked up at their approach. One lady, though, detached herself from a group and sauntered over towards Hamilton, her blue eyes sweeping over Crimson in an air of dismissal. Her red hair was perhaps a shade or two lighter than Crimson's own, and her superior air warned Crimson that this was a person of consequence. Crimson wasn't sure whether she should curtsey or not, but decided to wait until the intruder identified herself.

"George, my darling. I see you've found yourself another lady to woo. Your capacity is boundless, you bad boy," she murmured, her perfect mouth turning up slightly at the corners.

"Barbara, you flatter me, but I'm afraid this lady is destined for bigger game than I," Hamilton returned, his eyes sparkling as though he deliberately baited the woman.

The penciled brows went up in twin arches. "Surely you can't mean—" The blue eyes glanced sharply over the younger girl, than seemed to drill into her head. "This is the girl from France? From Madame?"

"Yes. Crimson Haviland, may I present Barbara Palmer, Countess of Castlemaine."

Crimson gazed shyly at the woman she had already heard so much about. So this was the woman who had held the king's heart in her hands for nearly eight years, the woman who had robbed the royal treasury of everything her greedy heart desired and had finally become tiring to Charles because of her temper and numerous infidelities.

"Lady Castlemaine, a pleasure," Crimson murmured swiftly, bowing her head a little.

The countess seemed pleased by her show of respect and deigned to smile. "Ah, she is quite inexperienced, it seems, George. I suppose you have already offered to educate her?"

Hamilton smiled. "Indeed, yes, Barbara, but you can be sure that my offer is only the first of many."

"Possibly, George, possibly," Castlemaine muttered, then swept away regally after turning sharply on her heel with a curt "Good afternoon."

"There's no need to look as though you've just seen some terrible dragon," Hamilton whispered to his charge. "Castlemaine's power has all but run out. The king only gives in to her demand for more wealth to keep her from screaming at him in the corridors of the palace. The woman can be a hoyden."

"I—I don't think she liked me," Crimson said more to herself than to the man who was once more hurrying her down the gallery.

Hamilton shrugged. "I wouldn't expect it. She doesn't really like anyone, except herself. I don't think she has a true friend in the whole court."

Despite his breezy words, Crimson shivered, remembering the look of calculation in those blue eyes that had
108

hardened as they passed over her. She had an instinctive feeling that she would do well to stay away from the Lady Castlemaine as much as possible.

They walked up to twin guarded doors which, Hamilton explained, opened into the royal apartments. After Hamilton identified himself, the guards allowed them entrance and Crimson found herself in the withdrawing room, where many lords and ladies were already in attendance, awaiting the king's pleasure.

"Beyond this is the king's bedchamber, which is strictly limited by court etiquette as to who may enter. But in your case, the king has made special instructions that you are to be brought into his private sanctum."

"Heavens, it sounds rather scary!"

Hamilton laughed, causing several heads to turn and stare disapprovingly. "Lord, no, mistress. 'Tis the king's closet, which can only be reached up a flight of stairs leading directly from his bedroom. Only the king and his trusted valet, old Chiffinch, have keys. So, you see, you *are* honored, my dear."

Feeling a little overawed by all this honor, Crimson walked with rapidly beating heart to the doors that led into the king's bedroom. After a sharp tapping, the doors were opened from within and, bowing, Hamilton left her in the care of the dignified servant who must be the one called Chiffinch.

"Follow me, mistress."

Crimson followed him through the immense private apartments to a small staircase that wound upwards to a closed door. After a short knock, the door was opened and Chiffinch had magically disappeared. Crimson found herself looking into eyes so dark that they had to be black. With shaking hands, she sank into a swift curtsey.

"Your Majesty."

Two long-fingered brown hands lifted her up by the shoulders, and she stood looking up at the tall, slender man who ruled all of England. At first glance, she could see the lines of worry and care etched into his dark face, which at thirty-seven years of age was, nonetheless, an arresting face with the extremely sensual lips, arrogant nose

109

and wealth of black hair that was streaked thinly with silver. She realized with a start that he was not wearing a periwig, and that his clothes were far simpler than anything she would expect a king to wear.

His hands were still on her shoulders and he was drawing her closer, inside the room so that he might shut the door against intruders. After doing so, he turned back to look at her.

"Crimson Haviland, it pleases me greatly to welcome you to England."

The words were heavily caressing, deep and sincere, and Crimson felt somehow as though she couldn't quite catch her breath. The sensuality of the man was incredible, and her extreme youth and naïveté were no match for it.

"Thank you, Your Majesty," she managed lightly, watching as he came towards her again.

Charles laid his hands once more on her shoulders, but this time to push back the hood that covered her hair. They moved surely to the ties at her throat, which allowed him to slip the cloak from her.

"My sister has sent me a jewel from her court," he murmured.

Finding her voice, Crimson managed a trembling smile. "You do me great honor, Your Majesty. I must admit, I was extremely loath to leave she who is so close in both our hearts."

"Ah, my little Minette. Tell me how she is. How does her husband treat her? How does Louis seem to favor her? Is she happy, do you think?"

Overwhelmed by the obvious love and devotion in the king's voice when speaking of his sister—his Minette, as he called her—Crimson did not know what to say. She remembered Madame's strict instructions not to leak any of her unhappiness and frustration to her brother.

As she was about to speak, the king interrupted. "Forgive me. May I call you Crimson? It would please me that we should be close friends. As you can see, I am so anxious for news of my sister that I have forgotten all my
110

manners. Please sit, mistress, and let me pour you a glass of wine."

Thankfully, Crimson took a seat, her eyes for the first time noting the contents of the room, which consisted of fine, old paintings, rare jewels in glass cases, and a large display of clocks, all of which were ticking softly in harmony.

King Charles handed her a glass of wine. "Please call me Charles in private." He glanced at her. "I should hope we can have many such talks as this without outside interference."

"Whatever pleases, Your Majesty." She looked up quickly at his exclamation. "I mean, Charles," she amended with a touch of embarrassment.

He regarded her for a long moment. "You seem quite young, Crimson."

"Seventeen, sire—Charles. Madame was kind enough to give me a position of importance despite my youth. I was most grateful for the opportunity."

"Sweet Minette. Her heart was always too large for her delicate exterior. Now, you must tell me of her, for my patience grows thin, I must confess."

"She is in good health despite her passion for staying indoors and reading much of the time," Crimson began, at which the king smiled. "She sends you her love, of course, and wished me to tell you that all is well with her at Saint-Cloud."

Charles frowned slightly. "She does not miss England?"

"With all her heart, she would like to come and visit with you, Charles, but she cannot do so. Her court is quite large and her husband—"

At her hesitation, the king leaned forward in his chair and tilted her chin up so that their eyes met. "Tell me."

"Monsieur is—difficult at times. He is not—he does not—" Crimson floundered helplessly for a moment.

"No need to go on, Crimson, I know of Monsieur's preference for men. But does he treat her decently otherwise?"

"Yes, he is most attentive to her at social functions and Madame does love Paris so. She delights in visiting Ver-

111

sailles, and I believe that King Louis is very fond of her. There are some, of course, who cannot understand her wit, nor her intelligence."

"Minette was always so," Charles agreed warmly. "I wish I had gotten some of her understanding. She would —she *should* have been a queen."

Crimson recalled that, at one time, Madame had been considered as a wife for the young King Louis, but the negotiations had never jelled and she had had to take second best.

Answering the king's probing questions, Crimson soon found herself unveiling life at Saint-Cloud, the court of Louis and her own early years with her father and her cousin. As she talked, she became more comfortable and the tightness in her relaxed. She laughed at the jokes the king made now and then, and asked him to refill her wine glass.

"You are delightful, Crimson," Charles said softly, placing the glass in her hand. "I do hope you will allow me to see quite a lot of you now that you have come to us. I shall expect you at court as much as is possible."

"Thank you, sire. I should be most happy to attend court. I would find it much preferable to staying at home with my father." She laughed a little and raised the glass to her lips.

"My sister speaks most highly of you in her letter. She even asked that I find a place for you at court that would insure your future security." For a moment, the dark eyes gleamed and he leaned closer so that Crimson was lost in their depths.

There was a magnetism about the man that attracted her irresistibly and she knew that his reputation was that of a woman-chaser, but still she could not turn away from the half-commanding, half-pleading look in his eyes as they bore into hers. His mouth was inches away from her own and she closed her eyes involuntarily as she felt its warm softness graze her lips almost tentatively.

Abruptly, though, he recollected himself and smiled ruefully. "You are much too beautiful to be kept away from court, Crimson. I think the position my sister had in

112

mind was as maid-of-honor to the queen. I'm sure she would be most happy to receive you, if you would make your greetings to her tomorrow morning. Does that suit you?"

Embarrassed at her lack of composure, Crimson merely nodded and looked down at her hands. She felt the king's fingers once more under her chin, forcing her to look at him. "Let us see what the future brings to us, Crimson."

12

After leaving the king's apartments, Crimson was more than grateful to see George Hamilton awaiting her entrance in the king's waiting room. With a smile of relief, she sailed over to him.

"You look as though you might be walking three feet above the ground," Hamilton whispered to her confidentially.

"Oh, yes. The king is so—so easy to talk with," Crimson put in, allowing him to take her arm in his. "He truly put me at my ease within the first few minutes and I know I could have remained talking with him for hours."

Hamilton smiled secretly to himself. "Ah, the king is truly a charming man," he murmured. "I'm sure you will be expected to be at court often. Your quarters in town are not far, I hope?"

Crimson shook her head. "I live with my father, Lord James Haviland, in St. Martin's Lane."

"Splendid! Then we will be seeing a lot of each other."

She glanced at him archly. "You presume quite a lot, sir, on such a short acquaintance." She wasn't really angry with him. How could she be? Everything now seemed to be taking shape for the better and she already felt that she might be very happy here close to Whitehall.

Hamilton was not remiss at reading her true expression, and he took the liberty of squeezing her arm, breathing in the warm odor of her perfumed flesh. "French perfume," he commented huskily. "Surely there is no better in the world, mistress."

"Thank you, sir," she answered him prettily, at the same time noting that they were once more in the long Stone Gallery, among a host of other courtesans.

They moved among them speedily, Hamilton hoping to corner this lovely young bird in somewhat more private surroundings, but before he could spirit her away, a voice hailed them from one side of the gallery.

"George, what have you got there? God's blood, man, you might save your dear brother some of the lovelies here!"

A young man stepped out from behind a bevy of young ladies, belying his careless words, and quickly made his way to where Crimson stood, feeling the tensing of her escort's arm muscles.

"James, you sop! Go back to your stable of pets and leave this one alone. She is already earmarked," George returned good-naturedly, but steering Crimson away from the man who approached.

"Stop! As colonel of one of the best regiments of foot-soldiers in England, I demand to inspect this young woman!" his brother replied laughingly. "Who are you, my dear?" He went on, bowing in front of an astounded Crimson who wasn't sure if she should laugh at his humor or be affronted by his boldness.

"She is Mistress Crimson Haviland, lately of France," George Hamilton put in, a little more sourly now.

"French! Aha! As I thought, most likely sent to spy on us!"

The man continued to play his role, circling Crimson,

his eyes passing knowingly over her as though seeking some hidden flaw. His dark, laughing eyes caught hers, and Crimson couldn't help but smile, completely won over by his wit. And certainly, he was handsome, more handsome than his brother, although perhaps two or three years younger.

"I really think, George, you had better hand this young lady over to me. Mistress, may I present myself? Colonel James Hamilton. You will give yourself over to me willingly, I hope?"

It was easy to see he had more than the joke on his mind, as his eyes gleamed suggestively into hers, causing Crimson to blush in confusion.

"Sir, I don't even know you," she murmured anxiously, glancing up at her escort for support.

"The young lady and I have other business to attend to, James. If you will excuse us?"

James Hamilton laughed. "On one condition only, fair lady, that you promise to be at the court ball tonight and favor me with conversation. Dancing with me, I can assure you, will be ever so much more enjoyable than with my dear brother here. He is, quite frankly, a clod on the dance floor, mistress."

George Hamilton looked up angrily and began moving Crimson away from his brother, who was clearly besting him with the young lady. "Good day, James. Do try and be good," he threw back at the laughing young man.

"Heavens, who was that?"

"My brother, of course," George returned tightly. "Deuced annoying, isn't he? Well, no matter, don't let him bother you. He has so many women dangling on his every word that I'll be surprised if he remembers to ask you to dance tonight."

His words served to dampen Crimson's enthusiasm, just as intended, and she followed him meekly enough until they were out of the Stone Gallery and proceeding into another set of buildings.

"Are you hungry?"

At his words, Crimson realized that she was. "Yes, all of a sudden dreadfully so, but—"

"Speak no more. Come with me. I have a small apartment in the palace that I share, unfortunately, with my brother, but I'm sure he won't be heading there now. I'll just get you comfortable inside and then go get us a bite to eat."

"You're most kind, sir," Crimson returned thankfully, her expression so trusting that, for a moment, Hamilton hesitated.

Swiftly, though, he resumed his worldly air and led her to the door of a small apartment, furnished quite sparingly with a bed, a small desk and a table and four chairs. There was no fire in the grate and, cursing at the forgetfulness of servants, Hamilton proceeded to build one himself until there was a cozy glow that began to pervade the chill of the room.

"No more than a quarter of an hour, my sweet," Hamilton said, blowing a kiss at her before disappearing behind the door, leaving Crimson to toast her feet before the now-blazing fire.

She watched him go, feeling her stomach rumble pleasantly at the thought of food, then turned back to stare into the fire. Everyone seemed enormously polite and interested in this English palace. It was not too different in that respect from the court of France, and she hoped that she would be able to fit in.

Her thoughts were interrupted by the brisk entrance of a young woman. The latter halted abruptly in her tracks at sight of Crimson seated before the fire, then a frown marred her pretty face as she folded her arms across her bosom.

"Who are *you*?"

Crimson rose hastily from her seat. "I am Crimson Haviland, mistress. I am waiting—"

"So I can see," the other cut in speedily, sizing her up and down with blue eyes that seemed too big for her face. "I am Elizabeth Stanhope, Lady Chesterfield." She said this last with a world of arrogance in her voice, as she awaited some reaction from the younger girl.

Crimson racked her brain for enlightenment and recalled that Lord Chesterfield had been dallying in the al-

116

cove earlier with someone who had looked far different from this lady.

"Pardon, mistress, but if you are here to wait for George Hamilton, he only just left to get me something to eat. I believe he will be back shortly."

The lady seemed to relax and an ironic smile shaped her mouth. Laughing a little, as though at her own folly, she moved closer into the room and sat down leisurely in one of the chairs.

"You are here for George? Please forgive me then, my lady, for I'm afraid I was much mistaken in my earlier assumption. I thought you were awaiting his brother, James."

"Oh, no. We just saw him in the Stone Gallery before coming here."

"No doubt with a host of young ladies attending him? My, he is a scoundrel, if you don't mind my saying. As groom of the bedchamber to the king, he is quite close to His Majesty and believes that all he has to do is crook his little finger to get whomever he wishes." The finely drawn brows drew downward and one hand reached up absently to pat at the wispy blond curls at her brow.

Crimson had resumed her seat and was now watching the other woman silently, a little bewildered, and anxiously hoping that George Hamilton would return before she made some unintentional slip of the tongue to engage this woman's anger again.

Lady Chesterfield did not seem to mind the other's silence, though, as she continued with a confidential air. "You know, I've been trying to catch my dear cousin for months, but he always seems to outwit me. I do hope he doesn't consider my—reputation—a deterrent to a comfortable, cousinly affair with me. You see, everyone knows that dear James is one of the most handsome, wittiest men at Court, and certainly the best dancer, believe me! Others say, too, that he is the most successful lover. Hmmm." Her blue eyes danced to meet those of the other young woman. "I'm afraid George has never been able to compete with his brother, my dear."

"I—I only met George Hamilton this day, my lady. I

117

really don't know too much about him or his brother," Crimson commented quickly.

"Then you must enlighten me, my dear. Just who are you?" The blond-haired woman cut in with a feigned sweetness that was not lost on Crimson.

"I have only recently arrived from France, where I was maid-of-honor to Madame, the king's sister. It was at my father's request that I returned to England. This is my first day at court, actually."

"Oh, yes! The little French girl who's already been hailed as the latest Frances Stuart. Why, how lucky for me to happen into you like this."

Crimson was once more at a loss and was grateful when the door opened to allow a startled George Hamilton entrance into the room.

"Lady Chesterfield! Good day, mistress," he stuttered in surprise.

She tittered deliciously. "I must say I have probably fouled up your plans considerably, George, dear, but I thought perhaps I might be able to catch your brother here at this hour."

"Well, he is not here, my lady, but I did see him not too long ago in the Stone Gallery. If you would like to try there?" His tone was hopeful.

"No, I think not, cousin. To tell you the truth, I am famished myself and that platter smells deliciously of food. Do you mind if I join you and Mistress Crimson?"

George let out an audible sigh, then shrugged and set the platter on the table. "Of course not, Elizabeth."

The three began to eat, although Elizabeth kept up a constant flow of lively chatter, describing the court and various members of its magic circle.

"I have met your husband, Lord Chesterfield, already," Crimson commented conversationally. "He seems most likable, mistress."

Lady Chesterfield's smile turned somewhat sour. "Oh, yes, my husband," she murmured vaguely and quickly changed the subject, causing Crimson to come to the conclusion that all was not well between husband and wife.

118

Certainly, it would not seem to be with both so eager to make merry with others.

When the meal was over, the three relaxed near the fire, although Hamilton remained somewhat unfriendly to his first cousin, clearly indicating that he would hope she would make her exit quickly. But the woman seemed to enjoy causing him discomfiture and remained for nearly an hour more, until Crimson noticed the darkening outside the window.

"I must return to my father's house to change for this evening, Lady Chesterfield. If you will both excuse me?"

Hamilton stood up wearily and gave his cousin a vicious scowl. "Let me escort you back to your coach, Mistress Crimson. I do hope to see more of you this evening."

He nodded brusquely to Lady Chesterfield, then took Crimson's arm and prepared to depart. Elizabeth threw him an amused glance before nibbling the last of the crumbs from the plate and winking almost imperceptibly at Crimson's retiring back.

13

Nicholas Brentwood eyed the sleeping form next to him with a certain amount of tenderness mixed with objectivity. He knew very well that he was treading on thin ice, bringing the English princess to his own rooms in order to make love to her. She had become terribly trusting and probably fancied herself close to being in love with him. He'd have to shatter that dream quickly, for it would do no good to leave emotional entanglements behind when he departed France at the end of his mission. Madame, Henriette-Anne, would go back to being the wife of Monsieur and the sister-in-law of the most powerful king in Europe. He, Nick Brentwood, would go back to the king of England, with his full report as secret agent to His Majesty.

Not that Brentwood disliked this work. It was easy, compared to other assignments he'd been sent on by Charles. Madame had been snobbish at first, then coy, and finally completely abandoned in her affection for him. She enjoyed making love, like a kitten enjoys catnip, and she was the kind of woman that Brentwood could appreciate. Not for him those cold, hypocritical ladies, those so-called gentlewomen who might pant in private after a man, and then, after the act of love had been completed, profess that they had been cruelly led astray.

He smiled slightly to himself, remembering the young English girl whom he had deflowered before her departure back to the land of her birth. He had thought she might be a little different. She was warm, uniquely vulnerable and very beautiful. Unfortunately, she had retreated behind dignified shock and accusation after he had shown her what it was to be a woman. He had been disappointed in her reaction, had hoped she would be more honest with him.

He shrugged. Well, the minx was gone now, probably enduring flirtation with every able-bodied Englishman at court, all the while pretending not to enjoy their attentions. God, why did women always have to hide behind false masks?

Beside him, the princess stirred softly, coming awake slowly as though loath to face the world of reality after their delightful interlude in bed.

"Is it very late?" she murmured, nestling her face against his side.

The muscles against his side quivered with anticipation as he felt her small tongue begin to lick sensuously over his ribs.

120

"A little before dawn, Henriette," he answered, bringing his hand down to caress the soft, brown hair that was unforgivably tousled.

"So soon," she breathed, taking her tongue away in order to bring herself up to his face. Her arms went softly around his neck and she kissed him ardently. "Every day is another chore for me now, until night brings you back to me," she continued between kisses. "What would I do without you, Nick?"

His hands were strong on her shoulders, as he forced her to look at him. "You are a princess of England and the wife of the second man in line to the throne of France, Henriette. You could have many lovers. No doubt, you *will* have many lovers. You're a warm-hearted woman."

"But you—you are different, Nick. I feel so splendidly alive when I'm with you. I don't feel like a princess or the sister-in-law of the king. I just feel like a woman."

She passed her hand over the dark-blond hair that curled against his neck. It was a few shades lighter than the dark-blond eyebrows and moustache. "I do love your hair so, Nick. It's a shame you have to wear that periwig in public. I feel privileged to be among the few to see what you look like undressed." She giggled faintly.

His dark-blue eyes laughed down at her, but his mouth was serious for a moment as she snuggled once more between his shoulders.

"Henriette, you've got to remember that I will have to leave one day soon. Your brother needs information that I will be bringing him. Although you, yourself, were a part of my duties this time, there is much else to tell."

The princess sat up and gazed beseechingly at the man. "Nick, you won't tell Charles how unhappy I am here? You mustn't. I do so want this treaty between England and France to be consummated. It would mean more gold for my brother's sadly dwindled coffers and a strong ally for him against the Dutch. Nothing must affect the outcome. If Charles thought that I was being mistreated here, he might not sign the treaty."

Nick's lip curled in disgust. "Your husband is a pig, Henriette. He—"

"Hush!" Henriette whispered quickly, laying a finger against his lips. "Why ruin a lovely night with his name? Besides, there is nothing Charles can do about my marriage to Monsieur. There could be no divorce between us. I, myself, wanted this marriage from the very beginning. I wanted to remain in France, to be near Louis and to be a rich and titled woman. I have gotten those things." Her voice was sad. "If I have given up my soul to obtain them, it is my own fault. Charles was against the marriage from the very first. It would do no good to remind him that he could have stopped it."

She looked up at him, her eyes pleading. "You have more important matters to discuss with him—the treaty, the tactics of the Dutch and the Spanish here at court. My life matters so little when you consider these things."

"It matters very much to Charles," Nick broke in.

"I know he loves me, and I love him, but there is nothing we can do."

Nick tilted her chin up and kissed her on the mouth. "I can see why he loves you, Henriette. You are a very brave, a very courageous woman."

They had begun to embrace again, when the door was suddenly flung open, allowing a stream of guards to pour into the room. Uttering a cry of surprise, Henriette huddled close to Nick's hard, brown body, but her exclamation turned to one of dismay when she saw her husband enter the room on the arm of the Chevalier de Lorraine.

Monsieur's soft, red mouth was pursed in disapproval as he hung against his paramour, eying the two in the bed. "Nicholas! I see you did not heed my advice, young man. Really! If you had only come to me I could have seen that you came away well satisified. But to go to my wife, of all people. The insult is too much!"

He turned his eyes away in false modesty and pressed his handkerchief to his mouth. "Chevalier, what do you think my brother would have to say to this?"

The Chevalier shrugged, his eyes boring into those of Henriette, his sworn enemy. "I doubt that our king would enjoy hearing of such distressing tales, Philippe. He might
122

even become enraged enough to order the demise of our dear Englishman."

"All right, you have found us together," Brentwood cut in swiftly. "Leave us some privacy in order to get dressed and I will accompany your guards to wherever you wish to have me sent." He was growing tired of the game, and could feel the uncontrollable sobs welling up within the woman next to him.

The guards were stationed incongruously about the bed as though awaiting some escape by the two from the room. Some had the temerity to eye the couple with lecherous grins.

"For God's sake, Monsieur, if you have any decency in you at all—" Brentwood began angrily.

"Decency? A strange word coming from you in this situation, dear boy! No, I hardly think you deserve any courtesy. Guard!" He nodded to one who was closest to Brentwood.

With rough hands, the guard shoved back the concealing bedclothes, revealing the two naked bodies beneath the covers. Monsieur stared appreciatively at Brentwood's masculinity, then gestured once more to the guards, two of whom seized him by the arms to drag him from the bed. He stood nude, unaware of his own embarrassment, concerned only for Henriette, who was trying to conceal her most private parts with her hands, her face red with shame.

"Leave her to get dressed," Brentwood demanded, pulling at the hands that held him. "I—"

"Be quiet, you English quid!" the Chevalier broke in angrily. "The bitch gets only what she deserves. From what I've heard, she would like nothing more than to allow each of these men into her bed."

Monsieur was shaking his head sorrowfully towards his wife. "Ah, Henriette, I'm afraid you have shown yourself to me now. A bad wife who consorts with what some might call France's worst enemy—an Englishman!"

Henriette, embarrassed and angry now, grabbed for the bedcovers and covered herself from her husband's disdainful eyes. "Order these guards to leave immediately and

123

allow me to dress myself!" she commanded, authority coming back into her voice.

"Henriette! I was unaware that you worried unduly about such things as nudity. Really, I—"

"If you don't leave this room immediately, Philippe, I will go to the king myself and tell him a few things that go on at Saint-Cloud, which might prove rather disastrous for your—your companion," Henriette went on, outraged now, her voice clearly threatening.

For a moment, Monsieur wavered, then shrugged his shoulders and signaled for the guards to retire and bring the prisoner with them. He threw Brentwood's breeches at him, then turned with his hand still on the arm of the Chevalier's, and quitted the room.

Henriette cast a despairing glance towards her lover, but Brentwood quickly shook his head and permitted himself a wry smile before donning his breeches and following the guards out to the corridor.

He was prodded down by the staffs of two of the guards, while Monsieur and the Chevalier went ahead, whispering to each other. The sight of their two elegantly coiffed heads bending near enough to touch, caused the smile on Brentwood's face to turn to one of pitying disgust.

"Where are you taking me?" he asked matter-of-factly.

"You'll have quarters below in one of the empty wine cellars of Saint-Cloud while I decide what to do with you," Monsieur returned airily, not even turning his head to look at Brentwood.

"And when will you decide what to do with me?" Brentwood pressed, at which one of the staffs was jabbed uncomfortably into his right shoulder blade.

"In my own time, Brentwood. I suggest you do as you're told meekly enough, or you may not find yourself with the ability to please any of the ladies any more." Monsieur tittered lewdly.

The implied threat was not lost on Brentwood, but he doubted if the prince would go through with it, although he had an idea that the Chevalier would be the one to carry out any torture. The man was a serpent, bent only

124

on his own gains. Monsieur was the biggest fool in the world if he really thought Lorraine was out for anyone but himself.

They continued downward, meeting no one but servants who quickly averted their eyes from the scene. Brentwood could smell the kitchens close by and felt his stomach growl at the thought of food. No doubt starvation would be one of the tricks Monsieur would employ to teach him his place. He only hoped that neither of the two men knew anything about his other activities while here in France. If they discovered he was a spy for Charles II, he would most certainly go to the Bastille, probably to remain there until he rotted away or was executed as a traitor. The memory of his father's execution suddenly reached up to engulf him, and he felt himself tremble a little with reaction.

They were below the kitchens now and a heavy wooden door was being unlocked and opened to reveal a moist cellar where stood empty wine barrels. Brentwood was pushed inside the doorway and one of the guards was instructed to tie him to one of the huge, wooden posts that supported the ceiling beams.

The rope bit deeply into his wrists, but Brentwood hardly noticed the pain. He wished them to be gone quickly so that he would have some time to sort out some type of escape plan.

"The door will be locked after us, and two of you shall remain on guard throughout the day and night," Monsieur was ordering the guards. "If the prisoner escapes, one of you will take his place!" The last threat was echoed in the room and then Monsieur and the Chevalier were gone after a few final instructions, which included, as Brentwood had surmised, that no food or drink would be brought to the prisoner.

The door closed heavily on hinges made of iron and the key was turned smartly in the lock. Brentwood was left, sitting on some dampish hay, waiting for his eyes to become adjusted to the gloom, which was lit only by the light from the corridor outside that reached him through the square window in the door. He could see the faces of

125

the guards as they marched back and forth across the window.

He must find a way to get out of this cellar. He doubted if Monsieur would go to the king with the scandal right away, but when he did eventually go, Brentwood knew that he would be transported to a prison of iron and steel that would not allow easy escape. Then, too, the king might become interested in Brentwood's true motives for being in France. If he were discovered, the possibility of a peace treaty between France and England would become even more remote.

For a moment, distant memory assailed him—memory of another prison, a wretched, narrow cell in Newgate Prison, nearly eighteen years ago in London.

He had been an eight-year-old boy then, jailed along with his father, William Brentwood, Earl of Dorset, for alleged conspiracy against the Lord Protector, Oliver Cromwell.

That night came back with a sudden vividness that left him sweating—the summer storm, the airless cell, the fear and hopelessness that were closing in on a small boy. He could remember the morning of his father's execution for treason. He had been separated from his father and taken below for a flogging—a reminder of what happened to conspirators. The scar at his temple twitched as he recalled how nearly he had lost an eye to the torturer's whip.

And then—his father as he walked slowly up the wooden steps leading to the scaffold, his blond hair catching the first rays of the dawning sun in the prison courtyard. The executioner's axe had forever taken a father from his son, and left in the boy a deep hatred for everything to do with Cromwell, and a determination to work for the cause of Charles II.

And so it had led to this moment, in another prison of sorts. An overwhelming need to escape washed over him.

Patiently, he began to scrape his hands across the splintery wood, hoping that after a time the rope would give way enough to allow him to untie himself. The process might take hours, and he steeled himself to remain patient. A splinter lodged in his wrist, causing a sharp prick of

126

pain, but he could not let that deter him from his goal. He must escape.

Some hours had passed, and Brentwood judged that it must be terribly late, perhaps already past midnight. He had continued off and on to scrape away at the binding ropes and felt some loosening, but still not enough to free his hands. Tired and feeling the hunger pains sharply now, he continued with his task.

Outside the cellar door, his ears picked up the sound of voices—probably the guards changing. But then suddenly, a woman's voice broke in and sounds of a scuffle ensued. Quickly, the key was turned in the lock and the door swung open to reveal Madame standing in the light of the corridor, searching through the gloom.

"Nick?" she called out softly.

"Here." His voice was thick from lack of water, but she came towards him, holding a small torch to see.

Behind her, two bodies sprawled on the floor and were being dragged inside the cellar by two burly men dressed in peasants' clothes.

"Nick, oh, thank God, it was easier than I dared hope. Hurry, we must get you away before the guards are changed again! Look, I have brought you some clothes, and these two will see you safely to the borders of France." For a moment Madame's voice was tear-filled, but she straightened up quickly after untying him when he would have embraced her.

"No. You must go, I know that. You haven't much time." Her eyes avoided his.

"Henriette, you have my eternal gratitude," Brentwood said hastily, reaching for the clothes she held out to him. "But your husband, he will know this is your doing. What will he do when he finds out I have escaped?"

Henriette shrugged. "He will do nothing. The embarrassment would be too much for him. I have already warned him that I will go to the king and tell him everything that has gone on between him and his paramour. Despite his foppish ways, Philippe has a true sense of what it would mean to be king. If there comes a day when he

127

might attain such a thing, he would not want the past to catch up and taint him. No, he will do nothing to me, nothing he has not already done before."

"For God's sake, Henriette, if only there were something I could do——"

She shook her head quickly. "Please go, Nick. I shall remember you fondly always." She reached up and kissed him lightly on the lips, aware of the two men waiting by the door. "You shall have to go by the way of the eastern road and escape through Holland. They might be waiting for you at the Channel. Good luck, my love."

Despite her anxious attitude, Nick lingered another moment and kissed her tenderly on the mouth, taking her in his arms. "I shall always regret such a hasty good-bye, Henriette," he murmured sincerely.

Henriette held back a sob, then hurried him out the door.

14

Crimson was standing as near to the window as possible, feeling with relief the slight draft it afforded from the chill January air. She had felt faint all day, and this evening, attending the glittering ball as one of the queen's ladies was nothing more than a tiresome affair, when normally she would have been laughing and dancing with as much exuberance as the other women.

She had been in England now for a little over two

months and had realized with a sense of guilt that she had become absorbed very quickly into her new English surroundings, despite her first feelings that she would never be happy in London.

She had made some friends among the ladies of the queen's household, although, as first Lady of the Bedchamber, Barbara Palmer, Lady Castlemaine, was still no more than polite when they met, as they did out of necessity quite often. Crimson had no choice but to dismiss Barbara's actions with a wry shrug of her shoulders. Although Barbara no longer held the king by his coattails, she was still jealous of any other woman who attempted to gain a hold over him. This puzzled Crimson because the king had never approached her in any other way but as a friend and eager listener for any anecdotes she could recall from her days spent with Madame in France. In fact, he was much more interested in the earthy Moll Davis, or the actress, Nell Gwyn, who was the same age as Crimson but had already been mistress of two men.

Standing nearer to the window, Crimson felt the faintness creeping strongly over her and swallowed deliberately a few times, feeling a small panic somewhere inside her that, perhaps, she had unknowingly encountered the pox. She knew already the tale of Lady Castlemaine's successful bout with smallpox when she had been younger, when she had found herself cured and with no scars or marks to mar her beauty, only the relief of knowing that she would never again contract the disease.

"You look a little flushed, my dear. Aren't you feeling well?"

Crimson looked up to see her father staring at her with a look of clear concern on his face. She shook her head and attempted a smile.

"It's nothing, really. I think I must have eaten something that disagreed with me earlier."

"Perhaps you should ask the queen to allow you to retire?" he suggested, taking her arm in his and rubbing it with a half-caressing motion that disturbed her more than her swimming head.

"I think not, my lord. Poor Queen Catherine. She has

129

so few friends among those at court, and I do try to remain with her at these affairs."

Haviland nodded reflectively, knowing the truth of her words. Queen Catherine had the respect of no one at court, least of all her amorous husband. Her first years at court as wife of the most licentious monarch in Europe had been filled with pain and angry arguments between herself and Charles, especially in regard to Castlemaine. But finally the queen's better judgment had been worn down by her husband's constant unfaithfulness and the virtual snubbing of her at Whitehall. She had given in, if only to have her husband come to her on those nights, once or twice a month, when he did his duty to try to beget the heir that everyone prayed for.

It wasn't really that Catherine was an ugly woman. The Portuguese princess was small, delicate-boned and had large, brown eyes that could look quite innocent, like those of a fawn. It was not her fault that she had slightly protruding front teeth that stuck out over her lower lip whenever she opened her mouth, or that her hair was too unruly for the smooth hairstyles at court and, many times, was virtually tortured into frizzled curls that stuck out unbecomingly on both sides of her small head.

Turning his thoughts away from the queen, who was somewhere about on the other side of the ballroom, Haviland glanced once more at the girl who thought herself his true daughter. Lately, he had begun to feel more towards her than would behoove a real father, and he had felt a superstitious relief that there was no blood relation between them. His eyes would stray longer than necessary over her small breasts as they emerged from the froth of lace at her neckline, or his hands linger on the warm flesh that seemed too tempting for him at times. He had even wondered what it would be like to awaken her to the delights of making love with a man and had carried his fancies to the point where he consciously sought her out when he knew she was undressing in her room or taking a bath in her closet.

Realizing that Crimson was looking up at him now with a shade of concern mixed with embarrassment in her eyes, he quickly roused himself away from such illicit thoughts.

"Have you seen Sir Reginald this evening?" he asked quickly, glancing about the room to keep his eyes from staying too long on the expanse of white throat about which a gleaming pearl necklace was clasped.

Crimson shook her head quickly, her slim brows drawing down over her eyes. "No, I have not, my lord," she answered curtly.

"You do not like him, do you, my dear?" he asked curiously. "Is there something so terrible about him that disturbs you enough to avoid his company?"

"I have only met him three or four times, my lord, but each time he looked at me as though I were some marble statue with no breath of life in me. His eyes were—calculating. No, I don't like him!"

Haviland felt anger building up within him. Sir Reginald had already met privately on several occasions with him to talk about a planned marriage between himself and Crimson. The match would be most advantageous to Haviland because Sir Reginald had already agreed to wipe out the huge debt that was owed him if only the young lady would say yes.

"She has, as you have said, definite possibilities," Sir Reginald was fond of saying. "Even though the king has not singled her out as yet, I have no doubts that he will not let her escape his clutches long. He slakes his thirst on those sluts that the Duke of Buckingham pimps for him, but he will soon grow tired of their boorish, peasant ways and long for a woman who carries herself like a lady."

"I'm sure you are right, sir," Haviland had returned, almost smacking his lips together at the thought that he would be free of the man once Crimson would accept his proposal. "When—ah, when do you intend to ask her?"

Gardner shrugged. "I have no intentions of asking her. You, Haviland, will do your duty as a loving father and tell her that the marriage has already been arranged. She has, after all, no choice in the matter. Why consult with her?"

And then he had yawned and put on a bored air, as though the matter were neatly taken care of already and the date only had to be set. Haviland had hoped to have time to get Crimson used to the idea of marriage to the other man, but it had been too obvious from the beginning that the girl had no liking for Sir Reginald, and would be most unhappy if she knew of the events taking place behind her back.

"So, you do not like Sir Reginald," Haviland continued after searching the girl's obstinate face. "But do you know how many wives hate their husbands here at court, my dear? How many married couples stay faithful to each other? No, at Whitehall, marriage can only provide a degree of financial security. Other than that, there are no binding social or moral ties."

"You talk of marriage, my lord!" she said, surprised, looking up at him with narrowed eyes. "With whom?"

He shrugged carefully. "Someday, Crimson, I must do my duty as a father and provide you with a suitable husband."

"Suitable? Do you say that Sir Reginald would make such a husband?"

He smiled without emotion. "He is as good as any other, my dear. And he has a considerable amount of money. His position at court is well established, helped, no doubt, by the fact that King Charles personally appointed his father as comptroller in Jamaica. You will be eighteen in June, will you not? You are not too young to be married."

"To Sir Reginald? He disgusts me. Please do not talk of it again, my lord," Crimson burst out angrily, feeling the dizziness overtake her again in waves that caused her to stumble backwards a little, to find something to brace her.

Quickly, Haviland caught her in his arms when she would have fallen to the floor. He glanced around, noting that several people were watching them with curious interest. He smiled collectively, feeling suddenly embarrassed, and managed to take his burden over to a small settee, where he slapped her wrists and patted her cheeks, which had gone white.

Crimson's eyes fluttered open after a few moments and she gazed into the eyes of the man above her, noting a sudden sharp suspicion lurking there that she could not divine. Carefully, she raised a hand to her head, then let it drop to her stomach where a churning feeling threatened to make her sick.

"I—I think I should retire for a few moments," she said faintly.

Haviland nodded quickly and helped her escape the crowded room without attracting undue attention. Crimson hurried to a private closet and was only just in time to vomit into a chamberpot. The swirling in her head ceased abruptly afterwards and she found a pitcher of cool water which she soaked her handkerchief in, to pass it over her mouth and face.

Her digestion was not working properly lately, and she hoped that she had not contracted some dire disease. She was too ashamed and worried to complain to the other ladies in the queen's household and could only hope that the strange affliction would soon pass.

Outside in the corridor, she was surprised and ill-pleased to see her father still waiting for her, joined by the unwelcome figure of Sir Reginald Gardner. The latter bowed at her entrance and his dark eyes passed swiftly over the slight disorder of her hair with a look of consternation.

"Good evening, Mistress Crimson. I was lucky enough to pass your father on my way to my rooms and he told me that you were—indisposed—inside. I hope you are feeling well?"

She nodded sharply and prepared to move away from the two men, casting a reproving glance at Haviland.

"Crimson, do you think you should return to the ball already? Another attack might overcome you. You were lucky to depart the throng without any embarrassment," her father was saying, his gaze sweeping over her figure with a look of calculation that caused a deep flush to spring to Crimson's cheeks.

"I—"

"Perhaps a short walk along these cool corridors would benefit you more than a return to the stuffy ballroom," Sir Reginald suggested, very correctly offering her his arm.

He was already touching her elbow, forcing her hand into the crook of his arm, giving her no chance to object. Glancing angrily at Haviland, Crimson once more made to open her mouth, but he stopped her with a look.

"I shall go inside and make your excuses to the queen."

Crimson watched him go with the feeling that he had deliberately deserted her with the enemy.

"Come, my lady, I'm sure the walk will do you good, and you needn't worry about my trying to take advantage of you." Sir Reginald's voice was sarcastic as he pulled the obviously reluctant girl beside him.

"Oh, I'm not worried, Sir Reginald," she said, falsely sweet, feeling her energy return at his words, "but I daresay *you* might be."

He looked startled for a moment. "What do you mean?"

"You might very well find yourself exposed to the pox," she replied demurely. "I'm afraid I haven't been feeling well for several days and I would hate—should the affliction prove to be serious—to infect you as well."

His hand came away from her arm as though stung. "Are you sure, girl? Could it be the pox?"

Crimson watched him, enjoying the dismay on his face as his eyes searched her exposed flesh for some sign of the disfiguring disease. At that moment, she could almost have wished she had been exposed to it. At least that would insure his staying away from her!

"Perhaps, then, you are right, mistress, and you should retire to your own rooms." His voice was flat, decidedly without any real sympathy. "I shall, of course, call on you again when it is positive that you are in no danger."

"Oh, Sir Reginald, how brave you are to risk such exposure!" she threw at him insolently.

He flushed angrily and his eyes darkened. "You seem to enjoy taunting me, mistress. I wonder if all this is merely a charade to keep me away from you. If so, I must admit it would be most insulting to me." In spite of the small fear that still lurked in his eyes, he leaned closer to her. "Tell me, has your father spoken yet of our coming marriage?"

"Our—marriage!"

134

At her thunderstruck expression, he smiled unpleasantly. "Yes, my dear, you have the honor of being asked to become my wife. It fills me with the greatest joy to behold your suitable expression of happiness." Sarcasm once more infected his words.

Actually, Crimson's face was anything but happy. She looked as though she might faint again, and, indeed, a faint dizziness was once more beginning in her head. "But —but I was never told. Lord James Haviland didn't—"

"Oh, forgive me, my dear. I suppose it is somewhat of a shock for you then. I do hope your—illness—does not postpone our marriage date unduly. I would grow terribly impatient if that were the case. Your father might have to suffer pangs of nervousness if I once more were made to press him for the money he owes me."

"You aren't marrying me just to erase my father's debts?" she demanded. "I suppose I should consider myself honored to be worth over a thousand pounds!" Her snort of derision was lost on him as he laughed.

"As you say, mistress, but someday, I should hope you would prove yourself worth even more."

His words and their meaning were lost on Crimson, who was still smarting from the lack of courage her father had showed in dealing with this man. He had actually bartered his own daughter in order to clear himself of his gambling debts! Oh, it was too much to bear!

He seemed to be awaiting her next words patiently and when she said nothing, he shrugged. "I see there are to be no glad cries, no loving kisses or embraces. I must say, my dear, my first two wives were at least capable of showing some emotion, if only at the thought of inheriting all of my money." His face was smug.

"Your money interests me not at all, Sir Reginald," she flung back at him. "But it seems that my father has a definite weakness where that commodity is concerned. I suppose it does no good to say that the thought of marriage to you makes me quite—unhappy?"

He shook his head, still smiling. "No good at all, my dear. In fact, I daresay your predecessors had the same initial feelings towards me, but they soon evaporated when they found out how truly obliging a husband I can be."

"I'm sorry, Sir Reginald, but I cannot—"

He held up his hand. "All that needs to be arranged is the date, my dear. I have already made up my mind, and the king has given his blessing. What else can he do? He knows you are too young to make up your own mind. And I am a favored courtier."

"But we don't even know each other!" Crimson continued, feeling as though she were talking to a brick wall.

"We will know each other very well after we are married, my dear."

15

The next few days were trying ones for Crimson. She was forced to retire to her father's house because of the continued attacks of nausea and dizziness that assailed her, and she had no wish to infect anyone of the queen's household. She was actually more scared than she admitted and hoped against hope that the symptoms would soon go away and prove only some odd indisposition.

Beth was helpful during the days that followed, more sympathetic than she had ever been, and offered to do any small tasks, no matter how irksome. Crimson was grateful to her and instructed her to keep her father away from her rooms at all times. She just could not face him with the knowledge that he had virtually betrayed her, sold her to Sir Reginald like a brood mare.

Her days in bed did little to improve her temper and she found herself given to screaming outbursts at Beth, after which Crimson would be instantly contrite and then burst into a torrent of tears that there was no explanation for.

As the days followed one after another in endless succession, she found herself feeling better. Extremely grateful, for the tiny red spots had never appeared, she began following a strict regime to bring her hair and skin back to their former youthful glow.

One day, a quick knock on her door was followed by the appearance of her father, an appearance that immediately put her on guard.

"You're looking much better, Crimson," he began, his eyes searching her face. "I think it time for you to return to court for a little entertainment. Perhaps you would care to accompany me?"

She shook her head. "No." The word was uttered flatly.

He had the grace to flush. "There is tension between us lately, Crimson, that I'm sure I know the cause for. You —you still have not resigned yourself to the marriage with Sir Reginald Gardner?"

"Did you really expect me to submit meekly, when you knew how much I disliked the man? How could you have planned all this so cold-bloodedly?"

"Cold-bloodedly! For God's sake, Crimson, you're not exactly coming out of this with nothing! You will have a husband who can provide well for you, as well as an honored name here at court. I fail to see how you can accuse me of being cold-blooded!"

"You know perfectly well what I mean." She threw her words at him. "I have only been in England a little over two months, and find myself betrothed to a man I hardly know. You had this planned all along. I know you did! Was this the reason you had me brought back to England?"

He started to shake his head, then shrugged. "Yes, if you want the truth, there it is. I needed you, Crimson, to

137

pull myself out of a bad spot I was in. I was fortunate that you are as beautiful as you are. You can be charming if you wish, but right now you are behaving as foolishly as your mother once did."

"My mother! The only foolish thing she ever did was most likely to marry you, although I suppose I must be grateful that she did, or I would not be here."

He laughed suddenly, startling her. The laugh was almost cruel, and he moved away from the door, shutting it behind him as he moved farther into the room. Some instinct drove Crimson away from him, afraid suddenly of his strange mood.

"Your mother got you before she even married me!" he said viciously, pent-up emotion causing his voice to tighten. Memories of his marriage returned with all the humiliation, the embarrassment she had caused him when she had announced that she was already with child, and that the child was not his. "You're no more my daughter than your maid, Beth, could be! Do you hear me, Crimson? I gave you my name, but the fact remains that you're nothing more than a bastard!"

White-faced, Crimson stared at him, unbelieving, wondering if his mind had become unhinged. What was he saying? That he was not her father, that there had never been any connection between them? A sudden, fierce joy overcame her and she smiled into the eyes of the man.

"A bastard! That does not displease me at all. I'm glad I'm not your daughter!" she flung at him haughtily. "Sir Reginald will hardly be overjoyed to be marrying a woman with no name!"

Her words temporarily halted the rage inside of the man, but then he smiled craftily. "Sir Reginald will never know that I am not your father, because there will be no one to tell him. I have given you my name, Crimson, and you owe me for that."

"I owe you nothing!"

"You'll marry Sir Reginald, or I promise you, you'll be ruined at court, my dear. No one will receive you. Not even the king, who seems to dote on you so because of your friendship with his sister. No, you will become an

138

outcast, a trull fit only to satisfy men like your mother chose to do!"

"You sicken me! Because I am not your daughter, you think I still do not have my honor. No man will touch me unless I wish it!"

"No man!" He laughed and his hands came out to grasp her shoulders, kneading her flesh through the silk of her wrapper. "I'll be the first, Crimson, to use you and when I'm finished and you are safely married to Gardner, there will be many others, as many as it takes for you to help your husband reach his goals. He'll pimp for you, my dear. You'll have nothing to worry about, for Sir Reginald will be able to arrange all your appointments, and see to it that they are kept!"

"You're insane!"

"Just remembering an old, old injury, my dear. You will pay very well for your mother's insult to me."

His hands were heavy on her, ripping away the gown, sliding it down her shoulders to expose the creamy skin beneath. Crimson, after the initial shock, began to fight him, seeking to claw at his face with her nails. He was stronger than she, and it was not hard for him to subdue her long enough to snatch the gown from her body.

He gasped at the sight of her perfectly formed breasts with their pink tips, and his hands covered them quickly, massaging them roughly with the fire of his passion.

"Let me go!" Crimson cried breathlessly, horrified at the look of desire on the man's face. Despite the fact that she knew he was not her father, there was a particular feeling of inexplicable guilt that he should see her nudity. It was more shameful, more destructive than any other feeling she had ever experienced.

He was pushing her backwards so that she tripped momentarily on the remains of her gown, feeling her shoulders pressed up against the wall as he steadied her. She wished she could vomit in his face as his mouth came down to capture hers, making the kiss a thing of indecency as he mashed his lips over hers, bruising them carelessly. She struggled against him, feeling wave after wave of hor-

139

ror break over her as his hands moved up and down on her body, plundering it blatantly.

Slowly, inexorably, he was pushing her down, sliding her back against the wall until she sprawled in a seated position as he crouched over her. She still struggled, but she could feel the dizziness in her head pounding over her, adding greatly to the emotional distress that was already running through her.

His hands were everywhere, it seemed, and through the pain in her head, Crimson felt his pinches and thrusting fingers in a swirling haze. Her body seemed to become somehow liquid as he continued exploring her greedily, his breathing becoming heavy and rasping.

"I'll be the first with you, little bitch. Your mother gave her virginity to the first soldier who asked her for it. Well, she should be squirming in her grave as she sees how I have exacted my revenge. Her husband will be the first to sample her own daughter!" His laugh was lost as he buried his mouth in the warm flesh at her throat.

Through the haze that enveloped her, Crimson reached out, her fingers clutching at his coat as she brought her flexed knee upwards. She must have hit her target, for he suddenly howled with pain and viciously knocked her head back against the wall.

Crimson slumped downwards, hardly knowing what was happening. Instinctively she tried to recover herself before Haviland could do the same, but her action had only infuriated him to the point where he would be content to beat her senseless while waiting for his potency to return. She felt his hand slap her on the cheek.

"Bitch! Ah, you're Deborah's daughter all right! She hated me at the end too, the ungrateful sow. Just like you, I gave her my name, the right to hold her head up in public when her belly grew big with you inside of it." With each word, his hands moved hurtfully on her body, bruising her thighs as he tried to separate them. "But at least with you, I'll be the first. Perhaps you will carry *my* child when you go as a bride to Gardner! Christ, I'd like to see his face!"

Weakly, Crimson attempted to focus her eyes as she

140

whispered, "You'll not be the first. You'll not be the one to take my virginity. It is no longer there to take!"

"What?" His face seemed suddenly to crumple. "You lying bitch, what are you saying? You've whored your body to someone else?"

"In France, before I came to England, on the night before I was to leave Saint-Cloud," she went on, enjoying his look of incredulousness despite her own pain and humiliation.

His face darkened ominously. His hand suddenly pressed itself into her abdomen and Crimson could not help the small cry of pain that was wrenched from her tight throat. For the first time, Haviland really looked at the naked form beneath him and then, suddenly, he let out a whimper of rage.

"So, I was right! And your maid—she confirmed my suspicions with her reports on the progress of your 'disease.'" He laughed cruelly. "A disease older than time! You're with child!"

Dully, Crimson considered him, then as the full import of his words came back to her, she found herself reliving that one night in the gardens of Saint-Cloud when a man had taken her virginity and—obviously—given her a parting gift to remember him by. Helpless tears rolled from her eyes. How could she not have guessed that she was pregnant! And she had thought it the pox! She laughed stupidly at her blindness, hiccupping at Haviland, and jerked her chin towards him.

"Breeding already! Two—almost three—months along! You'll show soon enough and I'll not be surprised when Sir Reginald withdraws his offer of marriage! Goddamn you! I'll not let this ruin my plans for you to marry him!"

He stood up suddenly, brushing at the disorder of his clothes, smoothing the tangled hairs of his periwig as he looked down at her with disgust written in his face. She had given herself to a damn Frenchman! The stupid bitch could not have picked a more hopelessly entangled mess to get him into. Well—and his eyes suddenly narrowed with a sharp brutality—there were ways to untangle this mess with Sir Reginald none the wiser.

16

Crimson would recall very little of that night. After Haviland had left the room and allowed Beth inside, Crimson had promptly thrown up and had had to have Beth bathe her face and neck to bring her back to full consciousness. She had a lump on the back of her head that hurt dreadfully as Beth busied herself with her hair. Her cheek was smarting and her whole body was shaking with the enormity of what had just passed between the man she had thought was her father and herself.

He had ripped apart any feeling for him with his brutal description of her own conception and his subsequent treatment of her mother. And then, on top of that, to stun her so completely with the news that she was pregnant— that she, a bastard herself, would bear another man's bastard, just as her mother had. It was too much to comprehend and her brain reeled at the thought of it.

"Which dress, my lady?" Beth asked, going to the armoire as she glanced back at the motionless girl.

"What—what?"

"Which dress shall I bring out for you to wear?" Beth repeated patiently. "Lord James said that you would be accompanying him tonight on a short journey."

Her words hardly penetrated the tight cocoon of Crimson's humiliation, and so the maid shrugged and drew out a serviceable heavy serge that would protect the girl from the icy winter blasts from the cold winter winds. She laid it carefully on the bed, smoothing its folds, then turned to finish dressing her mistress.

It was three hours later that Lord Haviland knocked curtly, then entered the room before Beth had a chance to answer it. By that time, Crimson had recovered some of her poise, and to see Haviland enter her room so calmly brought her, raging, to her feet.

"Get out of here!"

He smiled slowly and shook his head, signaling to Beth that she would leave them immediately. "You are coming with me, Crimson. I see that your maid has dressed you for the journey."

"What journey is this? I will go nowhere with you!"

He brushed at the sleeve of his coat, then eyed her speculatively. "You will come willingly, Crimson, or I shall have one of my men bind you. I am in no mood for one of your childish tempers."

"Bind me! You speak as though this journey could be my last. Have you sunk so low that you would murder me just to keep the scandal from your own name—a name that I heartily wish I were rid of!"

Once more he smiled. "And so you shall be, very soon, my dear. When you marry Sir Reginald, you will have your wish most assuredly. Now, see, doesn't that please you?"

"His name does not suit me any better," she snapped back waspishly.

He shrugged. "But it so happens that it suits my plans perfectly. I have no wish to find myself back in the predicament of owing Sir Reginald his thousand pounds again. No, it is much easier to rid myself of a young person who has grown tiresome to me."

"The king—I shall tell him what you are planning to do! He—"

"He is not here at the moment, my dear. And after to-night, I think you will be glad to marry Sir Reginald. You will be glad to leave my house."

"You speak truly there, my lord. Tell me where we are going!"

"Come along. I shall tell you when it is time, and I am fast growing weary of this useless chatter."

Because she knew he was quite capable of carrying out his threat to have her bound ignominiously by one of the servants, Crimson decided reluctantly to follow him outside to the waiting carriage. The driver seemed to have already been given his instructions, for he whipped up the horses immediately after Crimson and Haviland climbed in the carriage.

Seated opposite Haviland, Crimson kept her eyes carefully averted from his face. That he still wanted her to marry Sir Reginald was quite obvious, but how was he going to manage it with her soon to begin growing big with the child? She bit her lip unconsciously, chastising herself for not reading more into those first signs of queasiness than she had thought. But then, what could she do about it? She smiled bitterly at the thought of the father of the life within her. It was useless to think that he might be persuaded to marry her. She did not even know where he was now—most likely enjoying the caressess of Madame of France, and sparing no thought for the girl he had deflowered and left pregnant. How many others might he have left the same way, she thought, and it rankled deeply to think that she had been foolish enough to let him have his way with her.

Sunk in such dispirited thoughts, the time passed quickly for her and when the coach stopped abruptly, she sat up slowly as though just remembering where she was. She became aware of the freezing chill outside that seeped in the coach door as the driver opened it.

Hugging her arms about her, she stepped down to the frozen earth, gazing at Haviland with a faintly alarmed air. They were somewhere in the country, possibly on the outskirts of London, for she didn't think they had driven too far. The coach had stopped at one side of a poor-looking shanty, from which issued a feeble light under the edges of tightly pulled shutters.

"Where is this place?" she demanded of Haviland.

"Not too far from London," he replied calmly, taking her arm firmly in his grasp when she would have pulled
144·

away from him. "It is a place much frequented by the great ladies of court, I am told," he continued, chuckling crudely under his breath.

Crimson noted the presence of another carriage on the other side of the house as they crossed the rutted yard to knock lightly at the door. It took several minutes for it to be opened, and Crimson stamped her feet against the cold while they stood within the porch awaiting entrance.

When the door was finally opened, an old, wizened woman glared out at them as though they had interrupted her in sleep. "What do ye want?" she demanded ungraciously.

Haviland stepped into the circle of light and bowed. "Lord James Haviland, Mistress Abigail. I was here earlier this evening to make arrangements for my—daughter."

"Aye, aye. I remember ye now, me lord," the old woman cackled and opened the door to allow them to come in.

Inside, the place looked larger and was partitioned off by dingy sheets into three small cubicles, one of which was obviously used for the woman's personal needs, as there was a table with a chair and a roaring fire upon which hung a large caldron of water. A straw pallet lay in one corner, and a tiny cupboard stood against the wall farthest away.

Crimson could not see beyond the sheets to the other two partitions, but shadows moved behind one and she could guess that they must be the occupants of the other carriage. Curiously, she wondered what this old woman did that would number her clients among the "great ladies of the court" as Haviland had said.

"Mistress Haviland, if ye will please move to the far side there, I'll be another moment before I can attend to ye."

A sharp groan issued from the curtained alcove, followed by a woman's panting breaths and then a hard, imperious voice calling for the woman. "Get in here, Abigail —I—I think it is time!"

Crimson started at the sound and glanced up quickly at

145

the man beside her. "Sounds like—is it Lady Castlemaine?" she wondered aloud.

By the look of genuine surprise on Haviland's face, she could see that he had had no idea that the king's former mistress would be here also on this night. A definite nervousness increased over her, and Crimson heartily wished to be gone from this place which suddenly loomed evilly in her mind.

Continued groans and shouts of pain were coming from the cubicle where Abigail had disappeared, and she could hear the old woman clucking sympathetically and talking reassuringly to the woman in pain. "Only a little more time, me lady, and ye will be rid of this unwelcomed brat. Tell me, would not the king have been pleased at yet another addition to his family?"

"Shut up, you fool. This is not the king's child! If there had been a way to foist it on him, I would have, but he would not be fooled this time! No, if I had revealed to him that I was pregnant, my hopes of a duchy would have disappeared. Ah, no, 'tis that damn Jermyn's brat that I would expel—and quickly. What is taking so long this time?"

"I've an idea, me lady, that ye were further along than ye thought—perhaps five months. 'Tis almost like a birthing, it seems, but have no fear, it will soon be over. Ye should stay in bed longer this time, though."

"Don't tell me to stay in bed, you old crone! How can I stay in bed, at my leisure, when there are so many who are ready to usurp me? No, I cannot allow the king to suspect what I have done. He would never forgive me. Children are a damn delight to him! He would take it ill if he knew that I—" Her words were cut off by a sharp cry of pain, followed by murmured words from the lady who must have accompanied her.

Crimson, petrified by fear, understood that Lady Castlemaine was expelling a child—an unwanted brat, as she had named it. It was far too early for the child to live outside its mother's body. She turned, wide-eyed, to Haviland, who was watching her covertly.

146

"Why have you brought me here? To witness this? Is this some sort of threat or—"

"Silence. Follow me."

He pulled her along past the first partition and then on to the last area where stood a long, wooden table and a woolen blanket. Quickly, Haviland thrust her on the table, holding her down forcibly when she would have struggled to get up. For a horrified instant, Crimson felt like some sacrificial lamb and her head spun crazily with fear.

It seemed like only minutes before the old woman was back, throwing up Crimson's skirts in order to examine her. Crimson could feel the rough fingers on her thighs and groin and her skin flinched at the contact.

The woman laughed softly. "Ah, this will be easy, me lord. The child is very young, her hips still slender. I doubt if she would have been able to carry the child anyway through the nine months. Has she had much illness?"

Haviland nodded affirmation, not looking at Crimson's beseeching eyes as he held his hand firmly over her mouth. "She had bouts of nausea, vomiting—"

"Perhaps we had best leave her to miscarry then. I have no doubts that she will. She—"

"I want it done now," Haviland said tightly. "Give her the potion."

Abigail shrugged. "How far along?"

"A little over two months."

She disappeared around the sheet, and Crimson, straining to get away from Haviland's hand, could hear her talking softly to Lady Castlemaine.

"Now, now, me lady, ye must rest here a while. Ye're bleeding quite freely now and—"

"Shut up. I'll not stay here a moment longer than necessary, woman! Here is your gold. Only hand me my cloak, and my maid and I will be away from here!"

"As ye say, me lady. I will bind ye tightly."

Crimson stared, able to see Lady Castlemaine clearly now as she walked slowly from the cubicle to the door. She turned at the door as though to say something else to the old woman, and her eyes caught those of Crimson's.

For a moment, complete surprise was replaced by curi-

147

osity. Then as Crimson's stare pleaded silently with her, the penciled brows came down and a look of hatred stole into the blue eyes. Without a word of recognition, Lady Castlemaine went out the door, and moments later, Crimson could hear her coach departing quickly.

"I'm afraid you've made a permanent enemy of the lady," Haviland whispered, not without some pity. "She'll not forgive you for witnessing this."

Casting him a look of silent loathing, Crimson relaxed suddenly, hoping to deceive him. As his grip slackened, she was able to open her lips enough to bite his palm deeply. With a howl of pain, he released her, and quicker than he could catch her again, she had slid from the table and bolted for the door.

Outside, without her heavy cloak, the chill air hit her like a blow, but she stumbled on, hoping to lose him in the dark night. She would not have that horrible old hoyden commit some foul deed on her body. She shivered, partly from the cold and partly from the enormity of what had nearly befallen her. Bastard or not, she could not give up the child within her. She had been reared too strictly by her Catholic cousin, and the fear of hell burned brightly within her at the thought.

Moving haphazardly over the frozen earth, she stumbled twice, hitting the ground hard enough to cry out in pain. The ruts caused by the summer rains had been hardened by the freezing weather, and her foot would slip into one, only to turn at an angle and throw her off balance.

She could hear Haviland puffing somewhere behind her, and she increased her speed so that when she stepped on the patch of ice, there was nothing she could do to stop the fall as her feet slipped out from beneath and she landed heavily on her back. Almost immediately, a pain shot through her, and she thought she had broken her spine.

She was still lying supine, in the grip of intolerable pain, when Haviland located her and angrily reached down to take her in his arms. Quickly, as her groans became louder and more wrenching, he carried her back into the warm interior of the cabin.

Once more, she was made to lie on the wooden table, tossing her head from side to side, nearly unconscious from the terrible pains that gripped her stomach and abdomen. Mistress Abigail hurriedly examined her once more and her toothless smile was ironic as she addressed the man who sat by the fire warming herself.

"The girl has accomplished herself what she had tried so desperately to avoid. There will be no need for the potion, me lord, for your daughter has miscarried from the fall outside."

Haviland stared back at her, incredulous.

The woman nodded vigorously. "As I warned ye, she is as yet too immature to bear children with ease. This one was not lodged properly within her body and it was a simple matter to jar it loose. I will bind her tightly, and ye can take her home within the hour. She will be sore for a few days, but no other ill effects should be forthcoming."

Haviland nodded dumbly. He waited a while longer before the fire, his mind lost in thoughts of another time when he had waited in a poor cabin such as this while his wife died giving birth to a child that was not even his. To his own consternation, his eyes were moist at the unwelcome thought, and with an angry hand he rubbed his eyes to clear them. Providence had taken a hand in this, he thought to himself. The girl had miscarried by her own carelessness, and would have done so anyway, according to the old woman. Tomorrow, he would pay a visit to Sir Reginald and make the plans for the wedding.

17

"Oh, how lovely you look, Crimson!" Philippa cried out with envy, hugging the girl to her breast. "My dear, your husband must realize what a prize he is getting!"

Crimson stood quietly, allowing the loquacious woman to appraise her charms. The serious set of Crimson's face did nothing to inhibit the beauty and grace of her form as she stood in her wedding finery, only minutes before she would descend to the chapel below for the marriage. The gown of shimmering white satin was drawn back in the front of the skirt to reveal an underskirt of silver lace dotted with tiny blue bows of velvet. Lace dripped from the sleeves, identical to the lace in the long veil, which was secured to her hair with more blue bows, to fall quite freely over her shoulders and down past the train of the gown itself. White gloves encased her arms to the elbow, and a white cloak trimmed in ermine would keep her from shivering in the February chill, as she would have to cross the yard outside to get to the chapel.

Only six weeks had gone by since the miscarriage, a memory that still caused a strange, hollow feeling inside of her that could bring the ready tears to her eyes. She had not spoken a word to Lord James Haviland since that night when he had returned her to his house, and hence the quickness with which he had set about having the banns for the marriage read and the date for the wedding set.

Sir Reginald had insisted that the wedding take place in his country seat of Mayfield, in Kent. It would not be a Catholic wedding, as King Charles was too well aware of the opposition of the people towards that religion. A wave of anti-French, anti-Catholic feeling had swept over England, and the marriage would be carried out under the laws of the Anglican Church of England, much to the satisfaction of all those concerned.

The king himself had deigned to attend, but the thought could not cause more than a stir of excitement in Crimson's breast. She had not wanted this marriage, had fought vehemently against it, until all her defenses had been overpowered by the man she had once thought was her father. How glad she was that he was not! She could almost see him rubbing his hands with glee at the thought that after the ceremony, Sir Reginald would hand him a piece of paper forfeiting the right to collect on all his gambling debts.

It sickened her to think that Haviland would be gaining so much by this marriage, but at least she would be rid of him. Sir Reginald might be a cold, aloof man, but from his dealings so far with her, she assumed that he would not require too much more from her than to hostess parties and assume her place beside him when necessary at court functions. She was well aware that he dallied with several ladies and had a more or less regular mistress among the ladies at court: Lady Anne Brownwood, a vivacious brunette, whose surly husband was not often seen at court, as he preferred to go where there was a war.

"My beautiful *daughter*," a voice called from the doorway and Crimson turned to see Haviland in the doorway awaiting her. His sarcastic emphasis on the last word infuriated her.

"Don't ever call me that again!" she hissed, and she would have thrown something at his grinning face, but Philippa, foreseeing her movement, caught her arm quickly.

"Goodness, Crimson, the king is waiting downstairs

151

with all the other guests. Is it really worth it to degrade yourself in front of them for the small pleasure of venting your spleen today?"

Her words were true enough, and Crimson subsided, telling herself that there might be another, more profitable, time to get even with this man. Quietly, she took the bouquet of flowers from Philippa, who would serve as her matron of honor, and made her way to the door, where she avoided the outstretched arm of Lord Haviland. Nonetheless, he forced her hand through his crooked elbow and led her down the stairs. Below, a group of sparkling ladies and well-dressed men looked up expectantly. She could see the dark eyes of the king on her, approving what they saw.

Unconsciously, Crimson lifted her head higher. Bastard she might be, but none here knew it except herself and Haviland, and she had no fear that he would give her away. He had too much to gain by keeping to the lie that she was his daughter. Feeling a sudden, inexplicable urge to laugh in the faces of all these insincere courtiers, Crimson had to rebuke herself sharply, and she succeeded in keeping her face in placid lines.

At the bottom of the staircase, the king extended his arm, much to the excited whisperings of some of the ladies, who noted that the queen had not attended the ceremony, even though Crimson was one of her household. The king had assured everyone that the queen's latest miscarriage had required her to remain in her bed, but the ladies assured themselves that they were not fooled one bit —and that Charles had, once more, cast his eye on one of the lovelies of his court.

Haviland bowed low before the king and gave him Crimson's hand, so that it was the king himself who escorted the young bride to the chapel where her husband-to-be waited patiently. Sir Reginald was dressed in dark blue with pure white lace at his wrists and throat and he looked, despite Crimson's hasty dismissal of him, quite handsome.

Music swelled through the chapel, which was barely large enough to hold all the guests, and Crimson felt like a queen, as the king of England escorted her down the short aisle to the sacristy where the minister waited, his prayer-book open in his gnarled hands.

The king gave up her hand to Sir Reginald, who clasped it tightly in his as the couple turned to face the minister. Crimson, her veil still covering her face, felt her hand squeezed midway through the ceremony, her husband's fingers warm against her cold ones. She did not respond to the squeeze and the rest of the ceremony went flawlessly.

Afterwards, the couple was showered with snow as they ran back to the safety of the country house, their guests filing quickly behind them.

"Are you hungry?" her husband asked Crimson as they were seated at the head of the traditional long table filled with food so that the legs of it fairly groaned with the weight. The guests had already begun to eat ravenously, and their noise effectively covered any conversation between the bridal couple.

"Not very hungry," Crimson replied stiffly, toying with the slice of mutton he had just served her.

Beside her, the king overheard and laughed merrily. "Not hungry for food, eh, my dear? Just as a bride should be. What are the appetites of the stomach when compared to the appetites of the heart?" Those who had heard his comment laughed appreciably.

"Sire, you—embarrass me," Crimson murmured, her eyes on her plate.

She felt his hand seeking hers beneath the table and was startled when he caressed it softly. Her glance flew upwards and looked into the black eyes that were just then staring into hers with a curious mixture of understanding and desire that caused her to flush uncomfortably. Immediately, he released her hand.

"You are a most beautiful bride, Lady Gardner. I hope your husband appreciates what a flower he has snapped up," the king went on, busying himself with cutting his meat.

"Sire," Crimson said in a whisper, "I believe you know the reason for this marriage. Please do not make mock of me now."

Charles looked up, his black brows knit. "You are young, Crimson, and certainly cannot truly know your own mind in this matter. Believe me when I say that I weighed Sir Reginald's proposal to you very carefully. I decided that it would be best to see you married quickly before one of the young blades at court ruined your reputation." He leaned closer. "Now that you are married, my lady, you are fair game to me."

Crimson cast him a startled look and her blush deepened. "I consider you a true friend, sire," she murmured quickly, hoping that her husband had not overheard their conversation. "I hope that it will always be so between us."

King Charles smiled and his eyes were shuttered as he looked away from her to respond to some quip of the Duke of Buckingham's.

Throughout the rest of the long meal, Crimson glanced anxiously at her husband, who seemed to be consuming great quantities of wine and liquor—whether to fortify himself for the coming night, or just to quench some passing nervousness, she could not decide. After all, he had already been a bridegroom twice before. Surely, he would be used to the festivities that attended the wedding by now!

Crimson herself was too nervous to eat. The king was making merry now with Lady Winifred Wells, another of the queen's ladies who enjoyed his favors. Some said it had been Lady Winifred who had dropped an aborted baby on the very ballroom floor two years ago, and that the baby had been the king's own child. Fortunately, someone had had the foresight to snatch it up from the floor and everyone had gone on with the dancing, although it had been noted that shortly after Lady Winifred had retired early to her rooms and had pleaded sick the next morning when called to the queen.

Soon, the revelry had reached a pitch where most of the guests were clamoring that it was time to send the newly married couple to their bed. Men's eyes gleamed drunkenly and leered down the table, causing Crimson to avert her eyes in embarrassment. The women were not much

154

more sympathetic and, laughingly, two of them pulled Crimson up from the table to escort her to her rooms in order to undress from the bridal gown.

Philippa, whose hands were clutching her arm more for support than any help she might offer, hiccupped drunkenly and insisted that she act the part of mother tonight. On Crimson's other side, Lady Chesterfield was tugging her along impatiently. A bevy of laughing, raucous ladies followed in their wake and Crimson's dressing room was filled to overflowing.

Meanwhile, the men were quipping jokes and winking lewdly at Sir Reginald in his own dressing room. One man, whom they had left outside to act as sentinel, called back when Crimson emerged from her closet to enter the bedroom. Quickly, Sir Reginald, clad in a dressing gown of rich, burgundy velvet, was shoved forward.

Crimson, her hair cascading in deep, gleaming auburn waves down her back, was dressed in a long, white silk gown, through which tantalizing glimpses of her skin could be seen in lacy inserts. She was pushed forward to the edge of the bed in order to await her husband.

The king, his dark, merry eyes never leaving her face, claimed the first kiss. He walked slowly to the bed, leaned down to Crimson's obediently upturned face and planted a warm, intense kiss on her cold lips, warming them from his own so that she swayed towards him involuntarily. Disregarding the gawking courtiers, Charles' hands moved up to her shoulders before dropping regretfully to caress her breast above the neckline of the nightgown.

"Good night, Lady Gardner. Sleep well; and I trust you will not honeymoon too long and keep your delightful presence away from the court." The words were exceedingly correct, but the look in the king's eyes promised a warm welcome when Crimson returned to Whitehall.

He was sensitive enough to note the trembling that had taken hold of the girl and, holding up his hand, as the next courtier came forward to kiss the bride, he said, "It is time for us to leave the bridal couple alone, gentlemen and ladies. Come."

A disappointed sigh welled up collectively, but the

courtiers had no choice but to obey their sovereign and soon all had filed out of the bedroom, leaving Sir Reginald alone with his bride.

"The king is pleased with you," Sir Reginald commented slowly, untying the sash from around his waist.

The robe dropped carelessly to the ground and Crimson flushed to view her husband's nakedness. Despite having already known one man, she had never seen one entirely naked, and it distressed her that he merely stood next to the bed, without making any attempt to cover himself. Perhaps he was very drunk.

"Come to bed, my lord," she whispered, keeping her eyes on his face.

He chuckled. "First, you must show yourself to me, Crimson. I admit that our time of wooing was too short and without much intimacy. I want to see this piece of goods I have bought for a thousand pounds."

His words made the breath catch in Crimson's throat, but dutifully, she rose from the bed in order to struggle out of the nightgown. When she had lifted the garment over her head, she quickly dived back beneath the covers, pulling them up to her chin and blinking up at him in trepidation.

"No, no! Out of the bed. Over here by the firelight so that I can truly look at you," he commanded petulantly.

"But, I—"

"Stand here!" he said with more authority, pointing to a spot on the floor directly next to him.

Trembling and blushing to the roots of her hair, Crimson scrambled from beneath the covers and forced herself to stand across from him, feeling the glow of the fire caressing her with its warmth. There was no sound for a time, but she knew her husband's eyes were skimming over her as thoroughly as he might check out a prize colt or judge a cow for new stock.

"Please, this is embarrassing for me. Can we not go to bed now?" Crimson pleaded, nerving herself to look directly into her husband's flushed face.

He licked his lips reflectively, then came closer to her so that his hands were able to reach out and touch the

156

warm, silken flesh that quivered slightly under his touch. Heavily, his hands felt the texture of her shoulders, her breasts and moved lower to her belly and hips.

"A well-made young woman," he breathed, clasping both hands around her hips to draw her closer.

Crimson felt a shock run through her as her flesh made contact with his, and she was able to feel the proof of his desire for her, hard and alien against her. She steeled herself not to struggle away from him, but endured his touch, telling herself that this was her husband, that he had every right to do what he wished with her.

However, when his hand insinuated itself between her thighs, she could not help jumping back, her eyes flying to his in silent flinching. Careless as to her emotions, Sir Reginald drew her back and continued his exploration until she cried out in genuine hurt.

"I warn you, Crimson, I am not a gentle man," he said thickly. And then, "Are you still a virgin?"

The question caught her off guard and she gasped.

"Don't bother to lie to me. I would find out the truth soon enough," he cut in meaningfully.

Crimson could not face him, and she turned her head away as she shook it quickly. "No."

He sighed. "I expected no more. How many men have you known?"

She took a deep breath. "Why must you question me so? I don't understand why you wish to know these things. Surely they do not matter now?"

He tilted her chin up with his hand, forcing her to look at him. "How many men have taken you, my little bride?"

"Only—only one," she said between clenched teeth. "And that man, only once."

"The king?"

Startled by the question, Crimson flushed deeply. "No!" Then, because he still seemed to be waiting, she continued, "A man I knew in France."

"A damned Frenchman!"

For a moment, Crimson thought he was going to strike her and she flinched involuntarily at the look of deep rage

157

on his face. His hand, however, stayed at her shoulder, although he had doubled it into a fist.

Thinking that she ought to enlighten him about the true nationality of her first seducer, Crimson started to speak, but the ridiculousness of the situation suddenly hit her, and she shrugged her shoulders. Let him think what he liked! It was he who had insisted on knowing. For what purpose she could not fathom.

Suddenly she smiled wickedly and looked at her new husband archly. "And now tell me, my lord, how many women you have known?"

His brows rose sardonically. "Such a foolish question from a new bride. Really, my dear, I shouldn't think you would particularly want to know the answer."

His rebuke caused her embarrassment to return, but she hardened her jaw and repeated it, "But you know about me, my lord, and so I wish to know how many other women you have had before our marriage."

He shrugged. "I have been married twice before, little fool, and have known women both during and after those marriages. It is not a man's way to go without women's company, and there are always plenty who are willing."

He seemed to grow tired of the conversation, for he stopped abruptly and pushed back a lock of gleaming auburn from her breast so that his hand could cover the round, rosy-tipped peak. His other hand pressed her forward once more so that she would be able to arouse him by mere contact of their flesh. Embarrassed, but curious, Crimson could feel him growing hard beneath her belly, and the sensation caused strange little quivers to run through her. She would have liked to look down and watch this strange metamorphosis, but her upbringing forbade it and, instead, she fixed her eyes on a point midway between his mouth and nose.

"Can you feel it, Crimson? Can you feel what your presence does for me?" Gardner was saying, punctuating the words by kissing her along the length of her jaw.

She sighed and nodded.

"Come, shall we go to bed now? You have a lovely little body, my sweet, and despite its having already been initiated into the art of love, I have an idea there are still many things I can teach you."

He pulled her towards the bed now, holding her hand tightly until he could push her down onto the sheets which were warm from the heat of the fire. Crimson let herself be lowered heavily to the bed and lay, sprawled out before his eyes which were gazing intently at her so that she could feel tiny prickles of sensation all over her flesh. In another moment, he had joined her on the bed, his body immediately covering hers from thigh to breast so that it was impossible not to feel the state of his arousal.

"Ah, now let us begin, Crimson," he breathed in her ear.

Lulled by the sensations he was arousing in her, Crimson put her arms around his neck and pressed him tightly against her. Perhaps, she thought dreamily, this marriage would not be as bad as she had thought at first. Perhaps, they could grow to love one another. Perhaps—

A tiny shriek of surprise was torn from her throat as she felt him pull her legs apart with sudden brutality. Gone were the caressing hands, the whispering mouth—and in their place, a man intent on satisfying his own aching drives. Struggling to accept this new facet of her husband, Crimson tried to drift with him as he positioned her expertly beneath him, but it was to no avail.

As though he had suddenly gone mad, or were punishing her for something, Gardner thrust himself mercilessly into her, tearing at the tender flesh that had only recently undergone the trauma of miscarriage.

Crimson, forcing herself not to scream as her outraged flesh was subjected to her husband's sexual attack, closed her eyes tightly and prayed that he would be finished quickly. The act itself was closer to rape than to love, and she could not help the silent tears that ran down her cheeks. The pain was nearly too much to bear and involuntarily her hands reached for his shoulders to push him away.

Gardner, too absorbed in his own pleasure to worry about his wife, had reached the point where he was about to release his seed into her body, when he felt his wife

159

thrusting him away. With a cry of frustration, he felt her body slide from beneath him, even as his hands clutched at empty air to bring her back. Too lost in his own sexual release to have the strength to pull her back, he lay down heavily on the bed, his seed dripping ineffectually from his body.

Crimson, staring at him in horror, thought perhaps she had wounded him in some way by her abrupt withdrawal. She hadn't realized that a man's release was accompanied by such complete loss of composure and strength. Tentatively, she crept closer to him on her knees.

"Reginald, Reginald—what has happened? I—"

He turned on her, his face livid and snarling. "Get away from me, you teasing bitch! Go elsewhere before I throttle you with my bare hands!"

Confused and a little frightened by the intensity of his wrath, Crimson backed carefully off the bed, her eyes never leaving his angry face. Meekly, she retrieved her nightgown from the floor and put it on. Then, after a last look at her husband, she scurried into the safety of her own dressing room where she could curl up on the pallet put there for her maid's use.

It was very late before she could fall asleep, and just before doing so, she thought she heard a feminine giggle coming from the direction of her bridal chamber.

18

Lady Chesterfield looked closely in the mirror, her white hands passing over her smooth, round face, looking for blemishes and wrinkles. She was nearly
160

twenty-eight years old, ten years older than Crimson, who stood behind her waiting impatiently for her to finish her primping so that they could return to the masque in the great ballroom.

"Elizabeth," Crimson sighed, "you look so beautiful tonight in your costume that no one will even notice the red pimple over your left eyebrow."

Immediately, Elizabeth bent closer to the mirror and frantically examined that area on her face, but was relieved to see nothing. "Oh, Crimson, please stop teasing me. You know how I've been hoping to snare the Duke of York all these weeks. I would just die if I weren't perfect tonight, especially since he seems to be sniffing at the bait more and more."

"Such terms you use, my dear," Crimson replied, tucking a loose curl behind her own white velvet mask that sparkled with diamonds. Her own costume was the perfect foil for Elizabeth's, as Crimson was depicted as morning in a gown of palest blue silk, overlaid with white lawn that made her seem almost ethereal, while Elizabeth had chosen a black ensemble to represent evening. Crimson had taken the further precaution of covering her telltale curls with a white velvet snood, but Elizabeth, hoping the duke would recognize her, had allowed her yellow hair to be bound in sequined netting, which left little for the beholder to guess.

"Do you think James likes me a little?" Elizabeth sighed, putting her round chin in her hand and staring dreamily into the mirror.

"Which James?" Crimson replied impudently. "Hamilton or York? I'm never sure which one you are after from day to day."

"Silly! The duke, of course. My dear cousin James is a wonderful diversion, but heaven knows he's got so many women after him, I'm too soon lost in the crowd. Don't tell me he hasn't been paying you lavish court since everyone knows that you and your husband—"

There was a pained look in Crimson's face that stopped the other woman before she could go on. Recalling her wedding night, just two weeks ago, Crimson nearly

161

blushed at the shameful memory. She remembered the next morning, particularly, as she had arisen from the pallet in order to ask her husband's pardon, when she had been put to a standstill by the presence of Lady Anne Brownwood beneath her husband's wildly churning buttocks. Without a word, she had left the bedroom and her husband had not come to her since.

Crimson had decided that theirs would probably be a sterile marriage, and she wondered if this was some deserved punishment that had been bestowed on her by God because she had lost her baby. It was all too clear that Reginald had no more interest in her, whether because he was satisfied with Lady Anne's ministrations, or because of Crimson's humiliating performance on their wedding night.

He had seen her set up in his townhouse on King Street, while he obligingly stayed in apartments at Whitehall so that their paths rarely crossed except on those occasions when they were both at court. Sometimes she could feel his eyes on her, but he would never speak, and she was too proud now to ask forgiveness from him.

"All right, then, I'm ready, Crimson," Elizabeth muttered, pulling at the neckline of her dress so that even more of her powdered bosom was exposed. "If the Duke of York doesn't ask me to his rooms tonight, I vow I shall simply have to give up the chase."

"The chase," of course, was everything to Elizabeth, Crimson thought wryly as the two ladies left the dressing room. Once caught, the quarry became too boring for her to continue the affair. Crimson had never asked her why she could not simply live the life of a good and faithful wife to her own husband, Lord Chesterfield, who was one of the handsomest men at Court, and considered a great catch by all of the tittering, calculating ladies who set their snares for their all-too-willing victims. Crimson was sure that should she have been so gauche as to ask Elizabeth such a question, the other would stare at her as though she had lost her mind. It just was not considered fashionable to be faithful to one's husband these days.

162

After all, the king, himself, set the tone of the court, and they were only too willing to follow his lead.

The two young women descended the staircase and made their way back to the ballroom where brightly masked and gowned people swayed back and forth in time to a stately court dance. King Charles was leading the dance with Lady Castlemaine, whose plunging neckline far outrivaled anything that Elizabeth could display. Barbara's full breasts were nearly popping out of her costume, which was that of a coy, innocent shepherdess. The idea must have appealed to the king, for he was eyeing her through the slits in his mask with evident enjoyment.

Someone touched Crimson on the arm and she turned to see a tall gentleman lavishly outfitted in the costume of a courtier of Elizabethan times bowing to her.

"Lovely maiden of the morn, I must claim the very next dance, which promises to be a sprightly bransle, if I have bribed the orchestra enough. Will you honor me, my lady?"

Immediately, Crimson recognized the slightly arrogant tone of James Hamilton, and she smiled, determined not to allow him to guess at her identity. Instead of replying, she nodded silently, causing him to smile in amusement.

"So, you will not tell me who you are, fair lady," he sighed mockingly. "Then I shall have to be content with intriguing guesses until the hour of midnight when I shall be sure to maneuver you into some quiet corner. 'Pon my word, the figure that I can barely distinguish among those gauzy robes could only belong to Aphrodite. But we shall see," he promised meaningfully, winking broadly at her through his mask.

Crimson struggled not to blush, hoping to seem only one of the many court ladies who would take such a compliment with an easy shrug. It amused her for the moment to keep this Don Juan of the court guessing, for she was sure that he did not know her.

Hamilton took her arm casually and filled her ears with small talk, while Crimson kept obstinately silent, only nodding now and again at some particular remark. Soon the

163

bransle began and Hamilton led her out to the dance floor, his hands clasping hers firmly.

Other dancers soon formed a long line, or chain, and Crimson found Hamilton to her right with another man, dressed as a dashing pirate, to her left. The dance was lively as they stepped first to the right, then to the left, with only the youngest dancers remaining in the line after some minutes. Breathless and laughing with enjoyment, Crimson noted that Hamilton was, indeed, a very good dancer and easily kept up the lively steps until the dance was over.

Afterwards, leading her to an alcove for Crimson to recover her breath, Hamilton leaned over swiftly and placed a light kiss on her mouth. "Thank you for the dance, sweet maiden," he murmured. "Dare I hope, that should I stay, I might find even more approval in your eyes?"

Of course, he had noticed her pleasure, and Crimson immediately cast her face into more somber tones while she shrugged, hoping to keep him tantalized. For a moment, he seemed exasperated by her obstinacy, but quickly laughed and bowed over her fingers before disappearing to court some more sociable lady.

Feeling rather deserted, Crimson gazed after him, wondering why she had been so foolish as not to have revealed who she was. It would have been a delightful game to while away the hours, for she was fairly certain that she could control young Hamilton should he become too amorous. And besides, what did it matter? Her thoughts became bitter as she realized that her husband scorned her, did not care with whom she went to bed, and was probably propositioning some giggling courtesan at this moment. Crimson sighed and for a moment felt the burden of unwanted wife so heavily that tears came to the surface.

"What's this? Venus left alone?"

The warm, male voice brought Crimson's head up and she stared into the dark, warm eyes of the king.

"Sire, I—"

"Hush, you shouldn't let on that you know me, morning maiden. Isn't it always so? The lover deserts as soon as the

164

sun peeps over the horizon. It is said that the night belongs to lovers."

"Perhaps," Crimson answered, suddenly unsure, not knowing if the king really knew who she was.

"But then, there are exceptions," he murmured softly, drawing her deeper into the alcove.

Crimson allowed him to press her back into a small settee, unconsciously relaxing as his hands rubbed soothingly across her shoulders. His caress made her sigh and helped to soothe her troubled nerves. She leaned back, allowing his hands to smooth her dress back and pass gently over the fullness of her upper breasts. Her lashes drooped mysteriously over her aquamarine eyes as she tried to hide her thoughts from the king.

"What are you thinking, little one?" he asked softly, murmuring the words close to her ear, nuzzling her neck so that his black moustache tickled her a little.

Crimson leaned back further with sudden abandon and brought her hands up to trace the lines in the dark face of the king. "I am thinking, sire, that morning is indeed honored that the king should see fit to remain with her when there are so many others who command his attention."

"Command?" he queried humorously.

She shrugged. "It is said that the king cannot resist a lovely face or an inviting look." Her own boldness surprised her.

"And yet I cannot see your face, nor do I detect an invitation about you," the king remarked, drawing her into the circle of his arms.

Crimson smelled his clean, manly smell and snuggled deeper into the strong arms that seemed to be able to keep out the rest of the world at that moment. His dark hands moved more deliberately across her bodice and began to fondle her breasts with increasing skill beneath her gown. Crimson caught her breath and, for a moment, struggled involuntarily against the encroachment.

"Quiet, little one, I wouldn't hurt you," murmured the king in his rich voice, moving his mouth against her cheek, closer to her lips.

He had captured them in another moment and was kiss-

165

ing her firmly with a slow-simmering desire that would soon begin to blaze and demand more. His arms tightened, pressing her close to his chest, while his lips continued to play against her mouth. He forced her head backwards, arching her slender neck until he could feel the rapid pulse in her throat. Unknowingly, a thick lock of auburn escaped the white snood and the king, seeing it, chuckled deep in his throat and renewed his efforts to win this desirable young woman completely to his will.

Crimson, her head whirling pleasantly, was aware of the consummate artistry of the king's kisses, and allowed herself to flow along with them. It seemed as though no one was near, that nothing else mattered, that she wanted this kiss, this gentle mastery to go on forever.

When the king finally took his mouth away, Crimson could feel his hard breathing against her cheek. His hands at her shoulders tightened as though to push her back into the settee, but with sudden, inescapable quickness, reality came rushing back as a servant bowed deeply and presented the king with a sealed note.

Frowning, Charles took his hands regretfully from Crimson's shoulders and took the note, opening it to scan briefly its contents. A slight smile crossed his tightened features.

"So, he has returned finally, the scoundrel," he muttered.

Crimson, attempting to correct any damage to her costume, wondered fleetingly who had returned, but quickly dismissed the thought as the king turned to her with a tender look on his face.

"Will you come to me tonight, my lady?" he asked in a low voice that was almost supplicating.

"Sire, you do not know me," she floundered helplessly, wishing to avoid so direct a confrontation. Despite her pleasant sense of well-being in the king's arms, she couldn't help remembering that she was lady-in-waiting to his wife.

"Crimson, I am not so blind as you might think," he said, making her blush with confusion. "Who else has eyes the exact color of yours, or that delightful habit of flushing

166

when anyone gives her a compliment? Besides," he added teasingly, "I did peek beneath your hat."

Crimson couldn't help smiling at the king's easy manner, and she allowed him to take her hand in his. "Sire, I hardly know what to say," she said in a low voice.

"Only say that you will come to me. The back staircase. Chiffinch will let you in." He gazed longingly into her face. "Please."

His humble tone impressed her more than any haughty command, and despite any hesitation, she finally nodded her acquiescence.

The king pressed a kiss into her open palm. "Tonight, after the unmasking. I will be waiting, sweetheart."

He stood up and bowed before her, then left the alcove to mingle with the others of his court, many of whom already knew exactly what he had been doing in the alcove, and with whom.

Crimson, biting her lip with slight apprehension, looked up suddenly to see her husband, who had not bothered to appear costumed, staring at her with a smile of amusement and satisfaction on his face. With an exaggerated bow, he saluted her, making a sudden lewd gesture towards her.

Furious, Crimson turned away from him. It was disgusting to think he had seen and approved her actions with the king.

19

Crimson felt her heart beating rapidly beneath the cloak she had thrown over her costume as she ascended the short flight of stairs that would end in a door, through which she could enter the king's bedroom from the back way. Each step upward seemed harder and harder until, three steps from the arched doorway, her foot faltered completely and she stood still, her eyes huge in her face as she stared at the door.

Could she go through with this? Could she go to the king and let him make love to her, knowing that she was married to a man who *knew* what she intended to do, and approved because of some twisted idea of glory? Was she only sacrificing her own moral integrity to advance her husband's position? Was she so like all of the other ladies of the court who would give anything to sleep with the King?

No! She was not so naïve that she could lie to herself and say that the king loved her, or she, him. She just couldn't do it. But while her head told her no, her bruised emotions kept willing her to say yes, to forget her husband, her honor, everything but the warmth and promise of the king's kiss, his gentle touch and soothing voice. Did she really want to make him her enemy?

Her thoughts were in such a jumble that she did not

hear the door opening before her to reveal Chiffinch on the topmost step.

"Madam, you will catch cold standing there. Please come in and wait by the fire," the servant said with his usual quiet dignity.

Crimson stared up at him, but could not find her voice. Almost as one without volition, she forced herself up the last steps and into the comforting warmth of the king's bedroom. Nervously, she glanced first at the huge, curtained bed, then at the somber face of the servant who was inquiring if she would like a glass of wine.

"Yes, please," she murmured, clutching the cloak even tighter about herself.

Chiffinch bowed and poured her some claret from a cut-glass decanter which stood on a nearby sideboard. He handed her the glass, bowed again and disappeared from the room through a doorway cleverly concealed in the wall pattern. Crimson did not even notice his exit.

She drank the wine quickly, gasping for a moment as its warmth hit her like a sudden shower. Her fingers drummed a fitful pattern on the table next to her as she took a seat. Outside the room, in the king's withdrawing room, she could hear a jangle of voices, all wanting to talk to the king, petition him or complain about something. Somehow the sounds of other people so close only increased Crimson's nervousness and she arose from the chair to pour herself another glass of wine.

Afterwards, she let the cloak slip from her shoulders. The fire was hot and its glow had already caused a slight film of perspiration on her face. She wiped her brow with her handkerchief and walked idly to the window, looking down into the courtyard of frozen ice and snow. Restless after a few moments, she took two turns about the room, then settled herself once more in her chair to await the king.

Nearly an hour passed before she heard him come in and she sprang quickly to her feet. "Sire!"

The king smiled at her, his eyes glowing with pleasure. "Charles in private, Crimson," he said quietly. "God's blood, it's good to be in here with you and away from all

169

those magpies outside." He pressed one long-fingered, beringed hand to his brow and pressed into his temple. "My head aches tonight with petitions." He looked up and smiled again at her. "But now I can leave all that behind me."

Crimson smiled tentatively, not able to meet the king's eyes as thoughts of her near-betrayal of his trust in her came back. She had almost turned away from this moment, she recalled. What would the king have done had she not been waiting here for him?

He was coming towards her now, clasping her two hands to bring her up to stand before him. He noted her trembling and brought her gently forward so that his strong arms enfolded her against his chest. Musingly, he looked down at the crown of rich auburn hair, and smiled to himself, then touched it with his lips.

Crimson could feel his hands slowly picking out the pins that held her hair in its coiffure until the thick waves came loose and flowed softly down her back. She felt somehow more defenseless against the king's charm with her hair hanging loose, and, in an involuntary gesture, she reached back to bundle it into a thick knot against her neck, but the king stayed her hands, running his own through the thick, living silk.

"Your hair is beautiful, Crimson," he murmured, his lips close to her ear.

Words stuck in the girl's throat and she could only stand silently while the king caressed her neck and shoulders with his strong hands. He lifted the heavy auburn mane away from her neck and began to kiss her there. A sensitive tingling ran through her body, and her breath came a trifle faster, matching the king's own.

"Sire, I think—"

The king brought his mouth back to her face and sealed her lips with it. Crimson felt the command in that kiss, the unspoken pleading that demanded she subject her will to his. His arms were tight around her, pulling impatiently at the fastenings at her shoulders. In another moment, he would push the gown from around her and she would be naked before the king of England. . . .

170

A soft, distinct tapping at the door barely gave Crimson time to spring away from the king's arms before Chiffinch, his eyes downcast modestly, entered the bedroom.

"Your Majesty," he said, bowing low and came closer to the king to give him a message that Crimson, in her highly distraught state, did not hear.

The king's tightened features relaxed, and he slapped Chiffinch on the back. "Well, then, send him in immediately," he said. "I'm sure that our friend can understand the needs of the king and will not mind my lady in the room. Bring more wine, Chiffinch."

Crimson had only gotten her clothing settled to rights when the secret side door through the paneled wall was opened and a man stepped through, heavily cloaked against the chill from the outside. She did not even glance up, but attempted to make herself as small as possible on the settee while the king hurried over to clasp the younger man about the shoulders in a hearty welcome.

"Brentwood! God's blood, it's good to see you, my lad!"

Brentwood? The name rang like lightning through Crimson's brain and her eyes flew upwards in mingled surprise and shock to see the tall man shaking hands with the king. It could only be the same! Furtively, her eyes passed over the dark-blond hair, cut short and curling at his collar, different from the pale blond wig he had worn in France, but framing the same lean, tanned face with its startling blue eyes under perfectly etched eyebrows that were shades darker than his hair and exactly matched the arrogant moustache beneath his nose.

"Oh, my God!" The small cry was torn involuntarily from her, as she half-stood in order to flee the room.

Her movement caught the eyes of the gentlemen, and the king immediately hurried over to place an affectionate arm about her shoulders.

"Come here, Brentwood, and see what a beauty those treacherous shores of France have placed within my grasp. Lady Gardner, may I present Nicholas Brentwood, Earl of Dorset, a special friend of mine."

Crimson tried to clear her throat to acknowledge the introduction, but failed dreadfully and could only gaze pleadingly into narrowed blue eyes that held laughter and surprise in them.

"Lady Gardner. I believe we have met, my lady," Brentwood murmured, bowing very correctly over her hand. "In Madame's court, very likely."

Crimson took a breath and nodded. "Yes, my lord. I—I believe I recall seeing you there." She glanced sideways at the king and smiled. "What a coincidence, sire, wouldn't you agree?"

Charles nodded. "Perhaps a coincidence where you two are concerned, my lady, but not a coincidence that Brentwood has returned to me at this time. I sent him to France to watch over my sister and bring me news of her."

"Oh! So that is why you—" Crimson stopped abruptly and flushed.

"Excuse me, sire, but I am sure you are eager to hear my news. Might I suggest that the lady await us here, while you and I talk in your closet? I have much news for you."

As Brentwood turned back towards the king, Crimson was able to perceive the lighter streak of skin that led from the corner of his eye down his cheek and she could not help gasping as she realized that it was a scar of some kind.

Brentwood turned back to her, guessing what had caused her reaction. "My scar? Please don't let it bother you, my lady. Made by a whip when I was very young."

"But—but I never noticed it—"

"Skillful makeup applied by those masters of art, the French, can hide many defects, my lady. After my hasty departure, I did not see the need to conceal the mark any longer."

The two men bowed, the king kissing her hand with a look of longing that was not lost on the other man, from the look of Brentwood's sarcastic smile. Crimson had the feeling that he was telling her, "I told you so" and refused to rise to the bait, but curtseyed at their departure and prepared herself to wait on the settee.

"I'll sleep with the king if I wish!" she declared to the

172

four walls of the bedroom after they had gone. Why should she care if Brentwood knew it or not!

She settled her skirts about her and kicked off her slippers in order to tuck her feet beneath her. Chiffinch appeared after a time, offering more wine, and Crimson took another glass, then another as boredom made her chafe at the men's long absence.

She had allowed herself the well-being of a huge yawn when the clock struck half-past two in the morning, and in another few moments she was sound asleep.

She was still asleep when Brentwood came down the stairs that led to the king's closet, alone. He watched the graceful, young form for a few moments, a slight smile on his face as he took in the disarrayed hair, spilling leisurely over the side of the couch, the long lashes casting shadows on the smooth cheeks by the firelight. He could feel the tightening in him, remembering her nakedness beneath him in the gardens of Saint-Cloud.

He walked over to her and laid a warm hand on her shoulder, shaking her awake.

Crimson opened heavy-lidded eyes and gazed at the face above her, expecting to see the dark visage of the king, and surprised to see the features of the man she had dreaded seeing again.

"Where is the king?" she asked, raising herself quickly from the settee and avoiding the other's eyes.

"He is still upstairs. The news of his sister—" Brentwood stopped and grinned knowingly at her. "I'm afraid the king has left you in my hands for the rest of the night, my lovely. He has charged me with your security and asked me to take you home."

"You! Take me home? But I—" Crimson flushed and bit her lip.

"The king's mind is on his sister and the problems with France, Crimson. He will find time for you later, I'm sure," Brentwood continued with cruel sarcasm. "Where do you live?"

"I live in King Street," she said absently, her hands to her livid cheeks.

"King Street?" he repeated, eyebrows raised to sardonic cresents. "With the other redheaded king's whore?"

Crimson drew in a quick breath as though she'd been struck. "W-what do you mean?" she demanded breathlessly.

"Castlemaine has apartments in King Street, my dear. Surely you knew that when you chose your own accommodations?"

"No, of course not! The house in King Street is my husband's and he bade me live there."

"A husband, too! I swear the situation grows more and more like the royal whore's. Good Lord, Crimson, you and Barbara must have hit it off well."

"Shut up. Shut up! How dare you be so righteous with me when all the time it was you—it was you—"

"Now, now, my dear. You're quite right, if you were going to say it was I who introduced you to the game. But I never thought you'd enjoy the playing so much!" He laughed wickedly. "Really, Crimson, you do amaze me, and—I'm sorry we had so little time together. But who knows? Here in Whitehall, anything is possible, isn't it, my sweet?"

"I don't need to stay here and listen to your devilish insinuations, sir! If you will only call me a hackney, I'm sure that I can get home on my own."

"I'm sure you can, Crimson, but the king has charged me with seeing you safely home. Call it a command, if you wish, but I'm bound to carry it out." He continued grinning at her with that insolent air that was infuriating her to the point of near rage.

"All right then," she said in exasperation. "Take me home, if you insist, but please do so quickly. I cannnot endure your company much longer!"

He bowed and retrieved her cloak from the settee in order to settle it about her shoulders. His hands lingered for a moment, and Crimson felt their warmth like heavy weights on her flesh. She shivered, then caught herself up and broke away from him abruptly.

"Have you your own carriage?" she asked tightly.

He nodded. "Hired, of course. I hope you don't mind

the lack of luxury." Again, sarcasm laced his words and she felt his overbearing mockery with a slight wincing inside of her.

"Since it is a short drive, I'm sure I will be able to contain myself until I arrive home," she returned, keeping her temper in check with an effort. It would never do to engage this man in a battle of wits, for she was not quite sure if she would emerge the victor.

Chiffinch appeared, opening the door which led down the back stairs. The two antagonists left the warmth of the room for the chilly corridor, and Crimson pulled her cloak tightly about her as she hurried ahead of her companion.

At a curve in the stairs, he abruptly caught up with her, catching her by the arm in order to swing her around against him. Crimson took a sharp breath of surprise as he pushed her ungently back against the wall. His hands stayed on her shoulders, the palms pressing just above her breasts.

"How could I resist the setting, sweetheart?" he murmured, bringing his face close to hers. "Doesn't it bring to mind Madame's staircase at Saint-Cloud, when you first aroused such passion in me?" he inquired sardonically.

Crimson tried to push him away. "Don't speak to me of your—your passion!" she spat at him. "Let me go!"

"Oh, my dear, how can you keep denying yourself— and me? Come, we both know you want me to make love to you. It's in your eyes." He was laughing now.

"You pompous, arrogant—"

"Words of tender endearment," he sighed in mockery. "One kiss, Crimson, and I will let you go."

Crimson looked at him with narrowed eyes. How conceited he was. Did he think she was ready to fall into his arms after what he had done to her? She thought for a moment of the small life within her that he had begun, and that had been extinguished by a man's greed. No! She would not give in to him so easily!

"Let me go now, sir, or I will be forced to scream for help. What would the king think of his friend trying to seduce the woman who—"

"—who will be only too glad to whore for the king of
175

England, but won't take a smaller fish?" the man suggested, with that infuriating air of disdain.

"Ooh, you! You should be whipped, put in the tower!" Crimson sputtered, reaching up to slap his grinning, arrogant face.

He caught her hand easily enough in his. "You're too late, my dear," he put in smoothly, imprisoning her face with the fingers of his right hand pressed into the flesh on either side of her chin. "I've already been whipped, as you can see by the scar I carry as a memento. I was eight years old when they put me into prison, and since then I've seen the inside of quite a few. I'll be damned if I'll endure another for the sake of a willful girl!"

"Willful girl!" she repeated in fury. "You're insufferable, sir! You can leave me at once and I'll find my own way home!"

With his hand still holding her face taut, he laughed slowly and tightened his grip until she cried out. "Yes, willful, stubborn—a girl who plays at being a sophisticate with the king of England. How old are you, Crimson? Sixteen, seventeen? Not any older, I'll be bound. I've seen too many women, and been with too many, not to know the difference between you and someone like Castlemaine, and yet, you seem to insist on playing her role."

As Crimson started to speak, his mouth suddenly swooped down to capture her lips. He kissed with a knowing passion that was held in check by a mastery of his own will that would wait until he had broken her own will power. His lips were smooth and warm and encompassed her whole mouth with a totality that overwhelmed her for a moment. The kiss was long, drawn out and breathless, his lips moving deliberately against hers, forcing a response that she could not help.

It seemed to Crimson, as he kissed her, that time stood still for a tiny moment, and all that there was in the world was his mouth on hers, drawing the very life from her body, sucking the breath from her lungs, making her head spin dizzily. She felt nothing else, and when he finally took his mouth away, she swayed towards him involuntarily, as though seeking to regain again what she had lost.

176

She opened her eyes slowly and saw him staring at her with a mixture of arrogant mastery and smoldering passion —a clear desire written on his face that told her he was thinking of that time in the gardens of Saint-Cloud. Suddenly, she was furious with herself and with him.

He had released her hand during the kiss, and without thinking twice, Crimson raised it to slap his face. The suddenness of the attack made him release her, and she took advantage of the moment to slip from his grasp and run quickly down the staircase.

Breathing hard, she took the stairs two at a time, nearly risking a broken neck in her headlong flight. She could hear his boots behind her and knew that he would catch up with her at any moment. She did not care to think about what he might do with her should he apprehend her in the darkened corridor and hurried her pace even more, intent on reaching the hallway below where she knew there would be people walking about, even at this late hour.

With a sigh of relief, she rounded the last turn in the staircase and found herself in a lit hallway, two or three servants scurrying quickly about their duties and a yawning couple walking by on their way to their rooms.

Crimson nodded to the courtesans, not recognizing their faces, for she could hear Brentwood's footsteps directly behind her now. In another moment, his breath was quick against her neck, and then his hand was grasping her arm, spinning her sharply around to face him. She could see his face and was surprised to see that he was laughing.

"Now, Crimson, do you feel better, after having given the terrible Englishman seducer his well-deserved slap? Now that the proprieties have been duly observed, do you think you might invite me to your apartments tonight? I have a craving to feel your sweet body again, my dear." He ducked from her swinging palm. "Ah, ah, now. One slap is enough, sweetheart."

"You make me sick!" she retorted. "Just because you happened to be the first man to take me, do you think you're the only one who has any rights over me?"

"I hardly think so, my dear," he returned calmly. "I be-
177

lieve that is your husband's so-called right. Then, of course, there is the king, and God knows who else. No, I certainly wouldn't presume to keep you exclusively for my own use, my dear, but I don't see why you would have any objections to my sharing you with everyone else." The arrogance on his face made her choke.

"Leave me alone! Get out of my sight before I kill you!" she lashed at him. "Your presumptions are too disgusting to even argue with. I'll have my husband call you out and kill you!"

"Your husband must not take his conjugal rights too seriously, Crimson, or else he might have raised some objections to the king's intentions tonight."

"My husband—" She stopped abruptly and glared at him. "Oh, go away!" she finally ended desperately, feeling an absurd need to cry suddenly.

To her own horror, tears were already sliding from the corners of her eyes and she was in the greatest danger of beginning to sob openly. She did not want this odious man to see her at her weakest moment. She could imagine how he might laugh or offer some sarcastic remark to humiliate her further.

To her surprise, though, he did nothing of the kind. He only led her slowly and gently away, his arm around her drooping shoulders, taking her down the corridor to the crisp chill of the outside air.

"You're overly tired, Crimson," he said close to her ear. "It's nearly four o'clock in the morning, and, no doubt, you've been up since sunrise. I'll take you home, sweetheart."

His voice sounded so soothing in her ears and his arm felt so protective around her that Crimson allowed him to bundle her into his waiting carriage. After getting her address from her, Brentwood gave instructions to the coachman and jumped in beside her, pulling the lap blanket over both of them.

The drive to King Street was short, and they were in front of her dwelling before Crimson had quite finished removing the last traces of her tears from her face.

"Come on, Crimson. Let me get you inside before this

cold freezes those tears on your cheeks," Brentwood was saying softly, soothingly.

Crimson hurried inside the house with him, where a sleepy-eyed servant, trying vainly to suppress a yawn, lit the way upstairs to Crimson's bedroom, where her maid, a new, young girl named Diane, was waiting to help her undress for bed.

Crimson felt her head swimming with exhaustion and nerves and sat limply on her bed while Diane took off her costume and helped her don her nightdress, then unpinned her hair and brushed it out. Crimson wanted only to lie down and forget about this whole, horrible night. She hoped that she would not see Nicholas Brentwood again.

Diane slipped out, after tucking the blanket up around Crimson's chin and snuffing out the remaining candles, casting the room in darkness except for the faint light that came from the edges of the curtained windows. Crimson snuggled deeply into the sheets, stretching tiredly and feeling her own body heat warm the bedclothes.

Without any warning, a darker shadow appeared next to the bed and Crimson half-sat up to utter a scream of fright. A strong hand closed over her open mouth and pressed her backwards into the pillows. A warm, lean body slid beneath the covers and she felt a man's nakedness next to her with a start of alarm.

When he released her mouth, she took a deep breath and demanded, "Who are you?" But before he answered, she knew—she knew who it was by the small mocking laugh. How stupid of her! He had come into her house with her, the beast! And without even a word of warning, come into her bed, expecting—

"Get out of here before I scream," she whispered furiously.

"Don't scream, Crimson," he murmured, pushing his hand lazily into the wealth of her silky hair. "It wouldn't do to have the servants gossiping about you, would it? Besides, you shouldn't object to me being here. After all, I've had you before. I'm not a stranger. Just relax and let me make love to you. I want to, and, if you'd think like a woman instead of a spoiled child, you might find that

179

you'd like me to." He kissed her silk-clothed shoulder as his hand continued playing with her hair.

"W-what do you mean?" she asked him, quieter now, as she suppressed a shiver.

"Darling, I find you very attractive. I could even grow to like you if you behaved more like an adult. Despite your faults, though, you excite the hell out of me and I find myself itching to possess you again." He kissed her with slight, soft kisses on the cheek and jaw, and downwards on her neck.

Crimson lay back breathlessly and let him kiss her, aware of the tingles that were running up her spine in rapid succession. She shivered again and closed her eyes as he took her lips with his. His kiss was artful, full of the kind of mastery that a woman had no power against. She succumbed to him with a certain relief that she need not fight him anymore. She was too tired, and the sheets were too warm, and he was too experienced and too determined.

His hands were sure on the ties of her nightgown, pulling it off her shoulders and down to her waist to expose her bosom to the mastery of his hands and mouth. Crimson arched her back instinctively, offering herself up to him as his hands alternately teased and appeased her. Her own hands came up reflexively and her fingers tied themselves in his hair, pulling him down to her.

"I shouldn't—" she murmured, her one last resistance to him, as he pulled the gown from her hips and thighs, leaving her completely open to him.

"Hush," he whispered back, sealing her protests with his mouth. His hands continued their efforts, playing her as though she were some kind of instrument that he was tuning for some grand finale.

With a sigh of release, Crimson gave herself up to him. After a time, she forgot that she hated him, that she blamed him for that horrible scene in her life at the abortionist's cottage, that he had so casually slipped back into her life and resumed almost literally where they had left off in France.

He was kissing her all over her body, leaving a trail of
180

moist imprints that raised goosebumps on her flesh. Crimson's breath came faster now as she moved her body as though to escape his caresses, only to seek them a moment later with feverish curiosity.

Brentwood found himself pleasantly surprised at the perfection of her body—the small, tightly rounded breasts, the willowy waist that curved into still-girlish hips. He had hardly had time to really look at her before in the darkness of the gardens, but here, in the semi-light of her room, he took his time with her, moving his hands over her flesh with a sureness that would keep her form in his memory.

He smiled to himself, wondering if she would hate him again in the morning, or whether she might consider becoming his mistress. He had never really had a mistress— a woman exclusively for his own pleasure—because he had not wanted such ties between himself and anyone else, especially since his business for the king kept him away from England for long periods of time. He would not expect any woman to stay faithful to him for months at a time. He had had women, of course. Many of them. He enjoyed women and they, it seemed, found him reasonably attractive enough to allow him to enjoy them.

As he continued his stroking of the marvelous little body next to him, he wondered just how deeply involved with Charles she actually was. Had Nick interrupted one of several meetings between them, or had they not become lovers yet? Brentwood liked Charles too much to let a woman come between their friendship, but this particular woman had suddenly become rather special to him.

He had desired her in France and had bided his time, not wanting to frighten her off, for he had already perceived her to be an innocent. He grinned to himself. Why was it that men always knew a virgin when they saw one, and immediately took off after her with the tenacity of a bloodhound? Perhaps because, these days, virgins were rare indeed, especially with the sexual license that had been decreed by the king's own actions.

Had it been sheer coincidence that had brought him to the king's apartments on the very night that Charles had

had in mind to seduce her? He remembered telling her in France that the king would have her sooner or later; he hardly let any beautiful woman escape him for long.

He looked down at the writhing figure that he was so carefully molding, and his mind no longer could concentrate on anything but her own pleasure and his. His hands, which had been caressing her absently, with the habit of long practice, began preparing her in earnest for the act of love. He moved over her, his knee insinuating itself between her legs.

His fingers moved to that spot that now lay open to him and he doubled his artistry until he could hear the sweet sounds of her moans, begging him to go on. His hands moved to her hips, his fingers curving around her sides to bring her up to meet his downward thrust. He heard her gasp, a small choked-off cry, and realized that she was as tight as a virgin. Had no one had her since he initiated her into the art of love? He frowned and realized that he had no idea who her husband was. He could not even recall her last name now. Perhaps the husband was no more than a figurehead, in order to give some sense of propriety to the king's advances.

As he began moving within her, Brentwood's mind gave up such thoughts and concentrated instead on the mindless pleasure of the act of love. He could feel her arms clutching him, her hands digging into his shoulders, whether from pain now or passion he wasn't sure. Her mouth was open, the lips soft and full as he kissed her deeply. He moved his hands from her hips to cup her buttocks as he lay down against her, feeling the tense points of her breasts nipping his chest.

My God! She was so hot, so moist. He felt that part of her snug around him as he continued to thrust deeply. He could feel the excitement settling over him, causing the waves of passion to roll over him. The sensation settled in his groin, and he groaned against her mouth as he doubled his rhythm in order to effect his release.

As he reached the climax, he heard the tiny scream that was torn from her throat and quickly covered her mouth with his. He kissed her passionately, his hands still digging

182

into the flesh of her buttocks. When it was over, he settled his weight on his arms. She really seemed too fragile at this moment for him to collapse on top of her.

"Crimson, you delight me beyond hope," he whispered softly, nuzzling her ear.

She was silent, breathing deeply, her hands stilled, one curled around his neck, the other limp at her side. He bent and kissed her breasts, then rolled from above her to lie next to her.

After a moment, he reached out to pull her next to him, his arm clasping her firmly beneath the breasts. She curved her buttocks into him as naturally as though they had slept together always, and he moved his face into her hair in order to smell its sweetness. As she still did not speak, Brentwood shrugged to himself and pressed her closer. Women who weren't forever talking did have their advantages, he reminded himself. At least this one wasn't demanding if she had been as good as his other women or if he was satisfied with her technique. He smiled against her hair. Damn! Yes, she would make the perfect mistress, he thought before falling asleep.

20

Crimson awoke slowly, moving her head until she felt a small tug at her hair, preventing her from moving further. An arm, thrown carelessly around her, tightened as a strong-fingered, tanned hand groped upward to find her breast. She felt something hard and alien probing the flesh of her buttocks and moved away from it, only to be followed.

"Let me go, Nicholas Brentwood!" she gasped. It had taken her less than a moment to remember last night's events and presume who it was that was sharing her bed with her.

"I can't let you go, Crimson," he murmured back, his mouth searching for the nape of her neck as he nuzzled through her hair.

"My husband will probably be home any minute and—and you'll be sorry if he finds you here!" she said angrily, reaching behind her to pull her hair from beneath him so that she could turn to face that insolent smile.

"Ah, yes, the missing husband. Tell me, Crimson, just who this obliging man is that you're married to now?" His dark-blue eyes made mock of her and she felt irritation welling up inside of her.

"My husband is Sir Reginald Gardner. He is quite close to the king."

"I would say so, my lady, if the two of them share you with such ease. I suppose the reason why your husband isn't here in bed with you right now is because he thought you would be entertaining the king all night. Am I right?" His sardonic inference was plain.

With quick anger, she slapped his hand from her breast and moved away from him in the bed in order to sit up. "Get out of my bed immediately! What my husband does is certainly not your concern! I—I won't tell him about—about last night—"

Brentwood laughed, then quieted as he stared up at her with eyes narrowed in passion. Crimson was unaware of the lovely sight she afforded him in the morning light, exposed to the waist, her breasts high and rounded, around which her auburn hair curled invitingly as it cascaded over her shoulders. Her aquamarine eyes gazed back at him for a long moment before she looked away.

"Crimson, look at me," Brentwood demanded. "We made love together last night. Can't you admit that you enjoyed it?"

184

She flushed and kept her eyes averted. "I—I shouldn't have let you," she answered in a low voice. "If my husband found out—"

"Your husband! Christ! If my memory serves me right, Sir Reginald isn't exactly an angel himself. If I were you, my dear, I'd keep him out of my bed, if only to avoid getting the clap!"

"How dare you speak to me like that! Say instead that I would probably risk much more going to bed with you! No doubt you've known enough women to give me more than one disease!" She glanced at him angrily. "I'm telling you now, you'd better leave!"

"Crimson, don't lie to me. Sir Reginald is greedy, and enjoys women too well to leave you alone in your bed last night. No, if he were coming, he would have interrupted us well before now. My guess is, he's having himself a good time with some willing lady, and thinks himself lucky to have a wife who will oblige the king in order to get her husband extra favors."

"What are you implying?" she breathed, her eyes bright with fury.

"He's using you like a whore, Crimson. Call him a dandified pimp if you like. Hell, the Duke of Buckingham even stoops to provide the king with women. Why not your husband? I hardly think his morals are a paragon of virtue. Whose are? I'm not blaming you. Lord, if you feel like going to bed with the king of England, that's up to you! But don't give me this nonsense about your husband finding us in bed together and demanding satisfaction. I don't like women who play games with their lovers, Crimson."

"Their *lovers!* So, you think we are lovers already?" she asked incredulously. "One night, and I suppose you own me!"

"Hardly, my dear," he answered her, lying back against the pillows in order to watch her at his leisure. "But as long as you've brought it up, I was going to offer you a more permanent position than an occasional romp in bed. I want you for my mistress, Crimson."

Crimson could hardly believe her ears. How could he

be so casual about it? As though he were asking her out for a drive in the park. She took a deep breath.

"I will not be mistress to you, Nicholas Brentwood, nor will I allow you 'an occasional romp in bed.' Last night, I don't know why I—"

"Don't tell me you were so hot for the king that your disappointment in missing his arms forced you into mine. That *would* sound whorish, Crimson," he observed drily, folding his hands behind his head as he continued to watch her. "Can't you admit you like me a little bit?"

"I hate you! You—you took advantage of me last night. I was tired, and you sounded so obliging, ready to take me home and see me safely retired for the night, when all the time you were plotting to seduce me again."

"Come now, you make me sound like the darkest of villains, Crimson." He laughed indolently.

"I daresay you've got enough black marks against you to qualify you for that title," she snapped back.

Before she could say any more, he reached for her and drew her down on top of him, holding her struggling form against him as he planted kisses on her face, laughing when she tried to bite him. As she continued struggling, he pulled the covers from between them and she could feel his nakedness against hers. Her struggles only heightened the sense of intimacy, and his arms pressed her ever more tightly to him so that she could not escape the fact that he was becoming aroused once more.

"Crimson, Crimson," he murmured in her ear. "It's early yet, and we have a good part of the morning before you must return to court. Why not spend it together enjoying each other? I'm bound to have you again before I leave, so you might as well give in now."

"Nicholas Brentwood, I—"

"Call me Nick," he prompted lazily, biting her ear gently.

"I have never met a more conceited, arrogant, overbearing—"

"Tender words of love," he sighed, still at her ear. "My God, Crimson, you've excited me beyond belief. Let's get
186

on with it, my dear, before I have an embarrassing accident."

"You're laughing at me!" she accused, but was annoyed to find herself becoming a bit excited. His laughter was almost infectious. "Oh, go away!"

Still grinning, he turned her onto her back and rolled on top of her. His body moved on hers with an expertise that took her breath away and she let herself flow with his touch despite the fact that she assured herself that she loathed him.

His hands were once more skillfully bringing her desire to the surface, and she sought his caresses even as her own hands moved over the sinewy muscles of his arms. Her thighs quivered as he separated them in order to position her for his entrance, but she did not wince when he lowered himself to her.

"God, you feel good," he muttered as he moved within her.

Crimson was silent, her eyes closed, pulling his head down to her so that she could feel his lips on hers again. She had never known that it could feel so marvelous to have a man's lips on hers, that they could be so soft and yet so hard, so warm and full, and yet so demanding. His kiss thrilled her more than she could have believed, and she wondered if it would be like this with any man. Would she feel like this if the king took her to his bed?

But she could not think of the king now, not with this man with her, doing such exciting things to her emotions. She abandoned herself to her feelings and kissed him with a passion that she was not aware of.

When they had once more reached that pinnacle of shared feeling which they had experienced earlier, Crimson lay back, exhausted, feeling the strength draining slowly out of her limbs.

Brentwood propped himself up on his elbows and looked down into her sated face. He kissed her softly on the mouth, then continued his perusal until she opened her eyes, feeling annoyed that he was staring at her so.

"Well?" she demanded, feeling slightly foolish after her expressions of avowed hatred.

He grinned devilishly. "You really are delicious, my lady," he said. "I must have you as my mistress."

Stung, she glared at him. "I will not be your mistress!" she said. "I am a married woman and I—"

"Don't tell me you're already promised to the king. I know that," he went on ruthlessly. "As for being a married woman, I fail to see what that signifies anyway, considering that we've already been to bed together."

"I'm not promised to the king. I wish you would stop saying that!" she returned hotly. "And much as you like to ignore the fact, I *am* married and—"

"*I* like to ignore the fact," he interrupted with a slight disdain. "I would say rather, madam, that you are doing very well in that area yourself."

"If you must know, my marriage was arranged by my —by Lord James Haviland without my knowledge or consent. He sold me to Sir Reginald in order to pay off his gambling debt to him!" Crimson retorted.

"I would hardly call your situation unusual," Brentwood said with deceptive silkiness. "I don't know a lady whose marriage hasn't been arranged for her, usually from birth, by her parents. Did you, perhaps, have the misguided notion that you should wait until you find a man who suits you perfectly, a man whom you can fall headlong into love with? Sweetheart, it just doesn't happen. That's why men have mistresses and women have their lovers. Love is just too damn fickle to survive very long between the same two people."

"You make it sound so childish," Crimson returned petulantly.

"Love *is* for children, Crimson. Adults settle for passion and sex." He shrugged expansively. "Be my mistress, Crimson, and when the time comes that you've grown tired of me, or I of you, we'll part on good terms. I'm gone a good deal of the time anyway on the king's business. I'd just like someone like you there, waiting for me, when I return. Of course, what we both do when I'm gone is our own business."

"You make it sound like some hateful business deal," she complained, surprised that she was actually thinking of accepting the proposal. She had to admit that this man intrigued her. He was exciting, passionate and willing to keep the affair quite casual. Had she grown into such a sophisticate that she could handle it?

"I don't know," she finally said in a small voice. "My husband—I'm not sure what he would do if he should find out. He doesn't—that is, we don't—"

"You don't sleep together?" Brentwood finished for her. "But he has a mistress, I presume. Be honest with me, Crimson. Would you like to be my mistress?" The dark blue eyes were serious for once, gazing into her face with a fierceness that made her look away.

"You're the only man I've known," she finally managed.

He smiled. "I'm flattered, truly. I can offer you much more than what we've had today," he went on, "although I must say, what we had today is all I really need from you. But you would have an escort, a protector, someone who would furnish you with any material needs you might have. A husband can sometimes prove quite cheap when it comes to buying gifts for his wife. Life at court is not easy, Crimson, as I'm sure you may have already come to know. There are always those people who will use you, hurt you. Men ready to seduce you and then throw you away the next day. Women who say they're your friends only to betray you to your worst enemy. Tell me, Crimson, have you made any enemies at court yet?"

"Yes, one," she answered him, remembering the look on Castlemaine's face when she had left the cottage of the abortionist. "Lady Castlemaine."

"God's blood, Crimson. You do do things royally, don't you? If she is your enemy, you can bet there are others who may hate her guts but will do anything to gain her favor, which means you've got more than one enemy. You need someone to look after you, my dear."

"And how can you do that when you say that you are gone so much on the King's business?" she asked him.

He shrugged. "I do have my own friends," he returned casually.

"Among them the king, himself, who, if you are correct, would like very much to get me into his own bed," she said with a touch of spirit.

"As I said, what we do when we are apart is not the other's concern," he reminded her.

"Oh, I don't know what to do. You talk as though you're my one chance for survival at Court, that without you I will be eaten by the wolves."

"And so you will, my lady, so you will." He straightened up and jumped out of the bed in order to stretch, and then walked to the window to look out. "I'll give you some time, Crimson. I don't want to press you too much right now. But—" and he turned to look at her, "I'll expect an answer from you before the end of the week. I won't wait forever, Crimson."

She clutched the blanket belatedly over her breasts as she sat up to answer him. "Why—why do you want me to be your mistress?"

He smiled with an inscrutable expression. "Because I want you, Crimson. Because there is something about you that I like enough to want to protect from any harm, and because we're so damn good in bed together."

21

"Your Majesty, I'm sorry I'm late," Crimson said, curtseying swiftly before the queen of England.

Catherine of Braganza smiled at the young woman whose head was bowed low before her. She noted the richness of the auburn hair, coifed so perfectly, the translucency of the peach-tinted complexion, the perfection of the trim figure beneath the handsome gown, and she sighed expansively, knowing that her husband, the king, would not let this girl slip through his fingers without tasting her himself. Catherine thought fleetingly that Charles was becoming too greedy with his desires, but shrugged the thought aside, knowing there was nothing she could do to curb those desires. They were a part of him that she had come to know very well and to accept with as much grace as she could muster. It was too bad, though, because she liked this girl.

"Please do get up, Crimson," she said, touching the girl on the shoulder. Her English was imperfect; it still had that slightly intriguing accent in it that could please the king when he was in the right mood. "I'm sure you would have been here earlier if it had been possible."

Crimson rose, smiled at the queen, and took her place on a low seat in order to begin reading a book of poems that the queen had especially been eager to learn. The queen settled herself on her chair and took up her embroidery once more, nodding to her other women to resume their seats.

Before Crimson could begin, there was a flurry of movement into the room and, looking up, she saw Lady Castlemaine entering. She was dressed superbly in a gown of rich velvet, the color of spring grass, which made her red hair seem even more vivid in the bleak, wintery glare of the room.

"Good morning, Your Majesty," Barbara offered, bowing slightly. Her haughty gaze swept the room carelessly and lit on Crimson's face. The blue eyes narrowed perceptibly and Crimson could feel their chill like a physical blow.

"Good morning, Lady Castlemaine," the queen returned, her voice holding a world of weariness in it. She had long ago been shown that she must learn to tolerate this heartless bitch, or Charles would surely send her back to Portugal. The earlier years of her marriage to the king had been peppered with frequent quarrels over this same

191

woman, and it had been at Charles' insistence that Catherine had been forced to accept her as her Lady of the Bedchamber. Catherine had hated Barbara at first with a passion that threatened Catherine's health, but through the ensuing years, there had been so many other women in the king's life that she had learned to ignore his mistresses. Barbara, though, was hard to ignore, with her flamboyant airs and overbearing arrogance.

"And how are you this morning, Crimson, my dear?" Castlemaine was asking the other with deceptive smoothness.

"In good health, my lady," Crimson replied guardedly.

"And the king's health is good also, I trust?" Barbara went on maliciously.

A collective indrawn breath spread through the queen's chambers as all eyes were turned towards Crimson in expectation. Crimson, her cheeks flushed, gazed swiftly towards the queen, her eyes pleading.

"Of course, the king's health is good, Lady Castlemaine," the queen interjected, her brown eyes hardening. "Everyone knows that he is hardly ever ill."

"Of a certainty, Your Majesty, but I thought, perhaps, my Lady Gardner might have first-hand knowledge, as she was seen entering the king's bedchamber last night at a very late hour." Castlemaine's face was smug, and Crimson could not believe her bad manners. She must be mad, or drunk.

"Lady Castlemaine! You will please leave here at once!" the queen ordered, thunderstruck at the woman's audacity.

"Your Majesty must forgive me, but I only thought it in her best interests to point out where Lady Gardner's true affection lies."

Gathering her courage, Crimson looked up at the woman squarely. "My lady, your spies must have been very mistaken. Perhaps you do not pay them well enough to insure that their work is thorough. It's true that the king summoned me to his chambers, but only for conversation. I left his apartments in the company of another gentleman and returned home."

192

Castlemaine's face was livid, and her hands curved involuntarily into talons, as though she would have liked to claw at her rival's face. "You had best be wary of your speech to me, Lady Gardner," she spat out, "or you might find your pretty little nose quite out of joint."

"Ladies, please!" the queen interrupted, frowning. "Kindly refrain from airing your opinions of each other in my presence. It is most unbecoming and I'm afraid I shall have to speak to the king of your quarreling."

Barbara Castlemaine looked at the queen with a mixture of pity and disgust. The queen winced and looked away, hoping only that the hateful woman would leave quickly.

"You are dismissed from your duties today, Lady Castlemaine," she said in a dignified voice.

Barbara opened her mouth to say something, then shrugged. She inclined her head towards the queen, gave Crimson a darting look, then retired from the room.

"Your Majesty, please allow me to explain," Crimson began.

"Not now, Crimson, please," the queen replied, waving her hand as though to clear the air of Barbara's perfume. She nodded discreetly to the other women, whose faces wore the avid expressions of eavesdroppers.

Crimson dropped her eyes. She opened the book of poems once more and began to read aloud in her clear, easy French.

Afterwards, when it was time to prepare the queen for dinner, Catherine drew the younger girl aside and patted her shoulder.

"Don't allow Lady Castlemaine to frighten you, Crimson," she said kindly. "The woman has the manners of a fishwife and the morals of something much worse, but you can hardly blame her for her attitude when her world seems to be crumbling around her ears. I listen to court gossip too, you see, and I've heard everyone saying that the king grows very tired of the lady, so tired that he has promised her a duchy just to get rid of her. Of course, it's common knowledge that the king has other women. He has always had other women." She sighed regretfully. "He is a man of lusty appetites. He enjoys women like no other man I have ever seen."

"Your Majesty, this talk must be painful for you. It is not necessary for you to comfort me. Lady Castlemaine hates me." Crimson shrugged, trying to appear confident. "I'm sorry for it, but there is nothing I can do to change her thinking."

"She can cause her enemies a great deal of unhappiness, Crimson," the queen said in a low voice, remembering all those years that she, herself, had suffered.

"Please, Your Majesty, I want you to believe that the king and I are very good friends, but nothing else. He enjoys speaking of his sister with me."

"Ah, yes, his sister," the queen said sadly. "Perhaps she is the only woman who truly has his love."

Crimson was silent, feeling guilty that she had almost commited adultery with this gentle woman's husband. It was ironic, but she supposed she should be grateful to Brentwood for interrupting last night when the king would surely have seen her in his bed.

"Let us go have something now, Crimson," the queen said, resuming her accustomed manner. "Enough of such talk for now."

"Yes, your Majesty."

Crimson followed with the other ladies as the queen went into her antechamber in order to have dinner. Most of the courtiers elected to have dinner in their own quarters, or if especially favored, with either the king or queen. There were very few people eating with the queen, except for her own household, and Crimson felt a renewed pity for the little foreigner who, since she could not provide the king with an heir, was categorically shunned.

After the meal, there was to be a play in the Cockpit Theater in Whitehall Palace, and the queen excused her ladies to dress themselves for the evening. Crimson had been given a cubicle within the queen's apartments where she could dress without having to return home and, as she was going to accompany the queen to the play she went directly there in order to choose a new gown for the evening.

194

The maid, also provided by the queen, helped her undress down to her silk chemise and then scurried out with the chosen gown in order to press it in the kitchens before Crimson could don it.

Shivering from the chill, Crimson rubbed her arms, then stood up to take out a warm dressing robe from the armoire, when suddenly, two hands settled on her shoulders, causing her to stiffen in alarm. A warm mouth placed a kiss on the exposed nape of her neck, then traveled slowly around to her jaw. The hands on her shoulders dipped lower to her breasts, cupping them gently within the bodice of her chemise.

Crimson gasped and struggled out of the embrace, but the hands were firm once more on her, and pulled her backwards into a man's waiting arms, pressing her against rich velvet.

"Please, who—" she began, then stopped as the hands began to untie the laces at her bodice. Despite herself, she began to tingle with growing awareness of the man's desire. Could it be Brentwood? The man's audacity was astounding, but she allowed him to caress her a moment more before she pushed his hands from her breasts. "Nick, don't," she whispered, turning.

Her eyes met the black eyes of the king, which just now held both desire and a question. Crimson returned the look, astounded.

"Your Majesty!"

"Crimson, I came up here to ask your forgiveness for leaving you so abruptly last night. Seeing you in your state of half-nakedness so inflamed me that I would have taken you here on the floor, but—" His eyes sparked with some angry emotion. "You thought I was someone else," he accused warily.

"Sire, I thought—I thought—"

"You called me Nick. Do you mean Nick Brentwood, my beauty? I must confess, I hardly like to be mistaken for another man, but it also piques my curiosity to wonder what might have happened between you two last night."

"Sire, I believe you requested that Lord Dorset take me
195

home last night," Crimson returned stiffly, hoping to buy some time before the maid returned.

The king released her, noting her stiffness. "Of course, I asked him to escort you home," he retorted with a definite air of jealousy, "but I did not give him leave to bed you!"

"Sire, I hardly think it your business to wonder how my nights are spent," Crimson muttered, angry now.

His black eyes seemed even blacker with a kindled anger. "It is very much my business, my lady," he answered swiftly, "as I myself have every intention of spending your nights with you!" He was breathing hard and Crimson was surprised at his temporary lack of control. "I am offering you an esteemed position, Crimson. Don't be coy with me and pretend you don't know what I'm talking about. Surely I am not mistaken when I remember that you came to me last night with the intention of letting me make love to you. You did come to my bedchambers, did you not?"

"Sire, please let me explain," Crimson began, feeling embarrassed now. It was her own fault. She should never have gone to the king, should never have led him to believe that she was willing to succumb to him.

"Don't explain, Crimson. I am your sovereign and I expect you to obey me in all things.!"

"In all things, sire!" Crimson returned, her anger rekindling. "You would *order* me into your bed, sire?" she demanded with evident sarcasm.

The king reached out for her, his hands tight on her arms, bringing her up against his body. He would have kissed her if a deliberate cough had not been made by the maid returning with Crimson's gown. Slowly, reluctantly, he released her and they stood, staring at one another for a long moment.

Finally, the king regained command of himself. "Forgive me, Lady Gardner. You will do me the honor of accompanying me to the theater tonight."

"Forgive me, sire, but I am already bound to accompany the queen," Crimson retorted, still angry.

196

"You will accompany me, my lady, or you will not go at all," he said, his voice level, but his eyes commanding.

For a moment, Crimson hesitated, wondering just how far he would allow her to push him. Then, suddenly, she relented. It would do her no good to make an enemy of the king. With Lady Castlemaine already her enemy, she would need the king for protection.

"Of course, sire, if you wish," she murmured.

He smiled tightly at her. "I shall return for you in half an hour, my lady."

After he had gone and the maid had helped her lace the bodice of her gown, Crimson felt very much like crying. What a mess she was in now! The king desired her and expected her to share his bed. Brentwood had already come to her bed and had asked her to be his mistress. And then there was her husband who hated her—who would hate her even more if she did not accept the king's advances.

She stared at herself in the mirror of her room, noting absently the excellent fit of the russet velvet gown, the pristine whiteness of the lace at her bodice, which provided such an exquisite setting for her rounded breasts. How had she come to be in this mess? Of course, she had been stupid to let Brentwood back into her life. He had admitted he would be gone a lot, would expect only one thing from her during his stay at court. She must refuse his offer of protection. She must never see him again, not alone at least. She had to admit there was something about him. . . .

She shook her head. What to do about the king? She could not just send him a polite note, telling him that she was honored at his proposal, but she must refuse! The king was not used to being refused by a woman. She had heard about Frances Stuart, who had refused him and married another man, and had been banished from court. Although the king was generally an easygoing man, he must not be made a fool of in public. He would avenge such an insult and, unfortunately, Crimson did not have a husband who would stand by her, as Frances did. No, Sir Reginald Gardner had only married her so that she could help further his situation by using her influence on the

197

king. Once that influence was gone, she would be thrown to the wolves. There would be no one to protect her.

Crimson bit her lip. Not even the queen would dare to offer her protection should the king banish her from court. How Castlemaine would enjoy her humiliation! Ironically, it was the thought of Barbara's satisfied smile that caused Crimson's spine to stiffen.

Let the king bed her! At least it was no worse than being the mistress of Nicholas Brentwood. Certainly, after a time, the king would grow tired of her and give her some barony, or a title which would satisfy her husband immensely. God, how bleak it made the future seem, she thought wearily.

22

Crimson could not remember what the play had been about. She could hardly recall what she had eaten or drunk afterwards or whom she had talked to. All that she remembered was the king's eyes looking deeply into hers, the king's hands slipping inside her bodice to fondle her as he pulled her into a secluded alcove, the king's thigh, tight against hers at the table. He wanted her, it must be obvious to everyone else at court.

At midnight, after he had sat for an hour watching his friends play at cards, the king had taken Crimson's hand and led her out of the room. Crimson thought she could feel every pair of eyes boring holes into her back. Especially a certain pair of blue ones belonging to Lady Castlemaine, who had fairly seethed with hatred so that she had lost terribly at whist and had cursed out everyone at her table.

"Sire, should you be leaving so early?" Crimson muttered, not even making it a question.

"I am impatient, Crimson," he murmured back, his hand around her waist, drawing her down the corridor swiftly. "You eluded me last night, but you will not escape me this time. I will have no interruptions, even if it were the king of France, himself!"

It seemed to Crimson that they were in the king's bedroom so quickly that she had barely caught her breath. The king ordered Chiffinch out of the room and told him that no one was to be allowed entrance until morning.

Then he turned to Crimson and reached out for her, drawing her into his arms, turning her face upwards to receive his kiss. To her surprise, he did not kiss her with impatience, but took his time, molding her lips to his, working her mouth with infinite care so that both could receive full enjoyment from the kiss. She responded slowly, feeling a kind of tension begin to leave her as he continued to hold her, still kissing her slowly and deliberately.

When he finally released her, Crimson was breathless, leaning involuntarily against him as though to recover herself. She felt the rich black of his jacket against her cheek and rubbed it absently, feeling the king's hands in her hair, loosening it from its pins so that it fell down in deep waves nearly to her waist.

"Let me look at you, Crimson," the king breathed into her hair, his hands tense at her bodice.

For a long moment, Crimson hesitated. The king wanted to undress her, and once she was naked before him, there was no turning back. Briefly, the queen's unhappy face moved into her mind's vision. How long would it take for gossip to reach her that Crimson had become the king's mistress?

"Sire, please let us part now and remain only good friends," she whispered, after taking a deep breath.

"Crimson, why do you continue to hold me off? You

199

know how I feel about you. It is not a shameful thing to be the mistress of the king. Most women would deem it the highest honor."

"But it brings so many other things with it," Crimson sighed, pressing her forehead against his shoulder. "I don't know if I'm strong enough to be your mistress, sire, the woman who might hold your attention for a few weeks or months, but can never be sure where your heart lies or how long it will be before her place is usurped by some other pretty wench."

"Crimson, you wound me greatly with your doubts. I like you very much. I know that you will please me in bed and I would hope I would be able to give you pleasure also. We are both married and this is all there can be between us."

"You remind me of my husband, whom I have promised my fidelity in the marriage ceremony and your wife, sire, who is my dearest friend." Crimson lifted her face from his shoulder to look directly at the king. "You ask me to betray the confidence of a friend."

The king clenched his teeth and groaned. "Crimson, why do you make it so difficult for me? I want you. I want you so much that my hands are trembling, waiting to unveil the perfection of your breasts. Why do you torment me with your loveliness, and now that we are alone and can consummate our attraction for each other, do you defy me?"

"Sire, I don't wish to make you unhappy."

"Then make me happy, Crimson. Let me make love to you."

"I don't know, sire. I—"

"There's someone else. Don't tell me that it is your husband who makes you so reticent. I am well aware of your relationship, and I know all about Lady Brownwood. Why do you think I have given her husband another war campaign? As long as he is away, Lady Anne Brownwood will be free to amuse your husband, and thereby release you from any conjugal duties he might decide to demand."

"Sire!" Crimson was shocked at so bald a truth coming from the king. That he would admit keeping a man in the
200

field so as to allow the man's wife to be unfaithful to him was barely beyond her comprehension.

"Don't hate me for it, Crimson," the king went on. "Just tell me why you deny me."

"There is no one else, sire," she said in a small voice.

"Yes, there is. You called me Nick earlier. How well do you know my friend, Brentwood?" The king's voice had taken on an edge of steel.

"I knew him slightly in France, sire. I was completely surprised to see him here in England. I had no idea that he was an agent to you, that his mission in France was to report, among other things, the state of Madame's happiness."

"You haven't answered my question, Crimson," the king accused.

"We met in France at Saint-Cloud, but his interests were with Madame. He had no time to flirt with me, sire."

"Not true, Crimson. Any man would find the time to flirt with you, and I am well aware what attraction Brentwood seems to hold for the fairer sex. He is a man used to getting whatever woman he sets eyes on. You are not telling me the truth, Crimson."

Crimson tore herself out of the king's arms and buried her face in her hands. "What do you want me to tell you?" she cried out. "That Brentwood was the first man to lie with me? Yes, yes! He seduced me in the gardens of Saint-Cloud. I swore that I would hate him forever, but last night—last night—" She turned tear-filled eyes to the king's face. "Last night you had him to take me home and —and he—"

"He seduced you again?" the king asked sarcastically. "Crimson, why did you let him take you when you knew that I—"

"Sire, don't talk as though I were some piece of goods bandied about between friends! Brentwood has asked me to be his mistress!"

"And so have I! So what will you do, my lady? Which man will you have? The king of England who can give you wealth, position, a title—or a man who works secretly as my agent, who travels far and lives dangerously much of

201

the time he is away, who can offer you only a pittance compared to me?"

"You push me, sire. Why are you doing this? What would you have me do? At least Brentwood is not married, and my marriage to Sir Reginald is a laughable shame, as you have pointed out. Wouldn't it be more honorable, if such a thing is possible, for me to accept Brentwood's proposal?"

The king, normally the most easygoing of men, flushed a dark red and his black brows drew downward to match the thin curve of his lips. "If it is more honorable for you to be the mistress of Brentwood than to enjoy the glory that would come to you from being my lover, then do as you wish, my lady. Go to Brentwood, and I shall await the day that he casts you out for some other lady! You will not find me joyfully asking you to return to my arms!"

Crimson glanced up at his angry face and feared that he might have an attack of apoplexy. She started to speak, but the king held up his hand to keep her silent.

"Please go, my lady. I would not have you risk your reputation any more than you might already have. Let us hope that your conscience is clear now and that you will be able to give Brentwood his answer quickly. Good night!"

"Good night, sire, and I hope that you—"

"Good night, madam. You may leave me immediately!"

Meekly, Crimson curtseyed and hurried out of the room. She heard the king roar to Chiffinch to fetch the Duke of Buckingham quickly, and wondered if he was going to ask Buckingham to bring him one of his whores for the night. She felt the ready tears in her eyes, slipping softly down her cheeks. What had she done?

In the corridor, she ran past curious couples who nodded slyly to each other and tried to speak to her. Once she bumped into someone, and, without apologizing, went on, deaf to his questions.

"Crimson, wait!" A man's voice pierced her muddled thoughts and she felt a hand catch her arm to bring her around to him. "Crimson, what on earth is wrong? You look like a scared rabbit fleeing from the pack!"

202

Crimson looked up to see Brentwood staring down at her, a question in his blue eyes. Somehow she felt relieved to have him here with her, but the tears would not stop flowing and she sobbed all the harder when he pressed her against him.

"Come with me, Crimson," he ordered softly, drawing her down the hall.

She followed him without question, leaning against him, oblivious to anyone else. Dimly, she heard someone questioning Brentwood, heard him answer briefly. Then a lady's laughing titter floated across a room.

"Nicholas Brentwood! I swear I didn't know you were back in London!"

The voice was familiar, and Crimson looked up warily to see malicious blue eyes on her. Barbara Palmer, she groaned inwardly. Oh, God, she wasn't sure she could stand another confrontation with her.

"Lady Castlemaine, I didn't know you were so concerned about my whereabouts or I would have come to you directly from Portsmouth. You are looking lovely as always," Brentwood returned smoothly, releasing Crimson in order to bow before the countess.

"And I see you have already claimed one of the stars of our court, Nicholas," Barbara cooed. "Lady Gardner, it seems, is very much sought after these days. I'm sure most men at court have been trying to catch her for a private moment, isn't that so, my lady?"

"Hardly, Lady Castlemaine," Crimson answered. "But if you will excuse me, I have a raging headache and Lord Dorset has kindly consented to take me home."

"Oh!" the other woman tittered. "He is taking you home, and I daresay you will not be left alone tonight, eh, my dear? Yes, Nicholas is certainly a good choice for you. He's a strong lover and infinitely satisfying." She smiled disarmingly up at the man. "I have some fond memories of our time together, darling," she ended, licking her lips with a lewd air.

"Barbara, our time together was relatively brief and happened some time ago," Brentwood said insolently. "If you will excuse us?"

He hurried Crimson out of the room and through the last corridor, which led to the carriage yard. Once in the carriage, Crimson leaned back with a sigh, closing her eyes, strongly aware of Brentwood's hands on her as his arms encircled and pressed her close to him. She wondered if he would appreciate what she had done tonight for him. She had refused the advances of the king of England in order to be the mistress of a man who lived much of the time in danger, for she knew she was going to be his mistress. There was no one else to turn to now.

"Are you feeling better now?" His voice seemed distant, reflective.

She nodded. "Yes. I'm so glad you found me. I—I have had a terrible argument with the king."

"Really?" The insolence in his voice again, just when she wanted him to be kind and supportive. Why was he being this way now? "And what did you argue about, and when did you argue? Before or after he'd had you in his bed?"

"What do you mean?" she roused herself enough to straighten and look at him.

"It is all over Whitehall by now, I'm sure," he returned disdainfully. "The king took you to bed tonight."

"The king wanted to take me to bed, but I couldn't."

He wasn't listening. "I suppose this means that you have decided against my offer." He shrugged. "I'm sorry for you, Crimson. You'll only get hurt this way."

"Listen to me!" she cried out. "I am not the king's mistress! We argued because he found out about you and me!"

"You and me?" he repeated scornfully. "You mean that I had first taste before him. I suppose that wouldn't set too well, but he couldn't have expected you to be a virgin, surely."

"Don't be cruel, not now," she pleaded, swallowing her pride. "I told the king the truth about what happened between us in France and—and last night." She took a deep breath. "I told him that I couldn't be his mistress."

"Not mistress to the king of England! God's blood, Crimson, did you have an attack of conscience? I suppose you've decided to become the good little wife and remain faithful to your husband, despite the fact that he carries on with any game piece he can lay hands on!"

"Why do you have to twist things so?" she exclaimed angrily. "If you weren't so mean, you would listen to what I have to say. I'll be your mistress!" It didn't really come out quite the way she had anticipated. Her anger made her fling the words out as a challenge. They were staring at each other, breathing hard, more like combatants than lovers now.

Finally, he smiled, but the smile did not warm her heart. "So, you consent to be my mistress, to risk everything for my sake! Hmmm. I suppose I should consider myself the luckiest of men, indeed, I should be grateful, honored by your acceptance!"

"Stop it!"

He caught her hands in his and drew her roughly against him. "All right then, if you're going to be my mistress, you must learn to do as I say. Lift your skirts, wench, for I've a mind to have you right here and now!"

"What are you saying? Stop this at once. I'll not be used like a whore!" she answered back, fighting him.

He pushed her into the opposite seat and scooped up her skirts in his hands in order to throw them back over her face. Crimson felt the chill of the air hit her body, covered only by the thin chemise, and shivered. She attempted to right herself, but already Brentwood had moved over her, ripping at the chemise in order to expose her to his sudden lust. His hands readied her for his entrance and in another moment he was upon her.

"Get off me!" Crimson choked, outraged at this abuse. She tried to push him off, but he was firmly lodged now and in no mood to be denied.

"Quiet, my sweet! You are my mistress now and I want you. It's that simple. Lie back and try to give me some pleasure, will you?"

"Ooh—oh, you! You—"

She was sputtering futilely, feeling him arousing her treacherous body despite her anger. After a few moments, she was quiet, closing her eyes, willing herself not to enjoy

<205>205</205>

the act, nor to help him achieve his own pleasure. Despite her nonparticipation, he was able to gain the sensation he wished and soon lay atop her, breathing hard, satisfied.

"Now, will you get off me?" she inquired icily.

He kissed her mouth. "It would have been better if you would have been more cooperative, my love," he murmured, his good spirits returning as though by some magic.

Seeing him this way only irritated Crimson more. The selfish pig! She must be completely loony to be his mistress. His mistress! Another thought suddenly entered her mind.

"I didn't know that you had known Lady Castlemaine before. I mean—she made it sound as though you had been rather—intimate—at one time." She tried to read the expression on his face in the poor light.

"I'm sure you must know by now, sweeting, that at one time or another, Lady Castlemaine has known most of the men at court—intimately." He was not in the least sorry. "She invited me to her bed two or three times, I think. How could I refuse the most notorious woman at court?"

"But you knew her reputation?" Crimson accused sulkily.

"Her reputation is just what draws the men to her, my dear," he replied laughingly. "She is one of the most erotic women I have ever been with. She's not afraid to try anything and has done most everything I could ever teach a woman, and some things that even I couldn't believe."

"Well there's no need to sound so smug about it!" she cut in. "I suppose you think you're going to be able to teach *me* those things?"

"Of course!" he returned, licking her cheek wickedly. "By the time I'm ready to leave on my next mission for the king, you will be able to outdo Castlemaine, herself! I expect you to be an apt pupil, wench."

"You are really intolerable!" she said, put out. "Why I ever consented to turn myself over to you—"

"Admit it, you like me a little bit," he laughed.

Before she could say anything, he was kissing her again. She sputtered for a moment, fighting him again, but he
206

was not about to release her and she finally gave in, succumbing to the strength and mastery of his kiss. His mouth was so warm, so experienced, she didn't have the strength to resist it.

When he released her, they both realized that the carriage had stopped in front of her house. Brentwood sprang out and helped her to the door and together they made their way upstairs. Once in her bedroom, Crimson turned to him.

"Are there any rules we should abide by?" she asked, hoping to sound casual. She was terribly afraid suddenly that she might find herself falling in love with this arrogant man and she wanted to make sure she understood the regulations they would put on their affair before it started.

He shrugged, peeling off his jacket to throw it carelessly on a nearby chair. "I suppose it is up to me to inform you, isn't it? I mean, considering that this is your first time and I've been through it so many times before." His charming smile told her he was teasing her. "All right then. As my *mistress*," he said the word lasciviously, his eyes raking her from head to toe, "you will promise to make yourself available whenever I am in London. I suppose we can use your house, since you and your husband have an—understanding. I will make sure that all your living expenses are paid. It's that simple."

"It sounds simple," Crimson agreed, feeling somehow that she should be embarrassed holding this conversation with a man, but surprised that she was not. "When you are here, you will stay with me and when you are away—"

"You are free to pick from the many stallions available at court," he finished for her. "Of course, you will grant me the same license."

"Of course," she said slowly, biting her lip. "God, this all sounds so—so sordid. Is it always this way?"

He shrugged. "It's better to get the preliminaries over with, my dear. Then we both know where we stand. Agreed?"

Crimson nodded, but another thought had suddenly come into her head. She looked at the man opposite her, this man who had been virtually a stranger to her before last night and yet had fathered the first seed of life within her.

"If there are no more questions then—" He gestured to the bed.

"Wait." She took a deep breath. "What if—what if there are children?"

She was afraid to look at him, but kept her eyes on the floor, feeling a great lump in her throat.

"Children?" She could hear the frown in his voice. "Most women seem to take care of these things without too much bother," he said. Crimson's heart dropped inside of her. "But then again, if you want a little bastard running about, I don't mind," he continued, at which Crimson was able to breathe normally again.

Somehow it made a difference to her that he would accept children. She thought once more about the life that had drained away from her and felt herself on the verge of tears.

"What's the matter, sweetheart?" he asked, noting her distress. He came closer to her and settled his hands on her shoulders.

Crimson shook her head. "Nothing, nothing," she answered in a muffled voice, and began to undress.

23

"Thank God we've seen the last of the snow," Lady Chesterfield sighed expansively. "I am heartily sick of cold weather."

"But 'tis only the first of April, Elizabeth," Crimson answered from the depths of her closet, where she was trying to choose a suitable outfit for their morning excursion. "Surely, there will be more cold weather?"

"Oh, no, not like we've had, I'm sure," Elizabeth put in firmly. "We'll have lots of rain, though, which does have a way of bringing those nasty coughs with it. Still, rain is better than freezing cold any day."

"Does it ever get truly warm here in London?" Crimson asked longingly, remembering her last summer in France.

"Of course, silly. Don't you remember hearing about that horrible summer of the plague? Believe me, it can get very hot in midsummer here. God spare us another year of sickness!"

"Amen!" Crimson agreed fervently.

She had been Brentwood's mistress for a month now, and she realized that she was in the greatest danger of falling in love with the scoundrel. It was not only that he was an ingenious and tantalizing lover, but he could be so amusing and charming when he wished. And he was, indeed, one of the handsomest and most virile men at court. Of course, there were times when his mood would darken and he would treat her little better than a street prostitute. Crimson hated him when he was like this, and they had raging quarrels. After one of the worst of these, Brentwood had left without a word and had stayed away for nearly a week. She had seen him flirting outrageously with the women at court and had been hard put to keep back her jealousy, but had succeeded in keeping her head high, despite the knowing looks from the king and courtiers. Perhaps it was this immense pride which had prompted Brentwood to return.

"Crimson, you're daydreaming again!" Elizabeth accused her teasingly. "I swear, that's all you ever do these days, ever since that handsome Brentwood has come into your life. Are you in love with him, my dear?" And then as an afterthought: "I certainly hope not, for your own sake."

"What do you mean, Elizabeth?" Crimson demanded. "I'm sure it's obvious to everyone that my husband and I do not have a real marriage in any sense of the word. The marriage has really never even been consummated. Divorce—"

"Divorce is a dirty word, Crimson," Elizabeth sighed. "If it were possible, don't you think that I would have divorced Philip long ago? Sometimes I don't know if I can stand another day being married to him. He can be alternately cruel and mischievous—at my expense!"

"Elizabeth, your husband seems one of the most charming men at court," Crimson objected. "While it's true that he amuses himself with other women, your own record is not exactly blemish-free!"

"If only he would have been kinder to me in the beginning," Elizabeth went on. "If only he would have tried to be a husband to me, but all he could think about was Lady Castlemaine. In comparison to her, I was merely a toy to play with as long as I amused him. He told me once that no other woman could come close to Barbara. She was more erotic, more uninhibited than any other female he had ever been close to. So, to prove that I could attract men too, I began playing up to the courtiers, flirting with any man who was remotely interested. After that, our marriage truly fell apart."

"I'm sorry, Elizabeth," Crimson said sincerely. "Castlemaine is a most cunning woman, it's true. Sometimes I wonder why the king could ever allow himself to become ensnared by her."

"He's not the only one," Elizabeth went on, gazing sharply at the other girl. "My dear, don't you ever listen to gossip?"

Crimson shook her head. "I try not to, otherwise I'm sure I'll hear something that might hurt me or infuriate me!"

"Well, perhaps you should start listening. One can hear some of the most interesting things through a little constructive eavesdropping."

"For instance?"

"Your handsome lover is becoming a steady target for Castlemaine's claws. Every day she tries to catch him in some secluded corner in order to work her wiles on him.
210

Let's be honest, Crimson, Brentwood isn't made of mush. He's sure to be attracted to her."

"We've made a bargain," Crimson began unsteadily.

"Bargains are for the shopping market, Crimson. You had better open your eyes and watch Castlemaine. Perhaps it would be best if you didn't let your heart get too involved with Nicholas Brentwood. He might end up breaking it." Elizabeth shook her head. "I know what it's like, believe me. You know how hard I tried to catch the Duke of York, and that little, simpering Arabella Churchill somehow managed to hold onto him."

"But you would have settled for your cousin, James Hamilton," Crimson pointed out archly.

Elizabeth shrugged. "Even James eluded me after a time. You know that. It seems I'm unlucky at love, my dear, but I just keep trying." She smiled. "Unfortunately, I don't think you're made of the same stuff as I am. You'll get terribly hurt if this affair ends badly."

Crimson straightened. "I'll not get hurt, Elizabeth. If Brentwood chooses to leave me, it certainly is up to him. How could I expect anything permanent?"

"But admit you were thinking of divorcing your husband if it came to that." Elizabeth leaned forward. "You know you would have to get the king's permission to divorce your husband."

"And why wouldn't he give it if it meant my happiness?" Crimson asked her with false bravado.

"Because, of all things, he still wants you, Crimson. He has not quite forgiven you for turning him down the first time, and, naturally, Castlemaine does her best to keep his rage towards you alive with her little innuendos and lies. She wants to turn the king completely against you, and take Brentwood away too. It would suit her completely to have you miserable."

"I know she hates me," Crimson murmured.

"Even to the point of letting her old rival, Frances Stuart, or should I say the Duchess of Richmond, climb into the king's bed! Yes, the gossip is all over court. That the king climbed over Richmond's house wall and finally received consent from Frances to bed her. No doubt, with the scars that the smallpox left on poor Frances' face, she is no longer a serious threat, but the fact remains that Castlemaine was seen leaving her house just the day before the king was said to have climbed over the wall. It's not beyond that woman to persuade Frances to allow the king to have her."

"She's diabolical," Crimson agreed, feeling the goosebumps start on her neck suddenly as though with some premonition of danger from Castlemaine.

"Just listen to me then. Don't give too much of yourself to Brentwood. Between Castlemaine's claws and the king's jealousy, you might not have anything left."

"It's a lot easier to order me not to than to actually be the one to do it," Crimson returned, trying to laugh. She failed, then shrugged. "Oh, please, let's not talk about it anymore. Weren't we going to do something nice today?"

"I'm sorry, Crimson. I didn't mean to spoil your day, but I just thought I'd better tell you. What are friends for? At any rate, you're right. We were going to do something delightful, weren't we? Let's take a drive through Hyde Park first and watch all the gallants trying to charm their latest lovers. We could take cream and syllabub at The World's End in Knightsbridge, or visit Vauxhall. It should have some early spring blossoms, and I'm sure the birds will all be singing on such a sunny day. Would you rather drive over to Bedlam and make faces at the naked lunatics?"

Crimson shivered. "Good Lord, Elizabeth, no!"

She smiled teasingly. "Sorry. We could drive to the Tower and walk through the zoo. See how flexible I am today. I'm willing to do anything that pleases you, my lady. Oh, I have a lovely idea. Let's visit that new French house in Covent Garden, Chatelin's, I believe it's called. It has simply marvelous salads and fricassee. There is always a gay crowd there and lovely music. I've heard it's fast becoming one of the most sociable places around. Perhaps we could persuade some gallants to pay our bill!"

Crimson forced a laugh, determined not to be sad on this first fine day of the spring. "All right. Chatelin's it will be. We must dress for the occasion. The mulberry satin, don't you think?"

"Perfect, but let's do hurry," Elizabeth laughed. "Oh I've a feeling that the day is going to be perfect!"

The two young women were soon inside their carriage, directing the driver to take a few turns about Hyde Park and then on to Chatelin's. It was pleasurable to see the first brave blades of green dotting the lawns of the park and even the trees beginning to bud.

"Oh, look, Crimson. There's your father, of all people, driving with Lady Betty Norwood. Do you think she's his new mistress? I heard that Philippa's husband finally returned from Ireland and that put a stop to her liaison with your father."

"I hardly care what my—father does, Elizabeth. It's his business and I don't meddle, nor do I expect him to meddle in mine. In fact, I don't care to see him again, if it comes to that."

"Whew! I knew you didn't like his arranged marriage for you with Sir Reginald, but I didn't realize you hated him so! You two have a bad quarrel? Perhaps that's why he's been drinking so much lately, eh? The king has been displeased with him more than once because of his conduct while under the influence of too much wine."

"It would suit me perfectly if the king exiled him from court forever!" Crimson declared flatly.

Elizabeth was silent then, thinking it best to remain so until Crimson recovered her good spirits. When they arrived at Chatelin's, it was quite crowded with all manner of people, mostly aristocrats, who were practically the only ones who could afford the high prices.

The two entered the house and received a table close to the window, from which they could watch the colorful flow of people who were shopping or doing other tasks. Suddenly, Crimson stiffened and opened her eyes wide, as though in disbelief.

"Elizabeth, look there! Isn't that Castlemaine's coach that Nicholas Brentwood has just stepped from?"

Immediately, Elizabeth's eyes were riveted to the vehicle. Brentwood, dressed superbly even to his periwig—

213

which he so seldom wore in London—had just stepped out and was extending his hand to help a woman out. Lady Castlemaine!

"That shrewish bitch!" Elizabeth exclaimed heartily.

"Oh, my God, they're coming here!" Crimson said nervously. "Oh, Elizabeth, I just can't face her!"

"Hush, Crimson. There's no way you can escape it now. They'd see you if we left now for sure. For God's sake, behave yourself, and don't wear your heart on your sleeve."

Crimson bit her lip. She followed the couple with her eyes, hopelessly wishing that it was someone else who was acting so attentive to Barbara's witty comments, who was holding the woman's arm so tightly.

When they entered the establishment, many people turned to look. Who didn't know the celebrated mistress of the king? The owner hurried up to the couple in order to give them the best table, a table so close to Crimson's that her heart sank. Surely, Castlemaine would spot her sooner or later. Miserable, Crimson slunk down in her seat and stared steadfastly out the window.

"Lady Gardner! Lady Chesterfield! How delightful! Do come and join Nick and me!" Castlemaine's voice was bright, triumphant with a cruel undercurrent.

Forcing herself to leave her contemplation of the window, Crimson turned her head and smiled, her eyes carefully remaining averted from Brentwood's face. "Lady Castlemaine, Elizabeth and I were only just leaving," she said, relieved that her voice sounded normal.

"But Nick and I would so love to have you join us," Barbara went on, enjoying herself fully now. "My dear, I'm sure you and Nick—that is, well, I wouldn't want you to think that I was trying to take him away from you."

"Please forgive me, Lady Castlemaine, but I'm sure that Lord Dorset can decide for himself the company he keeps. If his judgment does seem poor at times, that is his own affair."

Barbara's eyes glittered at the intended insult and she turned to Brentwood, a slick smile on her face. "Nicholas, did you hear that impertinent wench? Are you going to let

214

her speak of you in such a manner, darling? After all, I do believe you hold some influence with her, do you not?"

Brentwood looked as though he were just barely keeping himself from laughing. "My lady, I'm afraid that she has a mind of her own and there is little I can do, short of a good lashing, to keep her in her place." He glanced over to Crimson's angry face and smiled with amusement. "Bravo, Crimson!" He saluted her.

"Oh, Elizabeth, we are leaving right now!" Crimson huffed, rising from her seat.

"Oh, Crimson, you can't leave now," Elizabeth whispered back.

"I'm leaving with or without you, Elizabeth," Crimson warned and when the other looked back at her balkily, she got up quickly. "A fine friend you are!" she hissed, and retreated from the room.

Once out in the spring air, she breathed deeply, well aware that everyone could still see her from the windows. Well, she would not leave looking dejected! Damn them all! She held her head up high, walking past the carriage which belonged to Elizabeth. It would serve her right if she used it to take her home, but she wouldn't want to see Elizabeth later on anyway. She mingled with the passing crowd and walked quickly until she was far enough away from Chatelin's to look back. Both carriages were still there. She ground her teeth and walked on.

She bumped squarely into a gentleman and looked up, slow to recognize the familiar features.

"Lady Crimson Gardner, I believe?" The gentleman bowed and she saw that his blond hair owed nothing to a wig. Her mind flew, trying to dig up the name that was eluding her so infuriatingly.

"Philip Stanhope, Lord Chesterfield," he supplied her easily.

Crimson's brows flew upwards. Elizabeth's husband! What tricks fate enjoyed playing on people, she thought, even as she smiled most charmingly. Some devilish quirk of temper prompted her to engage in a little flirtation with this man.

"Lord Chesterfifield, of course. Please forgive me, but

my mind was on something else at the moment." She looked up at him impudently, her lashes sweeping high.

"You're alone, my lady?" he questioned, sensing her abandon with the sixth sense of a man accustomed to divining a lady's thoughts.

She nodded. "Yes, I'm afraid so. It was such a lovely day that I had to get out and couldn't wait for anyone to escort me."

"Then, may I offer you my carriage?" He was putting out his arm, and Crimson did not hesitate in taking it.

"Of course, my lord. You are so kind."

The two walked to his carriage where Lord Chesterfield helped her in, then looked inquiringly at her. "Where to, my lady?" He was smiling seductively.

"Hmmm. Not home already, my lord. Why not Vauxhall? That is, if you have no other pressing business."

He laughed. "None at all, Lady Crimson. May I call you Crimson?"

She nodded.

"Good, and you must call me Philip. I must say I've been hoping for a chance alone with you since you arrived at Whitehall, my dear."

What those words might mean, Crimson was not certain, but she felt so angry with Nick that she could not have cared less if Chesterfield did try his wiles on her. Certainly it wouldn't hurt Elizabeth, who most likely had met someone else at Chatelin's. It was common knowledge that Elizabeth never slept with her husband.

As the carriage started moving slowly among the crowds, Crimson allowed herself to relax and listen to what Chesterfield was saying.

"I do hope your husband is in good health," he murmured with evident sarcasm.

"I'm sure he is," she answered in the same vein.

"And Nicholas Brentwood? Gossip has it that you and he have an—arrangement, my lady." Chesterfield's brows arched upwards, emphasizing the teasing insolence in his blue eyes.

Crimson drew herself up, feeling shocked at Chesterfield's candor, and feeling the heat in her cheeks. "It
216

seems my name is the topic of much gossip, my lord. I can hardly say that I like it!"

He smiled. "Crimson, having your name bandied about in public is only bad when one wants to remain an anonymous entity. Surely you don't wish to be just another faceless courtier?"

"And if I do?"

"Then you should try not to be so apt at drawing attention to yourself. I mean, marrying a man whom you hardly know, and then both of you taking lovers—well, perhaps that isn't so uncommon in this age. But what about refusing the king's bed? Something like that is bound to get you notoriety. Then also, you've made a bad enemy in Lady Castlemaine, my dear."

Crimson tossed her head. "I've heard that Castlemaine's day is over, that she no longer has any power over the king. So what does it matter if she doesn't like me?" she asked flippantly.

"Believe me, Barbara is still someone to contend with, my dear. For one thing, she still has people at court who owe her favors."

"And you, my lord?" Crimson wondered. "Are you one of those who still owe her?" She smiled sweetly.

Chesterfield laughed. "I think we've both parted company for good, Crimson. Barbara is far too grasping, too avaricious to suit me. She was a beautiful, healthy young animal, filled with a love of life, when I first met her. I taught her how to love and she proved, in the end, far too excellent a pupil to stay with me. With her talent, she knew she could move to the very top of the mountain, which she did, in short order. Now, I'm afraid she's going to have to topple a bit from her pedestal, but that won't bother Barbara, as long as she gets her duchy from the king and has as many lovers as she can handle."

"Are you, perhaps, the tiniest bit bitter, my lord?" Crimson asked skeptically.

He shrugged. "She wanted to marry me then. After she found out she had contracted the pox, she wrote me a letter, proclaiming her undying love for me. Thank God, I had the sense not to ask her to be my wife. After she survived the smallpox unscathed, she was so sure of her beauty, that, even if she had been married to me, I doubt that I could have stopped her from becoming the king's mistress. It's just part of Barbara's nature. She loves to love."

"She is beautiful," Crimson murmured absently. "I can see why the king was attracted to her."

"No more beautiful at seventeen than you are, Crimson," Chesterfield answered. "With the color of your hair so close to hers, and the same fair complexion, no doubt the king was attracted to you because he might have seen a memory of the girl Barbara once was."

"I'm not sure I like being compared to her," Crimson replied.

"Then let's not talk of her any more, all right?" Chesterfield broke in quickly. "Let's talk of you."

"Since you seem to fancy listening to gossip, I daresay you already know all about me," Crimson said impishly.

He smiled. "Touché. Crimson, you delight me. Yes, you're quite right—I do know quite a bit about you. For instance, that you were born in England, but have lived practically all your life in France, that you were lady-in-waiting to Madame of France, and that you came to London at the request of your father because he owed Sir Reginald a large sum of money, which was canceled out when you married Sir Reginald. Am I right so far?"

She flushed. "I'm afraid so. It scares me to think that everyone knows so much about my personal life."

"Ah, but there's more. After marrying Sir Reginald, you were immediately expected to become the king's mistress. Instead, you became the mistress of Nicholas Brentwood, who has been seen, by the way, with our good friend, Barbara Palmer, Lady Castlemaine. The king still desires you and is only waiting for you to quit your liaison with Lord Dorset before he will, no doubt, approach you again. Of course, with all the gossip flying about and with Barbara buzzing in his ear constantly about you and Nicholas, I'm sure that the latter will be sent off on one of his long journeys for the king very soon. It would certainly be the easiest way to be rid of a rival."

218

"You mean the king will send Nick away because he is my lover?" Crimson asked incredulously. "But that is ridiculous. Besides, I doubt very much whether our relationship will last out this day," she added woefully.

"Didn't I tell you Barbara was the worst enemy to have in this world?" Chesterfield guessed accurately.

"Oh, I don't want to talk about it!" Crimson exclaimed angrily. "If you persist in this odious conversation, I must ask you to turn around and take me home!"

He shook his head. "I promise not to speak another word about Barbara or Nicholas. I should hate to lose your lovely company, my dear."

Crimson settled back in her seat, silent, aware that she didn't feel at all lovely at this moment. She would have preferred to be alone with her thoughts, but Chesterfield seemed bent on keeping her company and she resigned herself to the ride to Vauxhall, which no longer appealed to her.

The ride was not too long, and despite her black mood, Crimson had to admit that seeing the green fields and blooming flowers helped somewhat to revive her spirits. Vauxhall was an old manor to the south of London, which had had formal gardens laid out around 1661, and had proved a popular attraction for the city folk who enjoyed leaving the soot and smut of London for the country atmosphere of Vauxhall gardens.

Early spring flowers were blooming in abundance already, tulips, daffodils and lilacs, all permeating the air with a delicious scent that assailed Crimson's nostrils even before they sighted the remains of the old manorhouse. She leaned towards the window, lifting the curtain in order to gaze out at the scenery. She breathed deeply of the air and turned to Chesterfield gratefully.

"I'm so glad you consented to bring me here after my horrid display of temper," she said.

" 'Twas my pleasure, Crimson," he murmured, watching the transformation of her face as she smiled. She really was as beautiful as Barbara, he thought, noting the pinkened cheeks, the even, white teeth and sparkling gray-green eyes that so complemented the rich, dark auburn of

219

her hair. He couldn't help but let his mind slip back for a moment, remembering Barbara as she used to be, young and vulnerable, before power and wealth had changed her. Unbidden, the thought came to him that he would like to make love to this girl, for a moment recapture his youth. He sighed. Was he really thirty-five years old, and had it really been over ten years ago that he had first awakened Barbara's sensuality?

The driver stopped the horses in front of the entrance to the gardens and Chesterfield roused himself in order to help Crimson out. He took her arm, inhaling the fresh, clean scent of her that was more intoxicating to him than the smell of the flowers.

"Everything is so beautiful," Crimson sighed. She turned her head up to meet Chesterfield's gaze and smiled saucily. "Must we return to London ever?"

Chesterfield's answering smile tightened. "Whatever you say, my lady. Today, I am your vassal to be ordered about as you wish. We need not return to London tonight." His eyes held a question that Crimson was either too inexperienced to, or refused to, see.

They walked together along the rows of greenery, passing several other couples, some noble, others middle- and lower-class, all enjoying the awakening spring day.

A rather short, chunky man, dressed in very dapper finery, towing along his plump wife, waved a hand to hail Lord Chesterfield as they walked toward him. "Ho, Lord Chesterfield! Good day to you, sir!"

"Mr. Pepys, I see you and your wife know how to enjoy a sunny day," Chesterfield answered.

"My lord, I had no choice in the matter as my dear wife insisted on the outing." Mr. Pepys gazed with studied interest at Crimson. "And I see you also know how to enjoy a sunny day, my lord. At your service, Lady Gardner." He bowed and winked at her boldly.

Crimson, not quite sure how to react to this beaming man, looked up to Chesterfield for support. The latter grinned.

"Crimson, may I present Mr. Samuel Pepys and his wife? Lady Crimson Gardner, friends."

220

"Ah, I already know of Lady Crimson," Mr. Pepys cut in, giving his wife no chance to say a word. "As you know, my lord, I am never one to listen to gossip, but sometimes one cannot help overhearing people talk, if you know what I mean."

"Mr. Pepys, you're a bald-faced liar and we both know it! I happen to recall that time we talked and you told me about the journal you've been keeping for posterity, as you so pompously informed me. No doubt, you're still keeping it?"

Pepys had the grace to flush. "Aye, that I am, my lord. Shall I enter our meeting in it tonight?" He winked once more at Crimson.

"By all means," Chesterfield laughed, "and be sure to write that I have every intention of getting to know my lady better before the day is out."

"Good luck to you then, my lord," the other returned, then bowed and bustled his wife off before either of the two women had been able to exchange a word.

"Goodness, who was that?" Crimson asked.

"Samuel Pepys, a kinsman of Edward Montagu, Earl of Sandwich. Mr. Pepys holds the king's favor and is a most likeable man. He is, furthermore, one of the biggest of those gossips you claim to abhor. What do you think he will have to say after seeing us together today?" His tone was half-serious.

"What could he say?" Crimson wondered. "You were kind enough to escort me to Vauxhall on the first decent day we've had this spring!" She tossed her head and eyed Chesterfield with a slight challenge. "Surely there is nothing to fuel his gossip in that!"

"Ah, now, there is where Mr. Pepys would disagree. He would most likely conjecture that we came out here to be alone, far away from the king's eyes and those of your lover and mine." He shrugged at her raised eyebrows. "Since he well knows that I am a most accomplished libertine, and you, ripe for such lechery after your quarrel with your lover—"

"How would he know that I had quarreled with Nick?"

Chesterfield winked confidentially. "He would know, Crimson."

"Well, I hardly think anyone would believe him. You have enough women to satisfy you, and I have too many men in my life already." Crimson shook her head. "I'm beginning to think 'tis better to be born ugly and undsirable."

"Don't talk such foolishness, Crimson," Chesterfield responded gruffly.

They were walking beneath a rose arbor that led in one direction into a relatively secluded area walled on three sides by tall greenery. Chesterfield clasped Crimson's hand and drew her inside to sit on a stone bench placed there for just such a tête-à-tête.

Once seated, he turned towards her and drew her firmly into his arms. Crimson, surprised at the embrace, allowed him to hold her until his lips came down searchingly against her face.

"My lord! I can hardly believe what you're about! Haven't you listened to anything I've said?"

He shook his head and continued placing kisses on her face. "Not a word, Crimson. How can I listen to you when my heart tells me that I must have you?"

"Please, let me go! I have enough troubles without—"

"How can there be trouble in this, Crimson?" he asked softly. "Is it so terrible for a man to desire you?"

"Yes, yes! All you want is that which any woman can give you! What is in my mind, my heart, does not interest you at all."

"Ah, my dear, but that is precisely where the trouble lies. As long as a man desires you only for your beauty, there can be no involvement of the mind or of the heart. Once a man begins to care for a woman to the point of love, that is where trouble begins. All I wish is to comfort you, Crimson. Let me love your sweet body, let me teach it the ways of pleasure."

"No!"

He shrugged, but did not stop kissing her. His mouth traveled to hers and captured it fiercely, pressing her lips apart in order to plunder the softness of her flesh. Crimson

222

fought the slow tide of passion that seemed to wash over her, ashamed that she could feel desire for this man whom she hardly knew.

She struggled to free her mouth. "Please—stop," she pleaded.

He shook his head brusquely and captured her mouth again while his hands moved surely over her bodice, reaching inside to caress her breasts. He could sense her on the brink of yielding and his efforts continued.

Traitor body! Crimson thought desperately, feeling a warmth in her flesh, a moistness that had nothing to do with the heat of the day. How could she be doing this! She, who would not allow the king to make love to her, and yet was panting in the embrace of this libertine after being in his company only a few hours. What was wrong with her?

Chesterfield was already lowering her to the lawn behind the bench, determined to seduce her now, uncaring as to who might come by and see them locked in such ardent embrace. In a few moments, he had pushed her bodice from her shoulders and lifted up her skirt. He was fumbling with his own breeches, breathing hard as his mouth licked at her flesh.

A blurred memory rose within Crimson as she recalled just such a moment in a different garden. A man whom she hardly knew, determined to possess her body. Somehow the remembrance added to her passion, and she clutched at Chesterfield, forgetting who he was, hardly caring, only wishing a release from this terrible, aching need that was filling her.

His hands were smooth on her thighs, his fingers sure as they teased her flesh so that soon she was groaning for him to hurry. He found her mouth with his once more as he lowered his body onto hers and entered her writhing flesh. Crimson shuddered, then pressed his body close against hers, straining to meet him.

Chesterfield's skill at making love was common knowledge at court, and Crimson had to admit that he was thoroughly expert with her. He brought her body to a fevered pitch before finally allowing her release as he collapsed against her. She could feel his heart beating furiously in time to her own and waited a moment before speaking.

"My lord. Philip, I feel so foolish," she murmured tentatively.

"Why? Because you were so determined not to let this happen?" he asked her, smiling a little as he kissed the tip of her nose. "You pleased me a great deal, Crimson. I'm glad we found each other today."

"I'm glad too," she sighed, suppressing the guilt as she pictured Elizabeth's face.

Neither of them heard the slight chuckle, nor saw the amused face of James Hamilton, as he tiptoed by, his disappointment at having someone else use his trysting place overshadowed by the juicy bit of gossip he would have to tell tonight.

24

Crimson was awakened by a deep voice close to her ear, and she opened her eyes quickly to look into dark blue ones that were gazing at her with mixed contempt and mockery.

"Good morning," he was saying abruptly.

Crimson sat up, pulling the covers up to her chin, gazing about the room quickly to see if they were alone. She remembered Lord Chesterfield bringing her home in the afternoon yesterday and then staying to make love again in her bed. She must have fallen asleep before he left.

She turned her eyes back to meet Nick Brentwood's, and cringed at the sweeping look of disdain he bestowed upon her.

"Oh, yes, I waited until I was sure he had left," he said tightly.

"He had left?" she repeated faintly, wishing she had thought to put on a nightgown instead of falling asleep completely nude.

"Lord Chesterfield. Was there someone else?" he questioned icily.

Crimson struggled to bring her wits about her, then cast a cool glance at her inquisitor. "I'm not in the mood for your insufferable insolence," she said. "I would appreciate it if you would leave immediately!"

He smiled and sat down on the bed, causing Crimson to move slightly, but when she would have crossed to the other side of the bed, he caught her arm and forced her to remain where she was.

"Don't act so terrified, my dear," he said lazily, his eyes darkening. "You don't think I'd be so uncouth as to try to force myself on you when your other lover has only just left. I dislike using another man's leavings, Crimson, especially when his seed has only barely dried on you!"

"Oh!" Crimson turned red under his cruel gaze, totally embarrassed at his lack of tact. "If you only came here to humiliate me—"

"Hardly worth the trouble, my dear, but neither did I come here to bed you. I only came to assure you that I will not hold you to our bargain. You have decided, obviously, that being mistress to only one man is not as enjoyable as entertaining two, or more."

Crimson frowned, "And what of yourself? Didn't I see you with Lady Castlemaine, the royal whore—yesterday?"

"I wouldn't fling such titles around so casually, Crimson. You never know when you might be labeled something worse," he observed drily.

"Well! Are you going to tell me that you didn't take her

to bed last night!" she demanded. "At least for old times' sake, I'm sure!"

He laughed in amazement. "I can't believe you're jealous! Perhaps it's best then that all this has happened," he added.

"I'm sure it is!" she snapped back. "You don't have to worry about me and all my problems any more. You can whore merrily along now for the rest of your days!"

"For your information, I didn't go to bed with Barbara," he said. "I came back here, instead, and found you otherwise engaged. I admit it wounded my pride a bit, but," he shrugged, "there are other fish in the sea, as they say."

"Wonderful! I'm sure you will be able to catch at least one without much fuss!" She threw it back at him.

He stood up and looked down at her. "I'd like to wish you good luck in all your endeavors," he said, "but I have the feeling that you hardly need my good wishes. Women like you will always find ways to survive."

"Thank you for the compliment," she snapped waspishly. "Good-bye!"

He hesitated. Suddenly, he reached down and tore the sheet from her grasp. He leaned towards her and pushed her, floundering, back into the pillows. Struggling to sit up, Crimson felt his hands on her breasts, toying with them as he exerted pressure to keep her down.

"Damn, but you're almost too beautiful to let go!" he cursed. Then he recovered himself and released her, letting his hand stray across her cheek in a gesture of regret. "Good-bye, Crimson."

He was out the door before she had recovered her wits and, to her dismay, she felt a tug of remorse, emphasized by the threat of tears in her eyes. Damn him! She wasn't going to let his rejection bother her, she told herself firmly. Besides, and she lifted her head proudly, she was sure she could get him back if she wanted him. . . .

Crimson glanced at herself in the mirror briefly before entering the huge salon where most of the court were gathered today. The king had already been up for hours and had taken his morning physic, strolling at a fast pace along the palace grounds and playing five or six sets of tennis. He had declared his wish to go boating on the ice-free Thames, a suggestion greeted by most of the ladies with resigned impatience. Only those lucky enough to enjoy the ride on the royal barge were eager to go.

Crimson hoped that she might escape the outing, especially as she had already been told to ride with Lady Chesterfield, but hadn't the heart to do so after her assignation with the lady's husband yesterday. She pressed her hands against the pale green watered silk of her gown and entered the salon, hoping not to meet Lord Chesterfield.

"Oh, there you are, Crimson," came a female voice close by.

Crimson turned to see Lady Anne Carnegie, sister to the Hamiltons, gesturing her over.

"Lady Anne, you wished to speak to me?"

Anne Hamilton Carnegie let her eyes travel over the younger woman in swift appraisal. "It's all over court, you know," she said finally. "You and Philip, Lord Chesterfield. I must say, my dear, the king was not at all in a congenial mood this morning after his physic. I daresay he ordered this boat excursion just to vent his spleen out on all of us other poor ladies."

"But how—" Crimson began at a loss.

"Oh, you know, someone must have seen you at Vauxhall yesterday. News like that travels fast when there's nothing else to talk about. Everybody gets so bored with all the usual affairs, that this was something new to talk about. Really, my dear, you do have a knack for getting your name on everyone's lips."

"Well, I'm sorry for it, but I suppose there's nothing I can do about it now. The king is already upset with me."

Anne shrugged. "There's a difference, Crimson, in being upset-mad, and upset-jealous. I would guess that the king's ardor is only fired by all your little affairs." She winked. "I don't blame you in the least for succumbing to Chesterfield's charm. He can be quite—persuasive, when he wants to be."

Belatedly, Crimson remembered that here was yet another of Chesterfield's earlier conquests, for he had known both Lady Anne and Barbara Palmer at the same time. Anne and Barbara had been friends, quite close, until some trifling quarrel caused them to drift apart after Barbara became the king's *maitresse en titre*.

"What makes you think the king is jealous of Chesterfield?" Crimson asked curiously.

"Because only this morning, Chesterfield was—umm—*asked* to return to his country estate. Something about trouble among his tenants. My dear, there is *always* trouble among one's tenants. Why the king should take this time to order Chesterfield home is certainly a matter for some conjecture. Don't you agree?"

Crimson sighed. Had the king really been so jealous of Chesterfield that he had sent him to his country seat, in effect banishing him from court, simply because Crimson had let him make love to her? She could hardly believe it!

She said as much to Lady Anne. "I hardly think the king would go to such measures for so trifling a matter. After all, they are great friends, despite the fact that the king knows very well that Chesterfield and Castlemaine were quite close at one time. Didn't someone tell me that the king forgave Chesterfield and freed him from all guilt when he killed some poor young man over the sale of a horse? Surely, if he can forgive murder, he can forgive him this?"

"My goodness, don't act so defensive, my dear," Anne chided with a superior air. "For one thing, Chesterfield, bless him, did not kill the man in cold blood. He challenged him to a duel when the horse the man sold him proved lame. Secondly, that was a long time ago. The king, alas, has grown older and more easily provoked, though 'tis true he is still an easygoing man compared to some of our more hot-tempered youngbloods. I'm afraid it would be foolish for you to try to convince yourself that the king will lose interest in you. The only way for him to do that would be for you to go to bed with him, my dear," she finished wisely. "Otherwise, the king will never let you go."

"You're forgetting, Lady Anne, that I have been the

228

mistress of Nicholas Brentwood for a month now, and the king has not intervened."

Lady Anne smiled pityingly. "My poor innocent, didn't you know that your Nicholas Brentwood left London early this morning? Bound for Plymouth, I've heard, to catch the first ship to the Americas."

"What!" Crimson felt all the blood slowly drain from her face. Nick was gone! But he hadn't said a word this morning to her! Oh, Nick! It was all her fault. She hadn't given him a chance to say good-bye to her. She'd been so angry, so mixed up about Lord Chesterfield.

"Take hold of yourself, Crimson," Anne advised, putting a sympathetic hand on her shoulder. "He always comes back from these mysterious business trips of his. You'll see him again, I'm sure."

Crimson shook her head despairingly. "He would not seek me out at any rate," she murmured more to herself. Well, at least he did not have to think of excuses to leave her, she mourned. Chesterfield had come along at a convenient time for him. And now, the king had taken Chesterfield away from her too.

"Crimson, do pull yourself together, my dear. The king!"

Indeed, it was the king, all-powerful, completely in control. He was dressed handsomely in olive green, white lace dripping from his wrists and the jabot at his collar. On his curled periwig, he wore a wide-brimmed hat, jaunty white feathers waving slightly as he walked into the room, a broad smile on his dark face.

"My ladies and gentlemen, let us make haste to the river stairs. The day promises to be sunny and only slightly breezy, according to my alchemist." His dark, satyr's face was completely composed as his black eyes searched the crowded room and came to rest on Crimson.

She swallowed hard and returned the look, endeavoring to smile bravely as the king's eyes bored into hers, all the while wishing that she could flee the room and leave all these grinning, staring courtiers.

"The queen has decided not to come, Lady Crimson,"

the king began, holding out his hand towards her, "so you shall accompany us on the royal barge."

The king had used the privileged, royal "us," and Crimson realized that she dare not refuse. She nodded gracefully, curtseying to the floor.

"I should be honored, Your Majesty."

She moved forward to take the outstretched hand of the king. As his hand clasped hers tightly and they turned to start out the door, Crimson's ears could pick up the furious buzzing behind her. Briefly, her eyes touched on Lady Castlemaine's and the blazing hate in them made her shiver. Barbara, also, was invited to the king's royal barge which promised that the journey would not be pleasant for Crimson. Why did the king insist on antagonizing his former mistress?

"Are you pleased to accompany me?" the king whispered as they stepped outside onto the steps that led down to the river side.

"I am honored, sire," Crimson returned ambiguously.

His black brows drew together and she knew that he was not happy with her answer; however, he said nothing as he waited on the oarsman of the barge. When everyone who had been invited was seated in the king's barge, the others came down the steps in order to await their own boats. Crimson caught a glimpse of Elizabeth chattering away with the Duke of York, and Crimson waved to her, but Elizabeth did not wave back.

"Lady Crimson, how nice to see you again." It was the Duchess of York, her round, pleasant face smiling invitingly at her, while she patted the seat next to her. "Come, sit next to me, my dear." Her pale, protuberant eyes did not even deign to watch the flirtation between her husband and Lady Elizabeth. York's current mistress, Lady Arabella Churchill, was nearly eight months pregnant and had been confined to her own quarters by her physician for the duration of her pregnancy. The duke, of course, was not by nature a faithful man, and so could hardly be disinclined to the attentions of another lady. Anne, Duchess of York, had become immune to her husband's flirtations. She had her two daughters, which, if King Charles did not

230

produce an heir from his wife, would seem to have very good chances at the throne of England. She had been a plain, plump young woman of no aristocracy when the duke had married her. She was still, despite her title, the same woman.

"Your Highness, I appreciate your invitation," Crimson said, casting a glance towards the king. The duchess had very neatly kept the king from keeping Crimson next to him.

The duchess smiled, whether or not because she could tell what was in the young woman's mind. "I know that you are still a relative newcomer to the court, my dear. Tell me, truthfully, what do you think of it?"

"I can hardly say, Your Highness. Whitehall is a beautiful place and the court so immense, it is hard to make a judgment. I suppose one can be happy there."

"You don't make it sound easy, Lady Crimson. Do you still miss France, perhaps?"

"I don't think so, madam. At first I thought I would never lose the love I had for that country, but if I were to be given the chance to return tomorrow, I am sure I would refuse. This is my country now."

"You are very wise in your decision, my dear. And I see you are losing a tiny bit of your French accent, yes?" The duchess smiled at this last as Crimson flushed.

"Truly, I hope so, madam." Then, as she saw a flash of pain cause the other woman's face to flinch, "Madam, are you all right?"

The duchess made a poor attempt to smile. "Yes, my dear. Just a little pain in my belly. 'Tis always so in the morning. My physician assures me it is only a temporary condition, although, I daresay, rumor has it that I have contracted a cancer."

"Perhaps, it would be best to ask the king to stop the barge so that you may return to your rooms," Crimson suggested.

The other woman shook her head. "No, no, I'll be quite all right in another moment. You're very sweet to be concerned, Lady Crimson, but I certainly would hate to

231

dampen the king's high spirits this morning. I know how he was looking forward to this excursion."

Crimson looked at the pale face doubtfully, but was aware that the duchess would never think of stopping any function of the court's. She had not that many friends at court, and was, in many respects, in somewhat the same position as the shunned queen.

The oarsmen had taken up their oars and were rowing the barge at a leisurely pace down the Thames River. Crimson leaned back in her seat, feeling the sun on her face with a distinct pleasure. Beside her, the duchess had recovered and had opened a box of sweets. She offered them to Crimson, who declined politely and returned to her contemplation of the river.

The river flowing to the sea. She wondered if Nick had reached Plymouth yet. Did he spare a thought for her? Or was his mind filled with this new adventure the king had sent him on? The Americas—but they were a vast place. He could be going anywhere. She sighed and trailed her finger along the side of the barge. Would she ever see him again?

Her reverie was interrupted by the voice of the king. "Lady Crimson, I wish for you to sit beside me."

Reluctantly, Crimson relinquished her seat next to the duchess and moved to the cushion beside the king. She settled herself tensely, aware of so many eyes on her. There was little privacy on the barge, except for the small canopy that had been erected over the king's seat which partially enclosed them on both sides.

The king had turned to Lady Castlemaine, who was sitting near him. "If you would, my dear? I wish to speak alone with Lady Crimson."

Barbara moved further away with bad grace, an expression of rage clearly written on her face. She murmured something under her breath which Crimson could not hear, but which caused the king's face to darken. However, he said nothing, but turned back to Crimson, smoothing his face into more pleasant lines.

"Now, my lady. We have some privacy, and I wish to ask you something."

"Of course, sire."

Suddenly, his face became more intense, his eyes questioning as he captured her hands in his beneath the screen of her gown. "Oh, Crimson, why? Why did you betray me a second time? And with Chesterfield, of all people! He is nothing more than a user of women. He has so many whom he has used once, then discarded without mercy, with no more thought than you would throw away an old gown!"

"Sire, please do not question me on this," Crimson pleaded. "I cannot say I planned it, but—it just happened. I had been hurt and—"

"If you were hurt, why didn't you come to me, Crimson? I would have sheltered you from anyone!"

"Sire, you talk of Chesterfield and his women. What of yourself? You, too, use women for a time and then discard them with little feeling. What difference between you or Chesterfield?" she sighed.

"Crimson, you wound me terribly," the king returned in a low voice. "But you know already that I will forgive you anything, if only you will consent to give me that which you have freely bestowed on two others. Why do you torture me?"

"Sire, I have no wish to torture you," Crimson whispered, her eyes averted. "You tell me that you desire me, but there are others that you have desired in just the same way. You are the king, you are never disobeyed. You only desire me the more because I do not say yes. If I surrendered to you, you would no longer want me after a time and then I, too, would probably be given some title and perhaps an estate in order to ease my wounded pride."

The king's brows drew downward. "How little you think of me, Crimson! If you loved me only a little bit, I would remain faithful to you. You would be my only mistress. I am not a hard man. Look to Castlemaine, if you wish proof of it. Did I not put up with curses, bitter quarrels and the screaming rantings of her greed, because I thought that she cared for me in her heart? God knows I grew sick of it, but I did not leave her to starve, nor did I cast her out when opinion was strongly against her and, without my support, she would have been torn to pieces by her enemies."

"I know that, sire, but I am not as strong as she. If I became your mistress, I would be hurt by your other casual affairs, I would be jealous of every one of your women, even those you no longer see. You have your children by them to think of."

He leaned closer, his lips nearly on her ear, and Crimson could feel his breath teasing her flesh. "*You* could have children too, my sweet. I would love them more than any of the others. Our children would be beautiful and sweet-tempered."

"Your other children are beautiful and obedient," Crimson pointed out.

He shrugged. "Bah, they're stupid for the most part. Their mothers have drummed into them the fact that they have come from the king's seed and so they neglect their studies, believing that there is no need to prove themselves."

"And what of your firstborn, sire?" Crimson asked softly. The king's devotion to James, Duke of Monmouth, was widely known. He had been born to the king's first mistress, Lucy Walters, when the king had been nineteen years old. Monmouth was still the king's favorite, and there were some who whispered that he would name him to be successor to the throne should he have no legitimate heirs.

The king's face had lightened at her mention of the boy. "Ah, James. Yes, Crimson, he, of all my sons, is both beautiful and intelligent. I am proud of him." He glanced quickly at her. "Would you begrudge me my affection?"

"No, of course not, sire!" Crimson returned quickly. "But you see that you cannot love any of your other children as much as your firstborn. He is closest to you and that is as it should be."

"Oh, Crimson, you twist things around so cleverly. You make me feel ashamed of my tenderest declarations. I cannot please you no matter what I do. If I would take you by force—and the thought has entered my mind—you would probably hate me. I don't want your hate, Crimson. I want your love."

"Sire, you have my devotion and obedience as a loyal subject," Crimson stated softly.

The king put his hands to his face, rubbing his temples in agitation. "God's blood, you are a stubborn wench, Crimson. Sometimes I could shake you in anger. You seem to be able to find ways to make me lose my temper at one minute, and then I want to hold you in my arms the next." He shook his head as though baffled. "What shall I do about you?"

"I suppose you shall leave me to the tender mercies of my husband, sire," Crimson answered, lifting her head up, her voice laced with petulance. "For I have heard that you have ordered Chesterfield to his estates and—and have sent Nick on another mission."

The king frowned. "Chesterfield deserved to be banished for a while. He knew that I—" He stopped for a moment, realizing the anger that was held in her eyes. "Are you so upset that I sent Brentwood away, Crimson? I cannot believe it, knowing that you willingly gave yourself to Chesterfield."

Crimson flushed and some of the anger left her. "I am to blame for that, sire, but—"

"Perhaps, you were falling in love with Brentwood, Crimson?"

She shook her head. "I don't know, sire, but I shall never find out, shall I?" she answered with renewed insolence.

"Crimson, it was for your own good. Brentwood could never stay with you for long. He is an adventurer. He enjoys his job as my agent. He could never stay tied to one woman for long. And you, you are a married woman. If he would decide to make a permanent tie, he would probably marry. There could never have been anything for you with him."

"I don't care!" Crimson's face was bleak for a moment and her voice rose. "You sent him away before I could find out! You didn't give us a chance together before your

235

jealousy caused you to use your power to separate us! I hate you for that!"

The king shook her by the shoulders, calming her down by force. "Be quiet, Crimson, for God's sake! Everyone is watching you! Do you want to make a fool of yourself and me? Don't think any of them would be sympathetic to you. They only wait for you to make a mistake to tear at you with their gossiping tongues. Think of your pride, at least!"

Sobbing a little, Crimson attempted to recover herself, not daring to look at the other occupants of the barge. The king wisely allowed her to her own thoughts and did not speak to her for the rest of the ride. Crimson remained silent, thankful when the barge pulled up at the Whitehall steps.

The king rose to help her to her feet, then walked ahead to accompany the Duchess of York off of the boat. Crimson waited for a moment, then held her head up high, and moved forward to the edge of the barge. The wide wooden plank wavered under her slippered foot for a moment and she waited for the oarsmen to steady the boat. Behind her, several others waited for her to cross the plank.

Crimson stepped onto the plank at the same time that the barge moved again, listing a little towards the river steps. People behind her were thrown forward and Crimson felt a sudden weight against her, causing her to lose her balance. The next thing she felt was the cold, clamminess of the Thames closing around her.

For a moment her mind was blank and she opened her eyes to a murky darkness. Then something struck her on the head and she was shaken from her fantasy state as her lungs started to ache from lack of oxygen. Hysterical, she tried to reach the surface, her chest feeling as though it would burst, but her heavy gown and petticoats caused her to sink further like a rock.

It seemed like long minutes, but in fact it was only a few seconds before an arm suddenly snaked out of the greenish void and closed around her neck, forcing her upwards with a strong tug. Crimson's head broke the surface of the water and she drew in a lungful of air, her

236

breath rasping strongly in her throat. The arm about her neck eased up a little and then was pulling her towards the shore where she could dimly see figures leaning down to catch her in order to pull her up onto the steps.

Gasping and choking, she was pulled out of the water and lay, like a grounded fish, blowing heavily. The Duchess of York was squatting down beside her, her face worried, her hand warm against the coolness of Crimson's wet cheek.

"Thank God, you're all right, my dear," she gasped. "If it hadn't been for the king's quick thinking—"

"The—king?" Crimson managed. She turned her head as she was lifted into strong arms and pressed against a tall, wet body. Charles II of England looked down at her anxiously.

"Are you all right, Crimson?" he asked.

She nodded feebly. The king had saved her life, had jumped into the river to keep her from drowning. "Thank you—Charles," she murmured.

He smiled then and hugged her closer, starting up the steps with the others following. In the background, Crimson could hear the buzzing and murmurings of the courtiers. The sounds followed her up to her small apartment in the queen's suite, where the king brusquely ordered everyone to leave. Only the duchess remained, kindly offering to watch over her while the physician was fetched.

"My dear, you are lucky the king is an excellent swimmer. Everyone else was gaping like stupid magpies while you were struggling in the water. I think we were all too shocked to move."

"How—how did it happen?" Crimson asked feebly from the small pallet, wondering if the queen had been told yet.

"You lost your footing," the king put in, leaning down to place a hand on her brow. "I shall have to have a wider plank made." He looked at her tenderly. "Rest, my dear, while they fetch my physician. I shall inform the queen and then go to my rooms in order to change. I shall return immediately afterwards." He reached down, caught one of her hands, and pressed it to his lips, before leaving.

Crimson coughed, then turned quickly in the bed in order to lean over the side and retch into the chamberpot.

"Oh, my dear, you must have swallowed some river water," the duchess said with concern. "Better now?"

Crimson nodded. "I still don't understand, though, how I could have fallen. I—I think someone may have pushed me from the barge. Accidentally, of course." She looked questioningly at the duchess.

The older woman shook her head. "I don't know. There were several others waiting to get off behind you. Poor Lady Castlemaine was furious because you had walked in front of her when—" She stopped suddenly and gazed sharply at Crimson, who stared back at her.

"Was she—was she close behind me?" she whispered, her eyes wide.

The duchess looked frightened for a moment. "Yes, she was—right behind you," she answered.

25

Castlemaine had tried to murder her! The thought kept spinning through Crimson's brain. Had Barbara really wanted to push Crimson into the river, or had she merely let the listing of the barge throw her forward just enough—either way, Crimson had no doubt that it had been Barbara Palmer who had pushed her into the river, pushed her to what easily could have been her death. If it hadn't been for the king. He had been so concerned, so anxious when the physician had examined her. Why couldn't she love him, just a little, enough to give him what he wanted?

Lying in her own bed on King's Street, Crimson tried to examine her feelings for the king. She had been hurt and angry when she had found out that he had had Brentwood sent away, but was it because she truly cared for Brentwood, or because of the sneaky way the king had gone about it?

And what of the queen and her loyalty to her? And Barbara Castlemaine? Always there was her to consider, especially now when her desperation had nearly caused her to commit murder in order to keep the king from becoming her lover! It was a matter of pride—and greed—to Barbara. She would not give the king up to this little foreign usurper, this girl, not yet eighteen! She wanted more power, more wealth before she would unhook her talons from her royal lover.

Crimson's head ached from all her thoughts. She wanted nothing more than to sleep. When the king's coach had taken her home, after he had been assured that all she needed was rest, she had been more than glad to go to bed, directing Diane to allow no visitors.

Tiredly, she started to close her eyes, when she heard a man's hard stride coming up the stairs and to her room. For a moment, she wondered if the king had actually come here, expecting, perhaps, a night of love for his bravery.

"My dear wife, good evening!" It was Reginald, opening the door, then closing it behind him with an easy air that aroused Crimson's suspicions.

"What do you want?" she asked him abruptly, wanting to be left alone.

He came up to the bed, pulling a chair over in order to seat himself next to her. "God's blood, my dear, I would expect a more civil greeting from you. After all, haven't I been a good husband to you? I've politely stayed out of your life up until now, letting you have your casual affairs without thought as to the honor of my name."

"Don't speak to me of honor, when you know how you
239

plotted to marry me in order to gain influence with the king!" Crimson threw back at him.

"You wound me, my dear, but—" His gaze sharpened as he leaned towards her. "Yes, I admit I had thought you could help my career. It seems, though, that you have a stubborn streak which I wasn't aware of when I married you. Your bull-headedness has caused me to lose some of the influence I had, my dear, and now that you have lost your lovers, I am wondering if you will show yourself more intelligent and accept the king's proposal?"

"If I do, you can be sure it wouldn't be because I have any wish to help you!" Crimson exclaimed.

"And why not? You help me and you help yourself. Remember, I *am* your husband. Whatever happens to me happens to you also."

"What nonsense! If, as you keep hoping I will, I do become the mistress of the king, I will have his protection."

"Now, my dear, we both know how fickle Charles can be. It's true he does have a way of showering his discarded mistresses with gifts, but how can you be sure he will be so generous with you? Besides, you are married to me for life! Ah, can you imagine us growing old together, with the help of all that wealth you will have picked up from His Majesty!" He sighed almost lasciviously. His eyes looked to her questioningly. "Without it, I have an idea I might be hard put to make your older years comfortable."

"I quite understand," Crimson retorted. "The Lady Anne Brownwood, no doubt, required a great deal of recompense for her role as your mistress. I daresay that is the only reason she remains with you!"

Gardner's eyes glittered. "My dear wife, I do hope you don't act this way around the king. He'll think he's laid another shrew like Castlemaine." Then he sighed and his face became more serious. "The truth is, Crimson, that Lady Anne Brownwood's husband has been injured on the field of honor and is coming home in a week. He is, to put it succinctly, very old-fashioned, and expects his sweet wife to be eagerly awaiting his arrival, having remained faithful to him all this time. I'm afraid I'm going to have to put up lodgings here for a while, until his wound heals."

"But you told me that this house would be mine!" Crimson burst out. The prospect of having Sir Reginald in the same house was not an inviting one, especially as her memory of their wedding night was still strong.

"I dislike the idea as much as you," he put in snidely, "but there is nothing else for me to do. Brownwood is extremely jealous."

"But—"

"Please don't turn me out, dearest. At any rate, with your lovers banished from court, it might be a good idea for me to stay here for your own protection."

"What do you mean by that?" Crimson asked, some of her anger slipping away as she remembered Castlemaine's threat.

"You know what I mean, Crimson," he said soberly. Then his face lightened. "I could bring Anne here and her husband would never suspect." He glanced at his wife. "Believe me, I would endeavor to remain discreet," he assured her.

Crimson looked at him, startled. "You would bring your mistress *here*?" she demanded. "You will not do any such thing, or—"

"May I remind you that this is my house, Crimson. When it comes down to it, I have every right to cast you out of it if I so desire. I would hate to think what you might have to do in order to gain a suitable shelter for yourself." He smiled blandly at her, challenging her to say anything more.

Furious, but aware that he was making no idle threat, Crimson subsided, casting him a murderous glance from beneath her lashes. "Do as you wish, my lord, but have the kindness not to make me a source of complete public ridicule." She pulled the bedclothes tightly about her. "And now, if you will allow me to get some rest?"

He started, as though just realizing the vulnerable position she was in. "How delightful! I'm afraid I've forgotten what you look like, my dear. Are you naked beneath those covers? No, how unfortunate. We could play some little games, if you were willing."

"Go away!" Crimson cried out.

He sighed in mock hurt. "As you wish, my dear."

Only after she heard him descending the stairs did Crimson breathe in a sigh of relief and allow herself to relax. She had a horrible premonition that these arrangements were not going to work.

Crimson was in the drawing room of the house when her husband paid her another visit. She looked up from reading some correspondence from her cousin, Violette, who was complaining of her lack of funds and the shocking depravity of King Louis' court. Crimson had to smile, wondering what Violette would have to say about King Charles' court.

"I'm glad to find you in, my dear. I'm having some things moved from my apartment at Whitehall over here."

"I take it Brownwood is back then?"

He nodded. "Turns out his wound is merely a grazed thigh, but I have a feeling he demanded to return home just to see how the domestic condition was, if you follow my meaning."

"Well, I can hardly blame him. Anyone would get tired of war all the time and no wife to comfort him," Crimson added. She remembered the king telling her that he had had Brownwood remain in the field in order to keep him away from his wife, so that Sir Reginald could dally with her as he chose. It seemed, though, that even the king could not keep a soldier at war forever. She could imagine the king's chagrin at hearing that her husband was moving in with her again.

"Let us hope his stay will be brief, though long enough, no doubt, to get poor Anne pregnant again." Gardner's mouth turned down in distaste.

"Well, at least the blame cannot be pinned onto you," Crimson retorted tartly.

He smiled sourly. "How clever you are, my dear."

He moved into the room and seated himself in a chair across from her. "A letter from some lover?" he asked, noting the paper in her hand.

"No, from my cousin in France," Crimson answered. "By the way, there was a letter for you too. I've had it

242

here for a few days and haven't had a chance to tell you. From the looks of it, it's from a great distance." She got up to go to the mantelpiece and retrieve a thick envelope which was half torn and stained by the elements. "Here it is."

Gardner opened it curiously, then smiled as he began reading. "It's from my father. He's the king's comptroller in Jamaica. Actually I haven't heard from him in some years. I wonder—"

Crimson watched him continue reading, his face taking on various expressions. The letter was not as long as it looked; Gardner was finished with the contents shortly. He looked up at Crimson.

"He wanted to tell me he's remarried. From the praises he's given her, she must be a beauty, although I suppose since she's only thirty years old to his sixty, he would think her beautiful even if she was plain as mud." He chuckled.

"You've never talked about your family," Crimson wondered curiously. "Is Jamaica far away?"

"Across the Atlantic Ocean, Crimson. It's an island, a beautiful little paradise, according to my father. He's been over there for about fifteen years. He helped to capture the island from the French and Spanish under Cromwell, and then proved himself loyal to King Charles after the Restoration and was appointed comptroller. He's in charge of sending contraband booty back to England for the king's coffers. Charles, no doubt, relies on the gold and silver from confiscated pirate ships to bejewel all his women."

"Pirates! That's sounds dangerous. How does your father manage to obtain this pirate booty?"

"Oh, he doesn't actually confiscate it himself. It's done by His Majesty's soldiers and privateers. Henry Morgan is making quite a name for himself with his raids on the Spaniards. They're supposed to split the monies with the king and my father collects the treasure and sends it back to England."

"What's to keep the pirates from keeping the booty for themselves?" Crimson asked, interested.

"Nothing except the hangman's noose. Any pirate who

is caught and found guilty of pirating is sent back to England for hanging. Lord, there must be hundreds of pirates in the Caribbean, more out for themselves than there are for the king and country, but those that do split the profits must be fairly considerable. My father seems to enjoy his work, although how he can survive in that rough and savage place is beyond me. I have a brother, Christopher, who lives there too."

Crimson gazed at her husband, amazed. "There's so much about you I don't know," she murmured to herself. "I would have liked to meet your family."

"I don't think my father will ever return to England," Gardner said, staring at the letter idly. "Now that he has a new wife after being widowed for twenty-five years, I'm sure he'll want more children."

"How did your mother die?"

"She died when Christopher was born. I haven't seen Kit since he left for Jamaica when he was nineteen. Kit's not one to write, so I doubt that I'll ever hear from him, although my father mentioned him briefly in his letter, saying that he was master of his own ship now, working under Henry Morgan."

"Perhaps someday you would like to go to Jamaica," Crimson suggested, trying to imagine what his family must be like. "It might be exciting."

He shrugged. "Not for me, I'm afraid, my dear. Give me the soft life of a courtier any day to such adventures." He smiled to himself. "Good Lord, Father doesn't even know I'm married again. I suppose I'd best write him soon."

26

The mid-April day was gray and dismal, promising a drenching rain at any moment. The condition of the weather did not help Crimson's spirits any as she gazed dolefully out of her bedroom window.

"Shall ye be going out today, madam?"

Crimson turned to her new maid, Jenny, a plain, little country woman who had appeared on her doorstep a few days ago, asking for work. She had been a godsend, as Diane had been called to her home in Kent where her mother had taken ill and needed her help. Jenny had been hired without fuss and had proved herself a remarkably adept lady's maid.

"No, I think not, Jenny. This weather puts such a damper on my spirits. I haven't the heart to go shopping and a drive would be pointless. No, I'll just wait until this evening when I'm to attend the performance at the King's Theater. Have the ivory satin pressed for me, won't you?"

"Aye, madam." Jenny took out the gown and whisked it out the door efficiently.

A sudden yipping caused Crimson to smile as a little spaniel pup came gamboling through the door into her room, making straight for the hem of her robe. He jumped on her happily, his feathery tail wagging madly as he waited for her to pick him up. Crimson cuddled him to her chin, scratching his ears and rubbing his head. He had been a present from the king, one of a litter from Charles' own beloved bitch, and Crimson had been flattered at the personal air of his gift. She had called the pup Charlie, and had sent the king an effusive thank-you.

She was grateful that he hadn't done more after the incident on the barge. He seemed to be biding his time now, perhaps feeling sure that Crimson would come 'round soon enough.

She sighed to herself. Perhaps the king was right. There was no need to press her for her answer, for where else had she to go? The king could afford to wait.

"Ah, Charlie, I just don't know what to do," Crimson murmured to the pup, which waved its tail enthusiastically at the sound of her voice. "Life is so simple for you, isn't it? But just wait until you're older and you see a pretty little female, then you'll find out how complicated life can be!" She chuckled to herself.

The rain began coming down in sprinkles, which quickly turned into a heavy shower and Crimson put the pup down and rang for Jenny. When the maid arrived, Crimson ordered a light breakfast and inquired if Sir Reginald had eaten and left yet.

"No, madam. He's had breakfast in his room, but hasn't left yet. Did ye want me to give him a message?"

"No, thank you, Jenny. Lay out a morning gown for me, and I'll change while you get my breakfast."

"No need for that, madam. I'll be gald to help ye with yer dressing. Just give me a moment," and she scurried out the door only to return in a few minutes with her breakfast.

Crimson ate slowly, her mind dreaming. She had purposely begged off from many of the functions at court in the last two weeks, because of her fear of Castlemaine's intentions. The thought of facing the woman sent a chill up her spine. She hoped that the king would hurry and publicly bestow the woman with enough presents to keep her satisfied. Then, perhaps, she would not feel such hatred towards Crimson.

Unfortunately, the performance tonight was one that the king had especially wanted the court to attend as he

246

had helped to write some of the lines. Nell Gwyn, one of the king's current lights o' love, would be appearing on stage. She was a good actress and a cheeky, saucy sort who had endeared herself to the common people. They loved her as one of their own.

She had only just finished her breakfast when her husband knocked tentatively on the door. She nodded for Jenny to let him in, then dismissed the maid.

"What is it?" she asked.

She noted that he looked a little pale and his hands flickered nervously. He had not troubled to dress yet and, without his periwig, she was surprised to see that his hair was thinner than she'd supposed. This made him seem older.

"My dear, how are you?" he began, taking a chair.

"Fine, and you?"

He shrugged. "I'm afraid I may not be so fine after tomorrow. You see, gossip has gotten around to Brownwood that his wife and I—well, you know. He's got a terrible temper, and I'm afraid he's challenged me to a duel. He calls himself an honorable man and won't have his wife's reputation tarnished any longer. It does put some pressure on me, you see. I'm not the best of swordsmen."

"Well, it seems a little ridiculous. Hasn't the king banned all duels? If you did promise to meet this man, it would be against the king's express wishes. All you need do is inform Brownwood and—"

"He would call me a coward. I would be a laughing-stock at Court. I couldn't bear that. Anne would despise me."

"Is she really worth getting yourself killed?" Crimson asked sarcastically. "I'm sure there is another lady quite capable of satisfying your—needs."

"Don't be snide, Crimson. It doesn't suit you. I can see the prospect of my death hardly concerns you."

"Of course it concerns me!" Crimson put in quickly. "I didn't mean to seem flippant about it, my lord, but I don't see why you feel you must go through with it, if you are so frightened!"

"I am not frightened!" he countered, rising from his

chair. "You do have a way of cutting a man in two, my dear. I only came in to inform you that I would be dueling with Brownwood in the morning and—I just wanted you to know that—if something should happen to me—"

"Nothing will happen to you! Don't be silly. Tonight at the King's Theater, all you have to do is explain the situation to the king. I'm sure he can calm Brownwood down. Or, I can say something to the king, if you wish me to."

"No! God's blood, wench, don't you listen to what I say? The duel will take place. It's a question of honor."

Crimson sighed resignedly. "All right, but for heaven's sake, have him call his honor satisfied after blood is drawn. Surely, if he wounds you he can't ask for more?"

Gardner shook his head. "Perhaps you're right, my dear."

He started to leave, then turned back and looked at his wife with a smile of irony. "I suppose it would be the best thing for you, wouldn't it, my dear, if I were to be killed tomorrow? You would be free."

Crimson looked at him, but said nothing. Free? For whom, she wondered.

The King's Theater was a magnificent structure, vying in importance with the Duke's Theater, both playing companies trying to outdo the other in spectacular performances. It was a friendly rivalry, and the king frequently attended plays at the Duke's Theater, as did the duke go to the King's.

Tonight, both the duke and duchess were in attendance. In fact, all of the court who weren't ill or in disgrace were there. The women had dressed in the finest gowns and jewels, and the men had tried their best to outglitter them.

Crimson, arriving on the arm of her husband, looked about at the shimmering, perfumed guests and felt a thrill of exhilaration that could only be dampened by the arrival of Lady Castlemaine on the arm of the king. The woman caught Crimson's eye and threw her a triumphant smile.

"The king attends with the royal whore tonight," Gardner observed drily. "Perhaps everyone is counting her out too soon, eh, my dear?"

248

"Perhaps the king finds certain facets about her irresistible," Crimson added philosophically.

"I can imagine." Gardner's speech halted abruptly as a young couple approached them. The man was soberly dressed in dark brown, with very little decoration, and the woman in vibrant red, which complemented her brunette hair beautifully. "Good evening, sir, and Lady Anne."

Crimson curtseyed at her husband's introductions, wondering at the congeniality between the two men. Brownwood was limping slightly, and Crimson thought that they must have called off the duel until she saw the suppressed tears in Lady Anne's eyes.

"Six o'clock at Kensington's grotto?" Lord Brownwood asked tightly.

Crimson saw her husband nod slowly. "As you say, my lord."

The other couple moved on and Crimson followed her husband inside the theater in order to take their seats. They had a box quite close to the king, and the latter signaled them to come over to his box for a moment. Crimson would have preferred to avoid so direct a confrontation with Castlemaine, but followed Sir Reginald with a resigned air.

"Sir Reginald, Lady Gardner, we're pleased to see you with us tonight," the king said, taking the opportunity to kiss Crimson on the mouth.

"We're happy to be here, sire," Sir Reginald returned. "Crimson and I both enjoy theater, and the King's Theater has the best productions around."

"I hope I don't sound too immodest if I agree with you," the king responded, winking at his brother who was also in the box.

"Sire, hadn't we best get ourselves seated? The play is about to begin," Castlemaine interrupted brusquely.

"Of course, my dear, but I had hoped to ask Sir Reginald and his wife to sit with us. Lady Crimson's conversation can be most amusing." The king looked to his mistress with a challenging air.

Barbara accepted his decree with poor acquiescence and turned to the duke in order to engage him in conversation, pointedly turning her back on Crimson as she sat beside her. Warily, Crimson looked to the king, a question in her eyes, but Charles merely smiled and nodded, his eyes tender.

The play began, but Crimson was hardly aware of the gist of the plot, for Castlemaine endeavored to make her at her most ill at ease by ignoring her throughout the program. At the intermission, the king beckoned to Crimson to sit beside him. She was aware of his thigh touching her skirts and he leaned toward her intimately.

"Are you enjoying the play, Crimson?"

"Yes, sire."

"Then tell me about it," he said teasingly.

Crimson flushed, aware that he had caught her in a lie. "You must have been watching me, sire, and not the play," she accused him.

He smiled. "I certainly would rather watch you," he admitted without shame.

"You're embarrassing me, sire," she said, glancing around and noting that Castlemaine was studiously endeavoring to ignore them.

"I don't mean to, my dear. You see how clever I was to bring Barbara tonight. No one will ever suspect that I was really hoping to meet you in a lovers' tryst." His smile brought lightness to his words.

"Least of all I, sire," Crimson smiled back. Then she became more serious. "Do you know of the duel that is supposed to take place tomorrow morning, sire?"

"Brownwood and your husband? Yes, I've heard. Very little escapes me, Crimson."

"Then have you ordered Brownwood to put a stop to it? Your dislike of dueling is well known, sire. These two would defy it for some silly notion of honor."

"What would you have me do then? Put them both in the Tower, perhaps?"

"Well, you can put an end to it tonight by ordering both of them to their country estates," Crimson suggested hopefully.

"You don't want to see your husband hurt, Crimson?"

250

the king asked in some surprise. "I hardly thought it would bother you one way or the other."

"Sire!" Crimson said, shocked. "He is my husband. Besides, I wouldn't want to see anyone hurt. You must put a stop to it!"

The king shrugged. "I cannot promise you they will listen to me, but I will speak to both of them tonight." He leaned closer. "Does that put your mind at ease? And, perhaps, bring you a little closer to liking me?"

"Sire, I like you already," she murmured, veiling her eyes.

"I am glad to hear it, sweeting," he answered softly. His lips were close enough to touch her, and she could feel his warm breath on her hair. "My patience grows thin, Crimson. When will you come to me?" he whispered urgently.

"I—I cannot say, sire," she choked, pulling away from him.

She stood up to resume her seat, hardly daring to look at her rival.

27

"Madam, your husband is dead."

The words were still ringing in Crimson's ears hours later as she sat in her drawing room, staring at the wall, hardly able to believe that Sir Reginald Gardner was actually gone forever. He hadn't even been a real husband to her, she thought despairingly. They hadn't had time to grow old together, as he had put it. The notion itself escaped her. She had hardly known him.

"Madam, the king is here!" It was Jenny, her round face wearing a look of astonishment as she nervously folded her hands inside her apron.

"The king? I don't want to see him now, Jenny," Crimson said absently.

Jenny's mouth went into a round "*O*" of disbelief, but she scurried out the door without another word. Crimson went back to her daydreaming, wondering what would become of her now. She would be comfortably well off for a time, practically speaking, but the idea of being a widow was hard for her to grasp.

"Crimson, let me talk to you."

She looked up to see the king's tall form, lean and dark in the doorway.

"It is late, sire. What are you doing here?" she asked him, rising automatically to curtsey.

He motioned her to be seated. "Please, Crimson, no formalities between us here, now. I wanted to see you. I wanted to make sure that you were—all right." He moved into the room and sat beside her, taking her hand in his in a gentle gesture. "I'm sorry that Sir Reginald is dead."

"Thank you, sire." She took a deep breath. "I cannot say that his passing has left me totally destitute, but I can't believe that he is really dead. It's silly, I know, but I miss the thought of him being there, even though we hardly ever saw each other until the last. If things could have been different between us, this would never have happened."

"Crimson, you can't blame yourself," he said firmly. "You couldn't have changed the way he was. What happened this morning was—such a waste. Brownwood has been put into the Tower for now."

"What will you do to him?"

He shrugged. "They were both informed of my wishes as far as having the dueling stopped, but they chose to go through with it anyway. Brownwood has disobeyed my express command."

252

"And murdered a man!" Crimson put in.

"Not murder, Crimson. The duel was a fair fight since they were both willing participants. I shall have to punish Brownwood, but not too heavily, for he is one of my best commanders in the field. I shall leave him in the Tower for a few weeks and then send him back to the wars."

"That would hardly be a punishment for him, sire, as he seems to love the battlefield," Crimson interrupted with a touch of sarcasm. She looked at him squarely. "Why did you allow him to come home when you knew what might be the result?"

The king flushed. "Crimson, I do hope you aren't accusing me of plotting for just such an outcome!"

"Forgive me, sire. I know you could not be capable of such cunning treachery," Crimson put in, but her eyes had narrowed at the possibility. Could the king have wished her husband put out of the way for good? The idea seemed possible. Was the king that desperate for her? She shivered.

"You look at me without pleasure, Crimson," the king said gently. "Has this changed everything that was beginning between us?"

"Sire, please don't press me now."

He came closer, pulling her up from her chair, to stand pressed against him so that he could look deeply into her eyes.

"Tell me, Crimson, is there no hope for me? I love you, my dear. I want you. Let me comfort you tonight in your solitude." His voice was nearly pleading.

Crimson knew she was treading on thin ice. She could not continue toying with the king's affections much longer. He was like a half-tamed animal on a leash, who begins to exert more and more pressure until the leash snaps finally and he flings himself at his victim. She must give him an answer soon or he might be pressed to use force. She could never forgive him for that.

"Not tonight, sire, I beg you. Tomorrow. Tomorrow, I will give you an answer."

He seemed satisfied with her answer. "All right, Crimson, I will wait one more night for you. Tomorrow your answer must be yes, my love, for I will not be able to bear it if you spurn me again." He kissed her mouth with passionate intensity. "God's teeth, how shall I let you go tonight! Crimson, you drive me crazy with your indecisiveness, but I shall wait. I shall wait."

He released her and looked down at her flushed face. "I had better go now before my will escapes me and I take you now on the floor. Good night, my love." He kissed her hand lingeringly, then strode out of the room, leaving her feeling drained and weak.

"Tomorrow," she echoed, feeling an invisible net tightening around her.

She walked to the mantelpiece and laid an arm on it, resting her head against her forearm to think. Her skin felt the crinkly touch of old paper and, looking up, she saw the letter her husband's father had sent to him. Curiously, she picked it up, wondering if Sir Reginald had been able to write him to tell him that he had married again.

Dear Son (she read):

I'm sorry that it has been so long since my last letter, but there has been no news to speak of. Today, though, I have finally taken a new wife. Her name is Juliette de Silva and she is as beautiful as your own mother was, perhaps more. As you may have guessed, she is half Spanish and half English, and she is thirty years my junior, but so demure and intelligent that I do not feel at all fatherly towards her! You will forgive the shortness of this message, but she is waiting for me now in our bedroom and I am in haste to join her. I should like to have more sons as I no longer am able to see you and hardly see your brother, Kit, except when he is in Port Royal after one of his raids. He is master of his own ship now and a better sailor there never was under Henry Morgan. I am doing well as always here, in Jamaica, my coffers growing ever fatter from all the Spanish gold that drifts through here. If you should ever find yourself in need of funds, please write to me.

Your father,
Thomas Gardner

Crimson frowned, noting that the letter was very short, considering that it came from a father who had not seen his son in many years. She gathered that Sir Thomas Gardner was more interested in his new, younger wife than in his son faraway in England. At least he had directed him to write, should he ever find himself in financial need. She fought back a sigh, wondering how to tell the old man that his son was dead now, leaving a wife, who had never really even been a wife.

She rang for her maid, who entered almost immediately. "Jenny, I think I shall be retiring soon, and I have this terrible headache. Could you bring me a glass of wine, please?"

The maid's face took on an almost sly look, which Crimson thought she must have imagined. Jenny curtseyed and left to get the wine, returning a few minutes later with the cocker spaniel puppy at her heals.

"Charlie! I suppose he's been begging for scraps in the kitchen?" Crimson said fondly.

Jenny nodded and set the glass of wine on a low table next to Crimson's chair, before hurrying out of the room.

"Charlie, you've been making a pig of yourself, no doubt?" Crimson murmured, picking up the puppy, who settled himself happily on her lap. "Ah, I think I've spoiled you, my boy. You'll grow fatter than a butterball!"

She scratched the puppy's ears for a moment, taking pleasure in the feel of the silky fur. Playfully, he reached around as though to bite her hand and nipped it gently, growling in mock ferocity. She swatted at him and he rolled in her lap over the edge of the chair onto the table, spilling the glass of wine. With a puppy's eagerness, he lapped up the wine immediately.

"Oh, you naughty boy, look what you've done! That wine was for me, Charlie, and now I shall have to call poor Jenny again."

She got up to ring the bell and waited a moment, but the maid did not answer the call. Again, she rang, and the maid still did not make an appearance.

"That's odd," Crimson murmured to herself, picking up the puppy. "I wonder where she's gotten to so quickly." She patted the puppy's head and started out of the room when the dog let out a small half-cry.

"Charlie, what—" she began and then gasped as the puppy began to convulse in her arms. Hurrying back to the chair, she laid him down gently and rubbed his belly. "You see what that wine has done for you. It's given you a bellyache, my friend," she chided him.

The puppy's large dark eyes looked up at her silently, and his small body stiffened suddenly before convulsing once more. His tongue hung out and the liquid eyes slowly glazed over. Horrified, Crimson put her hand to his chest and could feel no answering beat. The dog was dead, in hardly more than a moment!

"Charlie! What happened? What happened?" she wondered aloud. She stood up and looked down at the glistening spots of wine still on the table. The wine! It must have been contaminated, somehow! She must tell Jenny to throw away any other bottles like it. Jenny—

Crimson hurried out of the room, lifting her skirts, running down the hall to the kitchen. The cook was gossiping with her majordomo and looked up with surprise on her face when Crimson rushed in, breathless.

"Where is Jenny?" she demanded.

"Jenny, madam? Why, I don't know where she is. She came in here just a moment or two ago to fetch ye a glass of wine, but—"

"She's gone!" Crimson said with a sudden conviction. "Did you see her pour the wine?"

Both of them shook their heads, wondering what had gotten into the young mistress. Crimson could hardly believe the idea that was slowly forming in her brain. Jenny couldn't have wanted to poison her, could she? Why? Why? The thought, unbidden and frightening, came to her. Castlemaine! Castlemaine wanted her out of the way. It wouldn't have been too hard to bribe Jenny to slip the poison into her glass. And Castlemaine hated her enough to kill her. Hadn't she already proved that?

"Oh, my God!" Crimson's hand went to her mouth and she rushed out of the kitchen and up to her room for her cloak. She would go to the king right away. He would be back at Whitehall by now, perhaps laughing into Castlemaine's eyes, perhaps letting his hand slip casually into her bodice—

She had a sudden conviction that he would not believe her. He had never investigated exactly what had happened that day on the royal barge. He had no reason to suspect that Castlemaine would try to kill her. Crimson bit her lip nervously. The king had let her husband be murdered this morning and let the perpetrator off with a slap on the wrist. He would not punish the woman who had given him so much sensual pleasure for eight years. No, she would be free to try again, knowing that the king would never suspect her.

Crimson let the cloak slip, unheeded, to the floor. It was useless to go to the king. Castlemaine would be rid of her sooner or later unless—unless Crimson ran away, somewhere where Castlemaine would not find her. If Crimson were gone, away from the king, there would be no more reason for her life to be in danger.

But where to go? She knew no one in England. Her husband's country estates would not be safe from the king's amorous advances, nor from Castlemaine's murderous jealousy. She could count her friends on the fingers of one hand, and even those might be tempted to turn against her. After all, she was still the stranger, the foreigner, and Castlemaine the woman in power. She had no one left to protect her.

France? The possibility appealed briefly to her, but she realized that Madame would send her back if her brother requested it. Violette could not house her. Crimson did not even consider James Haviland. She had divorced herself from him forever.

Her mind whirled in circles and then her memory jogged her abruptly. Jamaica! Sir Thomas Gardner seemed a sudden welcome refuge. Hadn't he written his

257

son that should he need help, please write? Well, she was Lady Crimson Gardner by law, and her father-in-law was the only one she could turn to: an impersonal, faceless stranger who, at least, would have no previous convictions about her. She breathed a sigh of relief at the solution to her problem. She would gather her belongings, enough jewelry and money to see her safely on the sea voyage, and put the rest in the hands of her husband's solicitor. She would have to close the house on King Street, but she would instruct the lawyer not to sell it until he received instructions from her. Jamaica was a far-away place, and she didn't want to sell all her options in England in case this move proved untenable for her eventually.

A stream of excitement was suddenly pouring through her as she thought about the place she was going to. It was unknown, it was wild and dangerous, but at least she would be free to choose her own future.

PART THREE:
Danger in Jamaica

28

       Crimson gazed down into the sparkling depths of the greenish-blue ocean, fascinated by the dark shadows beneath the surface which the captain told her were dolphins. Now and then, one or two would break the surface in order to suck in air through the opening in their heads, and then drive their bodies upward in an arc and splash heavily back into the ocean. Their capacity for play seemed boundless, and Crimson had watched them for nearly an hour.

"Lady Gardner, I see you're back at ship's side," the captain's voice broke in. He was a middle-aged gentleman, the owner of his own trading ship which sailed back and forth between England and the islands, and he made a profitable business for himself.

"Yes, Captain Anderson. Watching these dolphins is so much more interesting than sitting in my cabin staring at the four walls," she answered with a touch of humor to soften her boredom.

"Ah, I know how you feel, my lady. 'Twas the same with my wife. She used to travel with me when we were younger, but she hated the long voyage and the bad weather and poor rations. After a time, she began staying home, and now I don't see her half as much, but at least I know she's happier in her own house with the children. I do miss her though," he ended with a sigh.

"I'm sure she misses you too, Captain Anderson," Crimson added.

He coughed brusquely. "Well, enough of that, my lady. I wanted to inform you that we'll be arriving in Jamaica in four more days, if we're lucky and the weather holds, according to my navigator. It should be a relief for you once we're on dry land again, eh?"

"Oh, yes, Captain. Your hospitality has been boundless and I deeply appreciate it, but it will feel good not to have this rolling deck under my feet anymore."

"Good. Now I must get back to the poop deck, madam. I shall see you for dinner tonight as usual?"

"Most certainly, Captain," Crimson smiled. She watched his tall, barrel-chested figure walk back towards the poop, his rolling gait accompanying itself readily to the caprice of the ocean waves.

It seemed forever that she had been on this ship. She remembered vividly the night of her escape from London, for escape it was, in her own mind. She had dismissed the servants, sending them back to the Gardner estate in Kent with instructions to carry on through her solicitor until she returned. She didn't tell them that she might never return.

She had packed two trunks full of clothes and taken her best jewels and all of her money in a large leather pouch, which she sewed inside her cloak. Then she had called for a hackney and had the driver bring the trunks down. She had left the house completely dark and had not looked back at it as the driver whipped up his horses.

It had taken only minutes to get to the public posting house and she bought a ticket to Bristol, traveling on the public coach with only three other passengers, thus affording her a full half of one seat. The other three had been merchants on their way to Bristol for a cloth fair and had been quite jovial and pleasant companions on the long journey.

Once in Bristol, Crimson had had her baggage taken to a reputable inn near the docks where she set about trying to find a respectable captain to take her to the Americas. There were many ships bound for the islands, but most of the crew and captains were not the sort that Crimson could trust, knowing that she was completely alone.

She had had to remain in Bristol for nearly three days before she had taken the innkeeper's suggestion to visit the *Margaret,* an idea which appealed to her when she learned that the ship had been named after the captain's wife. She had gone aboard the ship, noting its relative cleanliness and safety, and had found Captain James Anderson in his cabin going over his cargo list.

"Captain Anderson?" she asked after knocking and receiving permission to enter.

"Aye, what do you want, madam?" He was not in the best of humors, as his departure had been delayed by four days because of a broken mainsail.

"My name is Lady Crimson Gardner, recently widowed, Captain. I have relatives living in the West Indies and am willing to pay you fairly for a cabin on your ship. I understand that you will be stopping in Port Royal?"

The captain looked at her shrewdly. "And why is a woman of your title going about seeking a ship on her own, madam? Have you done something wrong?"

Crimson had been taken aback by his observation, but recovered herself stiffly. "No, of course not. But I have no one in England now and after my husband's death I wished to leave as soon as possible."

"I understand, madam, and you must forgive me for seeming rude, but I must check all my passengers carefully for I seldom take on anyone besides the crew. I could be thrown into prison were I found harboring a fugitive from the king's justice." He smiled gruffly, but his voice tried to be more gentle. "How much can you afford to pay me?"

She straightened proudly. "I can pay you whatever the normal cost would be, Captain. I do not wish to rely on anyone's charity."

He shrugged. "All right, then. It so happens that my wife used to travel with me and had her own cabin. You can use that and we'll talk about payment later. Where is your baggage?"

"At the Knight's Inn, captain."

"Fine, I'll send one of my crew to pick it up. We'll be

sailing first thing in the morning, Lady Gardner, so I think it would be best for you to sleep in your cabin tonight. Agreed?"

Crimson couldn't help the sigh of relief that escaped her and the captain's brows flew upward. "You're telling me the truth, aren't you?" he asked. "I might remind you that once you're on board, I will expect complete cooperation from you as far as my orders are concerned. If I find out that you have come aboard under false pretenses, it shall go the worse for you."

She shook her head. "I'm just glad to be leaving England, captain. There is nothing here for me anymore."

It was true, there was nothing there for her, Crimson thought, staring at the ocean again, but no longer seeing the dolphins. She had left the king a letter, telling him simply that she was leaving England and might never return. She hadn't the heart to tell him why, nor the courage, but had dispatched the letter quickly to a messenger service with instructions to deliver it to the king in five days. She was glad she had allowed herself that much time.

As she stood, leaning against the railing, she suddenly felt eyes staring at her and turned around quickly to see a thin, young man standing a few feet behind her. Her mouth turned down in annoyance, for she had noticed the boy watching her before. He was perhaps a year or two older than she, but the look in his eyes and his overall bearing seemed to make him double her age.

His dark, monkeyish face was always alert, the dark eyes almost frighteningly penetrating, the mouth sulky and turned down in a perpetual half-frown. One hand had a nervous twitch that would mysteriously go away when he was about his duties on the ship. Crimson had seen him shinny up the rigging with a dexterity and ease that amazed her, but she could not bring herself to like him. He was too secretive, his eyes sliding away guiltily when she caught him staring at her.

Now, seeing him watching her, she grew angry and stepped towards him. "You, there, why do you stare at me? I don't like it and I shall complain to the captain if you continue to do it!"

The young man's hand twitched against his side and he brought his other hand across to hold it. He said nothing, his eyes touching hers briefly, then jumping away as he turned to retreat from her.

"Wait a moment! Did you hear me? Do you understand what I'm saying?" Crimson cried out, determined to make sure that the boy would not continue his silent survey of her.

He twisted about and stared at her. "I heard ye, me lady," he replied in a quiet voice. " 'Tis no crime to look about, is it, me lady?"

Crimson was surprised at his insolence. "We'll see if it is, if you continue to do so. I promise you I'll speak to the captain!"

He shrugged. "Aye, me lady, as ye wish."

Then he turned and loped off to the other side of the ship, leaving Crimson feeling as though she had been summarily dismissed. The rudeness of the sailor caused her an uneasy twinge, but she quickly brushed it away. She would be sure to mention it to the captain tonight at dinner and he would see to it that the young man stopped his perusal of her.

She left the railing to return to her cabin and take a short nap before dinner. She was always careful to dress up for the meal with the captain as she knew he appreciated the gesture. Inside the cabin, she stripped down to her underclothing and lay down on the bunk which was nailed securely to the floor, as was all the other furniture. She lay staring at the ceiling for a time, wondering what kind of reception she would receive at Port Royal. She hadn't had time to write a letter preceding her to tell them of her arrival, and it probably wouldn't have arrived before her at any rate. She was restless, unsure now, at this late date, if she had chosen the wisest course.

When it was time to get up and dress for dinner, she washed herself with the water in a large wooden bucket, some of the fresh water that she had collected herself after the last rain. Without the aid of a maid, she had taken to

265

braiding her long hair in one thick tail and twisting it around the back of her head. She chose a cool, light gown of yellow silk and sprinkled her best perfume on her neck and shoulders. A lace shawl thrown about her, and she was ready to proceed to the captain's quarters.

"Ah, you look lovely as always, my dear," Captain Anderson said gallantly, holding a chair out for her.

Crimson seated herself and inclined her head. "Thank you, Captain. It does revive my spirits to attend your dinner table."

There were only two other guests, the ship's physician and the captain's first mate, both of them typical seamen, bearded and gruff, but trying to make an effort to be polite with a lady present.

Conversation was light, mostly between the captain and Crimson, who plied him with questions about Jamaica. He was as informative as she wished, firing her imagination with colorful pictures of the natives, the villages and the brawling, lusty port city of Port Royal.

" 'Tis not the easiest town to live in, my dear. Your father-in-law, Sir Thomas Gardner, lives above the city in the governor's castle. I'm afraid we're between governors there now, so to speak. So Mr. Gardner is acting governor until King Charles appoints another. There is usually a time lapse of six months to a year after one governor leaves or dies before another arrives." He shrugged philosophically. "So go the workings of government."

"Do you know my father-in-law personally?" Crimson wondered.

"Not very well, madam. Sir Thomas is a busy man and has a great deal to do without me adding to his appointments. As long as I have no trouble, I simply unload my cargo and stay long enough to give my crew some port time and then leave with a new cargo bound for England again. 'Tis an uncomplicated life." He winked. "My wife likes it better that way."

"I'm sure that this will be quite an experience for me," Crimson said, "almost like an adventure of sorts."

"Adventure!" the first mate guffawed after draining his wine glass. "Port Royal is no adventure, my lady. 'Tis a

266

wicked, wicked city, full of rogues and thieves, and, aye, even murderers. 'Tis no fit place for the likes of yourself, my lady, if you'll excuse me for being so blunt."

Crimson reddened and looked to the capain, who gave his officer a stern look of disapproval. "Smith is right, Lady Gardner, in that the city itself can be dangerous, but hardly more so than London or Paris at night. I'm sure you will be well supervised if you take any trips to the city proper. Sir Thomas won't let his daughter-in-law be—in-convenienced—by any of the rabble that lives in the city."

"Is it really that bad?" Crimson asked, unbelieving, wondering how Sir Thomas could have remained there for so long if the city was as wicked as she had been led to believe.

The captain's eyes slid away self-consciously. " 'Tis the pirates and looters that make it that way, my lady. The previous governor had his hands full trying to extract the vermin from the city, but it was no use. They're thick as bees. There's just too many of them. Let us hope that the new governor, when he's appointed, will have more luck, but I doubt it."

The physician nodded in agreement. "Being a port city, it's natural for the pirates to congregate there. Oh, they have other cities that they have infested through the years, Santiago, Santo Domingo, Barbados, but there is a certain aura, I suppose you'd call it, about Port Royal that brings them there by the hundreds. I'm afraid, my lady, that I agree with Mr. Smith. You may wish to leave Port Royal as soon as you arrive."

After this dire prediction, Crimson turned once more to the captain for confirmation. "Are there no city guards or soldiers to enforce the law?" she asked.

He sighed. "There are soldiers, but the garrison is short of men and many of them are in the pay of the pirates, themselves. Some of them are honest, but they have their hands full and the prison can't hold everyone who breaks the law in Port Royal."

Crimson shivered. "You do paint a black picture, Captain. You sound as though I should count myself lucky if we don't make port."

"A young lady like yourself, the daughter-in-law of the acting governor, will have all the protection you need, madam. It is only that some of your activities may have to be curtailed at times." He shrugged. "If it weren't for the pirates, Jamaica would be a most beautiful place to live, an island paradise, some would say, including Sir Thomas."

"Well, I suppose I shall just have to be careful," Crimson said stoutly. "After all, London is not such an easy place in which to live and Whitehall," she winced, remembering, "can be a nest of vipers if one is not careful."

"Enough of this gloomy talk, my dear. Eat up. The cook made the goose especially for you and the stuffing is his own recipe, learned, he says, from a French cook."

The four ate hungrily, for dinner was actually the only real meal on board ship during the entire day. Other meals were taken on the run, and even Crimson did not sit down to a formal midday meal.

When they had finished, the captain, as always, offered to walk Crimson to her cabin. On board deck, he glanced up warily to the starless sky and frowned.

"Looks like we're in for a storm, my lady. These squalls out near the Carib' can be pretty mean ones."

"Will it come tonight?" Crimson asked, noting the clouds that nearly obscured the light of the moon.

He shrugged. "Could come tonight, probably will wait until the morning though. You might be obliged to stay in your cabin tomorrow. The waves can get pretty high and I've known men who've been washed overboard without a chance to scream for help."

Crimson looked at him curiously. "You don't sound too concerned, Captain."

"Of course, I'm concerned, my lady, but I don't get myself into a lather over it. No use doing that. When the storm comes, she comes, and all the cursing and fretting I do won't change its course nor its fury. The only thing you can do is be prepared for it."

Crimson sighed. "It's good to know you'll be piloting us through the storm, Captain. I'll sleep soundly for it."

He chuckled. "If that storm hits before morning, you'll

268

be lucky to get any sleep at all. If a big wave throws you out of your bunk, I guarantee you'll wake up! But seriously, if the storm does come tonight, tie yourself in the bunk with one of the blankets, otherwise you'll be black and blue tomorrow morning."

They had arrived at her cabin door and he bowed courteously. "I'll see you tomorrow. Let us hope we all sleep undisturbed tonight."

Crimson bid him a good night and closed the door.

29

Crimson was awakened abruptly by two things. The storm must have hit because the ship had started to pitch about wildly, throwing her against the side of the bunk. Also, the door to her cabin had swung open, letting in the light from the outside lantern. She swung her feet from under the covers in order to get up and close the door, thinking that the wind must have blown it open, when a shadowed figure appeared in the doorway and then stepped inside her room, closing the door behind.

"Captain Anderson? What is it?" she asked, sticking her feet back under the covers.

As there was no answer, she sat up in bed and peered into the half-light. "Who is it?" she called louder. "Who—"

A hissing sound interrupted her and the figure moved quickly to the bunk, putting a hand over her mouth so that

269

she couldn't say a word. Crimson brought both hands up to tear at the hand on her mouth.

"Shut up, girl!"

The voice was thin, whining and the hand over her mouth stank from sea bilge and stale fish. Crimson struggled in earnest now, the age-old fear of rape sweeping over her. The hand tightened, slowing her efforts as it cut cruelly into her cheeks and pinched her nose so that she had to gasp for breath. Her hands fell away and she was pushed back into the pillow.

"Now, then, wench. I'll be looking at ye all I want, I think," the voice whined again, a note of eagerness creeping into it.

Crimson's brain clicked and she remembered the boy on deck earlier in the day. She had forgotten to mention him to the captain, a mistake that could prove her undoing tonight, she thought frantically. The hand on her face was pressing down harder and Crimson's eyes closed as she fought for breath. He was choking her and in another minute she would lose consciousness. Then, blessedly, the hand's pressure softened and Crimson was able to take in air through her nose.

"Come on now, wench. Promise ye won't scream and I'll not make it so hard on ye. Ye'll only make it worse on yerself if ye try to fight me."

Crimson shook her head furiously, the idea of the slick grin on the monkeyish face making her sick. She could imagine his other hand twitching nervously, itching to tear at her nightgown. That thought and the odor of his hand on her mouth made her nearly retch as her stomach shook with a spasm of disgust.

"Damn ye, bitch! All right then!" And once more, the hand pressed down on her face, allowing only a trickle of air to get through so that her struggles lessened quickly and then ceased altogether.

Dimly, she could feel his other hand clutching at the bedclothes to peel them back and leave her defenseless against him with only her silk nightdress between him and her shrinking flesh. In another moment, the hand was at the throat of her gown, ripping it jaggedly to the waist so
270

that it separated into two halves and fell away from her breasts which were heaving for air.

Desperate, she bit at his hand and he jerked it away, allowing her to take a deep breath, but slamming down once more on her face before she could scream for help. The pitching waves had begun to make it difficult for her to keep from rolling on the bunk, and she slammed into the side of the ship. The violent movement caused the boy to lose his own footing and fall on top of her.

"Ahh, yes. That is better, isn't it, me little beauty?" he breathed on her, his hand biting into her lips.

She could imagine the twitching hand out of control as it neared her flesh and she tried to heave his body off her, but another wave rolled her helplessly against the side of the ship again, jamming her between the wood and his body. His free hand was feeling her breasts now, shaking uncontrollably as it pinched the nipples. It smoothed over her flesh, moving from her throat to her waist where it pushed at the material to reveal more of her.

"Lord almighty!" he babbled, moving with deliberate intent against her leg.

Crimson could feel the hardness of him straining against his breeches as he rubbed against her and she brought her leg up, trying to knee him in the groin. He guessed her intention, though, and quickly placed his body over hers so that she could no longer move her legs. He slid his lower body up and down over hers, the motion suddenly becoming faster so that in another moment he had collapsed on top of her.

"Jesus, I've spent me load just being near ye like this," he sighed, breathing hard as he relaxed on her. "Now we've got to wait a bit until I can get to ye proper."

He reached down to rip away the rest of her nightgown so that her nakedness was completely open to him. Fumbling a little at his excitement, he forced his hand between her clenched thighs and moved it upward, nearly causing her to jump from beneath him.

"Now, now there. It won't be so bad, wench, if ye'll just relax. I know how to make a woman happy. Learned it early from me stepmum, I did. Here now, don't that feel

271

good?" he asked when his fingers were finally able to reach their goal.

Crimson squirmed under him, bringing her hands up to catch his arm, trying to pull his hand away, but he would not allow her enough air and she was nearly on the brink of going into a faint. His elbow was boring into her side painfully and his breath in her face was nauseating.

"Ha!" he crowed suddenly, triumphantly. "Ye're wet, my fine lady. Young Jack Hawkins is exciting ye, ain't he? Now, just give me another minute and I'll make ye flood the bunk!"

A sudden hard movement of the ship caused both of them to spill out of the bunk onto the floor with him on the bottom so that he struck his head sharply, causing his hand to slip away from her. Crimson took a deep breath and then screamed with all her might before Hawkins pulled her over him and then rolled on top of her.

"I told ye to shut up!" he screamed at her. One hand swiped with painful accuracy at her face, jerking her head sideways. She could feel the welt begin to bloom on her cheek. "Damn ye for a bitch!"

Quickly, furiously, he pulled his breeches down around his ankles and brought one hand down to pull at his organ, jerking at it rapidly in order to prepare it for entrance. Crimson could not see him, her head rolling painfully on the floor. But at least she could breathe, and with the realization that his hand was no longer on her mouth, she screamed again and again until he covered her mouth once more, cursing foully.

The door to her cabin was pushed open suddenly and, thankfully, Crimson could see figures pouring into the room—the captain and the doctor. Thank God!

"You were right, Matthew! My God, I hope we were in time!" the captain cried out angrily. With a sudden roar, he pulled the boy off of Crimson's body, catching him by the back of his neck. He shook him like a dead rabbit and Crimson looked up to see the grotesquely swollen erection quickly shrink into a nonexistent threat. Quickly, she averted her eyes and tried to cover herself with the remainder of her clothing.

272

"Did he—did he rape you, my lady?" the physician asked, leaning down to help her to her feet.

Crimson shook her head. "No, no, he didn't. You came before—"

She began to weep silently and the doctor patted her awkwardly on the shoulder. "I'm sorry we weren't here sooner, but the storm had everyone occupied and it was only luck that I had to come back down to my quarters for bandages. I heard you scream as I was going back on deck and called for the captain."

"Thank you, oh, thank you!" Crimson wept fervently, clutching the doctor for support.

Gently, he led her back to her bunk, forcing her to sit down as he collected the covers and drew them around her. Then he turned to Captain Anderson, who was inexorably squeezing Hawkins' neck so that the boy was nearly blue in the face.

"She's all right, Captain. You're killing the boy!"

"Damn him, the greasy little weasel! I knew I shouldn't have added him to the crew in Bristol. Didn't like the looks of him then, but I was short-handed." He glanced over to Crimson and gritted his teeth. "Call someone to take him below and have him manacled to the side of the hold!" he ordered. "After this damned storm passes, I'll have the bastard keelhauled!"

"But Captain, that lad will die if—"

" 'Tis that or hanging from the main mast!" the captain roared.

"Aye, Captain," the doctor muttered and went to fetch another of the crew to take the boy down to the hold.

Afterwards, the captain came over to Crimson and gently lifted her chin up. "I'm terribly sorry, my lady, that this happened. 'Tis a danger among men long at sea when a woman is placed among them day and night, but the little scum was only just taken on at Bristol and I hardly thought I would have trouble with him on the first voyage. Not one of my other crew members has ever molested any of our passengers. Please accept my apologies."

"I'm all right now, Captain, thank you. He scared me badly, but I was not really hurt." Crimson clasped his

273

hand. "Will he really die tomorrow because of this? I don't want his death on my conscience, captain."

The captain took his hand away abruptly. " 'Tis for me to say, Lady Gardner. The boy will be keelhauled in the morning. If he lives, I'll throw him into the hold until we reach Port Royal, and decide what to do with him when we get there."

Crimson, who had no idea what being keelhauled meant, was silent for a moment. Then, gathering her courage, she asked the captain.

"He'll have a rope tied about his middle and be thrown into the sea to be dragged under the ship from one side to the other," Captain Anderson answered her grimly. " 'Tis a punishment I have never had to mete out before, but I'll not stand for a defenseless young lady being mauled by one of my crew. I have more pride in my ship than that!"

Crimson had swallowed sickly at the description of the punishment. But she realized that she would not be able to dissuade the captain from his course, and so she remained silent until he gruffly bid her good-night and left her.

Crimson sat on the bunk for a long time, bracing herself involuntarily against the continuing waves, listening to the cries of the seamen outside as they struggled against the storm. Finally, she got up and washed with what little water was left in the bucket, trying to cleanse herself of the sickly odor of the young sailor. She brought out a clean nightgown from her trunk and tossed the remnants of the other in a corner. She felt better afterwards and lay down on the bunk, holding on tightly as the waves continued to crash against the side of the ship. She realized after an hour had passed that it was useless to try to sleep and resigned herself to lying wide-eyed until the gray dawn arrived.

30

Crimson dressed slowly the next morning, feeling sluggish and drowsy after her sleepless night in the cabin. The memory of the boy's attack still filled her with remembered disgust, but she could hardly believe that he was going to die because of it. It was horrible to think of him being dragged beneath the ship's keel, his body scraping against its rough, barnacled surface. Would he even be able to hold his breath long enough to keep from drowning? She suddenly recalled that moment when she had fallen into the Thames and had nearly drowned. The murky darkness, the cold clamminess—it had frightened her more than anything else she had ever experienced.

With a sick dread, she finished dressing and walked up to the deck, noting the still overcast skies and the dripping sails. The air had a sharp sea tang to it this morning and there was a slight chill left from the passing of the storm. She shivered and rubbed her arms absently.

"Lady Gardner, there's no need for you to come up here," the captain said grimly, coming up beside her. "I don't think you'll find the activity today much to your liking."

"Captain Anderson, I can't believe you're going to do this. He's only a boy, after all, and—"

"Boy he may be, my lady, but he was man enough to

275

have raped you last night if the doctor and I hadn't come when we did. Think of that, madam, and perhaps you will not be so merciful to him."

Crimson bowed her head, silent, realizing that she could not change the captain from his course.

"Now, I'm requesting that you remain below, my lady, while punishment is carried out," the captain ordered.

A sharp whistle was sounded and Crimson turned to the opening of the hold to see the prisoner, Jack Hawkins, being prodded on deck. His hands were bound behind him with stout rope and his shirt had been torn off, revealing his thin chest which had several black and blue marks on it, left, no doubt, from the storm throwing him about below.

Crimson shuddered at sight of the thin, white body, imagining it on top of her last night. She tried to hate the boy, but could not and turned once more to the captain to make another appeal, but the latter had already begun walking towards the prisoner, after ordering one of the sailors to take her below deck.

"My lady?" the sailor muttered, inclining his head toward the steps.

Crimson started to speak, but the sailor shook his head. She started to walk towards the steps when a sudden shout from the crow's nest halted everyone in their tracks.

"Ship sighted to portside, Captain!"

Immediately, Captain Anderson rushed to the forecastle to grab his eyeglass, peering into it for a long time before signalling to First Mate Smith to join him.

"I can't make out her flag, Mr. Smith. Your eyes are sharper than mine. See what you think it is."

The first mate took the eyepiece and looked into it, then turned swiftly to the captain. "She flies no flag, Captain," he said steadily.

Suddenly, the ship became a beehive of activity as Captain Anderson barked orders. The sailor who had been ordered to escort Crimson to her cabin had disappeared and Crimson hurried to the forecastle, wondering what was going to happen.

"Lady Gardner, get to your cabin immediately!" the

captain roared. "I can't be worrying about your safety, madam!"

"But, what is it, Captain? Is there a danger?" she asked quickly.

He turned to her, exasperated. "A ship has been sighted, Lady Gardner. In these waters, any ship can spell danger. She flies no flag so it is possible she could be a renegade. Now, will you please obey orders and get below!"

"Yes, Captain," she said meekly.

She hastened away from the forecastle as the captain called up to the crow's nest to keep a look-out and see which way the ship was moving. Crimson noticed several men standing at attention beside the ship's cannon, but she realized, even without experience, that the cargo ship would be woefully outgunned by the other ship, if it proved to be a renegade.

"Captain, she's bearing fast, straight for us!" the look-out called down.

Crimson paused at the steps leading to her cabin and turned back to look out along the gray gloom, making out the sleek shape of the other ship. It was bearing towards them at a fast clip, its sails billowed out like the wings of some handsome bird of prey. Even from the distance still separating them, Crimson could make out her figurehead, the face of a woman with long, flowing hair and the body of a winged bird, cutting through the waves with an ease that amazed her.

She stayed where she was, her hand on the railing, watching the approaching ship with a kind of fascination. It was a beautiful ship. Her captain must be very proud of her, she thought. Now, she could see the figures of her crew running about according to the directions of her captain, a man she could not pick out yet.

Suddenly, she felt the *Margaret* list hard to starboard and realized that the captain was trying to outmaneuver the other ship. But it was useless. The *Margaret* was a cargo ship, too heavy to outdistance the sleek schooner that was getting closer with each passing second. Crimson felt a sudden thrill of—what was it? Excitement, fear? She wasn't sure, but her breathing was rapid as she stared at the approaching ship, her lips parted, her cheeks flushed.

"She's gaining on us, Captain!" This from the crow's nest once more.

"All right then, Mr. Smith, can you see no flag yet?" the captain piped.

"No, Captain, but from the cut of the ship, she might be English."

"Let's not be making predictions, Mr. Smith. She must be pirate or she wouldn't be breathing down our necks now. It's clear she's no cargo vessel by the look of her twelve guns on board. Have the bosun signal them and ask them what they want."

"Aye, sir."

Crimson waited impatiently for the answer, hoping against hope that the other ship would prove friendly, but the chances for that seemed highly unlikely, especially when the bosun turned to the captain with a look of dismay on his face.

"Captain, the ship's captain asks that we pull up and allow him to board."

"For what reason?"

"He knows we're a cargo ship, sir, and requires that we give him everything that's in our hold or—"

"Yes, Larrimee?"

"Or he will blow us to hell, Captain," the bosun finished nervously.

"God's teeth, the man must be daft! I'll not submit to his demands like some damned coward! I'll blow a hole through his pretty ship and—"

"Pardon me, Captain, but we must think of the degree of danger. He could blow us out of the water three times as fast as we could put our cannonball into his side," interrupted the first mate urgently. "Besides, look how he has manuevered into an invulnerable position. We won't be able to get a good broadside on him now, sir."

Infuriated at the truth in the officer's words, the captain threw down his hat and cursed terribly. At the same moment, the other ship fired a warning shot across the bow, obviously in a hurry for their answer.

"Damn and blast them!" the captain said between his

278

teeth. "In all my voyages, this is the first time I'll have sur-rendered to the scoundrels without a good fight. I've not lost many cargoes, Mr. Smith!"

"I know, sir," the first mate answered quietly. "What do you wish the the bosum to signal to them?"

Captain Anderson took a deep breath and let it out in a rush. "Tell them to come aboard, dammit! But we'll have our men ready if they try to do anything more than take our cargo!" He turned around abruptly and his eye fell on Crimson's worried face. "Lord!" he groaned inwardly. Then he left the forecastle quickly to come down to her.

"Lady Gardner, you heard, I suppose?"

Crimson nodded, not wanting the captain to know how frightened she was. Would the pirates keep their word not to take anything but the cargo? Could they be trusted not to murder everyone on board? She tried to stop the trembling in her limbs.

"I can't promise you that this is going to go all right for us," he began grimly, "but I do know that it would be best if they didn't catch sight of you. Pirates have a known tendency for taking pretty young ladies who might have some ransom value. We've got to hide you, my lady."

"I understand, Captain Anderson. I'd best get to my cabin."

He shook his head. "Not a good idea, my lady. If they do decide to search for passengers, it would be the first place they'd look." He glanced around swiftly, and his eye fell on three wooden barrels which had held rainwater through the trip. "Let me dump the water out of one of those barrels and you can slip inside." He glanced at her apologetically. "It will be uncomfortable for a time."

She shrugged, trying not to look dubious. "It's quite all right, Captain. I would rather be uncomfortable than the prisoner of some pirate brigand," she assured him quickly.

He called for one of the men to empty the barrel and then helped Crimson inside. She crouched down on her haunches as the captain fit the lid back on. He took out the plug so that she could breathe easier in the confining space and told her that he would be back to let her out as soon as possible.

Crimson could see nothing beyond the tiny circumference of the plug, which allowed her a view perhaps two inches in diameter, but she found that by putting her eye directly up to the hole, her view was widened considerably. She could see the deck in front of her and the men at their posts. Then she felt the bump as the other ship tacked alongside and sent out grappling hooks to secure the ship from rocking.

She strained to hear the words exchanged between the two captains, but their words were partially obscured by the din of the boarding pirates. She could see some of them, dirty, half-clothed ruffians with their cutlasses lashed securely to their breeches.

"To the hold, men, and be quick about it!" came a voice so close to her that Crimson nearly jumped out of the barrel.

From her vantage point, Crimson could not see the owner of the voice, but she assumed that it must belong to the pirate captain. A sudden kick at the barrel knocked it to one side and she strained to keep from falling and overturning the barrel. She braced herself as another kick came.

"Damn, Sven's not keeping my boots polished," came an irritated mutter. "I'll have to speak to him about it." And then louder, "Hurry it up, lads, we've not got all damn day!"

"Darling, there's probably nothing in the hold but animal feed," came a laughing voice quite close—a woman's voice.

"Countess! What are you doing here? I told you to stay on board, wench!"

"Don't be mad, lover." The voice was almost caressing now. "That stupid captain doesn't know I'm a woman."

"I don't care, you disobeyed orders!"

"Oh, don't act the disgruntled sea captain with me," she returned, pouting.

"Jesus, I don't know why I let you talk me into allowing you to come with me. You could get hurt."

"Not me, darling. You know I take care of myself," she purred.

Crimson couldn't help wondering what kind of woman would want to dress up like a man and sail under a pirate flag. She was obviously the captain's mistress, but what else was she—perhaps a murderess, a pickpoccket or a woman of the streets.

The captain of the pirate ship was giving more orders, hustling his men along the deck so that they could be finished with their work and cast off. The pirate crew had worked surprisingly fast and Crimson could imagine Captain Anderson's groans of anger as he saw all of his cargo neatly brought up from the hold and taken aboard the pirate ship. It represented a great deal to him because now he would receive no money with which to buy cargo at the various island ports and he would be forced to return to England empty-handed, a wasted trip.

"Now then, that does it, eh, lads? Let's shove off then!"

The man moved in front of Crimson's vision and she could see that he was tall and broad-shouldered beneath the ragged clothes he wore. A heavy, ornamented baldric crossed his chest over the torn linen shirt that had once been white, and was tied to a purple sash around his waist that seemed to be holding up the scruffy breeches. His feet were encased in knee-high jackboots that were the only thing about him that appeared new. His collar-length hair was night-dark and had been greasily braided in two braids on either side of his head, over which a dirty red scarf had been tied. There was a black eye-patch over his left eye and a terrible scar that split across his nose. As he lifted his hand to signal the crew, Crimson could see, through a rent in his shirt, a raised, red scar that ran the length of his ribs on the left side.

When the pirate captain turned, she shrank away from her peephole, fearing that he might discover she was in the barrel, but he was merely gesturing to someone who turned out to be the woman Crimson had heard before. Although she was wearing men's garb, it was obvious to Crimson that she was a woman, for the big, round breasts strained against the shirt and the breeches were tight enough to allow the curve of the womanly hips to show

281

through. She could not see her face as it was shaded by a wide-brimmed hat.

"Ahoy, Captain! Another ship sighted bearing the English colors!"

Suddenly, the pirate crew began scurrying over the deck, wishing to get back to their own ship and away before the English ship closed in.

"Damn! Where did it come from?" yelled the captain. "Let's go, lads!"

The grappling hooks were reeled in and the *Margaret* listed heavily as the other ship got under way.

Captain Anderson appeared beside the barrel and lifted the lid to help Crimson out. She was grateful for his quick assistance, since her leg muscles had begun to cramp heavily. She stood on the deck, watching the other ship moving away when a sudden commotion on the deck of the *Margaret* caught her attention.

Like everyone else on board, she had forgotten about Jack Hawkins, and now, it appeared, he had used that inattention to pilfer a knife from somewhere and had cut himself free. Now, he was running across the deck, several of the crew running after him.

One of the crew caught up with him near the ship's railing, and Hawkins swung the knife in a vicious arc, cutting the sailor's throat with a single swipe of the blade. The dead man fell backwards on the deck and with final desperation, Hawkins dove into the ocean and began swimming after the pirate ship, screaming at the top of his lungs.

Crimson watched in amazement as the boy was thrown a rope from the other ship and eventually hoisted aboard.

"Damn the scum!" the captain cursed, running to where the dead man had fallen. "Damn him to hell!"

The captain of the English man-o'-war promised to give Captain Anderson safe conduct to Port Royal. The ship had come alongside the *Margaret* and had learned of the pirate attack, but there was no time to catch up to the schooner as it had already disappeared in the gray morning clouds.

Captain Anderson graciously asked the captain to come aboard for dinner that evening. Crimson was invited as always. The meal passed quickly, for Captain Talent was a most congenial guest and kept the conversation lively in an effort to play down the day's unhappy experience. Finally, though, the subject was brought up and everyone had to deal with it.

"From your description of the man, I'd say it was the pirate captain who calls himself Barracuda," Captain Talent began. Seeing Crimson's puzzlement, he explained, "The barracuda is a fish, my lady, that's seen in these warmer waters. It's treacherous and bloodthirsty and one of the most dangerous of the sea creatures—and so, too, is Barracuda, the pirate who makes his living off defenseless ships like this one."

"How long has he been in these waters?" Captain Anderson asked.

The other shrugged. "Not very long. Three or four years, perhaps, but there's tales that he was the scourge of the Mediterranean before he chose to come to the Caribbean. There's not many who get a close look at him and live, but they say he's an ugly devil. I've also heard he's got a woman who sails with him."

"He does," Crimson cut in. "I heard her talking with him."

Captain Talent looked surprised. "If you were that close to him, madam, you're lucky to be here with us tonight. He's known to take women prisoners for ransom quite often."

"I was hidden in a rain barrel," she said, throwing a smile to Captain Anderson. "He was so close he even kicked it! I heard him talking with the woman. He called her Countess, I think, and he was angry because she'd chosen to come on board our ship with the rest of the crew."

"Countess, eh? The name hardly fits, for I saw her spit one of my own men in a fight! Gad, the woman is a tigress!"

"You think we were lucky then, Captain, that all they wanted was the contents of the hold?" Crimson asked.

Captain Talent exchanged a look with Captain Anderson. "Aye, madam, I do think you were lucky. Pirates are a bloodthirsty lot who don't give a damn—excuse, me, madam—about how many lives are lost in a fight. Most of them have black pasts and can hardly look forward to a brighter future, so their own lives mean very little to them."

"It sounds rather tragic, Captain," Crimson murmured.

"Aye, I suppose it would to you, my lady, but their kind is hardly to be pitied. Too many ships have gone to the bottom and too many lives lost for me to feel sorry for any one of them."

"Is there nothing you can do about their activities on the high seas?"

He shook his head. " 'Tis hard to patrol all these miles with only a few vessels, madam. And those pirates are clever. They take their booty to one of their strongholds in Tortuga or Barbados or Santiago, and then sail into Port Royal free as you please with no proof against them. Once
284

in Port Royal they can gain all the information they need as to what ships are sailing when and what cargo they'll have. It's dearly frustrating to me, my lady, believe me."

"And my father-in-law, Sir Thomas? What does he do about it?"

"As much as can be done. Oh, he puts them in the prison, but most of them escape before they can be hanged."

"Lady Gardner, you must understand that Jamaica—all these islands—are too far away from the king's arm of justice," Captain Anderson explained. "There are no formal courts, no judges here. The king orders that all major felons be shipped back to England for trial. Only the menials can be sentenced and punished here on the islands."

"Well, it does seem a stupid law," Crimson put in.

Captain Talent smiled. "Stupid, perhaps, my lady, but it is the king's law and must be obeyed by all law-abiding Englishmen."

"Perhaps someday it will be changed," she added.

"Let us hope so, for it would make it a great deal easier to clear the waters of some of these riffraff."

Crimson nodded, then put as a question the nagging thought that had been in the back of her mind. "And this Barracuda, as he calls himself, Captain—surely you must have some clue to his true name and station? I mean, cannot you buy informers from his own crew? From what you've told me, these pirates are not a trustworthy lot and would be willing to sell information to you about the identity of this man."

"Aye, my lady, your reasoning is sound, but the truth of it is that no one knows who the man is, except, perhaps, his lady companion, and she's not about to tell us. Why, we don't even know who *she* is! No, Barracuda has kept his identity a guarded secret, and because of all the secrecy, there's been no end to the rumors about him. Some say he's a Spanish nobleman whose wife was killed in an English raid, but he doesn't limit his victims to English ships only. Others say he's the bastard grandson of Sir Francis Drake, who was himself a pirate of sorts."

"But you don't believe it?"

"I don't know what to believe, my lady, but until someone brings in Barracuda, dead or alive, I've got to keep trying."

"Well, my lady, 'tis getting late," Captain Anderson broke in, glancing at the enamel clock inside its glass case. "I think it might be a good thing for you to be bidding us good night after today and—last night." He coughed.

"Oh, I'd almost forgotten about that boy. He—do you think the pirates have accepted him?" she asked.

Captain Anderson shrugged. "It's hard to tell, my dear. I was surprised they took him out of the water, but if they give him a chance I'm sure he can prove to them what a scoundrel he is. If I ever see the likes of him again, I'll not wait to get him back to English justice," he said meaningfully.

Crimson paled, remembering the dead man whom they had surrendered to the grave of the ocean floor only a few hours before. She stood up and said good night to the gentlemen, then hurried back to her cabin. After a moment's thought, she sat down on her bunk and undressed, glancing warily at the door. When she had finished and lay in bed, she found it hard once more to fall asleep. When she finally dropped off, her dreams were troubled by pictures of bloodthirsty pirates and a one-eyed pirate captain in the midst of them.

32

Crimson leaned over the ship's railing, staring out at the green jewel that lay in the middle of the blue ocean waters. Jamaica! She could see the mountainous peaks that bisected the island from east to west, sloping down to dark green rain forests and then on to the sandy beaches of the coastal plain. Beside her, the captain was pointing out the city of Port Royal, which she could see as a collection of buildings of all shapes and sizes, all congregated on a narrow strip of sandy beach which was connected to the main portion of the island by an isthmus of sand.

In the bay, there was a collection of ships of all kinds, from the small pirogues, or canoes, made from tree trunks, to the three-masted schooners that waited majestically, their white sails billowing in the breeze. Vainly, Crimson looked for a ship with the figurehead of a woman with the body of a bird, but she couldn't find it among the amazing array of ships.

"Do you think the ship that ransacked us is moored in the bay, Captain?" she asked.

He shrugged. "She could very well be, as the town is a home base for many of the buccaneers in the area," he answered gravely. "It's very likely that the Barracuda, himself, is enjoying himself at one of the taverns, swilling ale and rum, patting his fellows on the back." He snorted in

287

disgust. "If I ever catch up to that Hawkins boy, he won't have a back to pat!"

Crimson shivered. "I'll go below and close up my trunks, Captain," she said, to change the subject. "How long before we go ashore?"

"An hour at most, my lady. I'll have your trunks rowed ashore after we get you on the dock. Is your father-in-law going to be there to meet you?"

"I didn't have time to write him," she admitted. "But I'm sure I will be able to find someone to take me to the governor's house."

Captain Anderson shook his head skeptically. "I hardly think so, Lady Gardner. You'll not want one of those wharf ruffians to take you. They're not to be trusted with your belongings. Besides, they'd charge you some exorbitant price for the use of some broken-down wagon. I'll have to make arrangements for you myself."

"Oh, I hate to bother you, Captain. You've been so kind already. I know you have things to do as far as the cargo and all—" She stopped lamely.

"I consider it my duty, Lady Gardner. Now, you'd better go below and get your things together."

Crimson went to her cabin, feeling not at all unhappy that she would be leaving it even though it had been her home for over two months. She carefully repacked the dresses and other articles that she had used for the voyage, glad that she had had enough water to wash them out. Then she opened the drawer to the sea chest that was nailed to the floor, in order to get out her leather pouch with all her valuables.

"They're gone!" Frantically, she searched the entire chest, but could find nothing, not a bauble, a loose jewel or one coin to indicate that her treasures had once been there. "They've been stolen!"

Desperately she went through her own trunks, thinking that she might have put the pouch back in there and forgotten about it, but it was not to be found. All her money, her jewels, everything of value that she had brought with her was gone! The thought of going to her father-in-law

288

without a shilling made her feel somehow defenseless. And he was still a stranger to her!

She ran back up on deck and found the captain on the poop deck. "Captain Anderson, someone has stolen all my valuables!" she cried out.

"Stolen! Lady Gardner, are you sure? All my men have proven themselves honest and trustworthy. Did you check everyplace?"

She nodded. "I'm sure I put my pouch in the sea chest in my room, but it's not there. I checked my trunks on the chance that I might have packed it away sometime during the voyage, but it's not there either. Captain, I'm sure it's been stolen!"

He shook his head then sighed. "All right, Lady Gardner, I'll order my crew on deck for questioning, and, if need be, I'll have the ship searched."

"Thank you, Captain."

Crimson returned to her cabin, realizing that her discovery of the lost valuables would probably delay the captain's schedule even more, and that he would not be too pleased about it. But she knew someone must have taken them! She had taken the pouch out several times during the voyage in order to wear a necklace or a ring to the captain's table for dinner.

Over an hour later the captain knocked on the door. "Lady Gardner, I'm sorry, but none of my men have seen the pouch. I have to believe them, for I made a quick search of their quarters, which revealed nothing."

"Captain Anderson, I remember taking out the pouch to wear that emerald ring to dinner on the night before the storm. I—" She stopped suddenly, her face a mask of surprise. "It must have been Hawkins! He must have taken my valuables!"

"Then they could only be somewhere in the hold, my lady, for he didn't have them when he dove into the sea."

But they couldn't be in the hold, Crimson thought quickly, not after the pirates had taken everything out! She said as much to Captain Anderson, who reluctantly agreed.

"You're right, Lady Gardner. If your valuables were in

289

the hold, I'm sure they're not there now. Those ruffians wouldn't have missed that."

"Then I have nothing left!" Crimson groaned. "Everything else in my husband's estate is still in England. It will hardly do me any good there!" She was on the verge of tears, so bitter was her despair.

"My lady, I'm truly sorry, but I'm sure Sir Thomas will be able to help you out. He can dispatch a letter to your solicitor in England in order for you to obtain more funds. I hardly see the need for tears."

Crimson attempted to wipe her eyes with her handkerchief, aware that the captain, too, had been left with nothing by those thieving pirates! She wiped her cheeks and sniffed hard.

"You're right, Captain Anderson. And now, I've delayed you long enough. My trunks are ready and so am I."

She went back out on deck and waited for the longboats to be lowered into the water. She was aware suddenly of the sunshine and heat of the place and was glad she had chosen a light silk gown to wear for her meeting with her father-in-law. The jauntily feathered silk hat on her carefully arranged curls made her appear braver than she felt and she clutched her skirts tightly as she climbed down into the waiting boat.

When the captain was seated beside her, they cast off for the shore, the sailors using powerful strokes to close the space between the ship and the docks in only a few minutes.

On shore, Crimson could see piles of dry goods, tightly packaged bales, and a morass of people, mostly men milling about, checking incoming goods and marking lists off as outgoing goods were loaded on board ships. Many of the men looked as though they might be pirates themselves, and she realized that it was very probably true. She was glad of Captain Anderson's protection as she searched the variety of faces, unconsciously looking for a black eye patch and a scar shaving across a broad nose. She was relieved when she did not find them, but, nevertheless, could not help a slight tingle of fear as they neared the docks.

The boat was tied to a post and Captain Anderson

climbed up a short ladder to the dock. Some of the men who were standing close by looked at the young lady stepping out of the boat with interest. Others ignored her, intent on the categorizing of goods. Two men a few feet away from where Captain Anderson was extending a hand to help Crimson up began quarreling drunkenly, interspersing their uncouth language with half-hearted swipes with their fists.

Even as Crimson was stepping onto the dock, the quarrel became a full-fledged fight as others joined in the foray. Suddenly, the dock was a storm of moving bodies and hamlike fists smashing into stubbled jaws. It was impossible to go through them, and Crimson shrank against Captain Anderson, wondering whether she should return to the boat or stand where she was.

"These filthy scum can't have a conversation without a fight breaking out," Captain Anderson muttered in disgust. "We'd best wait a bit, Lady Gardner, before we try to go through them. The fight could turn ugly, and I wouldn't want you to be in the middle of it."

It was more a drunken brawl at the moment, with several of the antagonists being thrown or punched into the water, only to emerge hiccupping stupidly and struggling to the beach beneath the docks to sleep it off.

Crimson nearly jumped when she felt Captain Anderson start forward, raising his hand and waving wildly in an attempt to be heard above the noisy brawlers. For a moment, she thought he was going to try to intervene in the fighting, but then she realized he was trying to get someone's attention.

"Mr. Gardner! Christopher Gardner! Ho, there!"

Gardner! It must be her husband's brother. Crimson remembered that Reginald had briefly mentioned Kit to her. Curious, she craned her neck to see above the men in front of her, trying to pick out the man whom Captain Anderson was signalling.

A tall, muscular man, with dark hair beneath his wide-brimmed hat, had stopped some yards away and was trying to locate the person who was calling to him. He was dressed in brushed leather breeches tucked into knee-high boots and a white linen shirt, over which a brown leather jerkin had been buttoned. She couldn't see his face, but was relieved when he finally located Captain Anderson and waved back in recognition. He began to make his way through the crowd, shouldering many of them aside.

Sensing that they were about to be rescued from their worrisome position, Crimson let go of the captain's arm and stepped a little to the side to avoid one of the brawlers. At the same time, two men who were clutching tightly to each other stepped towards her and then slammed heavily into her, causing her to lose her footing.

With a forlorn cry, she threw up her arms and tried to regain her balance, but she was too close to the edge of the dock and fell into the water below. For a moment, she was too disoriented to realize what had happened, and she opened her mouth to scream, succeeding only in taking in water. A horrible fear seized her as she was suddenly transported back to London and the Thames River with Barbara Palmer looming over her, watching her drown with satisfaction. Determinedly, she kicked her feet and surfaced, feeling sand beneath her and trying to get a foothold, trying to fight down her panic.

Strong arms scooped her up and held her high against a hard chest and she stopped struggling in order to take deep, rasping breaths of air.

"Quiet now, wench," a voice soothed her. "You're all right now."

She opened her eyes and realized that she was being held above the water, which had only been chest-deep above the shelf where she had fallen. She relaxed with a sigh of relief and looked up gratefully into the lean, sunbrowned face of the man who had rescued her. For a moment, she thought she was looking into her husband's face and drew in a quick breath of surprise.

"Christopher Gardner, wench, at your service," he smiled.

When he smiled, Crimson could see the difference, and noted the dark-brown eyes, the hawklike nose and firm-lipped mouth beneath a black moustache. At the same time, she was aware of the drunken shouts and clapping

292

coming from the dock and looked up to see several of the fighters staring down and cheering her rescuer. She flushed in embarrassment, aware of her drenched clothing, her ruined coiffure and her loss of both of her slippers.

At the urging from above, the man grinned up at them, nodded and bent his head to place a firm kiss upon her mouth. Crimson was so surprised she could only lie back in his arms and allow him her lips which were soon warmed by his own.

"Ah, come on, Kit, ye can do better than that!" called someone laughingly.

"Let's see ye bed her in the water, Kit, lad. 'Tis the only place ye've not tried yet!" put in someone else.

When he released her mouth, Crimson brought her hands up to shield her face from any further onslaught. "Please, sir, if you will hand me over to Captain Anderson."

Laughing, he handed her up to the dock where a red-faced captain helped her to her feet. "Are you all right, my lady?" he asked with concern.

"Y-yes, Captain, thank you."

"I'm grateful, Mr. Gardner, for your timely assistance," the captain said as the other man jumped up on the dock and shook himself like a wet dog.

"You're more than welcome, Captain Anderson, but I wonder if the young lady can't speak for herself. Have you no thanks to bestow on your rescuer, wench?" he asked insolently, taking the liberty of brushing sand from the front of her gown.

"I believe you have already taken your thanks, sir," she answered, slapping his hands away angrily. As infuriating as his brother, she thought with dismay.

"Pardon me, my lady. Mr. Gardner, may I present Lady Crimson Gardner, your—ah—sister-in-law. Mr. Christopher Gardner, my lady."

"Call me, Kit, please," he said, taking off his still-dry hat to bow jauntily before her, not at all flabbergasted by the fact that she was introduced as his brother's wife.

"I'm your sister-in-law," she repeated, wondering if he

293

hadn't understood the first time. "I was Reginald's wife for two months."

"*Was?*" he questioned, frowning. "I take it, madam, that that means you are either his widow now or a divorced woman. Which is it?" He was laughing silently at her haughtiness.

"My husband died several weeks ago in a stupid duel," she answered bitingly.

"Over you, I trust," he responded, letting his eyes travel over her figure with frank admiration. "How did my brother ever manage to land you, my dear? His other two wives were, I heard, quite dreary and not at all my type."

"Well, I don't think I'm your type either, Mr. Gardner," she huffed.

"Call me Kit, all my friends do," he said, reminding her deliberately.

She ignored his words and tried to tuck the wet curls away from her face. Disconsolately, she glanced down at her gown, aware of what a picture she made, dripping seawater onto the dock.

"I must get somewhere and change," she murmured to herself.

"Well, I had thought that as long as Mr. Gardner was here—" the captain began, silently appealing to the other man.

"Precisely, Captain Anderson. I'm here now and will take charge of my dear sister-in-law. I'm sure my father will be most interested in Reginald's latest wife. By the way, madam," he said, leaning towards her intimately, "were there any children coming along on the next boat?"

She reddened at his insolence. "Sir, I have already told you we were only married two months and—"

"Hardly enough time for a child, I suppose you're right," he said quickly, but there was no repentance in his smile. His eyes glanced down her body deliberately and Crimson felt an urge to slap him.

"If you please?" she said through clenched teeth. "My trunks should be along shortly."

"Of course, let me show you to my carriage." He offered her his arm which she ignored until she was offered the prospect of elbowing her way through the male crowd by herself. Then, in disgusted resignation, she placed her hand on his sleeve.

Turning back to the captain, she thanked him for everything, assuring him that she would welcome his company whenever he was in port again. The captain waved and smiled, then turned to his crew, relieved that he had dispensed with his passenger without undue fuss.

Crimson let her brother-in-law thread their way through the crowd until they reached his carriage, an open carriage, smartly outfitted and trimmed in gold. Once there, she shook off his arm in irritation, and proceeded to climb into the carriage herself.

Gardner shook his head, then smiled up at her. "You know you ought to feel lucky that I happened to take my father's carriage today. I doubt that you would have enjoyed riding double on my horse."

"I doubt that I shall enjoy riding in this carriage with you!" she returned flippantly.

"Well, we shall have some company, as I have to pick up my stepmother's maid at the dressmaker's."

"How far is that?"

"Only two streets away, so don't worry. I shan't have enough time to rape you before then," he whispered, ogling her.

She folded her lips primly and refused to rise to his baiting. He shrugged and got in the carriage, opposite her, folding his legs, carelessly letting his foot rise beneath her hemline. She moved her own legs to avoid any contact with his, and he ordered the driver to the dressmaker's shop.

He studied her silently as they rode. "You know," he said suddenly, "you're dripping all over the carriage seat. My stepmother won't appreciate that. She's very particular about her possessions."

"I thought you said this was your father's carriage," she returned.

He shrugged his shoulders. "Oh, what's his is hers, you understand. They share most everything, so long as dear

Juliette gets the bigger piece of the pie." His remark was made almost contemptuously.

"I daresay you and your stepmother don't get along, from the tone of your voice," Crimson observed curiously. "Perhaps you find it difficult to get along with most women, Mr. Gardner?"

He grinned. "You do have a talent for rubbing people the wrong way, don't you, Crimson? Perhaps we're a lot alike in that respect. Don't you think it might behoove us to get to know each other better?"

She shook her head precisely. "I doubt it, but I suppose I shall see a lot of you."

"Not much, as I do have quite a lot of traveling to do. I—"

Interested, Crimson leaned forward suddenly. "Yes, I remember my husband telling me that you serve under Henry Morgan in helping rid the Caribbean of pirates."

"Well, I do my best, but—"

"Tell me, have you heard of a pirate captain named Barracuda in these waters?" she asked intently.

He looked surprised. "Of course, everyone knows about Barracuda. He's one of the worst menaces to ships in the area. He's not too selective in his targets either. He preys on English as well as Spanish and French."

"Well, he attacked the *Margaret* a few days ago on the open sea and took everything in Captain Anderson's hold. I'm positive he stole my jewels and money too," Crimson said quickly.

"He stole your valuables? But, my dear Crimson, if he knew there was a lady on board, I'm surprised to see you here now. I've heard he has an eye for women, and I'm sure he wouldn't have missed you." He grinned engagingly, but his charm was lost on Crimson.

"Captain Anderson hid me in a water barrel," she said matter-of-factly. "Otherwise, I'm sure he would have kidnapped me." She shivered.

"The captain's a wise man. I must say I don't know him very well, but he does have a good delivery record. Tell me, what did this famed pirate look like? Did you get a look at him?"

296

"Ugly!" Crimson blurted. "Greasy dark hair and a black eye-patch and a terrible scar across his nose. Tall and broad, and he had a woman with him that he called Countess."

"We've heard of her, but no one knows who she really is," he frowned. Then he glanced at Crimson sharply. "But you said that these pirates stole all your valuables. Does that mean you have nothing but your clothing?"

She drew herself up stiffly and nodded. "Yes, but I can make arrangements with my banker in London should I need any financial assistance. I don't want you to think I came here to rely on your charity."

He leaned towards her lazily. "I don't know about my father, Crimson, but I wouldn't count on my charity at all. I exact payment for all favors done for anyone, and, in your case, I might prove rather greedy." He let his eyes slide over her body again.

Crimson pulled self-consciously at the stuff of her gown, feeling its wet stickiness against her skin. She did not deign to reply to Gardner's innuendo, but remained silent until the carriage stopped to pick up the maid, whose eyes went round with surprise when she saw the sopping young lady.

"It's quite all right, Maggie. This is Lady Gardner from England, the wife of my recently deceased brother. She will probably be staying at the house for some time."

"Aye, sir," Maggie replied. She sat next to him, quite close, and Crimson couldn't help be aware of the attraction between them. She was a little relieved that her brother-in-law had a love interest already, for she had no real wish to get involved with someone so like her husband.

"Well, Maggie, what did you pick up for Juliette today?" Gardner asked, chucking the girl, who looked to be the same age as Crimson, under the chin.

"Some hair ribbons, a bit of lace trim to fix the piece she tore off the other day when she got so furious with the groom." Maggie shrugged. "She's got a temper, that one."

The maid looked at Crimson as though wishing to impart important news which could prove useful. "The mistress can fly into a terrible rage because of the wrong color in a pair of shoes, or the fact that it's raining outside when she wants to ride her horse." She sighed. " 'Tis not easy working for her."

"Ah, but Maggie, my love, if you didn't work for Juliette, you would never have met me, eh? And that, sweetheart, would have been worse than what chores my stepmother has you do for her."

"I do hope your stepmother doesn't consider my coming an inconvenience," Crimson said tentatively. "I wouldn't want her to think—"

"Don't worry, Crimson. She'll think whatever she likes, but it will be up to my father to make the decision on whether you stay or not. Just hope that Juliette doesn't think you're as beautiful as she is, or she might influence my father to cast you out. She can be a heartless bitch at times."

33

Crimson was impressed with the governor's house, which was really a stone castle-fortress that stood on a sloping rise, commanding a clear view of the town of Port Royal and the bay. The castle was built on the main body of the island, and one had to travel out of the town and over a bridge that connected the two beaches.

"It's quite large, isn't it?" Kit Gardner murmured, noting Crimson's awestruck face. "So you see, there'll be quite enough room for you."

"Oh, but, Mr. Gardner, I—"

"Kit," he admonished teasingly.

Crimson gave in graciously. "All right then, Kit, I can hardly believe the castle was built just to be the residence of the governor. Why there's enough room to house a regiment of soldiers!"

"Quite right, Crimson. It's actually a fortress. See those cannon on the wall there? They can be aimed to fire directly on ships entering the bay. Actually, only about a third of the building is used for the governor's private needs. Most of it is used for housing soldiers, supplies and, of course, the treasure that must be sent to the king. Below the castle, built into the slope itself, is the dungeon, used for prisoners, a dreary place full of rats and moisture. I wouldn't recommend a visit there."

"I'm sure I'll take your advice," Crimson murmured.

The carriage traveled over a small bridge and pulled into the courtyard within the interior of the surrounding walls. Kit helped the two ladies out and they went inside.

"All right, Maggie, love, off to the wicked stepmother you go," Kit laughed, giving the maid a fond swat on her backside.

Giggling, Maggie wiggled her hips and scurried up the curving staircase, leaving Crimson standing with Kit in the vast hallway.

"I think Father is in the library, Crimson, if you'll follow me."

"Don't you think I should change first and arrange my hair?" she asked doubtfully.

He glaced over her skeptically. "It doesn't matter. You're still beautiful. Besides, it will take a while to have your trunks brought up. I'll send one of the boys down in the wagon for it. I'm afraid you'll just have to do as you are, Crimson."

He led her down the hall and into a large room filled with books of every kind, lining the walls in shelf after shelf. In the middle of all this collection of knowledge stood a handsome, polished desk, piled with maps and

299

documents, and behind the desk sat a man, broad-shouldered and tall like his sons, with pure white hair and dark, brooding eyes. Those eyes were fixed questioningly on Crimson now.

"Hello, Father, I'd like you to meet—"

"Not another of your hussies, Kit. This one looks as though she's arrived from some muddy fishpond. Aren't the taverns good enough for you anymore?" the old man muttered crossly. "Can't you see she's dripping on the carpet? Take her up to your room and get her wet clothes off. I'm sure you won't find it difficult." He sniffed disdainfully and prepared to go back to his paperwork.

Crimson flushed in humiliation and looked up to see Kit laughing silently. His apparent unconcern made her embarrassment all the more complete and she wished she could suddenly be whisked out of the room by some kind of magic.

"Father, if you'll allow me to introduce Lady Crimson Gardner, your recently bereaved daughter-in-law."

"What! What did you say? Kit, is this your idea of a joke? Why, Reginald hasn't written me anything about a new wife. His last one died a few years ago."

"Apparently he didn't like remaining a widower, Father, for he married this young lady in—" he glanced at Crimson.

"In February," she finished. "We were married in Kent, at his country seat. He lived only two months after our marriage and—"

"He's dead? Reginald is dead? Young woman, how do I know you're telling the truth!" the older man demanded, rising from the desk.

"Here is the wedding ring he gave me. I think it was his mother's ring. I had other of her jewelry that he bestowed on me, but it was stolen by pirates on the voyage over here. My marriage document is in my trunk," she finished defiantly, glad that she had thought to bring it. She really hadn't thought about whether the man would accept her as his daughter-in-law.

"Well, then, I'm sure I will need to look at it. How did my son die?"

"He was killed in a duel over a woman—his mistress." Crimson pinkened once more. "He insisted on dueling even though he knew the other man was a better swordsman than he. It was the lady's husband who killed him."

"God's blood, what a fool he was! Reginald, Reginald —I knew he would find trouble some day. He was too reckless, foolish." He glanced up to Crimson sharply. "But why did you come here?"

"I—I had nowhere else to go. I have no family of my own and I had to leave England because—because after Reginald's death there was no one to protect me."

"Protect you? Protect you from what?"

Crimson took a deep breath. She had a feeling that this terrible ogre would find her out if she lied. "There was a man who was attracted to me and—his—mistress tried to kill me. I know it sounds complicated, but it is the truth. She tried to have me murdered and when her attempt failed, I ran away. I had to leave England and I thought of you, here. I had hoped that you would welcome me," she ended with accusation in her voice.

"Is that all?" he demanded, coming around to the other side of the desk.

She looked at him blankly. "What do you mean?"

"I mean, young lady, that you appear in my house, dripping wet, and tell me an improbable story like that, and expect me to believe it?"

Angrily, she glared at him. "I'm telling you the truth! You wrote to Reginald and told him that if he needed help to write you! Forgive me if I thought that your help would extend to his widow!" She turned around to stomp out of the room.

"Wait a minute! You'll stay right where you are until I find out exactly what is going on," the man commanded. "Kit, what have you to do with all of this?"

His son shrugged lethargically. "Nothing at all, Father, believe me. I only just met the young lady myself on the docks. She just arrived on Captain Anderson's ship this morning. After she fell into the water, I gallantly saved her from drowning and found myself obliged to bring her up here."

"Hmmph! Well, at least I can be thankful she's not one of your tavern wenches parading as my daughter-in-law!" He turned once more to Crimson. "Where are your trunks, young lady?"

"They're still on Captain Anderson's ship, but he'll be bringing them ashore shortly. I would appreciate it, if you're not going to give me welcome here, that you let him know before he brings them in. I shall be happy to leave here tonight on his ship, rather than throw myself on your—hospitality," she said with a touch of sarcasm.

"A spirited little lady," Sir Thomas mused, rubbing his chin. "Tell me, how did you manage to persuade Reginald to marry you?"

"I'm afraid, Sir Thomas, that I was sold to him in order to pay off a debt that my—my father had incurred. Lord Haviland owed your son over one thousand pounds from gambling debts. Your son said he would wipe the slate clean if I would consent to be married to him. Naturally, my consent was never really needed, for Lord Haviland arranged the marriage himself."

"But why would Reginald agree to such a bargain? I always thought him a clever boy, but to wipe off a thousand pounds for the privilege of being your husband?"

Crimson bit her lips. "I was connected with King Charles' sister, Madame of France. Reginald thought that if I became his wife I would have some influence over the king, thereby helping him up the social ladder."

"Ah, I begin to see now. Perhaps Reginald wasn't being stupid after all."

"I assure you I wouldn't have taken the trouble to fabricate this story just for the privilege of being cross-examined by you, Sir Thomas!" Crimson explained furiously. "I dislike being called a liar by anyone, and especially so since the name is unjustifiable!"

Thomas walked up to her and looked into her face. "Perhaps you are telling the truth, my dear. I still cannot understand why you would choose to come to Port Royal when its reputation would hardly recommend it to a lady of your standing, but I suppose if you truly are my daughter-in-law, I had best give you a welcome here."

"Thank you, Sir Thomas, but I shan't be staying if—"

"Nonsense. If I say you may stay, you will stay," he contradicted her gruffly. "Kit, have her trunks brought up and she can show me the marriage license later. Meanwhile, she must have a change of clothing. Take her up to one of the empty bedrooms and have Maggie get something of Juliette's for her to wear."

Crimson opened her mouth to retort something scathing, but Sir Thomas was waving them away as he returned to his desk, apparently putting her out of his mind for the moment in order to do his paperwork. Feeling affronted, Crimson jerked her arm from Kit's grasp as he reached to lead her away. She stalked out of the room silently, indignant and feeling as though she had been summarily dismissed.

"Your father is—is—"

"He can be rather crusty, my dear. I'm afraid you'll just have to get used to it."

Kit forced her hand through his arm and led her back to the curving staircase and upstairs to the second floor. Two hallways branched on either side from the head of the stairs, and he chose the left one.

"My rooms are this way," he said by way of explanation.

She stopped. "Then I think we should go the other way," she said.

He laughed. "I don't think you'll want to be put next to Juliette, Crimson. Her perfume would probably nauseate you until you became immune to its scent, for one thing. Besides, she can curse like a banshee, and I'm not sure just how delicate your ears are."

"I'm sure her language couldn't be any worse than what I would hear from your own room," Crimson put in. "And then too, I should think Maggie might not like me so close to your room," she threw in with a slight challenge.

"Maggie would have very little to say about it."

He pulled her down the hall and opened one of the doors. The bedroom was large and sunny, its windows looking out onto the bay side of the castle.

"You can use this room. I'll have someone bring up a

tub and some hot water and you can wash off the mud and slime. Toss your clothes in a pile, and the maid will have them cleaned."

"Is there a lock on the door?" she asked.

He smiled. "Yes, there is. Are you going to lock me out?"

She nodded. "I'm used to bathing in private. I prefer it that way."

"As you say, Crimson. Let me call up the maid and you can undress."

He was gone only a few moments before a tall, thin Negress came into the room, bringing fresh towels, soap and a washcloth. Behind her, carrying a big copper tub, were two strong Negroes who placed it in the middle of the room. The maid left the articles on a seat and waited for Crimson to undress. Feeling a little uncomfortable at the maid's complete silence, Crimson stripped off the wet clothes and plopped into the warm water. The Negress picked up the clothes and left the room without a word.

"Wait. Did you lock the door?" Crimson called after her, but she was already gone.

Sighing and feeling as though she would like to be back in King Street at the moment, Crimson began to sponge her body and lather her hair. Lord, but it did feel good to be clean again, she thought when she was finished. She stepped out of the tub gingerly and reached for a towel, wrapping it like a turban about her wet head. She rubbed vigorously with another towel to get off the excess moisture from the bath.

"Just as I thought. As beautiful as a sea maiden," came a voice behind her.

Startled, Crimson looked up and saw Kit staring at her, leaning against the door to her bedroom with lazy ease. He had removed his own wet clothes and had dressed in soft, gray pants and a clean, white shirt, opened to the waist. His feet were bare as he padded into the room with a light tread.

Crimson had tightened the towel around the front of her, pressing her hands to her sides to keep it in place.

"What are you doing in here?" she demanded.

"I'm afraid I was so curious I couldn't resist catching you in your present state of undress. Dare I stay longer, Crimson, or will you throw something at me?" he laughed. But as he laughed, his dark eyes narrowed as they roved over the smooth, creamy shoulders and long legs that were exposed to the thigh.

"You, get out out of here at once or I shall call for help!" Crimson warned, backing up a little.

"Crimson, I only want to welcome you as a brother-in-law should," he smiled, coming closer. "Here, let me kiss you and—"

"You've already taken that liberty," she threw at him.

"Ah, yes, but those pink lips are so inviting, I'm afraid I've become rather greedy. Come here, Crimson, and let me kiss you."

"No! Leave at once or—"

He took two more steps and was towering over her, his hands suddenly catching the edge of the towel and whisking it away with ridiculous ease. Crimson shivered at the fiery look he bestowed on her as he raked over her nakedness with a practiced eye.

"My brother showed uncommon good taste when he wedded you, Crimson," he murmured, letting his hands move carelessly up her arms to rest just above her breasts.

He bent down to take her lips, moving over them with a hard, demanding sweep that took her breath away. His arm crept behind her back to settle in the curve and arch her closer against him. His free hand tore the towel from her hair to allow the damp, curling mass to fall free. He was kissing her with bruising force, parting her lips to taste the sweetness of her mouth, and Crimson felt herself swirling in a disbelieving whirlpool of emotions.

"Well, and I suppose this is our new guest?"

Crimson felt Kit's arms tighten about her in a strangely protective gesture as he turned his head.

"Juliette, you do have the worst timing, my dear," he muttered.

Her mother-in-law! Crimson wished the earth would swallow her up.

"I can see that, Kit, but if you will release the young

305

lady, perhaps, she can make her decision as to which of these gowns she would like to use, and then, I promise I will slip quietly away and leave you two to carry on."

Crimson gathered her courage and peeked out from behind Kit's shoulder to look at Juliette—Lady Gardner. She was, indeed, a beautiful woman, with midnight black hair that was curled in an elaborate coiffure, complementing her olive coloring and jet-black eyes. Her lips were very full and very red, and she had a black mole on the side of her chin that only seemed to emphasize the redness of her mouth.

"Good day, my dear," Juliette was saying in a syrupy tone.

Feeling ridiculous and embarrassed at the same time, Crimson stooped to pick up the fallen towel and wrapped it around herself. "Lady Juliette, I—I don't know what to say. I—"

"That's quite all right, my dear. Just let me know which of these robes you prefer, and I'll leave without bothering you further."

"But you don't understand, I—that is, Kit and I—"

"My dear child, Kit does have a way with women. I'm afraid he has quite a reputation in the town, and God only knows how many little replicas of himself running around." The voice was deceptively sweet while the black eyes narrowed as they noted the perfection of the girl's complexion, the curling mass of auburn hair, the wide-set aquamarine eyes. "You seem awfully young to have been married and widowed already," she said almost to herself.

"I'll be eighteen in June," Crimson responded.

"Eighteen? Kit, you are picking them young, aren't you?" Juliette said to her stepson, eyeing him with a teasing light in her eyes.

He smiled sardonically. "It seems more pleasant than picking them old," he returned.

Juliette's smile thinned. "Well, my dear, let me just leave both of these on the bed and you can choose at your leisure. I can see you have other things to do."

She laid the robes on the bed and, after a sly look at both of them, left the room. Crimson stared at Kit with
306

a sinking feeling, then, remembering how he had taken advantage of her and gotten her into this mess, she frowned.

"You! Get out of this room this instant! Look what you've done!"

He laughed arrogantly. "I haven't done a thing you didn't want me to do, Crimson. Be honest with yourself. Weren't you a little curious to see how the younger brother measured up to your husband?"

"No! You're both pig-headed, overbearing and obnoxious!"

"How touching! My, you are the picture of the sorrowing widow, my dear. I was wondering why you didn't bother wearing black, but I can see now that you weren't actually in mourning."

"I think I explained in your father's library that it was a marriage that was forced on me. It would have been hypocritical of me to pretend that I loved him."

"Perhaps, but as a young lady of rank, don't you think you could have made the effort to act the part?"

He was baiting her again, and she stubbornly refused to say anything more on the subject. "Please allow me some privacy while I dress."

"Since you said please, I will obey, little sister-in-law," he grinned. "But do hurry, for I'll only give you ten minutes and then I shall return to take you downstairs for something to eat."

Helplessly, Crimson watched him go, feeling somehow overwhelmed by his easygoing attitude. She slipped into one of the robes, a dark green silk that had a wine stain on the bodice. Juliette hadn't seemed like the type who would trouble to give her something suitable to wear, but she sighed, thinking that she should be grateful for anything at this stage. She rubbed her hair with the towel and searched the dressing table for a brush. From the pocket of the robe, she picked out a length of satin ribbon and tied it about her head to keep the hair away from her face. She had no slippers to wear, and resigned herself to appearing downstairs in bare feet.

True to his word, Kit reappeared a few moments later to take her downstairs. She realized she was ravenously

307

hungry and was looking forward to luncheon, no matter that she had to eat in the company of a man who seemed determined to seduce her.

Downstairs, he steered her into a small, private drawing room. "We'll eat in here, my sweet, since Father is having company for luncheon today."

"Of course, I doubt that he would appreciate me interrupting like this," she said, smiling for the first time.

He stared at her. "Ravishing, Crimson. You should smile more often, darling, and I'm sure you would have no trouble getting what you want."

"Even your father might believe my preposterous tale?" she questioned him, still smiling.

"I'm sure he would believe anything," he assured her, coming round the table, but she eluded him, putting a chair between them.

"No more of that," he said sternly, reddening at the memory of his eyes on her naked body and then his arms pressing her nakedness against him.

He, too, seemed to be recalling that moment, for his eyes held an intense excitement. "All right, Crimson, we'll call a truce for now, but I promise you I'll have you yet, sweetheart. You're much too lovely for me to leave unscathed."

He went off to the kitchens to order their meal, and Crimson seated herself in one of the chairs, noting the fine china in the sideboard, the plush velvet of the chairs, the exquisite pictures and knickknacks that littered the room in an ordered array.

When Kit returned, he found her studying a graceful ivory-carved figurine. "That's the goddess Diana, the huntress," he said. "She reminds me a little of our own Juliette, don't you think?"

Crimson smiled. "Yes, I think I do see the resemblance now."

He laughed. "I'm glad to see you do have a sense of humor. I can't abide women who don't."

"Let's not talk about your taste in women," Crimson said, chiding him. "Tell me about the island."

308

"Oh, you'll come to see most of it, probably, if you decide to stay."

"You mean, if your father lets me stay," she corrected him.

"If he doesn't, I'll hide you away in my rooms. He need never know," he returned, leering at her.

"You don't give up, do you?" she laughed, wishing she could make up her mind whether she liked him or not.

"Never, where a beautiful woman is concerned."

"What are we going to have for luncheon today?" she asked, to steer him away from the subject.

"We'll have what Father and his guest are having," he replied ambiguously.

She made a face at him. "Don't you ever answer a person in a direct way?"

He shook his head. "Not when she insists on avoiding the subject that I'd like to discuss." He came closer to her, but she eluded him once more.

"Tell me, who is your father having for company? Is it someone very important?" she asked, moving to the other side of the table and sitting down.

Kit shrugged. "I don't really pry into my father's business. He seems to be preoccupied much of the time with all this pirate trouble. As he is acting governor until a new one is appointed, we hardly have time to talk."

"He must be proud of the fact that you sail under Henry Morgan."

"I suppose Reginald told you that. Yes, I suppose he is. I almost wish I were with Morgan now. The old buccaneer is probably gaining loot and glory for himself in Panama now."

"Why didn't you go with him?" she asked.

"Father wanted me here to patrol these waters while Morgan was away. It gets around pretty fast that Morgan's expedition is gone and they'll become even bolder than they are now. That's probably why your ship was attacked."

She shivered. "It was frightening. I can see why your father has the problem on his mind so much. I'm sure he gets many complaints from the traders."

"The ocean's too big to make his job easy, Crimson, but he does his best, I suppose." He looked at her across the table. "Enough of that stuffy talk. Let's hear about you, Crimson. I'd like to know you better."

"You already know everything," she said. "You were there when I tried to explain to your father."

He nodded. "I can understand why your lover's mistress would try to have you killed. With you as a rival, she wouldn't have a chance to keep him."

"I didn't say he was my lover," she interrupted. "He was attracted to me, but I—I couldn't reciprocate the affection." She wondered why she was trying to explain to this man who was almost still a stranger.

"You mean you were faithful to my dear brother? God, he didn't deserve such luck!"

She felt the heat in her cheeks. She was silent for a time until the food was brought in. It was delicious—roasted chickens, cold tongue, lamb and fresh fruit grown on the island. She ate with relish, nearly oblivious to Kit across the table, watching her eat. When she was finished, she looked up, feeling slightly rude that she had ignored him throughout the meal.

"I was so hungry—" she began by way of explanation.

"I would have never guessed," he teased her.

She made a face at him, then smiled. "Oh, I feel better now. Your company doesn't seem half as bad as before I ate."

"Why, thank you! It seems there's hope for me yet. Shall I suggest a romantic interlude in the garden outside, or would you belch in my face?"

"Kit!" she broke in. "Ladies do not belch!" She was laughing, enjoying his company for the moment, and he was delighted.

"Oh, Crimson, I know what I'd like to have for dessert now. But the question is, how to bring you 'round to my way of thinking?" He reached across the table to capture her hand.

She couldn't admit to him how fast her heart was beating as his strong, rough fingers caressed her skin, but she admitted to herself that he was attractive and, despite his careless arrogance, there was a certain something about him that she had to like.

"You'll not get me 'round to your way of thinking, Kit, unless you behave like a gentleman," she chided him.

"Me, a gentleman!" he exclaimed derisively. "No, I'm afraid I'd much rather sweep you off your feet and ravish you deliriously. Give me lusty wenches, or give me no one!" he proclaimed, releasing her hand to stand up and come around to her side of the table.

"And how do you know I'm a lusty wench?" she asked him.

"Those eyes, that hair, that figure! They were meant to make a man's blood run as hot as lava, my sweet," he teased her devilishly.

"Oh, you're insufferable!" she put in, reddening again. "I don't know why I'm sitting here listening to your insults."

"Are they insults? I assure you I didn't intend them to be so, my love."

She made a face and rose from her chair, slipping out of his grasp when he sought to hold her. "I'd best get upstairs before—"

She was interrupted abruptly by Sir Thomas himself, coming through the door with his guest behind him.

"I'm sure you'll like these cigars, Nick. I keep the best ones in here," Sir Thomas was saying, when he stopped suddenly at sight of Kit and Crimson.

Behind him, his face carefully hiding his surprise at seeing Crimson there, was Nicholas Brentwood. After a moment's hesitation, he smiled directly into her eyes.

Crimson could hardly believe her own eyes when she looked into those of the man whom she had known so intimately for such a short while in London. What was he doing here? She remembered, with lightning swiftness, that he had been sent on a mission to the Americas by King Charles. But what sort of mission could it be, here with Sir Thomas? She was about to speak, to acknowledge him, when a slight narrowing of his eyes told her that he didn't wish her to seem to know him.

"Kit, what are you doing in here! And with this wench!"

311

Sir Thomas was sputtering in agitation. Then turning to Nick, "Forgive this intrusion, Nick. This is my son, Kit, and this—er—young lady claims to be my daughter-in-law."

"Claims to be, Sir Thomas?"

The other man shrugged. "She only arrived this morning with some highly suspect tale, and I'm waiting for evidence before I decide if she's telling the truth or not. I'm embarrassed that this all had to be brought out."

Crimson was flushed, aware of the robe, her flowing hair and her bare feet which would probably lead Nick to draw some unfactual conclusions about her relationship with Kit. She dared not look at him, but could feel his eyes assessing her leisurely, remembering the body beneath the robe that he had known most intimately for a short time.

"Excuse me, Sir Thomas," she began, "but Kit and I—"

"Crimson and I were having lunch in here, Father," Kit supplied quickly. "Forgive the intrusion, sir," he continued bowing to Nick.

"Dammit all, Kit, can't you take the wench to your rooms, or dispose of her somewhere else about the house when you knew I had a guest?" Sir Thomas cut in crossly.

"Please, Sir Thomas, it's quite all right," Nick said smoothly, keeping his eyes on Crimson's face. "The wench is quite lovely and I do assure you I can appreciate such a flower on this exotic island."

"Put like a true gentleman," Kit said softly, eyeing the other man closely now.

"Damnation, just let me find those cigars and we'll return to the library, Nick," Sir Thomas went on, casting an infuriated glance at the silent girl.

"Crimson, I think we'd best disappear," Kit whispered to her, leaning towards her. He took her arm and began to leave when Nick stopped him.

"But we haven't been introduced," he said indolently.

Kit stopped and glanced at Crimson's averted face. "Forgive me, sir, this is Lady Gardner, widow of my brother, Reginald."

Nick bowed lazily. "Charmed, my lady. Nick Brentwood, at your service. I'm here on business, thinking of

312

opening an import business in the town. I do hope I'll be meeting you again—soon."

Crimson murmured something inaudibly and tugged slightly on Kit's sleeve, indicating her wish to leave the room. Kit gave her a puzzled glance, then shrugged, bowed to Nick and escorted her out.

"Oh, Lady Gardner!" Nick said suddenly as they were about to turn the corner into the hallway.

Crimson turned back to him questioningly.

"I do believe you've mislaid your slippers, my lady," Nick finished, laughing with amusement.

Crimson's eyes narrowed, and she turned around huffily, hurrying out the door with Kit on her heels.

"You and Brentwood seemed to take an instant dislike to each other, my sweet," Kit observed as they climbed the stairway.

"He seemed an arrogant man," Crimson said shortly, walking rapidly back to her room.

She entered her room quickly and prepared to shut the door, but Kit stopped her with a booted foot lodged in the doorway. She gave him a narrow look and when he would have bent down to kiss her, she jerked away.

"What's this? That fellow downstairs had a bad effect on you, sweeting. You'll not let me in, I take it?"

"I wouldn't have let you in my room if I *hadn't* met Mr. Nick Brentwood," she snapped back at him. "I'll be sure to lock my door."

He grinned. "I'll let you know when your trunks arrive. Then we'll see if you'll be staying on a permanent basis." He blew her a kiss and left her, whistling softly to himself as he strode down the hall to his own rooms.

34

Later that day, when Crimson's trunks were brought up from the docks, Sir Thomas knocked on the door for a visit.

"I've seen the marriage document, Crimson, and I have to believe you. You're my daughter-in-law and you're welcome to stay here as long as you wish. I hope you forgive my earlier disbelief," he ended. He was stiff, formal with her, obviously embarrassed by the morning's episode and not willing to admit he was completely wrong.

"Of course, Sir Thomas," she said, folding her hands as she seated herself in a chair. "If you please, I would appreciate your having my trunks brought up here so that I can change into something more suitable." She indicated the stained robe.

"Certainly, my dear. If you like this room, I shall have one of the serving girls dust and tidy it up for you."

"Thank you, I would appreciate that."

"When you've changed, I'd like for you to come to my wife's drawing room. She hasn't met you formally yet and, since you'll be our guest—"

"Of course," Crimson returned, dreading the encounter already.

When her trunks had been brought up and she had changed into a violet silk gown that was trimmed in white satin bows, she sat in front of the dressing table to fix her hair. The atmosphere in the house was not the most congenial, she decided, but she had nowhere else to go at the moment and she was forced to remain here, in Jamaica, at least long enough for Castlemaine to forget about her so that Crimson might eventually return to England.

When she was ready, she made her way to Juliette's rooms and knocked softly on the boudoir door, steeling herself to stand up to what she was sure was going to be a confrontation.

"Come in, my dear, please," came Juliette's deceptively sweet voice.

Crimson took in a deep breath and opened the door, closing it behind her as she faced her mother-in-law. Juliette was beautiful in a black silk negligee bordered in brilliants, seated in a plush chair, reclining almost regally as she eyed Crimson speculatively.

"Do sit down, Crimson. Please don't be nervous. I promise not to bring up your little—interlude—with Kit," she laughed throatily. "He is a tempting man for any woman and I can certainly understand how you were swept away by his charm."

"He was kind enough to bring me here," Crimson murmured, seating herself some distance away from the glittering black spider.

"Oh, my dear, Kit is never kind without a reason. You must remember that. Did he tell you that he has a mistress in Port Royal, a French girl whom he saved from a shipwreck? She thought he was kind, too, but he exacted a high price from her. Ah, poor Delia, she pretends to fight him, but she gives in much too easily to be believed. Of course, working in a tavern, I'm sure she gives in to quite a few men."

Crimson wasn't sure if she liked the turn in the conversation. She wasn't interested in hearing about Kit's women and wondered why Juliette would be. Could it be that this beautiful, decadent stepmother nourished something more than motherly affection towards her handsome stepson? It was a question that Crimson truly did not wish to know the answer to.

"You're so quiet, my dear. Does the conversation shock

315

you? Please forgive me then, I only wanted to warn you about Kit before you made a serious mistake."

"I'm capable of taking care of myself where Kit is concerned, my lady," Crimson answered swiftly.

Juliette laughed. "Please call me Juliette," she insisted. "And as far as Kit is concerned, I'm sure you *think* you are capable, my dear, but you are quite young."

"I've been a married woman," Crimson put in.

"Yes. Poor Reginald. Of course, I never met Thomas' older son, but I was told a great deal about him. Thomas is not one to show his feelings to anyone, Crimson, but he is suffering over the death of Reginald, you can be sure." She glanced curiously at her. "Just what were the details of his death, my dear?"

"He had a mistress who had a jealous husband. When the husband returned from the wars, he found out about the affair and challenged my husband to a duel. Reginald accepted and was killed in the fight." Crimson recited the details in a monotone. She had some feeling that Juliette was prying for a reason other than sympathy.

"Reginald had a mistress! With you as his wife! Unbelievable, Crimson! You did not condone it, I trust?"

"I had little choice in the matter, since the marriage was arranged by my father. I barely knew my husband before he was killed. The marriage was one of convenience, madam."

"Oh, yes, such marriages are no doubt the mode in London these days. Ah, I am such a lucky woman that I had no one arranging my marriage to anyone. No, you see I waited until I found a man I could love and trust. Sir Thomas is a good husband, child."

Crimson privately found it hard to believe that Juliette would marry Sir Thomas for love or trust; more likely it was for his position in government and because he was probably the wealthiest man she could find. Her disbelief must have shown on her face.

"I know, I know. You're thinking of the age difference that lies between my husband and me, aren't you, Crimson? Let me assure you, it doesn't matter at all. We love each other."

316

"I wouldn't presume to think otherwise, Juliette."

"You're a good child, obedient, polite, well brought-up, I assume. I'm sure you had all the advantages of wealth and position, didn't you? I doubt whether Reginald would have married you otherwise."

She stopped and studied Crimson closely. "Have you thought yet about marrying again, Crimson?"

Crimson looked at her, baffled. "No, madam. I—there is no one."

Juliette stood up and smiled, coming over to pat her shoulder with a motherly air. "Of course, it's too soon after Reginald's death, I understand, but you are a lovely young girl and I couldn't help but be curious."

"May I remind you, madam, that I had to flee London for fear of my life and had no chance to meet a man between that time and now—"

"Except for Kit, of course," she put in smoothly.

"I hardly know him, and I certainly have no intention of marrying him!" Crimson exclaimed, wondering what she was getting at.

"Good, I'm glad. Kit is not the man for you, my dear, just remember that." Juliette's hand tightened suddenly on her shoulder. "I don't want to see you hurt by him, child."

Crimson suddenly wished that she could leave the room. The cloying scent of Juliette's perfume was indeed overpowering.

"If you wish me to stay away from Kit—" she began uncertainly.

"No, no, of course not! You two are fairly close in age and I'm sure there are some things that you might have in common. I would think it terrible if you never spoke to each other because of something I said, my dear." Juliette walked slowly about the room, absently twisting the glittering rings on her fingers. "But I'm just concerned that Kit may try to take advantage of your youth, your inexperience. I'm only looking out for your safety, dear."

"I appreciate that, Juliette," Crimson murmured, glancing about the room as though for a means of escape.

At that moment, a sharp knock on the door interrupted their conversation, much to Crimson's relief, but her relief changed to embarrassment when the caller turned out to be Kit. At Juliette's welcome, he sauntered into the room with the easy air of one who knew his way about, and Crimson's suspicions seemed to gain more credence in her mind.

"Juliette, you do look lovely in your disarray, my dear," Kit said, bowing over his stepmother's hand. He brushed it lightly with his lips, allowing his eyes to travel insolently over the expanse of flesh that was partially revealed by the sheer material.

"Thank you, Kit. You look as though you're going somewhere," she murmured, her long eyelashes fluttering coquettishly.

"I have to go into town, Juliette," he answered, releasing her hand, but her other hand came up to clutch at his sleeve.

"If you'll wait a moment, Kit, I'll change and go with you. That stupid Maggie forgot to pick up something."

"Sorry, Juliette. I've got business with some of the traders and I don't need you tagging along and slowing me up. I've already ordered my horse saddled and—"

"Kit!" she pouted, puckering her red lips invitingly. "I'm so bored here, my dear, and I would so like to go into town with you. I'll have my mare saddled too and we'll ride down together."

"Juliette, I—" Kit began, exasperated.

"No, no. Now you just wait for me downstairs and I'll hurry and change." Juliette glanced at Crimson as though just remembering her presence. "Oh, I'm sorry, Crimson, dear. If you excuse me, we'll continue our conversation after dinner this evening."

"Actually, Juliette, I came in here to see if Crimson would like to ride into town with me," Kit broke in impatiently. "I'm sure she's anxious to take a look around."

Juliette stopped abruptly and stared at Kit in rebuke. "Darling, you don't know how tired Crimson is after all the excitement today. She should go to her room now and take a nap, I think, before dinner. Don't you think so?" she asked, turning to Crimson, who had risen from her chair to quit the room.

318

"Yes, I—I am tired," she returned, wishing to get away from both of them.

She would not meet Kit's eyes as she murmured her excuses and quickly left the room. As she started to walk down the hall, she heard Juliette's door close, and Kit was beside her.

"Coward!" he laughed at her, catching her arm.

"It was obvious she did not want me to go with you, Kit!" Crimson snapped. "I wouldn't want to spoil her pleasure."

His smile vanished and he pulled her along the hall, out of sight should Juliette suddenly come out of her room. "I told you that she was a regular dragon at times, Crimson. I'm afraid you probably saw her at her best today. She can be a positive witch at times and is really only congenial to my father."

"I'd say that she likes *you* fairly well," Crimson retorted. "I was afraid she might drool all over you before I had a chance to retire gracefully."

He laughed, pulling her to sit beside him in an enclosed window seat. "Juliette does like me, as a matter of fact, but—"

"But being your stepmother, she can't quite make up her mind whether to treat you like a little boy or to take you to bed with her!" she finished, wishing he would just let her go back to her room.

He had the grace to flush. "You have to understand, Crimson, that Juliette is thirty years younger than my father, and she has the needs of a woman who has never known another man and has waited a long time to get married."

"I can hardly believe that!" Crimson returned. "She has as much experience with men as some of the whores on London Bridge! Why, she shouldn't be here in this isolated place, she should be in London, at Whitehall, where I'm sure she'd outshine Barbara Palmer!"

Kit caught both her hands tightly in his. "God's blood, you must be overtired!" he said sharply. "Could it be that we'll have two shrews in the house now? Listen to me, Crimson. Juliette is frustrated and—"

"I can believe that!" Crimson cried, jerking her hands from his grasp. "And she's not the only one with a problem. She told me about your French mistress in town and all the other women you enjoy!" She was on the verge of tears, a combination of pent-up emotions and exhaustion. "I should have stayed in London and slept with the king!" She stood up and ran to her room, oblivious to his voice calling her back.

She slammed the door furiously in her wake and when she heard him knock, she refused to open the door.

"Go away and leave me alone. Don't bother to explain anything, for I'm afraid I won't believe you. You and your father and stepmother can all sink into the ocean for all I care!" she cried and fell on her bed, sobbing, wondering how in the world she had come to be in this place, among strangers, people who obviously didn't want her here.

35

Crimson remained in her room for two days, refusing to see anyone, eating alone from a tray the maid brought up. She was utterly depressed at the bleak future that seemed in store for her and only wished to be left alone.

Then, on the third afternoon of her self-imposed exile, she was looking out her window, drearily watching the many ships on the bay, when she noticed directly below her, in the exotic garden that Sir Thomas had had terraced along the slope of the hill, a man and a woman. Her senses sharpened as she recognized Juliette's deep-throated laugh and then Nick Brentwood's answering chuckle of lazy amusement.

Nick Brentwood. She had forgotten about him being here! Curiously, she stepped back behind her drapes to watch them as they walked in the garden, wondering what he could be doing with Juliette. She remembered he had made up that tale about wanting to open an import business in Port Royal. But why was he really here? She couldn't hear their conversation, but found herself becoming unreasonably jealous when Juliette reached up to put one exquisitely shaped hand on Nick's shoulder. She pulled teasingly at the dark-blond hair, and he responded by bringing her up against him with sudden aggressiveness that pleased the lady immensely.

Crimson watched, biting her lip furiously, as Nick arched Juliette back into his arms and kissed her almost languidly. They locked in a tight embrace and while Crimson watched, Nick began caressing Juliette with casual skill. Crimson half-expected them to sink onto the verdant soil and make love, but Juliette suddenly laughed with a rich throatiness and pushed him away.

She picked up her skirts and started to return to the house, glancing over her shoulder to make sure he was following her. Crimson seethed with unwanted fury, amazed at the depth of her emotion, unaware whether it was truly jealousy over Nick or an intense dislike of Juliette. She suddenly realized that she had been hurting no one but herself by staying in her room and turned about quickly, running to the armoire to see what she had to wear.

She called up a maid to help her dress, impatient suddenly to see Nick again, to talk with him. She wanted to know why he was here and why he seemed intent on playing seducer to Juliette's coquette. She dressed in a turquoise dress that made her eyes seem more blue

321

than green and arranged her hair in a simple style, threading a blue silk ribbon through the curls.

When she was ready, she descended the staircase cautiously, listening to see if anyone was below. Trying to walk casually, she proceeded to the formal drawing room and knocked on the door.

"Come in," came Sir Thomas' voice.

Crimson opened the door to see Sir Thomas, Nick and Juliette seated, obviously engaged in conversation. They all three looked up at her entrance, Juliette with a look of displeasure, Sir Thomas with a look of surprise and Nick with a look of amusement and indolent scrutiny that took her in from head to toe.

"Good afternoon, Juliette, Sir Thomas," Crimson spoke. "I'm sorry if I've intruded. I was only wondering if anyone had seen Kit. He promised to take me into the town when I was ready and I do feel the need to get out." Her look challenged anyone to disbelieve her.

"Kit had to leave on patrol, Crimson," Sir Thomas answered her impatiently. "If you will wait a moment, I'll see if one of the servants can drive you down and—"

"I'd be delighted to accompany your—daughter-in-law," Nick broke in smoothly, looking steadily at Crimson's defiant face so that she pinkened slightly.

"Why, thank you, Nick, but that's not necessary," Sir Thomas returned.

"It's quite all right, Sir Thomas. I have to be returning anyway and I'd much rather make the trip with some company."

"But you've ridden your horse up, Nick," Juliette intervened, after a furious glance at Crimson.

"I can ride," Crimson broke in with a touch of arrogance that was not lost on the other woman. "Remember, Juliette, that I was brought up well."

Juliette eyed her with surprised haughtiness, aware of the defiance within the younger girl, and puzzled by it. "Well, of course, if you can ride, my

322

dear," she began, trying to sound graceful, "I will be glad to allow you the use of my own horse."

"Thank you. Whenever you are ready, sir," Crimson said, turning to Nick challengingly.

He grinned with delighted wickedness at her. "Of course, my lady." He bowed over Juliette's hand. "Excuse me, Lady Juliette. Please don't be concerned for her welfare. I shall send one of my men back with her."

"You are most kind to indulge the child," Juliette returned, smiling at him with a silent promise, which Crimson noted as she excused herself to change her garment.

Nick grinned, saluting Sir Thomas, who was not quite sure of the exact meaning of the undercurrent he sensed in the air.

When Crimson had returned, in her riding habit, Nick then offered his arm to her and took her out the door.

Once outside, Crimson felt her courage begin to abate at the prospect of being alone with this man who had been so sure of her in London. She was silent as they walked to the stables and waited quietly while her horse was being saddled.

"You've become quiet suddenly, Crimson," Nick said as he helped her onto her horse, letting his hand slide intimately along the side of her leg beneath her skirt.

Crimson pulled away from him, urging the horse forward. He shrugged and mounted his own horse, coming up beside her. "Has your courage deserted you, sweetheart?" he asked with amusement.

"I'm not sure if it was courage or foolishness," she retorted. "Please, let us get going and leave before Juliette decides to join us."

"The formidable beauty—yes, I can see where you might be at odds with her. You two are quite a bit alike, you know, except that Juliette knows what she wants and goes after it without a touch of compassion."

"I don't know what you mean," Crimson returned, exasperated. "I'm not like her in the least. She—"

"She's honest with herself, Crimson. When she likes a man, she lets him know it. You, on the other hand, insist on playing games."

"I'm not playing games with you!" she exclaimed. "It was you who offered to take me to the town."

"I seemed to get the impression, though, that you were aching for me to do just that. Tell me, Crimson, are you going to try and seduce me along the road? Or shall we wait until we arrive at my humble abode?"

"You make me sick!" Crimson cried. "How dare you be so casual about it! I saw you with Juliette in the garden. You were both so—so disgusting!"

"Whatever do you mean, sweetheart?"

"Don't pretend to innocence. She's a married woman!"

He laughed in cynical mockery. "And just exactly what were you when you agreed to become my mistress in London, Crimson?"

She flushed. "I—I—"

"Ah, now perhaps you can see what I mean. You really are a little hypocrite, Crimson."

"Oh, be quiet!" she flounced and urged her horse forward.

He laughed and shook his head, then followed her as she made her way down the side of the slope. They rode for a time without speaking, until they arrived at the bridge. Nick caught up with her and caught her bridle in his hand.

"What are you doing?" she demanded. "I'm quite capable of controlling my own horse."

"My dear, you're obviously too angry to notice those two sorry-looking fellows up ahead there. They're quite capable of throwing you down off your horse and stealing it from under your nose before I could do more than draw my sword. Now, will you shut your mouth and let me do what's best?"

Crimson was effectively silenced and watched wide-eyed, as the men Nick had referred to leered at her with oily grins when she passed them. She shivered and was grateful that Nick was with her, shuddering to think what the men might have tried if she had been alone.

They rode into the town, and Crimson could feel the ocean breeze, smelling of sea tang, on her face; it made her nose crinkle. The town itself was built haphazardly with all sorts of poorly constructed buildings, some of which looked to be in danger of falling down. The streets were narrow, rutted strips of sand and mud, and all along the street, men walked or sang or lay in the filth. As they neared the docks, the few places of legitimate business gave way to taverns and brothels.

Crimson could hear women laughing brazenly, men calling drunkenly and foul curses and oaths mixed in some places with the sound of crashing glass or breaking furniture.

"Where are you taking me?" she demanded suddenly of Nick.

"A timely question, my sweet, for we've just arrived at my residence while I'm here in Port Royal." He indicated the two-story, rambling building that bore the name the King's Privy. "As you can see by the name, I picked only the very best." He dismounted and smiled up at her lazily. "Well, are you getting down, Crimson, or would you rather remain out here as easy pickings for any drunken pirate that comes along?"

She hastily got down, slipping off the horse before he could help her. "Isn't this a—a tavern?" she asked uncomfortably.

"Yes, it is, but it was the best room I could get in the town, I'm afraid. The owner, a man named Hook, is a pretty decent sort. And the bargirls keep my room clean enough."

She glanced at him and saw that he was laughing at her silently. "What I would like to know is why you made up this story about starting an import business here in town, when we both know that—"

He covered her mouth with his hand and glanced about them warily. "Hush, for God's sake, Crimson. Let's get upstairs and I'll tell you what I can."

He released her and she followed him around to

325

the back of the building where they climbed up a narrow stairway and entered into a hallway along which were eight doors. Nick opened the first one and pushed her inside, locking the door behind them. Crimson was not sure she liked being alone with him, without an easy escape route, but she was determined not to show her trepidation as she faced him with folded arms.

"Well?"

"Sit down, Crimson, I promise I'm not going to devour you," he said with amused disdain. "Believe me, I was as surprised to see you here as you were to see me," he said seriously. "I gather that your dearly loved husband is dead and you decided to throw yourself on the mercy of your father-in-law, for what reason, I'll be damned if I can figure out."

"That is none of your business!" she said with growing irritation. "Why I left is—"

"Is of no concern to me, you're right," he interrupted. "I have an idea it had something to do with the king, but if you're too ashamed to tell me—"

"What do you mean, ashamed? I left because I was nearly murdered by Lady Castlemaine! She nearly drowned me and then tried to poison me! I should have gone to bed with the king and thrown myself under his protection. It would have probably stood me better than finding myself alone with you in this undesirable room without a friend in the world!"

"My, my, I suppose you are to be pitied," he sympathized with clear contempt. "May I remind you, Crimson, that if you had been faithful to me, I would have been able to protect you from Castlemaine through my friends in London? But, of course, that's all in the past, isn't it?"

"Yes!" she said emphatically.

He shrugged. "At any rate, you're here now, and despite my better judgment, it looks as though I'll have to tell you my business here." He seated himself on a chair, turning it backwards so that he could straddle it and lean against the back. "King Charles sent me here to delve into Sir Thomas' business in-
326

terests. There's been information concerning your father-in-law, my dear, that may brand him as a traitor to his king."

"Sir Thomas! I can't believe it! But how—"

"Quiet," he interrupted impatiently. "Lord, why is it that a woman can never keep her mouth shut long enough to hear the truth! It seems that Sir Thomas' shipments of gold and coin back to England are dwindling. It seems fair to assume that he must be keeping something back, possibly for his own gain. Confiscating monies directed towards the king is punishable by death, Crimson. It's a serious crime. That's why I was sent here."

"You were sent here as a punishment to keep you away from me!" Crimson objected. "Don't you see, the king wanted me for himself and you stood in the way."

"Your conceit astounds me, Crimson," he laughed. "Do you think the king would make up that story just to rid himself of a potential rival? He would have forced you to succumb sooner or later. After all, it was *you* who had already kicked me out of your life, if you'll recall." His brows, such a contrast to his bronzed hair, rose in sardonic dark crescents.

"Well, it's all over, as you said," she reminded him angrily. "And I'm glad it's so! Except that fate saw fit to throw us together again on this island."

He looked directly at her, his dark blue eyes insolently assessing her. "I promise you, Crimson, that I won't touch you. I would hope you have the self-discipline to take care of your own emotions."

She colored furiously. "How dare you! You think this is all a joke, don't you? Well, you won't have to worry about me sneaking into your bed at night, Nick Brentwood. I'm not stupid enough to—"

"I believe you, I believe you!" He laughed easily. "Besides, I'm afraid all of my spare time will be taken up with the lovely Juliette. She might prove pliable enough to give me some information as to what exactly her husband is doing with all the pirate loot."

327

"I can imagine how you'll obtain this information," Crimson sneered, realizing with a sudden twinge that she would hate to see that obnoxious woman in Nick's bed. She flushed at the picture, hoping that Nick wouldn't guess her thoughts.

"My tactics will be only those used by any loyal servant of the king," Nick chuckled. "Let us hope they will prove fruitful."

"Well, you'll have to share her with her stepson," Crimson shot back. "There is something between Kit and Juliette that hardly behooves their close relationship. She lights up with desire whenever he comes near her!"

"Kit, that's the younger brother, isn't it?" Nick frowned, ignoring Crimson's ill-concealed anger. "Do you know anything about him?"

"I'll not be recruited to help you," Crimson began furiously.

"Come now, sweetheart, just because I'm not obliging enough to satisfy that itch you seem to have between your legs doesn't mean we can't work together on this."

"Oh!" She gasped at his crudity, and sprang at him to slap his face.

He caught her easily and they wrestled for a moment, knocking his chair to the floor before he was able to throw her onto the bed where she lay breathing hard beneath him as he held her down. They glared into each other's eyes for a long moment.

"Let me up!" she demanded.

"I'll let you up when I'm ready, my sweet," he returned. "You should learn to control your frustrations. Now, I want you to answer my questions."

"And if I don't?" she challenged him.

He smiled mockingly. "I'm sure I can think up some deserving punishment for you." His lips were so close that they were almost touching hers.

Crimson held her breath, wondering if he was going to kiss her, and wondering at the same time if she wanted him to. Involuntarily, she closed her eyes, parting her lips for the expected touch of his mouth. His insulting laugh shocked her into opening her eyes.

"My God, you *are* ready for it, aren't you, Crimson? What's the matter? Didn't the king or Chesterfield have enough for you?"

She gasped with humiliation, hating him so that she spat in his face. He slapped her, not hard, but enough to bring the tears to her eyes. He pressed down into her arms with his hands until she cried out.

"Now be a good girl, Crimson, and help me in this," he said masterfully. "I don't want you to be in the middle of this thing and get hurt."

She sniffed back a sob and gazed doubtfully at him. "All I know is that Kit sails his own ship under Henry Morgan. He—he told me that Morgan was away, but that he would still patrol the waters for pirates."

"All right, then we should assume he is honest, at least for now. But his father?"

"I don't know. We haven't even seen each other except briefly."

He seemed to be thinking for a moment, his eyes staring into space so that Crimson was able to glance at him covertly. She studied the handsome face, lean, sun-browned and showing no signs of the dissipation of Charles' court. His dark blue eyes looked out from beneath thick blond lashes, crinkling a little at the corners from squinting at the sun. The darker eyebrows and moustache were an arresting contrast to the deep gold of his hair. Beneath the moustache, his mouth was firm, promising sensuality, but now folded in thought. Watching him, Crimson felt an unaccustomed ache rise somewhere within her and she looked away, afraid that he would humiliate her again. He had promised not to touch her. She supposed she ought to be grateful for it, but somehow she felt only a sad frustration.

He released her suddenly, standing up beside the bed to look down at her. "Listen to me, Crimson. I want you to see if you can find out anything while you're staying up there. I hate to use you like this, but the opportunity is too good to miss, and since you *are* here, you might as well make yourself useful. Will you help me?"

"I don't know, Nick. My welcome there has been so

329

cool already that I don't think anyone is going to tell me anything that might be of use to you," she said truthfully. "Only Kit—"

"Ah, yes, I remember seeing you with him in the dining room." His dark blue eyes narrowed with a mixture of scorn and desire. "The little barefoot waif—it was a pretty picture, except for the wine stain on the bodice," he said.

Crimson blushed. "It was the only thing that Juliette let me wear while I was waiting for my trunks. My own clothes were wet after I fell into the water, and Kit rescued me. He—he happened to be there and—" her voice trailed off uncertainly under his unwavering gaze.

"All this is interesting, Crimson, but the end result is then that you and Kit are friends?" His voice was flat.

"Yes, I suppose so, but Juliette doesn't seem to care for that, and I'm sure she'll try to do something." Crimson sighed. "So you can see I'll not be much help to you."

Nick was thoughtful for a moment. "Well, let's see what happens. Just keep your ears open for me."

"All right." She straightened her gown and glanced sideways at him. "Will you take me home now?"

He smiled with a devilish twist. "Are you so eager to rid yourself of my company now that we've struck our bargain, Crimson?"

"I wasn't aware it was a bargain," she countered.

"But of course, if you help me, then I will be indebted to you. You see, I'll be obliged to you. Is the idea appealing?"

"I—I think not," she breathed, looking away from his gaze, feeling her heart begin beating faster.

They were both silent for a long moment. Then Nick touched her lightly on the shoulder. "Come on, I'll take you back now."

Crimson felt a keen disappointment, but was determined to keep it from him. She followed him downstairs and outside to the horses. He helped her mount, but his hand stayed beneath her foot as he looked up at her gravely.

Crimson looked away and her eye passed absently over the other buildings on the street. Suddenly, her eyes sharpened. "There, there!" she gasped, pointing to a dingy tavern out of which poured three men, leaning against each other in obvious comradeship. They were laughing together, the tallest one imparting some ribald joke.

"He's the one who attacked the ship I was on," she explained to Nick, who had turned in the direction she pointed. "He's called Barracuda. That's him!" She would never forget the black eye-patch, the greasily braided hair and the scar over his nose.

The pirate captain had heard her shout and looked up briefly. Upon seeing a young lady pointing to him, especially with a man beside her, he must have thought it best to disappear, for he disentangled himself from his companions and ran down a side alley.

"Go after him! That blackguard has my valuables!" Crimson shouted to Nick.

"He's gone, Crimson, there's nothing I can do. Probably ducked into some pirates' den."

"Oh, he's escaped again!" Crimson said bitterly.

"He's not a man easy to forget, Crimson. I'll keep an eye out for him the next time," Nick promised.

He mounted his own horse and prepared to take her back to the governor's castle himself. Neither of them looked back to see the remaining two men watching them. The scrawnier of the two eyed the girl with unconcealed lust, and his partner slapped him on the back.

"Eh, Hawkins, can ye imagine a night with her? Ye'd not have to pick the lice off her!"

The boy called Hawkins licked his lips and smiled tightly. "Aye, ye'd have a fine time with a wench like that," he agreed softly.

36

Crimson did not see Nick again for two days. He did visit the governor's castle again, though, to call on Sir Thomas for more information on the technicalities of setting up his business. Juliette and Crimson were trying to convince each other they were not enemies, by sitting together in Juliette's private drawing room, drinking tea.

"What do you think of this Nick Brentwood, my dear?" Juliette asked the younger girl, sipping her tea nonchalantly.

"He's a handsome gentleman," Crimson answered steadily. "But I'm not completely sure I like him."

"Handsome, my dear? He's divine!" Juliette emphasized with a hearty sigh. "As for liking him, I admit he can be rather arrogant and caustic at times, but I find myself attracted to him anyway. He's like Kit in so many ways."

Crimson, sensing the drift of the topic, tried to turn to another subject. "Has there been any word yet when the new governor will be appointed?"

"No, not yet," Juliette said briefly, waving away the subject. "You know, my dear, Kit should be back in another week or so. I thought we might have a party when he returns."

"A party?" Crimson wondered who else they could invite. Certainly not the likes of those who inhabited the town. She said as much to Juliette, who laughed broadly.

"My dear, the townfolk are not all vagabonds and criminals," she said. "There are honest shopkeepers and a few middle-class merchants and their wives who would probably enjoy some entertainment. We even have some aristocracy, Lord and Lady Baldwin who live up from the town. Also a lawyer and two physicians and their wives. I'm sure they would all be interesting company and it would lighten the dreariness that has settled in around here."

"I'm sure it would be nice," Crimson agreed, warming to the idea. "I have a ball gown that I brought from England, which would be lovely for the occasion. I didn't think I'd ever get to wear it." She closed her eyes dreamily.

"I shall have to ask Sir Thomas, of course, but I'm sure he would applaud the idea. It would give him a chance to acquaint himself with others on the island. He can be so reclusive at times."

"He seems to have taken a liking to Nick Brentwood," Crimson pointed out, watching Juliette's expression.

"Yes, you're right. Somehow I can't see Nick Brentwood as an honest businessman, can you, my dear?" she asked.

Crimson was careful to keep her expression bland. "What makes you say that?"

"Oh, I don't know, a feeling, perhaps. He's too dashing, too much the adventurer to make a good businessman, I think. If I had to guess, I would say he'd make the perfect pirate—yes, it would suit him." She gazed into her teacup as though seeking an answer there.

"He, a pirate? Then why would he go to all this trouble to establish a business in exporting and importing?" Crimson questioned, hoping to find out exactly what was in Juliette's thoughts.

"Export and import are two things that a pirate does by trade, my dear," Juliette laughed. "If he *were* a pirate, wouldn't it make sense for him to have his own business in which to handle his own booty?"

"But I don't see how he would have time for it," Crimson pointed out. "Being away at sea for weeks at a time—he couldn't do it. Perhaps, though, he has friends among the pirates and has been assured of first look at their goods," she suggested.

Juliette nodded thoughtfully. "A sensible idea, Crimson. If he has friends among the pirates—I wonder. You know, my dear, that as comptroller of this island, my husband is bound to send all confiscated pirate booty to the king as his due."

"You mean that Sir Thomas actually is able to obtain pirates' booty?" Crimson asked breathlessly. "How—how would he go about it?"

Juliette shrugged. "Through others like Kit who capture a pirate ship and take its cargo. It's simple enough if one has a fleet ship and enough courage to command it. Of course, we can't always be sure that all under our protection are honest in dividing the goods. But it is the only way we have of obtaining it, so we are obliged to take their word."

"And—after the goods are received, where are they stored?" Crimson flushed as Juliette gave her a curious stare. "I mean, I would think it might be dangerous for Sir Thomas to hold the goods for very long for fear of an attack."

Juliette smiled confidently. "All the booty is kept below the castle in a room built into the rock of this mountain. The dungeons used to house prisoners are close by it. A fitting justice, I think." She gazed sharply at the girl's avid face. "There is no way to get into the treasure room without the key and there are only two. Sir Thomas keeps one on his person at all times and the other is hidden."

"I see, but how can Sir Thomas trust those whose ships he selects to take the treasure back to England? Surely there are dissolute men involved in such schemes?"

"We can only hope they do their duty. There are three captains whose ships we always use. They travel to Jamaica from England once every six months. We load the ships in a narrow cove on the lee side of the island. The treasure is taken there by mules. The only bad thing about the trip is the Maroons."

"The Maroons? What are they?"

"Who, my dear. They are runaway slaves, mulattos and the like who are kept armed by the Spaniards. They live in the mountains and dense forests and only come out in full force. They harry our mule trains constantly and several men have died." She studied her fingernail. "Sometimes I wonder why we must go through all this mess just to give the gold to the king, who does nothing for it!"

Crimson held her breath, wondering if Juliette would actually trust her enough to tell her something that might be damning to her husband. Crimson was convinced that Juliette knew about Sir Thomas' traitorous activities, probably even encouraged them. And what of Kit? Did he know of his father's extortion?

"I can see your point," she began cautiously. "All that gold and silver going through your hands, only to be sent on to England." She waited, hoping that Juliette would pick up the thread of her innuendo, but the other woman was silent, perhaps thinking she had already said too much.

"Bah! This tea grows cold, my dear. I suppose our delightful tête-à-tête must come to an end now." The dismissal was obvious.

"As you wish, Juliette. Please let me know if I can help in any way with the party plans." Crimson exited gracefully, then hurried to her rooms, her mind filled with the information that Juliette had given her. How to get the news to Nick, though? She couldn't trust a servant with a note, that was certain. And it would be too obvious if she called on him. It was maddening to have to wait for him to come to her.

She tapped her foot impatiently, excited with the element of danger involved. She would go to Nick tonight with the information! She knew the way and the tavern where he was staying. But how to obtain a horse without arousing suspicion? She frowned to herself. It would have to be very late indeed if she were going to get away with it. She sat down on her bed, her mind detailing a plan.

Crimson retired early, using the excuse of a bad head-

335

ache. She needed to get some sleep before the night's excitement, but found it difficult as her thoughts kept turning towards her encounter with Nick. Seeing him alone in his room at night, when he very likely would be asleep in bed, made her tingle with a strange sensation. Ah, yes, she remembered his promise not to touch her—but she would make him eat those words, she vowed, giggling to herself.

She waited, eyes staring into the dark until sleep caused her to doze a little. She awoke with a start, afraid she had overslept. She glanced to the porcelain clock near her bed and sighed with relief. Only half-past three. Time enough to get to Nick and back to the castle before anyone knew the difference.

She dressed quickly in a dark green dress, winding a satin scarf about her head like a turban to disguise her hair. It would have been better to wear men's clothing, but she had had no access to any. She would just have to be careful.

She stole down the hallway, glad that Kit was gone for there was no one else with sleeping rooms in this part of the house. At the top of the stairs, she listened for noises and heard, distantly, the loud snores of Sir Thomas in his room next to Juliette's. She descended the staircase and tiptoed to the back of the house, past the kitchens where the cook was nodding sleepily in a chair, and outside. She ran to the stables and ducked inside, listening for the snores of the stablehands in the loft above. She went to the first stall and drew out Juliette's mare. Hurriedly, she slipped a bridle on the horse, realizing that she would have no time to saddle the animal. Cautiously, she walked the horse outside and mounted her. It felt odd to straddle the bare back of the mare, but she dug her heels in her sides and the horse moved out of the courtyard, over the bridge and onto the road leading to the town.

It took no time to descend the slope and cross the bridge that connected the island with Port Royal on its shifting strip of sand. Even at this late hour, there were men and women up and about. It was not too bad at the upper end of town, but as she neared the docks, the people grew thicker, and she kept to the shadows, beginning to taste fear in her mouth.

She could have made better time ducking through the alleys, but she was afraid that she might get lost, or worse still encounter some band of cutthroats who would see her raped and her throat slit before making off with her horse. No one really paid any attention to her as the streets were dark and she had tucked her skirts tightly around her legs and under her.

Rounding a turn in the narrow street, she came across a group of randy, drunken pirates, singing at the top of their lungs and watching a pair of laughing women doing a bawdy dance in the mud. The two women had stripped down to their shifts and were lifting the material up high around their thighs, enticing the men slyly.

Crimson hurried past this scene, but not before she saw two of the men break from the group and topple the women on their backs. In a moment, the women were naked, the men's trousers pushed down to their ankles and they were copulating furiously in the street. Crimson choked back a cry as the others gathered around them in a circle, awaiting their turns.

Finally, she picked out the tavern called the King's Privy. With some relief she turned the horse into its narrow yard in order to tie her to one of the wooden stakes. She pulled her skirts up quickly, aware of raucous noises within the tavern, and went to the back, nearly bumping into a man who was relieving himself in the yard. Frightened, she hurried on to the steps, fairly flying up them before the startled pirate could do more than button his breeches.

She opened the door to the hallway and then turned the handle to Nick's door. Cautiously, she tiptoed in, hardly able to see in the dark, feeling her way to the bed. Her nose had picked up the scent of cheap perfume and, her senses suddenly alerted, she felt softly along the bed. Her hand glanced off a woman's naked breast and Crimson drew back as though she had been stung. She stood for a moment, breathing hard, a raging despair searing through

337

her so that a large tear ran down one cheek. She rubbed her eyes angrily and backed towards the door.

Outside in the hallway, she leaned against the wall, willing her heart to stop its furious beating. Damn him! Oh, damn him! Somehow she felt a curious sense of betrayal, of destroyed trust that could not be renewed. She stuck her hand in her mouth to keep herself from sobbing. A noise caught her ear and she saw a man coming up the stairs at the opposite end of the hallway.

Quickly, she turned about and fled the way she had come, back down to the yard below, around the noisy tavern and to her horse. A hand clamped on her shoulder unnerved her so that she jumped and screamed at the same time.

"Why so nervous, sweeting?" cackled a voice, hardly sober. "Don't run away, me pigeon! We'll have a good time!"

With only a moment's thought, Crimson reached around and grabbed the pirate's dirty beard, yanking hard, at the same time stamping hard on his foot. With a yowl of pain, the man let her go and she hopped onto the mare, grabbing the bridle and digging her heels into its flanks.

"Damn ye for a bitch! Stop that wench!" she heard the man cry.

Blurred faces looked up at her in surprise, but she urged the horse to a gallop and sped through the street like a she-devil, scattering people as she passed. It would be no use to keep to the shadows now. If the pirate gained a horse, she was sure he would be after her as fast as he could. She would have to rely on speed to get her to safety.

What a fool, what a fool she had been, she told herself over and over. To risk her life to give a message to a man who lay asleep, assured of a woman whenever he wished —a trollop! Well, she had been no less a trollop, running down to meet him in his room, excited at the mere thought of being alone with him again! Fool! Fool! She ground her teeth in fury and jabbed her heels into the horse. She vowed she would not be so foolish again. To hell with his mission for the king!

338

She had crossed the bridge and was flying over the smooth sand of the beach, heading for the trail that led up the mountain through the green, raintree forest. She leaned low over the horse, trusting it to follow the path, unaware of the tears wetting her face, the sobs welling in her throat. How could he have betrayed her so!

Her horse had slowed subtly as the pressure of her heels subsided and was trotting comfortably over the trail now. Crimson was oblivious to the change in stride, did not hear the hoofbeats behind her until it was too late.

Before she knew what was happening, someone had jerked the bridle reins from her hands. She gave a frightened cry as a dark figure caught her around the waist and pulled her to his own horse, allowing the mare to trot, riderless, up the path while he steered his own horse into the trees.

Crimson struggled instinctively, desperately afraid, imagining the drunken, leering face of any one of a hundred pirates laughing down at her. As she kicked and fought, the arm tightened about her midriff, causing her to fight for breath. Then, suddenly, the arm loosened and she was dropped abruptly to the ground, where she lay, her leg folded painfully beneath her.

The silent figure dismounted and stood over her, the light of the moon behind his head obscuring his features. She could smell him, though. The tawdry scent of a whore's perfume on his doublet, the rum on his breath, stale sweat and salt spray in his hair. She knew panic and tried to crawl away.

His voice was a hoarse, low whisper. "And where would ye go, beauty? Ye cannot run away from the Barracuda!" He laughed deeply.

Crimson was nearly beyond reason as she realized who had overtaken her. Images of that scarred face, the eyepatch. She cringed and wished the earth would swallow her.

But he was bending over her, picking her up beneath the arms, hauling her up to stand before him. Before she could take two breaths, he had pressed her tightly against him, his hands cupping her buttocks through the silk of the dress, causing her belly to touch his groin in an intimacy that nauseated her.

His hips moved slightly so that she could feel the hard length of him through the silk. She struggled, fear tight in her throat, her arms coming up so that her hands could pummel him. His hands left her buttocks and caught her wrists so that she thought he meant to break them. She cried out in pain.

"Don't struggle, wench. I'll have ye—now!"

His mouth searched for hers. She smelled the rum and reared back, but he only pulled her back with a jerk. His lips closed over hers, taking them with urgency mixed with a passion that seared her mouth as he forced it open to taste the honey-sweetness of her tongue. He kissed her so long that she felt her mouth was bruised, like some bitten fruit.

His hands left her wrists and seized her bodice, tearing it quickly so that he could capture the twin globes that peaked so proudly in the balmy breeze. His caress was rough, hurried, with a mind to better things as he lowered her to the ground.

Crimson wished she could scream, but her throat felt raw from her sobs, and her hands could only pound ineffectually at his back as he pushed her skirt up to expose her womanly softness. He pulled his breeches down and lay on top of her, his heavy frame mashing her soft flesh into the warm grass.

"Please," she sobbed, the only word she spoke.

He was silent, intent on the young body beneath his. Crimson valiantly tightened the muscles of her thighs to ward him off, but his knee was strong, separating her legs as his hands quitted her breasts to insure that they remained wide apart.

Rolling her head from side to side, she moaned, afraid of him, of what he would do to her body. For a moment, his fingers trailed along her inner thighs, feeling the silken flesh with evident enjoyment, before bracing himself to enter her.

Crimson felt as though she were being split as he sheathed himself within her. She gasped, would have
340

screamed, but for his mouth covering hers again. His hands moved from her thighs to her hips and then to her buttocks, cupping them once more to force her cooperation. Thrusting, thrusting mercilessly as Crimson tried to tear her mouth away from his.

She could feel sweat pouring from her body, feel an inner heat that had nothing to do with the warmth of the night. Desperately, she tried to quell the wave of sexual desire that was washing over her. Treacherous body! But it was no use—she could not fight him and herself!

Unconsciously, she relaxed her muscles and his thrusting became less painful. The softness within her met him eagerly and her hips arched instinctively to his own rhythm. She could not stand it! His mouth was tight on her own, forcing the cries to be stifled in her throat, changing them to tiny moans of utter defeat. Was he going to pound her into the very earth!

Finally, he released her mouth to gasp out his own need as he reached his own release. Crimson screwed her eyes shut to keep out the terrible image of his face, but the thought ruined the ending for her and she felt a deep shame that made her sob in earnest. She did not see his hand come up to stroke her cheek, then pause and turn back. The regret on his face was keen as he withdrew from her and stood up.

"Ye're mine now, wench," he said softly, under his breath. "Ye belong to the Barracuda!"

He rearranged his clothing, then bent to pull down her skirt. Crimson continued to cry uncontrollably, hardly aware when he lifted her onto his horse and mounted behind her.

The next thing she knew, he was swinging her down in front of the castle. He climbed up on his horse, looked down at her and galloped back to whence they had come. Crimson, looking after him, gulped back a sob.

37

Morning came too swiftly for Crimson as she awakened with a swollen lip and a tenderness between her legs that made her wince. One thought was burned into her brain. She had been raped, raped by a pirate, by the very same pirate who had attacked her ship and stolen her money. The memory of his face filled her with bitterness and she placed the pillow over her head as though to shut out all thought.

She could barely recall stumbling back into the house, climbing the stairs to her room and collapsing on her bed. Utter mortification swept over her as she looked down at the torn, dirty dress that she had not taken off. With a sudden anger, she tore it from her body and threw it into a corner of the room. Sobs overcame her and she lay, naked in the bed, pounding her fists into the mattress.

"Crimson! My dear, are you awake?"

Crimson's head jerked up in alarm. Juliette! What was she doing up so early? Had she seen her come in? Distressed that the other woman might discern what had happened, Crimson forced herself to stop trembling.

"Yes, Juliette, but I've not dressed yet," she called back. She hated to think of the smug look on her face should she learn of the rape, a rape caused because of her silly, foolish ride to meet Nick Brentwood.

"Well, may I come in?"

Resigned, Crimson jumped up from the bed and grabbed a silk robe to cover the telltale marks on her body. She grabbed the discarded gown and threw it into a chest.

"Of course, Juliette," she called.

Juliette was dressed in a midnight-blue riding habit, which set off the ripe curves of her figure almost indecently. Crimson was aware of Juliette's quick scrutiny of Crimson's person and clenched her fists within the folds of her robe.

"You have dirt smudged on your cheek, my dear," Juliette observed drily.

Crimson's eyes widened as she glanced in her mirror. "Oh! I didn't realize—"

"Have you been rolling about in the mud, Crimson?" The voice was flat, deadly as though at any moment its owner could strike out at her.

"Of course not! I—"

"Before you try to concoct some dreadfully inept lie, I may as well tell you that the groom informed me he found my horse standing outside the stable this morning with the bridle on. Do you know anything about this?"

Crimson flushed, realizing that she had been caught. But not completely so. Not yet. She had to think of something to explain her use of the horse. "I—I couldn't sleep last night," she began cautiously. "I thought some fresh air might do me good and—"

"And you took my horse for a moonlight ride? Where did you go?"

"I—I didn't get far actually. I couldn't remain seated without the saddle and I fell off halfway down the path. The horse returned without me and I had to walk back." Crimson breathed easier after the lie was told. "Do forgive me for taking your horse without your permission, Juliette, but my head was splitting and I simply had to get out."

Juliette was silent, weighing the truth of her words. "I don't know whether to believe you or not," she said bluntly. "Your actions are awfully suspicious, my dear. But I can't imagine you going into Port Royal by yourself.

343

I doubt whether you would have been able to return here if you had." She tapped her foot uncertainly.

"Juliette, I wouldn't want to arouse any false suspicions in you. I swear I'm telling you the truth." Crimson hoped her expression was as innocent as she was trying to make it.

"All right, we won't say anything to Sir Thomas—this time, Crimson! But let us hope it doesn't happen again or I shall be forced to use—other methods, to get the truth from you." She turned on her heel and walked out of the room, leaving Crimson weak with relief.

She called the maid to bring up water for her to bathe in. As she settled herself in the tub, she found herself thinking once more of the pirate last night. He had said that she was his now, she remembered with a shudder. That she belonged to him. The thought of that gruesome figure claiming her as his property made her stomach turn and she scrubbed herself vigorously as though to wash away his mark upon her body.

When she had finished and was dressed, she felt well enough to go downstairs, especially since her stomach had begun growling unforgivably for food. Downstairs, she entered the small, private dining room and found Juliette and Sir Thomas already eating.

Sir Thomas looked up, squinting narrowly at her. Crimson suspected that Juliette must have already informed him of her escapade last night, for he did not seem at all inclined to be friendly. When she had stood at the doorway for almost a minute, Juliette finally nodded graciously.

"Come in and have something to eat, Crimson."

"Thank you, I'm famished," the girl responded quickly, seating herself at the far end of the table.

When she had been served, Sir Thomas looked at her closely. "Juliette tells me that you went for a ride quite late last night," he said, as though questioning her.

Crimson's fork paused in midair as she returned his gaze levelly. "Yes," she answered shortly, waiting for him to continue.

"You are aware, I hope, that it is highly irregular and

dangerous for a young woman of your station to be riding about at night alone." The eyes turned hawklike as his stare never wavered from her face.

"Juliette made me quite aware of that this morning," Crimson said. "It shall not happen again, I can assure you."

"I'm glad you have *some* sense, Crimson. Since you are my daughter-in-law I would expect you to conduct yourself accordingly. You may ride whenever you like during the day, escorted, of course."

Crimson took a deep breath in order to keep down her growing anger. "As you wish, Sir Thomas," she murmured softly.

"Good, I am glad the matter has been cleared up," Juliette chimed in brightly in order to take some of the tension from the room. "And after you've eaten, Crimson, you may accompany me on a ride around the island. That way I can show you the paths that are safe to ride on."

"Oh, I really don't think I can," Crimson objected, aware of the tenderness of her bottom.

"Of course, you can, my dear. I do insist," Juliette smiled.

"Yes, I think it would be a good idea," Sir Thomas put in absently as his wife touched his hand for his approval.

"There, you see, if you are to stay in our good graces, my dear, you will simply have to humor me. If you have no riding habit, I'm sure you can wear one of mine."

Crimson would have defied both of them, but stopped herself with an effort, realizing what tenuous ground she was on. She nodded tightly and finished eating in silence.

They started out following the path that wound around the back of the castle, climbing the rising slope among the tangled undergrowth of fertile green. The path followed the face of the mountain, then curved off along a wide shelf that led away from the bay towards the open sea. The two rode abreast for a time in silence, Crimson taking in the beauty of the emerald-green forest, now and then looking down towards the castle to the golden sands far below.

"The path gets a little tricky here," Juliette said, pushing her mount ahead of Crimson's. "We'll have to take it one at a time as it follows the curve of the mountain."

Crimson followed behind her, guiding the mare over the muddy trail, now and then sending small rocks sliding down into the murky forest. When they turned the corner, she saw a line of tall trees almost blocking the path, and picked her way carefully through them, following Juliette's lead. It was impossible to see the ocean now and all around were only the tall, silent trees and green underbrush. The path wound through the trees, here and there, becoming lost in some dense bushes, but emerging again on the other side.

"When will we get out of all this?" Crimson asked.

"It goes on for about a quarter of a mile until we can see the ocean again," Juliette responded.

Crimson was about to ask another question when she thought she heard something rustle in the underbrush. She slowed her horse, trying to discern from whence the sound had come. There it was again! She looked up to see if Juliette, too, had heard, but the woman was riding calmly on, obviously not alarmed.

"Juliette!" Crimson caught up to her as she stopped her horse. "I heard something in the brush a moment ago."

"Probably just a wild animal. Are you sure?" she asked.

"Yes, I heard it twice. What kind of animal could it be?"

"Well, there are wild boars up here," Juliette began, becoming concerned at the thought. "Nasty, ugly creatures, but—"

Suddenly, a piercing yell sounded in their ears and, terrified, they turned around to see five or six dark-skinned men on foot, running towards them, waving long knives above their heads.

"Oh, my God, the Maroons!" Juliette screamed and dug her heels into her horse.

Crimson did likewise and her horse bounded forward through the forest. Terrified, she tried to remember what Juliette had told her about the runaway slaves, who were kept armed by the Spanish with the express order to harry the English as much as possible on the island. What would
346

they do to two defenseless women alone on the mountain? Crimson did not wish to find out and leaned low over the horse's neck to avoid low-hanging branches over the path. In front of her, she could see Juliette's dark blue habit, likewise spread low over the horse. The slaves might have guns.

The Maroons were not daunted by the fact that they had no horses, but continued giving chase, running as fleetly as wild deer over the path. Crimson tried to concentrate on the path ahead, praying for the break in the trees when they would be out of the dense forest. They would make better time with the horses once they were out in the open.

Suddenly, a wide gap opened up on the side of the path, made from a recent mudslide. Juliette was able to force her horse over to the side and avoid the ditch, but Crimson did not see it until it was too late and the horse slipped in the soft mud, losing its footing and throwing Crimson headlong into the brush. Snorting wildly, the horse regained its footing and continued on without her.

Crimson's breath had been completely knocked out of her and she lay in a tangled thicket, a little dazed, trying to reorient herself. She tensed, hearing the yells of the Maroons, but they passed her without even pausing, obviously not having seen her fall. She realized that her sable-brown habit had probably saved her from being discovered and said a prayer of thanks.

When the yells had receded, she scrambled out of the bush, scratching her face on a thorn. The collar of her habit was ripped, and hung down her bodice, exposing her throat. She sank in the mud for a moment to catch her breath and try to think what she should do. The path was too dangerous now, for she did not know when the Maroons might come back this way, or whether there were others following them.

She looked down the slope of the mountain, peering through the greenery dubiously. Should she try to go down that way? She shrugged, realizing it was her only choice. She clambered up from the fertile loam and began making her way down, holding on to branches and thick roots.

Several yards down, when she thought her legs would break from constant tensing against the slope, the descent leveled out somewhat, allowing her to stand upright.

She had lost her hat in the fall and realizing this, she started down again quickly, thinking that the Maroons might find it and somehow figure out a way to overtake her. She slipped several times in the soft earth and once slid down on her back until a gnarled tree root stopped her. She clung to it, breathing hard and pushing the tangled locks from her face.

Once again she descended, catching footholds tentatively. A sudden cawing sound startled her, so that she nearly tumbled head over heels before she realized that it was a large blue and green parrot, staring down at her beadily and scolding her shrilly. Another bird, its plumage as beautiful as the first, joined it, and Crimson hurried away, not wanting anyone to be alerted to where she was.

After nearly an hour of tense work, she finally found herself on a level shelf which gradually lowered to a large wall of boulders, with moss and straggly bushes growing from between them. She stumbled over to them and leaned against the stone, catching her breath and gazing back up to whence she had come, peering through the forest for any glimpse of pursuit.

She could see nothing and turned back to figure a way around the rocks. She hoped that once she could gain sight of the ocean again, she could make her way to the beach and walk around to Port Royal. That was of course, in the hope that the two beaches would connect.

She scrambled over a low boulder, slipping on wet moss and scraping her knee through a rent in her habit. She began to cry softly, pressing her face against the cool rock before wiping her eyes with a dirty glove and continuing her journey.

On the other side of the boulders was a rocky shelf leading down to a protected cove, where Crimson could see a ship riding peacefully at anchor. Excited at the prospect of imminent rescue, she began the twenty-foot descent down the face of the stone cliff, gaining easy footholds from the many irregularities in the rock.

348

Finally she was on level beach, the soft, golden sand cushioning her aching feet, and she sat down abruptly, laughing and crying at the same time in a delayed reaction to her escape. Fleetingly, she wondered what had happened to Juliette, but assured herself that Juliette must have escaped and was probably on her way back to the castle to get help in finding Crimson.

She stood up, brushing the sand from her clothes, attempting to rearrange them decently enough to approach the ship. The sails were down and she looked to be getting a thorough conditioning in preparation for a long sail. The crew must be somewhere about on the beach, mending torn sailcloth and painting rusty spars. She hesitated instinctively before coming out of the shelter of the rocks, searching the sunlit beach for signs of life.

To her right she suddenly spied a makeshift lean-to where several men were, as she had thought, tending to a sailor's duties. To her left, she saw a laughing woman emerge from a screen of bushes, and she started. Confused, Crimson squatted down behind a boulder to see what might develop. A sixth sense warned her to remain still as she watched the woman run towards the beach, then veer towards the water.

From behind the screen of bushes, a man followed, naked to the waist, laughing too as he tried to catch her. The woman, whose hair was as golden as the particles of sand, splashed water towards him and ran into waist-deep water, her hands on her hips as she stuck out her tongue saucily.

"Come back here, wench, or I'll lay the whip to you!" called the man.

Crimson continued her watch, engrossed in the two people, so that she did not hear the light tread behind her until a hand suddenly reached down and clamped on her shoulder. She turned, startled, to see a toothless, grinning ruffian staring down at her.

"What have we here?" He winked at her lewdly.

Crimson stood up so suddenly that he lost his hold on her and she ducked beneath his arm to run, but where? With a sinking feeling, she glanced out at the ship and finally noticed something which she had been too elated to see before. The figurehead on the ship was a woman with the body of a bird! No! No!

She ran haphazardly out towards the beach, her presence suddenly alerting the others who began whooping and running towards her. It was child's play for them to catch her, and she fell against the sand, shutting her eyes tightly to keep out the sight of their greedy, lusting faces. The attack by the Maroons, the flight down the steep side of the slope, the pirates' faces—all spun dizzily in her mind, pressing down on her senses. Very quietly, she fainted.

38

Crimson came to slowly, rolling her head, feeling the gentle swell of a ship beneath her. She didn't want to open her eyes. She was afraid of what she was going to see.

"Come on, girl. Open up and take a sip of this wine." The voice was feminine and had a pronounced French accent. A hand slipped beneath Crimson's neck and pulled her up a little, while a glass was pressed against her lips.

"Is she awake, Countess?" This voice was decidedly masculine, a little hoarse, and Crimson recognized it at once.

"Barracuda!" she gasped and tried to struggle up out of the bunk in which they had laid her.

The girl laughed. "Ah, she knows you, my love, but it does not seem that she wishes your company, eh?" The hand became insistent on her neck as the glass was pushed into her mouth.

Crimson drank the wine slowly, opening her eyes to look into the face of the French girl called Countess. She had a pleasant, open face that just missed being pretty. It was a face that smiled a lot, for Crimson could see the tiny laugh lines around the mouth and radiating from the corners of the blue eyes.

"There now. You feel better, don't you, *chérie?*"

Crimson nodded feebly, trying to peer over the girl's shoulder to see the man who stood in the shadows. She already knew what he looked like, could imagine the lusty greed in his one eye.

"Please, help me to get away," she whispered to the girl pleadingly.

The girl laughed once more. *"Chérie,* we will not hurt you, I promise. We only wish to make sure that you are all right after your faint. Where did you come from, eh?"

"From the side of the mountain," Crimson explained, noting the disbelief in the girl's eyes. "I was with Lady Gardner, on the riding trail, and we were attacked by a group of Maroons. My—my horse threw me and I had to escape down the mountain or risk being captured. You have to help me get back to the castle," she pleaded once more.

"Of course, of course we will," the girl assured her. "Just rest now."

She patted her on the shoulder and Crimson fell back on the bunk. She didn't want the girl to leave, didn't want to be left alone with the man who still lurked in the shadows.

"Don't leave me."

"I'll just be a moment. You'll be safe in here," the girl soothed.

She left the cabin and Crimson glanced uneasily to where the man still stood, watching her silently. Fear rose in her throat, and she could not take her eyes off the unmoving shadow. It seemed forever before the girl returned.

"The longboat is ready, darling. Do you wish to row her back yourself?"

"No, have Pitney take her."

"The men have their doubts. What if she talks about our cove?"

"She won't talk. I'll see to it, wench. Take her on deck now."

Crimson could barely distinguish the conversation as it was uttered in low tones, but she shivered as she made out those last words of the pirate captain.

"I give my word," she began desperately, "I will not tell anyone about this place. I—I couldn't even remember how to get back here again."

"You'll be blindfolded in the longboat, but Pitney will take you 'round to Port Royal. I'll be going with you," the French girl assured her.

She guided Crimson out of the cabin and up to the deck where the men were staring at her curiously. One young man in particular kept his gaze steadily on her, so long that Crimson's eyes were drawn towards him. She gasped inwardly as she recognized the boy who had attacked her on the *Margaret*, the same who had killed one of the crew before escaping. She took her eyes away from his quickly, hating the slow smile that distorted his face when she had met his gaze.

She was led down the rope ladder to a dinghy below where a stout man awaited her and the French girl. Once inside the boat, she was blindfolded. She could feel the powerful sweep of the oars as they cut through the water. She tried not to think of the man who commanded the ship with the haunting figurehead. He had raped her last night, taken her in the darkness of the night, but now in the light of day he had not touched her. What sort of phantom was he to her?

When the boat arrived in Port Royal harbor, Crimson's blindfold was taken off and the man called Pitney helped both her and the French girl ashore. He then took his leave, disappearing quickly among the other moored ships.

On the wharf, the girl turned towards Crimson with a friendly grin.

"You'd better let me get you through the crowd along the docks, otherwise you might be mistaken for fair game. Come on, I'll take you to my place and you can wipe your face and fix your dress. You can send someone up to the hill for a carriage to bring you back."

It sounded like a good idea to Crimson, who had no intention of trying to get through the crowds alone. She stayed one step behind the girl, her eys on the ground as they made their way to a tavern called the Green Jade. Along the way, the girl called to several men, received salutations from many more and grinned brassily at everyone.

Inside the Green Jade, Crimson was led upstairs to a small cubicle which held a pallet, a chest and a few clothes hung on nails in the wall.

"It isn't like the castle, but it's home to me," the girl said with a touch of defiance, when she saw Crimson gazing around the room bleakly.

"You do keep it—tidy," Crimson said lamely, not wishing to offend the girl who had kindly offered her hospitality.

"Yes, I do," she admitted candidly, "for the men don't like to tumble about in the slops, if you know what I mean." She winked and laughed at the expression of chagrin on Crimson's face. "Heh, I didn't even catch your name, *chérie*. Mine is Delia."

Delia. The name was familiar, but Crimson couldn't quite place it. "My name is Crimson Gardner."

"Gardner? You're related to them on the hill, then?"

"Not through blood. I was married to Sir Thomas' oldest son before he was killed. I came over from England only recently."

"Ah, no wonder I've not seen you around. Besides, I'm sure Kit would have told me about you if—"

"Kit! That's right, I knew I'd heard your name before!" Crimson shouted. "You're—you're Kit's—" She blushed suddenly.

"Kit's what?" the girl asked laughingly. "I bed with him

353

now and then, but I've got no exclusive rights to him as far as who he likes to tumble. I'm not the jealous type, *chérie*. We enjoy each other occasionally, but we both have other interests."

"You seem so—casual," Crimson commented, still red. "From what Juliette told me, you and Kit—"

"Juliette Gardner! That jealous bitch can't stand the idea of Kit sinking it into anyone but her! She's a man-eater, I'm telling you!"

"Well, I know she is fond of Kit—" Crimson began, not wanting to know the meaning of Delia's words.

"Hah! She would be unfaithful at the swish of a skirt if it were up to her! She wants Kit, she's always wanted him. That's why she married his father, to be close to him. Sooner or later she'll get him. A man can only say no so many times." Delia's expression grew stony. "That woman is no damn good for Kit."

Crimson was silent, sensing the other girl's angry torment. Perhaps she cared for Kit more than she would admit, even to herself. Crimson frowned to herself with a touch of irony. With so many women chasing after him, it was a wonder Kit had attempted to seduce her when she arrived. Hadn't he enough to satisfy him? But enough of him, she thought suddenly. She wondered if Delia would give her any information about the pirate Barracuda.

"The man you were with today, the pirate captain," she began slowly, "he is the one called Barracuda, isn't he?"

Delia turned to her, throwing off her previous thoughts. "Yes," she said, glancing curiously at the other girl. She seemed to be trying to gauge Crimson's intentions.

"He was the one who attacked the ship I was on, the *Margaret*." She took a deep breath. "I remember seeing him and a woman called Countess. He called you that today. You sail with him, don't you?"

For a moment, Delia was taken aback and her face paled a little. Then she nodded reluctantly. "Yes, I do sail with him sometimes when he allows it."

"I've heard that the woman who sails with Barracuda has killed her share of men," Crimson went on.

Delia gazed intently at her. "So you have heard, so you
354

should be warned," she said in a low voice. She took a step towards Crimson.

"You have nothing to fear from me," Crimson assured her hastily. "I only wanted to make sure that you were the same. I am curious about this pirate captain."

"Why?" Delia asked bluntly, but in her eyes there was a certain small lurking fear which bewildered Crimson.

"Because he—because he stole something of mine," she said. And because, she thought, he has sullied my body, has dared to call me his possession. "I was carrying all my valuables on the *Margaret* and they were gone from my cabin after the attack."

Delia shrugged. "Perhaps he took them, perhaps one of the crew. You are lucky that they did not search the ship for the woman who owned them." Her meaning was clear and Crimson could not help shuddering.

"But who is this man? Why?" She couldn't go on. It would be impossible for her to confide in this stranger her real fear: why had he followed her last night, why did he want her?

"Who is he?" Delia repeated almost to herself. "He is only another pirate, Crimson. Another of the thousand who dot the ocean from the colonies in New England to the Spanish territories to the south of us. He is no more than that. You would do well to forget about him, his ship and the secret cove. Should you try to inform on him, it would be your undoing." She was warning Crimson against the danger that awaited her.

But I cannot forget him, Crimson thought desperately. *I cannot forget that he took my body and claimed it for himself. Did he truly mean what he said, or will this be the last that I see of him?* If she could only be sure.

"I'll go downstairs and see about a messenger," Delia said, changing the subject abruptly. "There's water in the pitcher."

"Thank you," Crimson murmured, but the girl had already flown out the door, obviously wishing to avoid further conversation. Crimson wondered fleetingly how she could share her body with Kit and the pirate and with the many others who had called out her name on the docks.

She was a strange woman, indeed, one who had killed for the sake of gold, was protective of a renegade pirate, enjoyed the favors of the son of the highest ranking gentleman on the island. A remarkable woman! It would be best to keep her as a friend. She could prove a deadly enemy, she was sure.

Crimson performed her hurried ablutions and waited in the room for Delia to return. It took a few minutes before the latter stuck her head through the door and informed her that the messenger had left and the carriage would probably arrive within the hour. Then she was away again with a mumbled excuse about being needed below in the common room.

"You've been very kind," Crimson called after her. "I shall be sure to repay you."

She didn't know if Delia had heard her or not, but she knew that they would meet again.

Inside the castle, there was some chaos as Crimson arrived in the foyer. Juliette, looking bedraggled for once, rushed out of the library to clasp Crimson against her and Sir Thomas followed afterwards, a worried frown on his face.

"Those damned Maroons! There's got to be a way to stop these attacks on innocent townspeople!" he raged. "Good God, I think I aged ten years when Juliette came flying in here and told me what happened. Crimson, we weren't sure if you were alive!"

Crimson tried to explain what had happened, then caught herself up, recalling the promise she had made to Delia and the pirate captain. Stupid to feel responsible for such a promise, she thought to herself, but the memory of Delia's face, warning her, made her keep silent.

"I found a path back to the town," she ended lamely.

"Thank God, those savages didn't capture you," Juliette said, "I was only lucky that my horse was able to outdistance them, once we reached the flatlands."

"That does it!" Sir Thomas proclaimed. "You will not ride up into the mountain any more without an armed escort, Juliette, nor you, Crimson. It is far too dangerous.

356

I'll have to send soldiers up into the hills to scour those savages out!"

"Yes, dear," Juliette said approvingly. "Poor dear Crimson must think she has come to some wild, uncivilized world." She gazed at the younger girl with false sympathy.

"I think I'll go up to my room now, if you don't mind," Crimson said. "I'd like to change and take a nap before lunch. It has been an ordeal."

"Of course, dear. If you like I'll have a tray sent up when you awaken," Juliette called after her.

Crimson nodded and hurried up the stairs to her room, her mind whirling with the new disclosures she had learned today.

39

Plans for Juliette's ball went smoothly, and Crimson threw herself into the preparations fervently, hoping to keep her mind off her encounter with the Barracuda and her wistful anger towards Nick. The invitations were sent out and the hall was decorated by the time Kit returned from his voyages.

Crimson was in the sitting room, reading a book without much enthusiasm, when she heard Kit's expansive voice hailing his father in the hallway. Despite her thoughts of Delia and Juliette and all Kit's other women, she knew she was glad to see him, for he was probably the only friend she had on this island.

She hurried out into the hallway to greet him, her face smiling her welcome. "Kit, I'm so glad you're back!"

His dark eyes lit up in response to her smile and he walked towards her in order to embrace her warmly. His arms held her tightly and his mouth on hers was commanding so that when he released her she was a little breathless and looked away from the question in his gaze.

"Crimson?" he began.

"Kit! Oh, Kit, how wonderful that you're home again!" cried Juliette, flying down the stairs to throw her arms about him in anything but a motherly fashion. She seemed oblivious to Sir Thomas, standing a few feet away. "Darling, we've planned a huge party and—"

"Kit must be tired, Juliette," Sir Thomas broke in suddenly. "Why don't you let him go upstairs? You can tell him about the party later."

Juliette's lower lip stuck out petulantly as she sulked for a moment. Then her face brightened. "All right, Thomas, but as soon as Kit has refreshed himself he can drive me down to town to pick up my ball gown." She fluttered her lashes up at Kit. "You will, won't you, Kit?"

He grinned with easy self-assurance. "If you wish, Juliette." Then, turning to Crimson once more, "And what about you, sweeting? Have you a ball gown to pick up also?"

She shook her head, aware of Juliette watching her closely. "No. Mine was brought from England and it needed no alterations."

"I trust it will be suitably stunning," he laughed, tracing a finger down her jawline with easy arrogance.

"I hope you like it," she responded, moving her head slightly, just enough to keep him from touching her.

"If I like it, and I'm sure I will, you must make sure to dance all the dances with me, Crimson." His eyes were looking into hers, a silent question in their depths that caused her to feel uneasy.

"You're embarrassing Crimson, Kit," Juliette broke in. "I'm sure there will be many others who'll want to dance with our little widow," she added with a touch of sarcasm.

Sir Thomas stepped towards his son and put an arm about his shoulder in order to steer him away from the two women. "I must tell you what happened a few days ago, Kit, as soon as you've changed. We've got to do something about those Maroons up in the hills." His voice trailed off as he and Kit ascended the steps, leaving Juliette and Crimson staring at each other.

"You'd best be careful of my stepson," Juliette said softly, to break the tense silence. "You can see how easily he tends to overwhelm people, especially vulnerable young women like yourself."

"He was only glad to see me," Crimson put in defiantly.

Juliette laughed as though at some poor, simple-minded child. "My dear, it's easy to see you have had very little experience with men. Obviously, Reginald had no time at all to teach you anything."

"Please don't worry about me, Juliette," Crimson said shortly, to break off the conversation, and turned around to return to her book.

"Oh, my dear, I'll worry about you constantly," Juliette said, almost to herself.

It was later that day that Crimson was out in the gardens, walking aimlessly through the patterned rows of blooming flowers and flowering shrubbery, and saw Juliette and Kit returning from the trip to Port Royal. Juliette was laughing at some sally from Kit and she leaned towards him in the open carriage, her breast leaning against his arm. Kit laughed too and reached out to draw her closer.

For a moment, Juliette's face took on the expression of the predator as she turned her face towards Kit's, offering him her lips as she closed her eyes. Crimson held her breath as Juliette's hand found Kit's and led it to her breast which was spilling enticingly out of the froth of her bodice.

Kit's hand strayed across the smooth, olive-toned flesh, dipping once inside the bodice to tease the taut point, but he did not kiss her except to brush her mouth with his own almost tauntingly.

Juliette's eyes flew open and her expression tightened.

359

Crimson could not hear what she said, but saw Kit's eyes flick over the castle as he answered her as though warning her that Sir Thomas could be watching them. Crimson half-turned around, expecting to see Sir Thomas' face peering through one of the windows.

Juliette raised her hand as though to slap Kit, but changed her mind quickly, flouncing out of the carriage and calling back to him to bring in her gown. She disappeared inside the front door, leaving Kit gazing after her, his expression one of supreme confidence mixed with a fleeting desire. Crimson hurried back into the cover of the garden, lest Kit see her watching him.

That evening at supper, Crimson was surprised and a little concerned to see Nick joining them at the table. Sir Thomas explained that he had invited Nick Brentwood up to talk business after dinner and also to personally invite him to the ball the following week. Crimson was careful to keep her eyes on her plate, not wishing for him to engage her in conversation.

She needn't have worried, though, for Juliette monopolized him during supper, perhaps partly because she wanted to make Kit jealous and partly because she was attracted to Nick anyway. Crimson watched her lean towards him with open invitation in her eyes, her bosom bulging from her bodice, so that even Sir Thomas could not help but notice and spoke curtly to Crimson to assuage his own anger.

"Have you learned table conversation at court?" he wondered, making note of Crimson's silence. "God's blood, girl, you're as quiet as a mouse!"

Crimson flushed as all eyes were drawn to her face. "Excuse me, Sir Thomas, I didn't mean to be rude. I was just—thinking."

"Well, kindly do your thinking somewhere else," he sputtered on. "I would appreciate a little conversation myself," he went on pointedly, glancing towards his wife.

"Forgive me, Sir Thomas, your wife was entertaining me with some amusing stories of life on the island," Nick spoke up. "She was also telling me about the narrow escape that she and your daughter-in-law had a few days
360

ago. I understand you have sent soldiers to scour the hills for the Maroons."

"That I have, Nick. I'll not stand for my own family to be terrorized by those renegades. They're worse than the pirates."

"Ah, yes, the pirates. You know some of them aren't really a bad sort, only when they're drunk or out of luck. I've met quite a few in town and have spoken to some about providing me with goods to export to England. I'm hoping I can strike a bargain with a number of them."

"Bah, you can't trust the word of a pirate!" Sir Thomas argued. "He'll sign anything and then turn around and rob your own ships as they take the goods to England. I'm afraid, Nick, you'll find the business you're in rather a rough one here. Perhaps you should go into something else." He leaned across the table, his eyes sharpening. "You know I could use an assistant here with government affairs on the island. That is, until the new governor arrives. But it could turn into something permanent later on."

Crimson was aware of Nick's set smile and knew how he must feel having been invited to gain access to the secrets of the castle, so to speak. She waited to see what Nick would answer, knowing already that he would say yes.

"The offer is tempting, Sir Thomas," he began slowly.

In more ways than one, Crimson thought, noting Juliette's secret smile.

"I must warn you, though, I've had little experience in government affairs. I'm not sure I would be of much use to you."

"I need someone to help inventory goods, see to the prisoners. It wouldn't be hard," Sir Thomas insisted.

Crimson thought Nick must be thinking of his own luck to be handed such an opportunity by the very man he was sent to watch. His smile was slow, confident, his eyes narrowed.

"You might even wish to take rooms here in the castle," Kit offered lazily, intent on Nick's expression. "It would

361

be closer to your work." He smiled as Juliette turned to him with a scowl.

"Let me think on it," Nick said, giving Kit a sideways glance. "I'll give you my answer at the ball, Sir Thomas."

The older man nodded. "Fair enough, Nick. Keep in mind that I'm not just doing this as a favor. You will have quite a bit of work to keep you busy."

The rest of the meal passed quickly in pleasantries and Crimson was more than glad to say good-night, aware of Kit's bold looks and the air of tension between Nick and him. Juliette sat between them, looking as pleased as a cat licking the last of the cream from her face. Poor Sir Thomas, Crimson thought fleetingly, wondering if he really guessed at the depth of his wife's infidelity.

In her room, she undressed slowly, pacing the room restlessly after she had gotten into her nightgown. She wasn't sure if she liked the idea of Nick being so close. She knew he would accept Sir Thomas' offer—it was his whole reason for being here. She sat down in a chair, her knees folded beneath her, gazing out her open window into the balmy night. Everything seemed suddenly so confused. She didn't know what to do, didn't even know what she wanted. Should she ever have come here?

Hours later, she was awakened by a small sound close by. Startled, she looked around wildly for a moment, before realizing that she had fallen asleep in the chair. She stood up and yawned, stretching luxuriously. A knock on the door made her pause before climbing into bed.

"Who is it?" she called out.

"It's Kit. May I come in for a moment?"

"Kit! I'm dressed for bed. I was asleep until you woke me up," Crimson returned, grabbing for her robe.

"Please, Crimson, I want to talk to you."

Crimson hesitated. "Can I trust you to behave yourself?" she asked.

She heard his muffled laughter. "I won't make any promises, my sweet," he answered, "but I will do my best to keep a curb on my animal instincts."

Crimson sighed and gave in. She knew he was capable

362

of remaining in the hall for a long time, harrassing her so that she couldn't get to sleep anyway.

"All right, but only for a few minutes," she said, unlocking the door and closing it behind him. "What do you want?"

"You, of course, my beauty," he said with a mocking sigh. "You don't know how I've waited for this moment," he went on teasingly. "You and I alone."

"Kit, don't tease me," Crimson objected. "Was it something important?"

"You hurt me deeply, my love," he said, still playing his role. "Here I'm ready to declare my heartfelt devotion and you ask me if it is important!" He laughed softly, coming closer to her.

Crimson backed up a little. "Kit, I don't want you to——"

"Crimson, why don't you relent just a little?" he sighed. "After all, it's not as though you were a virgin any longer."

Crimson gasped. "How dare you! The state of my personal life is none of your concern!"

"Don't jump at me like an angry cat, Crimson. I just meant that you have been married and——"

"I know what you meant, Kit Gardner." She huffed, eyeing him furiously.

"All right, then, I ask your forgiveness. It was tactless of me."

She remained silent for a moment, but finally had to relent in the face of his pitiable expression. "If you only came up here to antagonize me, I would appreciate your leaving at once, Kit. I am tired."

"I dropped in on Delia today, on my way up from the docks," he shot at her suddenly, taking her off guard. "It seems you two have met."

"You—talked—with her?" she asked, sitting down abruptly on a nearby chair, her hand to her forehead.

He nodded, his expression strangely grim. "It seems you were captured by pirates and released through the kindness of the Barracuda. She said she took you to her room when you were returned to Port Royal and you were asking a lot of questions."

"She told you that?" Crimson asked weakly. "Why would she tell you such a thing?"

He shrugged. "Delia trusts me."

"But now you know that she allows that—that pirate to —" she gulped. "I mean, don't you care that you share her with that terrible murderer!"

"Delia does as she wishes. She makes no demands on me. When I want her, if she's free, we enjoy each other. It makes for a simple and satisfying relationship."

"You sound so callous about it," Crimson accused him.

"Crimson, I don't ask for your judgment on my actions," he broke in. "What I want from you is information on this Barracuda. Where is this cove?"

Crimson looked up quickly. "I—I cannot tell you, Kit. Delia warned me."

"You don't need to worry about Delia. She'll do as I say."

"Then why don't you ask her about the cove?" Crimson asked with spirit.

For a moment he seemed at a loss. "I know she won't tell me, Crimson. The Barracuda would kill her if she told anyone."

"And what about me, then? He would do away with me faster than he would kill his own paramour!"

He gave her a sidelong glance. "I think not, Crimson. From what Delia has told me, the Barracuda holds a special attraction for you."

"What! She's crazy! He—"

She stopped. Could she tell Kit that the pirate captain had raped her? But he might question how she came to be in Port Royal in the middle of the night. She glanced over at him and noted a curious intenseness about him. What was it? Jealousy over a pirate's feelings for her? Impossible!

"He would kill me without a touch of remorse when it came to saving himself," she finished awkwardly, not meeting his eyes.

He shrugged. "You will not tell me where the cove is then?"

She shook her head. "Truly, Kit, I only came upon it by
364

accident. I was trying to get down the mountainside, to get away from the Maroons and—and there it was! I wouldn't know how to get there from Port Royal, for I was blindfolded and besides, I just want to forget about it! If I never see the Barracuda again, I would count myself blessed. As for Delia, she was—kind to me," she admitted. Then she glanced up narrowly at Kit. "And she did some talking on her own about you and Juliette."

Kit seemed surprised. "She has no right to conjecture about something she knows nothing about."

"Perhaps not," Crimson returned, "but you sometimes give me pause in your relationship with your dear stepmother."

He grinned suddenly. "My dear stepmother's relationship with me is really none of your business, is it, Crimson?"

She flushed. "Well, I—I—"

"Crimson, don't worry yourself about what happens between Juliette and me," he said matter-of-factly. "If I want to bed the bitch, I'll do so at my own pleasure. Whether I do so or not has nothing to do with you."

Crimson had to admit to herself that he was right. "I suppose it has nothing to do with your father either?" she snapped waspishly.

He had the grace to redden. Then he folded his arms and gave her a look of amused wonder. "God's blood, Crimson, I come in here to question you about your little escapade with the pirates and the conversation somehow finds its way to the matter of my relationship with Juliette and my father. You do have a way about you, my love."

He stepped closer to her. "But let's not talk about anyone but us for a moment. Come here, Crimson, and welcome me home properly."

His wry grin was engaging, but Crimson shook her head firmly. "You've been welcomed enough for two men," she said ruefully. "I doubt that you need any more embraces tonight."

"Ah, but I do need yours, Crimson. Yours is the only one that would please me enough to make me wish for more. Come here, Crimson," he commanded softly.

"No! You get out of my room and let me get some sleep, before Juliette comes looking for you and discovers you here," she threw at him sarcastically.

He stood over her and grasped her arms to pull her out of her chair. "I simply won't believe you don't want me here, Crimson," he murmured.

His lips came down on hers, melting them until they parted to allow him the sweetness of her mouth. His arms were around her, pressing her against his body. Warm, so warm, she thought. It would be easy for her to let him make love to her, easy to accept the strength of his embrace as the illusion of his protection. But she knew she could not rely on him to protect her from the Barracuda, or even from Juliette.

Firmly she disengaged herself and pushed him away. "No more, Kit," she said, looking up at him. "Please go now."

He hesitated, but something in her eyes changed his mind. "All right, Crimson, I'll go, but I won't always let you slip through my fingers."

He released her and walked out of the room, closing the door behind him. When he had gone, Crimson sat back in the chair, running her hands through her hair distractedly. She could not hold him at bay much longer, she realized. Why must she hold him away from her at all?

"Thank God I wasn't forced to witness a sordid love scene," came a voice from the darkness of the window. "Are you recovered from his ardor, Crimson?"

Crimson jumped up, eyes wide, straining to see in the moonlight. Then her brow furrowed in outrage. "Nick Brentwood! Come out here in the candlelight, you sly snake!"

He laughed mockingly. "Oh, Crimson, I must admit I was hard put to keep myself hidden a few times there. I wasn't sure whether or not I should leap out to protect your—honor." He coughed sarcastically.

"Get out! Get out immediately or I will scream for help!" she exclaimed furiously. "It's not enough that I have one scoundrel keeping me from my bed, but now you!"

366

"My dear, I am certainly not keeping you from your bed. By all means, climb in and we can talk."

"Talk! I have nothing to say to you!"

He strode within the circle of light and Crimson was struck anew by the handsome, dark face, the arrogant tilt of his head, the challenging smile on his lips. She trembled, remembering him with that cheap harlot at the tavern. If she had found him alone, what would have happened? She shook her head abruptly to clear such thoughts.

"Crimson, do you remember our little talk? Have you any information for me?" he asked, noting her distress, but choosing to ignore it.

"Information?" She was tempted to say no, to let him do his own spying, but then she realized that he was quite capable of haranguing her all night. "Yes, Juliette told me where the treasure is hidden. There is a special room under the castle next to the dungeons. There are only two keys, though. One is kept hidden, the other is on Sir Thomas' person at all times."

"Is that all?"

She shrugged. "Juliette seemed suspicious when I asked her too many questions. I didn't want her to guess my intentions."

"You did well, Crimson. I seem to have recruited you into my task," he said, smiling warmly at her.

"Well, no longer, I'm afraid," she said warily. "You have slipped into the good graces of Sir Thomas now. You can do the rest on your own."

"I've got to get the key to get into the treasure room, Crimson," he began seriously. "It's the only way I can tell if he's hoarding some for himself, that, and his account books."

"It shouldn't be too hard to look over those," Crimson said. "I'm sure he keeps them with his other papers."

He shook his head. "It wouldn't be very smart of him, and I have a feeling that Sir Thomas is pretty careful about hiding such damning evidence."

"If he is so careful, why would he want a stranger like yourself helping him?"

367

He shrugged. "I'm not sure. It sounds as though I'll be doing a lot of menial, unimportant tasks to keep him from having to take up his time. Time he could use to gain more of the treasure."

"Do you really think he's extorting some of it?" she asked curiously.

"I think both he and Juliette are greedy little souls and if the opportunity presented itself, I think he would take advantage of it. What more golden opportunity than to have the governor be recalled, so that you are the only one in charge of shipping the goods back to England? I learned that Sir Thomas has an old grudge against the king. He had hoped for a title upon the king's ascent to the throne during the Restoration, but didn't get it. Perhaps he decided to take some of the wealth as just payment for his loss of a higher rank."

"Oh, Nick, I could care less if Sir Thomas is keeping some of the treasure for himself. What does it matter really? Hasn't the king enough to satisfy him?"

He smiled with amusement. "Oh, Crimson, how naïve you are, my sweet. The king, and the rest of England, never have enough to suit themselves. The king needs every bit of gold he can lay his hands on. The Parliament screams at him when he talks of raising taxes in order to keep his mistresses dripping in jewels that could pay for a thousand loaves of bread for the poor. The treasure from the New World is the king's tribute. He doesn't have to account for any of it to Parliament. Do you understand now?"

She nodded reluctantly. "But I still don't care. It's not my problem. You're the one he sent here to spy for him."

He agreed readily. "You're right, Crimson." He looked at her disdainfully. "I won't trouble you anymore."

He turned to take his leave, but Crimson stopped him with a hand on his arm. "Please don't be angry with me, Nick."

"Crimson, Crimson," he sighed. "You're just like any other pretty young woman of our times, her head filled only with her own hopes for wealth and titles. My dear, perhaps you ought not to have put Kit off like you did. He
368

might be a splendid catch for you." His words were biting, meant to wound her.

Stung, Crimson responded with her own anger. "Yes, perhaps I will then. It would be better than—" She could not go on. Better than loving you, she had wanted to say, but would have bitten her tongue before letting him think she cared for him. "I suppose you can enjoy yourself with the dockside trollops. It might be amusing for you and Kit to share Lady Juliette, too. You could have her on Sundays and Kit on Mondays. Of course, you would have to make allowances for Sir Thomas. After all, he is her husband." She was babbling anything, wanting to hurt him, wanting to cover her own hurt.

He turned to her, and his fingers were on her shoulders crushing them painfully. "I am quite capable of making my own choices where my women are concerned," he said tightly. He eyed her bed suggestively. "I could take you now, Crimson, but—" his eyes were cruel, "I simply don't have the inclination." He released her abruptly.

Crimson felt tears of raging hurt welling in her eyes, felt sobs in her throat threatening to break through. She watched him go out the door, hating him—and wishing he would have stayed. . . .

40

The day of the party dawned hot and sunny. By coincidence, it was the day before Crimson's eighteenth birthday and Juliette had graciously announced that they would celebrate the event at the party tonight.

Crimson was despondent, despite the maid's assurance that her gown was beautiful and she would dazzle everyone at the entertainment that evening. Nick had surreptitiously avoided her for the past few days, and Kit was strangely withdrawn as though he had something on his mind.

The guests were due to arrive at eight o'clock, and at seven, Crimson began her bath, luxuriating in the warm water, seeking solace in relaxation. The warm steam sent the tendrils of hair curling about her ears and put an attractive pink flush to her fair skin. When she had dried herself and had donned her silk chemise, the maid arranged her hair in shimmering, auburn ringlets, which resembled a Grecian coiffure and accented the girl's patrician nose and wide expanse of brow. Her gown of emerald-green satin made her eyes look like spring grass, and two large white blossoms pinned in her hair completed the look of mystery about her. She wore no jewels, but she wore a thin ribbon of black satin about her throat, to which another, smaller, blossom had been pinned.

Picking up her plumed fan, she gazed at her reflection in the mirror for a moment before shrugging and starting downstairs. After all, what did beauty matter when she wasn't happy? Her happiness, she had come to realize, had much to do with Nick's attitude towards her.

Downstairs, some of the guests had begun arriving, and she spied Juliette and Sir Thomas at the door receiving their company. Kit was in the great hall, flirting absently with the daughter of one of the merchants, and Nick was standing at ease by one of the windows, his eyes meeting hers as she entered the room.

Almost shyly, Crimson approached him. "Good evening, Nick. You look handsome tonight," she said.

He seemed surprised by her directness. "Thank you, Crimson, and you look utterly lovely. I am hard pressed not to take you away with me."

Crimson blushed and her heart beat faster. Was he flirting with her, or just teasing her, the words meaning nothing to him? She looked into the dark blue eyes, noting with a start the faint scar at his temple. She smiled tentatively, wanting him to smile back at her.

"You seem in a fair mood tonight, Crimson, especially since our last meeting. What has happened to change your attitude towards me?" he asked softly.

"Nothing, Nick. I'm—I'm sorry that I was so selfish before. I realize now that what you're doing is important to you and the king. My small trials can hardly be compared to your business, but I was upset."

"How goes it with your determined brother-in-law?" he asked abruptly, shifting his position impatiently.

Crimson blinked at the change in subject, then recovered herself. "I have hardly seen Kit since—that night. He seems preoccupied."

"Perhaps Juliette has finally gotten to him," Nick observed almost to himself. "A man can hardly hold out against her forever."

Crimson took a deep breath and hid her expression behind the wave of her fan. "Does that include you too, Nick?" she asked tensely.

He laughed mockingly. "Prying, Crimson?" Then at her furious expression, "Yes, I suppose it does, when there is no one else to compete with her." His dark blue eyes delved into hers, a subtle question in them mixed with a desire he was unable to hide. "I did make you a promise, but it is up to you to release me from it." His intention was obvious, Crimson thought. He wanted her as his mistress, the same relationship that he had enjoyed in England for so short a time.

Her brows drew down. "You enjoy making it hard for me, don't you?" she asked him. "Why can't we be friends, Nick?"

He shrugged. "Crimson, I'm a man who needs women for only one thing. You're a woman who can satisfy that certain need admirably. As far as anything else is concerned, what does it matter when we can enjoy each other's bodies?"

"Oh!" She waved the fan with growing fury. Why did he do this to her? "If I am only a body to you, then I suppose it hardly matters what's inside my head, does it? In that case, Juliette or some cheap tavern whore would do just as well!" She was almost crying. "I hate you! Do you hear me? I don't care if I never see you again!" She searched frantically for a handkerchief. She was succeeding only in embarrassing herself, she thought unhappily.

She felt Nick's hand on her arm, pulling her towards him, away from the room, out onto the small balcony, into the moonlight. Gently, he drew her into his embrace and sighed into her hair.

"I'm sorry, Crimson," he said unexpectedly. His fingers were gentle, turning her face to him. "I'm only lying to myself when I say I don't care about you. I'm not used to feeling this way about a woman, my sweet. I think I'm fighting it too hard."

She sniffed and looked up at him. "What—what do you mean?"

"I mean, my little beauty, that I'd be a fool to let you go again, after I already lost you once in London. Come to me tonight, Crimson. I want you," he murmured, his lips coming down on hers with urgent command.

Mesmerized by the kiss, Crimson clung to him with sudden passion. His mouth worked on hers with masculine confidence, molding the clinging lips to his own, tasting the sweetness of her mouth, his tongue touching hers. His hands pressed her against him, moving up the length of her back, reaching around to cup the soft roundness of her eager breasts. Their kiss was endless, and Crimson felt herself whirling in a dizzying eddy, wanting him to take her there on the balcony, wanting to seal this new-found caring with their bodies. He wanted her, he had admitted it!

But through the mindless joy of the embrace, a sudden, unbidden thought sprang to the surface. He wanted her, yes, but was that all? He had wanted the tavern whore too. Did he want Juliette? How many other women had he wanted? Wanting was a carnal thing, a word invoking an aching need only in that region below the waist. What of his mind, his heart?

Tearing herself from his embrace, she looked up at him.
372

They were both breathing hard, feeling that sweet, bitter ache that demanded satisfaction. His eyes were nearly black with his desire, and he reached to take her in his arms again. Crimson stepped back.

"What is it, Crimson?" he asked, frowning. "Come, we need not play games with each other now. Let us fulfill our desires." His eyes were ruthless.

She shook her head. "No, you will only use my body, Nick. You care nothing for what is in my mind, my heart. What of love?"

"Love?" he seemed genuinely surprised. "I want you, Crimson, and you want me. What else is there?"

She swallowed bravely. "After you tire of my body, Nick, what then? Will you go to another woman, leaving me alone again? I don't want that."

He glanced at her with a sudden cynical arrogance that made her heart freeze. "What do you want then, Crimson? Do you want me to tell you that I love you? Would that make everything right, would that give you leave to present me with the treasure of your body?"

She was trembling with her longing for him, but she shook her head. "No, Nick, for I know they would be empty words to you," she said sadly. "I do not want you to say something you wouldn't mean." She took a deep breath. "But I won't let you take me without love."

"Damn you, I'll take you when and where I want," he said savagely. His hands reached for her, crushing her arms, drawing her to him again. He pressed her against his body, not to cherish, but to hurt, to force her to submit. His mouth was heated, urgent, ungentle now as Crimson struggled to get out of his embrace.

With fierce strength, Nick pulled her down the short steps that led onto the grounds. Quickly, he pulled her to the side, pushing her down to the soft lawn beneath a patch of blossoming shrubbery. Crimson fought him, tears streaming down her cheeks, hating him for destroying her new-found love. Silently, they wrestled on the ground. Nick's hands were pulling up the skirt of her gown, not even taking time for preliminaries. He fumbled with his

373

breeches, trying to hold her down and ready himself at the same time.

"My God," he half-joked, "you fight like a tigress!" Then, clipping the words: "But I have you now, you teasing beauty! I'll take you here and now! It's what you've wanted since I saw you again on the island, isn't it?"

"No, no," Crimson sobbed. "Not like this, Nick, please not like this." She was remembering the first time he awakened her womanhood in the gardens of Saint-Cloud. "Be gentle, at least, Nick. Remember the first time you took me. You—"

"So, you remember that, do you?" he said tightly, finally succeeding in forcing her tautened thighs apart. "Well, let us see how much you've learned since then!"

Crimson hardly heard him as she thought back to that time. "You didn't even care about me then, did you, Nick? You left me with a child, but the thought never occurred—"

"A child!" He stopped just as he was about to thrust into her. "What child? You brought no child with you to the island, did you?" He shook her slightly by the shoulders. "What are you babbling about, Crimson?"

She laughed forlornly. "Oh, yes, I was with child when I arrived in England. Your child, Nick. But it wouldn't do for me to arrive pregnant at my own wedding, would it, especially when my husband was not even the father! So like my own conception, you see. My mother's husband was not my father either. It did seem as though the sins of the mother were being revisited on the daughter." She choked back a sob. "But I didn't keep the baby, you see. Lord Haviland was determined that I should not prove an embarrassment to him, and so he arranged to have the child aborted."

"Good God, Crimson!" Nick exclaimed, falling back weakly.

"Oh, it wasn't all that sordid, Nick," she murmured thickly. "I tried to run away to save the baby—foolish of me, of course—and I fell and miscarried. Justice is done, wouldn't you say?" She began crying in earnest, heavy sobs that wracked her body.

374

Nick shook his head, feeling a sudden, unexpected lump in his own throat. "Crimson, I—"

"Don't say anything, Nick!" she implored. "Just leave me alone!"

Silently, he rearranged their clothing and helped her to her feet. "Crimson, you can't stay out here by yourself. Let me take you inside or—"

"Go away!" she half-screamed.

He hesitated. "I'll have Kit come out to you," he said heavily.

She said nothing, leaning against the stone wall of the balcony, crying more softly now.

Nick hurried inside and found Kit engaged in conversation with one of the doctors who had been invited. "Kit, I'm afraid Crimson is not herself tonight," Nick began. "I think you had best go out and see to her."

Kit lifted one brow in surprise. "You mean you're leaving the young lady in my care, Nick? How sporting of you." The words were uttered with a trace of jealous sarcasm that Nick ignored brusquely.

"Just go out to her, Kit," he repeated flatly. "She's beneath the balcony."

Kit shrugged. "All right, I suppose it's my job to repair the broken heart you've given her." He strode out of the room, leaving Nick to reflect on the shattering news he had just received.

He wasn't able to reflect long, though, before Juliette came up to him, touching him teasingly on the shoulder. "Where did you send Kit off to in such a hurry?" she asked lightly, brushing a twig from his coat sleeve.

"To Crimson. She's upset and I didn't think it a good idea to leave her alone outside." His manner was abrupt, impatient with this cunning intriguer who, he suspected, would use her body to corrupt her own stepson.

"You sent Kit to Crimson?" Her dark eyes narrowed in controlled rage.

"Yes, Juliette," he replied, turning away from her impatiently.

Her arm stopped him. "Don't be angry. Let's forget about them," she breathed huskily. "You and I know what

375

we want. We don't have to play any games with each other, Nick."

Nick looked down at the eager, sensuous face. He despised the woman, but his near-rape of Crimson had left him with a very real need in his loins. This woman would do very well for what he wanted right now. Smiling with caustic amusement, he nodded slowly. "As you say, Juliette. We both know what we want."

41

Crimson was grateful to Kit for helping her through the rest of the night at the party, but found it difficult to sleep as she relived the memory of her first encounter with Nick, her subsequent pregnancy and miscarriage and the shock of learning that the man she had always thought her father was not. She was quiet, introverted for the next few days, avoiding both Kit and Nick.

On a gray, rainy morning, Juliette unexpectedly came up to her room for a chat. "God, it is dreary today," she sighed, seating herself on a chair close to where Crimson was writing a letter to her cousin in France. "There must be something to do on a day like today."

Crimson indicated her own correspondence. "Don't you have any letters to catch up on? Now would be a good time to do so."

Juliette sighed again. "I hate to write letters!" She idly picked at the sleeve of her gown. "I have an idea! Let's explore the castle. I've never really looked through it. You could come with me, Crimson."

"Well—" Crimson wasn't sure she wanted to be bound to Juliette's company for the entire morning, but she finally nodded. "All right, Juliette, it might prove interesting."

The two women strode downstairs and to the back of the castle where the kitchens were. A staircase led down to the wine cellar, and from there a locked door led down into the very bowels of the stone fortress. From her pocket, Juliette produced a key that opened the door and the two entered the dimly lit corridor. Rush torches were set at long-spaced intervals so that one could see where the corridor turned and dipped.

"It's rather scary, don't you think?" Juliette asked in excitement. Her eyes glanced at Crimson curiously to see if there was fear on her face.

"It is rather grim," Crimson agreed readily, although she wasn't really frightened. "Let's walk on and see what's at the end of this corridor."

"Yes," Juliette agreed softly, her eyes suddenly narrowing like a cat's. "Let's see."

They walked abreast until the corridor narrowed, and Juliette stepped forward to lead the way. As they walked, the air grew cooler and moist, the stone walls sweating. Crimson shivered a little, for she had only worn a thin silk day dress, which gave her little protection against the lowered temperature.

Deeper into the corridor, Crimson thought she heard someone calling and stopped to listen for the direction of the sound. "Juliette! Can you hear something?" she asked.

"What?"

"I don't know. Someone calling, I think."

Juliette shrugged. "Perhaps it's a prisoner, or the guards in the dungeons."

Crimson stared at her. "Are we close to the dungeons?"

"I'm sure we must be," Juliette returned nonchalantly. She turned down a fork in the corridor.

Crimson noted that she went left, and to the right was a closed door from which she could faintly smell the sea

377

tang. "What is through that door?" she asked, pointing as Juliette turned around.

"It leads through a tunnel that goes out of the mountain on the north side. I think the old governors used to use it as a means of escape when the fortress came under attack by the Spaniards. I think Thomas told me that there was a cave-in some time ago which closed off the tunnel, so he locked the door and no one uses it any more. I'm sure the other end is probably grown over with bushes and weeds. Let's go this way, Crimson. It may lead out to the soldiers' garrison."

Crimson followed her, becoming disturbed as the sounds of shouts and cries grew louder. They must be coming from the prisoners, she thought. It amazed her that she had been living on top of them and had never even thought of them before. She shivered, hearing distinctly the maniacal screams and moans.

"Why are they screaming so?" she asked Juliette worriedly.

"My dear Crimson, you are so sheltered!" Juliette laughed. "Why, they are tortured every day until they divulge any secrets we may wish to obtain from them. How else would we find out about their treasures and the rest of their crews? After all, they are murderers and thieves and have no right to be treated like human beings."

Crimson was silent, still caught up in the torment of the prisoners. Dear God, the noise was getting closer. Was Juliette taking her into the dungeons? They rounded another bend and came up to two more doors, each leading a different way.

"This one," Juliette explained, pointing to the right, "leads to Sir Thomas' treasure room. This one leads to the dungeons."

"Juliette! You knew all along exactly where you were taking me!" Crimson accused her in surprise. "Why did you pretend to be exploring the castle?"

Juliette laughed. "Just as a lark, Crimson. No harm intended, my dear. Come on, we'll have to go through this way to get out on the other side." She took another key
378

from her pocket to open the door and carefully locked it again after the two of them had passed through.

"You can see why we have very few attempts at escape," she said to Crimson. "My husband is very sure of his prisoners. Once they are caught, they escape only to the hangman's noose."

Crimson shivered at the matter-of-fact tone that Juliette used. Seeing the brighter light ahead, she guessed that they were coming to the guard room. Once in the room, Juliette greeted the three guards who were on duty, placing a gold coin in each of their hands. Crimson was puzzled by her action, but waited impatiently for her to finish her conversation with them as the moans and groans from the prisoners were beginning to prey on her nerves.

Suddenly, Juliette turned around to Crimson and pointed at her. "This is the one," she said quietly.

Crimson watched in stupefaction as one of the guards came towards her and pulled her hands behind her back in order to bind them. She was only mesmerized a moment, though, before she began to struggle.

"Juliette, what game is this?" she asked her crossly, trying to pull her hands from the guard's grasp. It was no use, and he had them firmly tied with a leather thong before Juliette had even answered.

"No game, Crimson, dear," Juliette purred maliciously, her dark eyes glinting with cruel amusement. "I brought you down here to keep you away from Kit—forever!"

"What are you talking about, Juliette?" Crimson cried, beginning to feel frightened. "Tell this man to release me at once!"

"No, my dear, you're going to have a little stay down here until I can arrange for someone to take you off my hands." Juliette stroked her chin thoughtfully. "You see, I simply could not stand by and let you turn Kit away from me. I've waited too long to trap him, and it's become important to me not to have any rivals sneaking about, trying to seduce the dear boy from under my very nose. He's mine, Crimson!"

"Juliette, don't be foolish. Let me go now, and I promise not to say anything to Sir Thomas," Crimson pleaded, struggling in her bonds.

"Too late, my dear. I knew you would be trouble the minute I saw Kit with you in your room that first time. He desired you, I could see that. I couldn't stand to see the need in his eyes when he looked at you. He was almost ready to give in to me before you came."

"Juliette, you're insane! No man is worth the trouble you'll find yourself in when Sir Thomas finds out."

"Sir Thomas won't find out. He hardly cares what becomes of you, my dear. He's an old man, content with what passion I can still prod in him. He can do nothing to interfere with Kit and me. And one day, when we have enough money, Kit and I can run away together, abscond with the treasure, so to speak!" She laughed crazily. "Yes, to satisfy your curiosity, it was my idea to keep part of the treasure. I persuaded Sir Thomas to defy the king's orders, and should he be caught, I will be able to sail away from this damned island, having had the king neatly dispose of my loving husband." She smoothed a wrinkle in her skirt. "Do I shock you, Crimson?"

"I never realized that loving a man could drive a woman to become a criminal!" Crimson said defiantly, feeling the woman's hate like a blow.

"I've wanted Kit for a long time, Crimson. I married his father to be near him and to have a means of obtaining enough wealth to escape this dreary life. Kit and I together."

"How can you be sure that Kit won't try to find me?" Crimson asked.

"Very simple, my dear. I'll tell him that you've run back to England, that your marriage certificate to his brother was forged, and when I found out about it, you escaped on the first available ship so that Sir Thomas wouldn't discover your lie. I imagine he will chafe a bit at first, but your loss will only bring him closer to me for—comfort." She grinned. "And I will be ready to comfort him, Crimson."

"You're forgetting about Nick Brentwood. He's not going to believe such a feeble excuse."

"Why not? What is he to you?" she asked, watching her closely.

Crimson opened her mouth, then closed it, realizing that she couldn't risk putting Nick in jeopardy, for he might be her only means of rescue when he discovered she was gone. He knew the marriage was valid, so he would not believe Juliette's lie, and then he would investigate. She was sure he would find her. Perhaps it was better to wait, to let Juliette think she had won.

"He was interested in me," Crimson began offhandedly.

"Hah! Well, my dear, I must tell you that your handsome Nick is not entirely immune to my charms either. He and I have enjoyed some passionate moments together these past few nights. He does help to solace me for the temporary loss of Kit's affections."

"You—and Nick—" she said, struggling to keep hidden her pain.

"He's a passionate lover," Juliette sighed. "If I hadn't already fallen in love with Kit—"

"How can you say you love him when you—"

"Enough of this stupid talk! Guard, put her in one of the cells, alone. I'll arrange for her to be taken out, and I'll send you word."

"Juliette! Wait!" Crimson cried as the guard pushed her forward to a narrow corridor from which emitted the groans and shouts she had heard before. The guard opened a rusty door with one of the keys from a large, iron ring and shoved her inside the dark hole. Crimson fell heavily on the cold, stone floor, banging her knee sharply. The door closed behind her, and she began to sob, her shoulders shaking. She knew now that Juliette was capable of leaving her to rot in this place, with no one the wiser. The guards had obviously been paid to forget her existence. If only Nick—but she didn't want to think about Nick now. How could he have gone to that woman's bed? Didn't he know that she was evil?

Crimson had no way of telling the time. There was no window in her cell and her eyes were only able to make out the bale of foul-smelling hay, which was supposed to

381

serve as a bed, in one corner. There was no bed, no wash-stand or chamberpot. She endured the cell for what seemed like days, before the door was opened to allow two men inside, one of whom was holding a torch.

"Jesus! This place smells like a pesthole!" one of the men swore, making a gagging sound.

"Where's the wench? Let's take her out of here before ye puke!" exclaimed the other impatiently. He lifted the torch high so that the light fell on Crimson, huddled in a corner of the cell. "Come on, wench. We're here to take ye out!"

Weak with relief, Crimson scrambled to her feet and walked hopefully towards the man. "I'm so glad you've come," she began.

"Aye, I can imagine," the man said. "Come on, let's be gone."

An iron hand clasped itself around her wrist and dragged her out of the cell into the guardroom, which was strangely empty. Crimson looked at her two companions uneasily. One was short and very stout, his ragged clothes emitting a smell that might have vied with that of her cell. His friend was a little taller and less fat, with a jagged scar across his face that had taken half his nose with it, drawing up his mouth in a macabre grin.

"Where are you taking me?" she asked.

"No questions, wench, or you'll feel the back side of me hand!" growled the taller one impatiently.

His companion snorted. "Ye'll know soon enough, wench."

They led her out of the guardroom, a different way from that which she had been led in by Juliette. The stairway curved several times, and finally opened out into a small alcove that faced the east. Looking back and up, Crimson saw the flat stone face of the wall surrounding the castle. Outside, it was night, and she squinted her eyes to make out the path by which they were leading her away from the castle.

They pulled her along roughly, not giving her a moment to catch her breath, and half-dragging her down the steep slope until the path connected with the main road leading down to Port Royal. Two horses were tied to a large bush. The men untied them and Crimson was forced to mount in front of the taller man. She didn't like the easy familiarity with which his arms went around her to hold the reins and tried to remain as upright as possible in the saddle.

"I don't think she likes ye!" the pudgy one hooted, noting Crimson's look of pained disdain.

"Shut yer mouth, Smitty. What she likes don't make no difference to us!"

They prodded their horses down the slope, over the bridge and into the town, making straight for the docks. Crimson was acutely aware of the night noises of the town —the loud laughter, drunken shouting and screams of glee. They passed the tavern where Nick had stayed, and went on to the docks where the crowd was spilling from the doors of taverns out into the muddy sand. Crimson shrank away from leering faces and grasping hands that slid lewdly up her ankles. Men were everywhere, dirty, ragged, some without limbs, one or two dressed richly with velvet coats and linen shirts. Most were drunk or dragging giggling dock prostitutes with them. Crimson's eyes sharpened as she caught sight of fair hair and a round, pleasant face.

"Delia!" she called desperately, trying to jump from the horse.

The girl turned upon hearing her name and her blurred gaze caught Crimson's for a moment. The blue eyes narrowed as if trying to remember, but Crimson's captors hurried her on before Crimson could tell whether Delia had recognized her or not.

They headed for a shabby tavern at the end of the long row and tethered their horses outside, before pushing Crimson forward into the door. Inside, several men held girls on their knees, their hands fondling breasts that spilled easily from loose blouses. One man lay in a pool of vomit, snoring contentedly in the middle of the floor while ale and rum splashed on him from the customers above. Everywhere was laughter and singing and loud voices.

Crimson was shoved past the common room and down a short hall and from there into a small room where sat an enormously fat man, playing cards with three or four others.

The fat man's beady eyes, set deeply into twin pockets of fat, surveyed the flushing girl closely, then smiled. "So, ye've gotten her, eh, mates? She's as good a piece as I've seen lately. Whew! We'll be able to get a lot out of this one, lads!"

"Lord, Captain, we're not to hold her for ransom," the scarred one answered tentatively. "Our instructions were to get rid of the wench for good!" The man pulled a large bag from beneath his coat. "Here's the gold, Captain."

The fat man took the bag, weighed it carefully in his hand, then stuffed it into his own coat. "Aye, ye did good, lads, but I can't imagine not getting more for this wench. She'd fetch a high price on the auction block."

The scarred man spoke again, letting his hand stray to the girl's bodice. "I'd say we could rent her out to the men for a shilling or two a round. We'd make some coin." His eyes were bright with lust, obviously thinking of paying for her himself.

"Bah! She'd be dead within a week and of no more use to us!" the leader spoke in derision. "No, we could make more at an auction. After all, the one who wants her gotten rid of won't know the difference, eh, mates?" He laughed, as though pleased at the little joke he'd be playing on Sir Thomas' wife.

Crimson, who had been trembling with fear, slapped the man's hand away from her bodice. "Don't you touch me, you animal!" she hissed.

The scar turned livid in his face and without another moment's thought, his hand cracked painfully across her cheek, snapping her neck back. Crimson struggled to keep her balance as her head whirled dizzily for a moment. The man, in a sudden fury, grabbed her bodice at the neckline and tore it to the waist, leaving only her thin chemise to protect her breasts. He would have ripped that away, but the captain held up his hand to stop him.

"Enough, Jake. We don't want scars on her, lad, or she'll not fetch a decent purse. Come on, there's plenty of
384

likely wenches in the tavern room for ye. Leave this one to me and I'll put her where she won't escape."

The man called Jake hesitated, obviously trying to calm the surge of lust for this desirable young girl. Finally, he took a deep breath and nodded silently. He and his companion left the room, leaving Crimson shivering before the fat captain and his card-playing friends.

"Excuse me, mates," the captain said, rising from his chair with difficulty. "I'll have to see to this wench first and I'll be back to finish these cards." His pig eyes bored into the faces of those present. "No cheating while I'm gone, lads, or ye'll feel my knife sliding 'tween yer ribs." He laughed cruelly and wiped his mouth with the back of his hand. Then he turned to Crimson, who was staring at him in disbelief. "All right, come on, wench!" he commanded gruffly. "I'll have to tie yer hands again."

He tied the rope about her wrists, pulling it tightly so that she gasped. It cut into her delicate flesh painfully with each step she took so that she had to bite her lip to keep from crying.

The captain was leading her back through the common room, disregarding the eyes that watched their progress with curiosity. A tall, wild-eyed pirate suddenly jumped up from his chair, putting an arm about Crimson's waist.

"Hey now, Thornton, where ye taking this wench, eh? She's too pretty a piece for the likes of ye, ye mound of fat!" He roared with laughter and others in the room joined in. "Leave her with me and I'll make it worth yer while!"

"She's mine, Spring, and I'll not be giving her up for any offer ye'd make," Thornton returned, casually taking out his pistol. "She'll be up for public auction in Barbados next week if ye'd care to join the bidding, lad."

The pistol leveled itself at the other man's chest and he released Crimson slowly. "All right, Thornton," the pirate said between his teeth. "Ye damned robber! I'll bet ye'll ask a treasure chest for this one." The man shook his head sorrowfully and returned to his seat, gazing at the odd pair as they disappeared through the door.

Crimson dared not ask the fat man any questions as he

prodded her along on foot to the dock. She was silent until he told her to climb into a longboat, which was drifting lazily in the water next to one of the piers.

"Where are you taking me?" she risked in a moment of terror.

As she had expected, he cuffed her smartly on the cheek, bringing the tears to her eyes. "Just get into the boat, wench, and keep yer mouth shut unless ye want a swollen cheek!"

It was difficult for her to get into the boat with her hands tied behind her back and the pirate captain was obliged to half-carry her down himself. Once in the boat, he took up the oars silently and began rowing out into the bay towards one of the schooners, moored in the channel. When they arrived at his ship, he cut her hands loose and told her to climb up the ladder that led up the side. Crimson obeyed quickly, fearing any more physical demonstrations.

Once on the deck of the ship, she glanced about fearfully, hearing the captain puffing laboriously as he climbed up. There were only a few of the crew on the ship as lookouts and they barely glanced at her. Obviously their captain was a strict disciplinarian.

When he heaved himself over the railing onto the deck, Thornton stood for a moment catching his breath before pushing Crimson to the cabin area. She entered what must be the captain's cabin and stood in the middle of the room, watching the big man as he locked the door behind him.

"Ah, now we've arrived, wench. Take off yer clothes!" he ordered.

Crimson blinked. "What?"

"Ye heard me, wench. Take off those clothes. I want ye naked!"

Crimson gazed about the room for a weapon, but her eyes came back to the captain, who had calmly taken his pistol and was directing it at her. "Come on, don't ye try anything stupid. I'll not kill ye, wench, but I can make it awfully painful for ye." His tone was quiet, reasonable as though trying to convince a child of what was best for him. "The clothes. Throw them on the bed!"

386

Slowly, Crimson's nerveless fingers moved to her waist where the torn halves of her bodice hung on either side. She pulled at them, pushing the skirt down until it lay in a pool around her feet. She threw the ruined dress on the bed and untied the straps of her chemise. Only a moment's hesitation before she pushed the garment down and threw it on top of the gown. Her slippers and stockings followed and she stood up, nude, her eyes remaining steadfast on the floor as she heard his appreciative intake of breath.

"Perfect form ye have, wench. Ye'll fetch a higher price than I thought." She heard him moving about, the rustle of his clothes as he stripped them off quickly. "Good Lord, I've got to sample ye, wench," he muttered excitedly.

Crimson's eyes flashed upwards in fear, but suddenly her mouth opened in a laugh at the ridiculous picture the fat man made without his clothes. She eyed his soft, flabby rolls of fat and couldn't stop laughing. Tears squeezed from her eyes and her shoulders shook with the intensity of her laughter.

The fat man's small eyes nearly disappeared in his face as his brows drew down in anger and embarrassment. "Shut yer mouth, ye cheeky wench, and lay down! Ye might laugh now, but ol' Thornton'll pin ye to the floor in short order!"

Crimson was still laughing helplessly, partly from hysteria, and partly from her scorn of this enormous man whose huge belly prevented her from even seeing his maleness.

Red-faced and breathing hard, Thornton could feel his erection go limp and the knowledge caused his anger to be doubled. In a rage, he drew his clothes back on and walked to the still-laughing girl to shake her by the shoulders. Crimson's head rolled sharply, as she stopped laughing on a forlorn hiccup.

"Blast ye, wench! I'll not be laughed at!"

He turned to the bed and threw her chemise at her. Quickly, Crimson scrambled into it, truly afraid of the wrath she had brought on herself. The man grabbed her wrist and dragged her out of the cabin onto the deck. Growling to himself, he led her to one of the cannons which were nailed to the deck.

"We'll see if ye're still laughing tomorrow morning!" he hissed, forcing her to bend over the cannon barrel, as his hand pushed her neck. He called for one if his men to bring some rope, and, in short order, Crimson found herself tied to the cannon, her hands and feet almost touched beneath the weapon.

"Now then, bitch!" Thornton laughed. He tore the back of her chemise to expose her back to the waist. "We'll see what a bit of sun on ye will do!"

He left strict orders to the crew not to touch her or give her water until he returned to the boat the following evening. As he was leaving, he reached down and patted her rump. "Ye'll be begging me to split ye tomorrow," he promised.

Crimson turned her head to try to spit at him, but he deftly moved himself away. "You big mound of lard!" she threw at him. "I'd rather suffer here for a week than give in to you!"

He laughed unpleasantly. "Ye may just do that, wench!"

He whistled softly to himself as he climbed down to the waiting longboat. After he had gone, Crimson was left to herself. The rest of the crew left her alone, per the captain's orders. She was relieved that they obeyed their captain so explicitly, and she allowed herself to relax against the cold metal.

The night passed swiftly, for Crimson was tired enough to fall asleep despite her awkward position. She awoke a little after dawn, trying to move her legs from their cramped position, but the rope was tight enough to allow her little room to move. Her hands and feet tingled from the reduced flow of blood and her head ached from being forced down. She tried to hold it up for a while, but her neck soon felt the strain and she was obliged to lower her head once more.

As the sun began climbing in the sky, the metal of the gun heated up and if she moved from her original position she would burn herself. She was obliged to remain still, although by now her legs and arms were nearly numb.

By noontime, she thought surely she was going to die.

388

Her head ached abominably and her tongue hung from her mouth, too thick from lack of water for her to even drool. The men passed nearby, not even looking at her, and she couldn't even speak to beg them for water, her throat was so dry.

She must have fainted for a time, for she awoke to see the sun lower in the sky and her ears picked up the captain's voice as he strolled on deck, bellowing orders to his crew to get the ship underway. Thankfully, she waited for him to untie her. My God, the villain was right. She would welcome his gross body now. Anything to relieve her cramped, aching muscles and the awful pain in her head.

But the captain seemed in no hurry and it was nearly dark, the ship under full sail, before he approached the still form, hanging across the cannon barrel.

"Well, now, wench," he purred, "have ye come to yer senses?"

No answer, and the captain scowled. "Don't play games with me, wench! I'll have ye flogged where ye lay! Answer me!"

Still no answer and the captain suddenly moved closer to lay a hand on her sunburned back. A slight flinching told him she was still alive, but he realized that he had nearly killed her through the ordeal. Quickly, he ordered one of the crew to cut her off the cannon and take her to his cabin. By God, he wasn't about to lose a good piece of flesh so easily. Damned he be if he couldn't get his price for her now!

When the man cut the rope and lifted her up to carry her, Crimson thought she would scream with the pain of the circulating blood, but her throat could make no sound. The mist of pain before her eyes cleared a little as she was lowered to the captain's bed, but she knew she would die if the man tried to take her now. She would suffocate from his sheer weight on top of her.

To her relief, a bottle of clear water was brought to her lips. Most of it slopped helplessly along her swollen tongue, but enough drained down her throat to revive her somewhat.

"Damn ye for a bitch!" the captain was swearing, even

389

as he tended to her with a rough gentleness. "I almost lost ye out there. How was I to know ye was too delicate for such! Damn!" He kept muttering to himself even as he massaged her wrists and ankles to speed up the flow of blood. At regular intervals, he would hold the water to her lips for another drink.

It seemed hours before her tongue felt normal again, and Crimson was able to speak. Her eyes opened slowly and focused on the captain's round sweating face. Her ribs hurt from being bruised against the heavy metal and her back felt hot to the touch from the sunburn she had received. But at least her head was clearing and her legs and arms were relaxing.

"Ah, ye're coming to now, eh?" The captain patted her cheek to force her to consciousness. "Ye almost died out there, wench," he told her slowly. "Ye'll not fight me now, will ye?"

"No." The word was little more than a husky whisper.

He smiled, pleased at her obedience. "That's a good girl. I'll not trouble ye—that way—again," he told her, much to her relief. "But ye'll prove docile during the sale or I'll give ye another taste of my methods, wench!"

Crimson nodded slowly. All she wanted to do was sleep and let her body heal itself. She would need her strength if she was going to survive this nightmare, she thought tiredly.

42

The rest of the voyage to Barbados, an
island to the southeast of Jamaica, passed in a haze for
Crimson. She was not allowed out of the captain's cabin,
and, although Thornton kept his word not to touch her,
he slept in his own bed every night, forcing Crimson to
sleep on the floor if she didn't want to arouse his desires
by sharing the bed with him.

The voyage took a little over a week, as Thornton was
in no hurry and wanted his captive to be in the best of
health again before the auction. He had made sure that
word of the sale had spread around Port Royal before
his departure, and he expected plenty of bidders, a fact
that caused him to rub his plump hands together every
time he looked at the girl.

Crimson was careful to keep silent except for those
times when the captain spoke directly to her. She had no
desire to arouse his wrath again, after seeing the results
the first time. She realized now that this man was someone who must be dealt with carefully and on his terms.

Despite the knowledge that she was to be sold at auction like a slave, Crimson was happy to hear the captain's
words that Barbados was in sight and they would anchor
the following morning. Whoever bought her, she must try
to convince him to take her back to Port Royal. She was
sure that Sir Thomas would ransom her back, out of

public embarrassment, if nothing else. What she would do once she was back at the governor's castle, Crimson was not entirely sure. She could not continue living in the same house as the woman who had so callously sold her to pirates, but she had to get to Nick to tell him what Juliette had told her. Then, she would take the first ship back to England, where, she realized, more danger waited for her.

Captain Thornton allowed her up on deck as the ship dropped anchor in a sheltered bay which led to a shore of golden sands, upon which makeshift buildings were scattered about haphazardly.

"What is this place?" she asked curiously.

Thornton, in a good mood upon reaching his destination, deigned to answer her. " 'Tis called Barbados, wench, a major base of the brotherhood."

"The brotherhood?"

"Aye, the Brethren of the Coast, the company of pirates who roam the Caribbean. The island welcomes us all when we're sick or in need of shelter from those cursed king's men!"

Crimson gazed out onto the beach, perceiving a lively little community springing up out of the sands. "Does anyone live here permanently?" she wondered, eyeing the shabby buildings dubiously.

"Aye, there's plenty of us that are retired, so to speak," he laughed. "We've a little store here and a tavern or two, even a kind of hospital run by a doctor who became a pirate after he was accused of butchering one of the king's men. He couldn't stomach the life for long, though, and stayed here on the island."

A few moments later, Crimson was in another longboat with several of the crew and the captain. They were rowed ashore to a small pier, and then Crimson was taken to one of the buildings occupied by a frightening-looking man of huge girth and stature.

"I've got a wench I want ye to watch for me, Nolan," Thornton said shortly. "I want no one sniffing about here after her. She's to be sold two days from now. Do you understand?"

The behemoth nodded stiffly and one giant hand closed

around Crimson's wrist to pull her inside. Crimson would have struggled, but it would have been ridiculous against so powerful a man. She was pushed into a room and was surprised to find two other women already occupying it.

"Well, company for us," smiled one of the women, a frizzled redhead with big, high breasts. "Welcome, dearie."

"Aw, she looks quite fresh, Kitty, not the same as the likes o' you and me," admonished the other, a small brunette with doe-brown eyes. "She looks frightened, she does."

"Aye, Lora, but so was I the first time," replied the other. "Who are you?" she asked Crimson.

"Crimson Gardner," she replied, glad to have two such friendly companions with which to share her trials.

"I'm Kitty. This here is Lora. Crimson, eh? 'Tis a pretty name, dearie, an unusual one. Are you gentry?"

"I'm English," Crimson began hesitantly, not wishing to offend the other two women. Then, to change the subject, "How did you both get here?"

Kitty shrugged. "My man got tired of me, dearie. Just up and got tired of me. So he brought me here to get some coin out of my hide."

"I worked as a bargirl in Port Royal. I was indentured for seven years, but I couldn't keep up with the work, so my master, he sold me to some rogues who came in one night. Gave them my papers and all. Now they're going to sell me to the highest bidder." Lora sniffed.

"More'n likely we'll all end up somebody's whore!" Kitty said ruefully.

Crimson shivered. "How can you let them do that to you?"

Kitty laughed. "Honey, there's nothing I can do about it. We got here same as you. You don't think there's a chance for you to escape, do you? Not with big old Nolan out there ready to break your neck if you so much as stick your nose out the door."

"I—I see what you mean," Crimson said. She slumped onto a stool, dejectedly.

"Honey, it won't be so bad," Kitty said sympathetically.

"You might happen onto a nice one who'll treat you well and won't beat you for every little mistake you make. You're young and pretty. You'll go high."

"It's not much consolation when you're used to being free," Crimson sniffed, feeling sorry for herself. "I don't think I could be a—a servant to a man's needs." She shivered again, imagining the pirate captain as a master.

"Well, no need fretting about it, dearie. Just be quiet and do as you're told and mayhap the Lord's luck will be with you."

Crimson had to admit that Kitty's advice was the only kind she could use right now. She had to hope that whoever saw fit to buy her would prove greedy enough to want to gain a ransom for her.

The day of the auction dawned with promise of a swelteringly hot day. Crimson could feel the stickiness on her skin, forming beads of perspiration all over her body. She had twisted her hair up and around the back of her head to keep it from laying its damp weight on her neck as she slept. Kitty and Lora had done the same and had taken to sleeping without their bodices. Crimson, who only had the ragged chemise, wished she had a dress to wear, and had asked Nolan if he would procure one for her, but the big man had simply stared at her as though he hadn't comprehended her question.

Captain Thornton arrived by mid-morning, yawning hugely and scratching his fat belly. "Aye, ye look a mite tamer than ye did when I first saw ye," he said approvingly. "Has yer back healed, wench?"

Crimson shrugged. "It's peeling."

"Well, that won't bother those randy goats today," Thornton chortled. "After all, it's not yer back they'll be interested in!" He winked at her. "Ye mind yer manners and be a good girl for me out there," he admonished her, "or I promise ye I'll send ye to the cruelest swab among them!"

"I'll try not to run away," Crimson agreed.

"Run away? 'Twould be foolish for ye to attempt that anyway!" Thornton said gruffly. "But I don't want ye acting like the queen of England, or the men won't buy. Most of them don't like the ones with their noses in the air. No, ye just be quiet and passive and I guarantee ye'll be off my hands before noon."

He left the room and in a few minutes Nolan called for them to follow him out to the sandy beach. An area had been penned off containing livestock and other goods which were being sold before the women. Crimson flushed at the idea of being sold like a cow or horse or bolt of cloth. Bitterly, she made out the form of Captain Thornton, and would have defied his orders, but the memory of her ordeal on his ship forced her to remain silent.

It was obvious that she was the main attraction, for the bidding on Kitty and Lora proved quick and neat. Crimson shivered when she watched Lora being taken to her buyer. The man was tall, very dark and had a wolfish grin that was truly frightening. He picked up Lora in his brawny arms and carried her hurriedly to the cover of some scanty bush before throwing her on the sand and stripping off his breeches. Lora's forlorn cry was lost in the howls of laughter made by the other pirates.

"All right, gents, now we have the prime piece o' flesh I've been telling ye about!" Thornton called to the eager listeners. He prodded Crimson forward, jerking her hair down so that it fell in a soft, gleaming cape about her shoulders. An "oh" of appreciation filtered through the men as Thornton took the liberty of running his sausage-like fingers through it.

"Where did ye steal that one!" hooted one of the pirates.

"Ah, my source of supply is a secret one," Thornton returned with an air of conspiracy about him. "But just look at her, lads, is she not the finest piece ye've seen in a while?"

"Aye, that she is," another man spoke up. "Is she still a maid, Thornton?"

Thornton shook his head sadly. "No maiden, lads, but she was only a wife a short while before he up and got himself killed."

395

"Aw, now why would he want to leave a nice wench like that behind!"

The pirates joked among themselves, behaving very much like a band of small boys, Crimson thought in some surprise. Were these the dreaded Brethren of the Coast? Were these those murderers, cutthroats and thieves that scoured the Caribbean, bringing terror to the Spanish gold ships? She would have laughed until she caught the look in their eyes as they watched her. A cold, calculating look that belied their careless words. They wanted her, she had no doubts about that.

The bidding began jokingly, but then as it reached higher sums became more serious, accompanied by growls of dismay by those who couldn't match the price. After ten minutes of easy bantering between four or five of the captains, the bids became heated, with more than one man laying a close hand on his sword.

Crimson turned her eyes away from the lusting faces and chanced upon the outline of a longboat out in the water, being rowed from one of the ships. She could hardly perceive the figure at the helm, but her hopes soared as she wondered if it might not be some last-minute rescue. Could it be Nick, or Kit? She squinted to shut out the glare of the sun, but her attention was suddenly drawn back to her immediate surroundings as she felt a tug on her bodice.

"Breasts like a goddess," Thornton was saying, smacking his lips in a lewd pantomime. "Not like those cow teats ye'll find on those tavern girls in Port Royal!" He was ripping her bodice in order to show the proof of his statement.

Uttering a shocked cry, Crimson slapped away his hands and reached up to pull on his straggly beard, causing a ripple of laughter among the pirates. Enraged, Thornton struck her on the cheek so that her head snapped away from the crowd, so that her face was covered by a curtain of gleaming auburn. A collective groan moved among the pirates as Thornton freed her breasts from the chemise. They stood, firm and taut, pearls of sweat on the flesh. The men surged forward hungrily.

"Aye, ye believe Thornton now, do ye?" he bellowed, catching Crimson's shoulder, forcing her to look out over the crowd. "Now what are my bids, lads?"

The bidding came fast and heavy, the sums floating in Crimson's brain until she heard the impossible sum of a thousand pounds. Ridiculous, her mind told her, but hadn't she been sold to her husband for just that sum? Her head hung lower, for she didn't want these animals to see her pain, her degradation as the tears slipped down her cheeks.

"Two thousand pounds!" The voice was low, intense.

Crimson pulled her head up to locate the owner, but shrank away from the black eye patch, the scarred nose —the Barracuda! Helplessly, she looked to the figure next to him and recognized Delia. So Delia *had* seen her on the docks. But why had she brought her pirate lover? Why not Kit, or even Sir Thomas?

"Aye, Barracuda, ye know the wench's worth, ye do!" Thornton cried, highly pleased. "Ye'll have her at yer mercy tonight!"

"Twenty-one hundred pounds!" This came from a hulking brute close to Crimson, whose trousers revealed his imminent desire for her.

"Captain Duncan! Ye're a lucky man—" Thornton began.

"Twenty-two hundred pounds!" Barracuda replied calmly.

Thornton's eyes bulged. "Duncan, can ye match that?"

The man nodded furiously, glancing with murder in his eye at his rival. "Three thousand pounds, Barracuda. I'll have this wench—now. Ye keep out of it or I'll slit yer gizzard for ye."

"Five thousand pounds, Thornton. I doubt that Captain Duncan can top that sum," Barracuda returned.

No word came from the defeated man. A tense silence was broken by Thornton calling the auction over. Then suddenly, the huge pirate lunged towards Barracuda, his blade drawn.

"Damn ye, Barracuda, I'll not be beaten out of the wench!"

A large circle was formed as everyone cleared an area for the two opponents to fight. The combatants threw off their coats and shirts, leaving their chests bare as they weighed their swords in their hands.

Crimson drew a breath of pain as she realized she would be the property of the winner of this contest. Both men hardly appealed to her, but as her eyes fell on Delia's tense face, she thought that perhaps she had better hope for the Barracuda to win, for at least he had shown her leniency before when she had come upon his secret cove. And she had Delia, who would support her too.

Her eyes flew to where the two men were engaged in a furious swordfight. The Barracuda was taller, but the other man probably weighed nearly twice as much as he. His weight was to his advantage as he swung with full force at the lighter man, causing him to lose his balance for a moment.

Crimson cried out in alarm as Duncan's blade sliced the other man's arm, causing a film of red to drip slowly down to the sand. Barracuda lost no time in regaining his footing and nearly missed being skewered by the other man's deadly steel. He stepped to one side, parried and then thrust, catching the other man off guard so that his sword drove to the hilt in the man's chest. A gout of blood rushed from Duncan's mouth and, as Barracuda drew his sword from Duncan's flesh, Duncan fell to the ground, his face lost in the sand.

Thornton mopped his brow and smiled weakly at the victor. "Ah, Captain Barracuda, ye have proved yerself and yer reputation! I congratulate ye, lad!"

"I'll take the wench now," the man replied flatly, donning his shirt and coat without bothering to staunch the flow of blood. "I'll have my man bring the gold to you in a strongbox tonight."

"Tonight?" squeaked Thornton weakly. "But I had hoped to sail—"

"Tonight," the other repeated in a deadly voice. "I want to make sure I've not been cheated, in case the wench has the pox."

Crimson flushed at this sullying of her character, but she remained silent. It would hardly do to cause her captor to become angry with her. She must remember to keep to her plan of persuading him to take her back to Port Royal.

She had forgotten that her breasts were bare until she was pushed forward to the waiting pirate and his hands reached out to cup them appreciatively.

"Truly those of a goddess," he remarked sarcastically.

She came to herself with a start. "You should know," she hissed, referring to his rape of her on the island path leading from Port Royal.

He smiled, obviously remembering also. "I told you then, wench, you were mine." He clasped her wrist, not ungently, and guided her to his longboat. "I'm sure Delia will have something for you to wear around my men. Eh, Countess?" He called back to his paramour.

"I know you've wanted her for a long time, darling," Delia replied with a sour note to her voice. "But if you expect me to give up my place without some rancor—"

"Countess, she'll never take your place," the man laughed.

"No? Well, it should prove interesting to see how well you can satisfy two women at once, my dearest!" she shot back crossly, as they climbed into the boat. "Perhaps I shouldn't have told you."

"Quiet, Countess. Let's get back to the ship and I'll let you dress my arm while I teach this wench some lessons in love!"

"You can bleed to death before I'll sit by and *watch* you, for God's sake!" hissed Delia indignantly as she folded her arms across her bosom.

The Barracuda reached over and kissed her full on the mouth. She refused to be completely mollified, though, and stubbornly kept her eyes averted, not even responding to Crimson's friendly overtures. The pirate captain shook his head and drew his good arm about Crimson's shoulders to press her against his chest.

Crimson felt her heart beating swiftly as his hand reached around casually to fondle her breast. She would have struck it away, but was frightened that he might abuse her further. Her face was turned away from his for she was afraid of what might show in his one-eyed gaze. She could see ahead the figure of the woman with the body of a bird, arched proudly on the bowsprit of the schooner.

When their party had climbed aboard, Crimson was taken to the captain's cabin, where she was locked in alone. She wondered at this unexpected turn of events, and then her heart lightened as she thought, perhaps, the Barracuda had decided to take her back immediately to Port Royal.

She sat quietly on a low chair, stilling her curiosity to rummage about the cabin. She attempted to repair the damage to her bodice and succeeded in tying it together so that she was at least covered decently. She had almost dozed off, when the door was unlocked and thrown open brusquely. The Barracuda stood, looking down at her fiercely, before closing and locking the door behind him.

Crimson steeled herself to remain calm. After all, this man might agree to take her back to Port Royal. What did it matter if he asked for a bout of love from her body? He had taken her before, and he hadn't hurt her then. She swallowed reflexively and waited for him to move.

He continued to stare at her, as though not quite believing that he had actually thrown away a king's ransom for her person.

"Five thousand pounds," he murmured to himself. "Are you really worth it, Crimson Gardner?"

"How—how do you know my name?" she asked, startled.

He shrugged. "Your name is hardly significant now, is it?" He moved to one side of the cabin, stripping his coat and shirt off. The wound on his arm had stopped bleeding, and there was caked blood around its edges.

"Your arm—" she began, standing up.

He looked sharply at her. "A small price to pay for what I'll demand of you, wench. It's the gold that hurts." He winced, and she saw he was laughing.

"You didn't have to buy me," she threw out challengingly.

"True." He cocked his head to one side and began to unbraid the two locks on either side of his face. "But I did buy you, wench, and I expect full value for my ill-gotten gold." He poured water from a heavy earthen pitcher into a deep bowl, then plunged his head into it. He doused himself several times, then dried his hair briskly on his shirt.

"Take off your clothes," he commanded casually as he was drying himself.

Crimson blinked and remained where she was.

Peering from beneath the shirt, the pirate frowned. "Your clothes, wench. They're no good to you now."

"I—I prefer to remain dressed," Crimson ventured tentatively.

"As you wish," he returned briskly. "I'll just rip the damned thing off in a moment anyway."

At his casual threat, Crimson proceeded to remove the chemise. She stood in embarrassment for several moments before she realized that the pirate was not even looking at her. He was staring into a small mirror nailed to the wall of the cabin. In surprise, she saw that he was deftly removing the scar from across his nose.

She gasped. "It's not real!"

He laughed. "I'm afraid not. Neither is this damned eye patch." He untied it from his head. "Damned nuisance!"

He turned around, smiling lazily at her and Crimson uttered a shriek. "Kit!"

"I'm afraid so, Crimson. No one very exciting. No swashbuckling stranger pirate to sweep you off your feet."

"Kit!" she repeated. Then she frowned in sudden fury. "You are the Barracuda!"

He nodded. "In the flesh," he said slowly, removing his breeches to stand naked before her.

"You—you keep away from me!" Crimson breathed furiously. "All along, you lied to me! You let me believe—" Her face flushed. "You raped me!"

"Crimson, I didn't rape you. I was as gentle as possible, but I just couldn't let such an opportunity go by. You were alone, foolishly risking your neck to see your old lover, Nick Brentwood."

"How—how did you find that out?"

"Well, my suspicions were aroused when I saw you and him outside his room at the King's Privy."

"That's right, I remember now seeing the Barracuda—you—when Nick was ready to take me home. Then you must have seen me go down there that night when—"

"When I followed you up the path and—"

"Raped me!" she declared with renewed anger.

He ignored her and went on, "I must confess I eavesdropped outside your room after I left, the night of my arrival back home, and heard most of your conversation with him."

"You heard?" Her hand flew to her mouth. "So you know what Nick has been sent to do?"

He nodded, his expression serious. "My real purpose for talking with you that night was to see if you would tell anyone about the cove and your discovery of my ship and crew there. When I had satisfied myself that you weren't going to do so, I let myself think of more romantic inclinations, but you forced me out the door. I thought better of it halfway to my rooms and returned to try again, only to find you already occupied." He frowned to himself. "You know, I thought there was something about Nick Brentwood. I don't know, it was just that his story seemed a little far-fetched. He didn't seem at all the merchant type."

"Did you know that your father was keeping the king's treasure for himself?" Crimson asked.

Kit shrugged. "It was none of my business. After all, I was joined to the Brethren in piracy. Not exactly something I would wish my father to know about."

"But it's all Juliette's fault!" Crimson objected. "She told me that—"

"Enough of all this seriousness, Crimson," Kit interrupted, becoming aware of her nakedness again. "I came in here to do something and I'm fast becoming impatient of all this talk."

"But Kit, now that I know it's you—" Crimson began

402

helplessly, her eyes flying downward to note his growing desire, then flitting away in embarrassment.

"I've had you once as the Barracuda, Crimson, without your consent. Let me have you now as myself, with your cooperation." His dark eyes looked into hers so that she flushed.

"Kit, please, I—"

"You've held me off a long time, Crimson," he warned her, coming closer to her. "Don't fight me any more, sweetheart," he urged gently.

His hands reached for her shoulders, caressing them briefly before drawing her closer to him. Crimson would not look up, but kept her eyes fixed on the curling hairs of his chest. She jumped a little as she felt the heat of his engorged manhood touch her belly and tried to back away, but his hands held her steady.

"Crimson, I care for you," Kit was saying softly, his hands reaching down to her hips to draw her up intimately against him. "Let me love you, my darling."

His lips were tracing teasing patterns from her temple to her jawline, even as he rubbed his lower body against her suggestively. Crimson trembled at his sensuality and tried to fight down the growing desires that were threatening to engulf her. A warm wave of wanting was seeping over her body as Kit continued to plant kisses over her face. His hands kept her pressed against him so that she could feel the crispness of his hair against her breasts.

"Crimson," he murmured once more before finding her mouth with his. He was kissing her, gently at first, and then harder with his need.

She knew she couldn't fight him. He was beating her with his sheer mastery of her body and she suddenly acquiesced, becoming the willing victim. He sensed her subjugation and opened her lips to his tongue, while his hands roved up over her sides and around to her back. Gently, he was leading her to his bed, lowering her to the sheet, preparing her for his entrance.

Crimson moaned softly, tossing her head on the pillow, bringing her hands up to clasp around his neck. His hands found her breasts and alternately teased and assuaged them while his knees introduced themselves between her thighs. Instinctively, Crimson's knees arched and clung to him, forcing him to satisfy her sensual craving.

They rolled about the bed, seeking sweet release from pent-up emotions. Finally, he steadied her with his body and drove into her, causing her to groan with mingled joy and hurt. Panting now, they made love with deep intensity, until their needs were fulfilled and each lay, breathing softly, satiated.

Kit kissed her softly. "Crimson, I can never let you go!"

Hearing his whispered words, Crimson trembled at his possessive tone. Unaccountably, her thoughts turned to Nick and Juliette. . . .

43

Nick Brentwood lounged indolently in the garden of the governor's castle, wondering if Juliette would keep their assignation today or not. The end of June had brought a terrific heat that caused many people to remain indoors, or take to swimming in the rivers on the island—with a sharp eye out for alligators. Sir Thomas was taking his usual afternoon nap, and Juliette, eyes gleaming with passion, had promised Nick to meet him beneath the rose arbor. She got a vicarious joy out of making love beneath her husband's very nose, so to speak, and had already met Nick in the garden on other occasions.

Today, she was late, but Nick didn't mind. He was becoming used to the feeling of apathy that seemed to assail him whenever she came to him. She was a vociferous lover, sucking his strength from him as animals drink at a spring to slake their thirst. She was more than possessive and Nick chafed at her demands for his time.

Another thing worried him, and that was a nagging feeling that Juliette had something to do with Crimson's sudden disappearance a few days before. Something in her expression when she had told them about her departure gave him pause for thought. He could read hate in her eyes, hate mixed with a joy of having rid herself of the younger woman.

Kit, too, had apparently left for some trip and Nick couldn't help wondering if the two of them had gone off together. It was obvious that Kit loved Crimson, he thought, feeling a surprising pang of jealousy. He desired her physically, but had not forced her into submission: something only a man in love would do.

Nick tried to assess his own feelings about Crimson and found that he missed her with an acute feeling of loss. God knew it had been hard not to take her, and his self-possession had flown that night beneath the balcony, but—good Lord—when she told him about the loss of her child— his child—she had defeated him finally.

Did he love the little minx? He shook his head in a kind of wonder. Was it possible that he had fallen into that age-old trap that women had spun for men for centuries, that trap that he had sworn he could avoid? And what of Crimson? Did she care for him? He doubted it, else she would have come to him in the town. She had known where he was staying. Why hadn't she come? The tiny memory of those few nights with the barmaid caused him some trepidation, but he quickly brushed those thoughts aside. Crimson had simply not wanted to come.

"Why so thoughtful this morning, darling?" Juliette broke into his reverie.

He looked up at the eyes and smiled lazily. "I was wondering what was taking you so long to get out here," he lied blatantly.

She smiled. "I wanted to wait until Thomas was sound

405

asleep. I think he suspects something between us, Nick."
She tittered silkily. "Of course, I couldn't care less, but I'm
afraid he does have the means to—ah—dispose of you if
he wishes."

"Maybe these little trysts aren't worth it then?" Nick suggested rudely.

She laughed uneasily. "Don't be mean, darling. Let's
just enjoy each other while we can." She sighed. "I don't
know what I would have done without you."

"Don't play games with me, Juliette. I'm sure I didn't
mistake the gleam of avarice in your eyes when you look
upon your stepson." His voice was deep with mocking sarcasm.

She veiled her eyes. "And what was that in your eyes,
dearest, when you looked at my daughter-in-law? Simply a
passing interest?"

He smiled at her. "Touché, Juliette. So you noticed?"

"Hah, you admit you were interested in the little chit!"
she exclaimed as though claiming some obscure victory.
"Couldn't you see that she had eyes only for Kit?" Her expression turned inward and Nick could see the jealous
spite lingering there.

He wondered anew if she knew something more about
Crimson's disappearance than she was telling. "Your face
is too transparent, Juliette," he said softly. "You'd best be
more careful about shielding your feelings for Kit."

She tossed her head willfully. "Sir Thomas is an old
fool," she said loftily. "He could catch me in bed with Kit,
and he could do nothing about it!"

"Ah, such wifely devotion brings the tears to my eyes,"
Nick responded sardonically. "I knew there was a reason
why I have always avoided the marriage couch."

"You and Kit are two of a kind," Juliette accused.

"Perhaps more than you can imagine," Nick said, thinking suddenly of Crimson again.

Juliette stood up and pulled at his hand. "Well, are we
going to make love or talk about Kit and that girl all day?"
she asked coquettishly. "Really, we shouldn't waste words
on either of them."

406

Nick rose from his seat, but his heart was not in it. Even as Juliette lay down in the thick grass and hoisted her skirts up to her waist, he felt a distinct feeling of disgust rising within him. Gazing at the olive-hued thighs, he felt no answering lust and realized that he no longer wanted her.

"Get up, Juliette," he commanded her roughly.

She blinked up at him. "What's the matter, Nick? Are you still worried about my husband?"

He shook his head violently. "Get up, now!"

She scrambled to her feet and looked at him questioningly. His answering look was harsh, contemptuous, and she cringed away from it involuntarily.

"I'm going into town for a while," he said abruptly, turning away from her.

"Why, Nick, why?" she asked him, her voice rising stridently.

"To get drunk," he answered her shortly, and hurried back into the house.

The drunken stupor did not help to erase Crimson from Nick's mind. Rather, it intensified her face, her figure, her voice until the thought of her was like a dull ache, a bittersweet pain that was totally alien to him. He slammed his glass down angrily and called to the barmaid to attend to it.

Her plump, pretty face smiled brassily at him. "Aye, sir. Ye wish it filled and then, perhaps, a room for to sleep it off?" she asked saucily.

"No room, wench, but hurry with that rum," he ordered, in no mood for a mild flirtation.

She pouted, then took his glass to refill it. Nick watched her in a haze, his chin propped up by his hands. Damn, why didn't the girl hurry! It seemed forever until she plopped the filled mug in front of him. He caught her hand and slipped a coin into it. She curtseyed, then flounced away to find more eager game.

Nick sipped the rum slowly, trying to bring his thoughts together. It didn't make sense that Crimson would take the

407

first ship out without saying something to him. Did she hate him that much, not even to say good-bye? Dammit, she knew he would see her again when he returned to London. Or did she care? Was she going straight to the king?

He chewed his lip at the thought of her in Charles' bed —another willing female to fall victim to the king's charm and power. Damn her! Another thought quickly replaced that one. Perhaps she would prefer the elegant Chesterfield. He remembered how she had cuckolded him once before with the handsome libertine. The thought still galled him. She was a devious bitch, he was quite sure of that now, with the rum making things so clear. Else why would she leave so mysteriously?

He frowned to himself. "But did she leave by her own choice?" he wondered out loud. Once again, Juliette's cat-like face appeared in his vision. What exactly did she know about Crimson's disappearance? Had she taken it upon herself to arrange it?

He stood up and slammed his fist on the table, upsetting the remaining rum in the glass. "Damn, I'll find out if I have to wring that bitch's neck!" he stormed and drained the last of the rum.

Throwing some coins on the table, he hurried out to his horse and mounted, weaving dangerously as he urged the horse forward. Nearby, two grinning pirates watched him and silently followed on foot as Nick navigated the horse through the streets of the town and over the bridge. Out of necessity, the horse was keeping a slow pace, as each bounce made Nick's head feel as though it was about to burst. Like twin shadows, the pirates ran on bare feet, closing in as Nick approached the trees leading up the slope.

Lost in his own thoughts, Nick didn't hear the pirates until they had overtaken him. One seized the horse's bridle from his hand. The other pulled Nick from the animal, causing Nick to roll over in the grass, striking his head on an old tree stump.

Despite the dizzy pain combined with the rum fumes in

his brain, Nick realized that he was being attacked, and he reached for his sword. He got slowly to his feet, his head shifting from side to side to eye the two men blearily.

"Ah, he's too drunk to do us any harm," one pirate said disdainfully. "Let's close on him, Harry!"

"Watch his sword," the other warned, circling to the opposite side.

Nick backed up to keep them both in his field of vision, but his reflexes were slowed by the effects of the rum and his fall from the horse. He tripped and would have fallen, but kept his balance with an effort. This was just the moment the thieves were waiting for and both sprang towards him at the same time.

Nick fended one off with his sword, but couldn't move fast enough to keep the other away. The pirate jumped on top of him, knocking him to the ground and, at the same time, seizing his coin purse and throwing it to his companion. The other caught it deftly, pushed it inside his shirt and took out his dagger.

"Move off him, Harry, and I'll finish the bloke off!"

Carriage wheels coming down the path caused all three men to tense and, after a second or two, the two pirates scrambled through the trees, obviously not thinking it worth their own lives to kill their victim.

Nick shook his head, trying to free it from the dazing effect of the rum, and got to his knees. "Ho, there!" he called, hearing the carriage pass by. He was relieved to hear the driver call a halt to the horses and out of the door sprang Juliette's maid, Maggie, her eyes round in her face.

"Oh, sir, you've been attacked by ruffians! Are you bad hurt?"

Nick faltered towards her and she reached out to help him to the carriage. "Turn this thing around and take me back to the castle. I have to talk to Juliette!" he said thickly.

"Ah, I don't think you'll be talking to anyone, sir," Maggie surmised after they were seated and she had given the order to the driver.

Nick found himself resting against her shoulder, but

409

fought the welcome drowsiness. He had to talk to Juliette, to make her tell him what she knew about Crimson.

When they reached the castle, he refused Maggie's supportive arm and walked slowly inside, searching the downstairs for Juliette. She was nowhere to be seen, but Sir Thomas was busy in the library and looked up in surprise at his bloodstreaked face and harried look.

"Juliette? Why, I'm not sure where she is, Nick." He got up from his chair. "What has happened to you, lad? Let me call a servant to help you to your room. You've been hurt!"

Nick waved his hands away. "Must speak to Juliette now!" he shouted and made his way upstairs, Sir Thomas following behind, determined to find out the reason for Nick's urgency.

"Now, see here, Nick, I—" Sir Thomas began in protest as Nick pushed open the door to Juliette's rooms.

Nick ignored him and searched her suite. She was not there and, with a sudden suspicion, he made his way to his own room. Swinging open the door, his eyes beheld her, bent over his sea chest, rummaging through the contents.

"What are you doing in here?" he demanded hoarsely.

She whirled around, her jaw dropping at sight of his rumpled appearance. "Why, Nick, I didn't expect you—"

"Obviously!" he returned, striding inside the room. "What are you doing going through my things?"

Juliette backed away, frightened by his tone and his disheveled appearance. "Nick, I think you're drunk. Why don't you sleep it off and we can talk later," she suggested.

"Damn you, bitch! Tell me what you were doing, sneaking in here while I was away!" He towered threateningly over her.

Juliette gasped, but her eye caught the figure of her husband entering the room, and some of her fear left her. Brazenly now, she looked up at Nick. "All right, Nick, darling, I'll tell you. I was looking through your things, I admit it! And I found certain letters, accounts—evidence, if you will—that could prove highly dangerous for you!" She smiled triumphantly. "You are a spy for the king,

410

aren't you, Nick? You were sent here to spy on my husband, to prove that he was confiscating the king's treasure and then see him sent back to England to hang for treason!"

"You sneaking bitch!" Nick roared, reaching out to clasp her neck with his hands. "So you've found me out. That's not going to keep me from wringing your neck if you don't tell me what you've done with Crimson!"

"Crimson!" she repeated, reaching up to try to unclasp his fingers. "That little whore is probably dead by now!" She coughed as his hands tightened.

"Thomas, help me!" she gasped, and before Nick could turn around, he felt something hard bounce off his skull. Slowly, he sank to the floor at Juliette's feet.

Rubbing her throat, Juliette kicked him viciously with her foot. "This bastard is a spy, Thomas, did you hear?" she said to her husband.

Sir Thomas, trembling a little from the shock of the declaration, stooped over to make sure that Nick was unconscious. "My God, the king suspects me then, Juliette! We've got to escape this island before—"

"Escape!" she cried. "Why? We can get rid of him easily enough. I'm not leaving without the treasure, nor without—" she stopped and glanced at her husband scornfully.

"Without Kit?" he asked, anger replacing his initial shock. "You want him very much, don't you, Juliette? Don't you?"

"Yes!" she threw at him, her own anger causing her to throw her caution to the winds. "Yes, I want him! I've wanted him since the day I first met you both, but he didn't want me. And so I married his broken, old father just to be near him! Yes, yes, yes! You don't think I could actually love you, do you! Your feeble attempts at satisfying me only made me sick!" Her hatred of all her wasted time without Kit came spilling out of her mouth, heedless of the pain she was causing. "I'll have him yet!"

With a suddenness that caught her off guard, Sir Thomas brought back his hand and slapped her with all his strength. Her head spun crazily and she fell back against the chest, breathing hard.

"I should never have married you!" Sir Thomas shouted at her. "All you've done is bring about my ruination. It was you who urged me to take a share of the treasure! You wanted it for yourself and for Kit! Well, you won't have both, my dear!" he promised.

She struggled to her feet, holding her flaming cheek with one hand. "What do you mean? I'll have Kit and the treasure too, and you can't stop me!"

"You'll have to choose between me and the treasure, or Kit and escape!" he said slowly. He backed away from her as though fearing she might attack him. "I'll put guards at the treasure room to keep you out. Make your decision quickly, my dearest wife, or I shall be forced to put you in the dungeon with your lover!" He looked down at Nick's still form.

Juliette took a deep breath. She took the safest way out. "The treasure then, damn you!" she said, but knowing that when Kit returned she would have both.

Sir Thomas smiled slickly. "All right then, my dear. Let me call a servant and we'll have this—spy—taken below and put in a cell for the time being."

After the servant had taken the unconscious form of Nick Brentwood downstairs, Sir Thomas returned to his wife's rooms to find her dabbing at her bruised cheek with some witch hazel.

"What has the girl, Crimson, to do with Nick Brentwood?" he asked Juliette slowly. "If she has been allowed to escape the island—"

Juliette laughed cruelly, triumphantly. "She has not gone back to England, Thomas, so don't worry yourself about her."

"How do you know?"

"Because it was I who arranged to have her kidnapped by pirates! She'll not be running back to the king with any tales of confiscated treasure. I ordered them to kill her, after they'd had their fun with her, of course." Her smile was pure malevolence, and her husband took a step back,

412

realizing the extent of his wife's hatred and beginning to fear it.

"Why did you have her kidnapped?" he asked. "Had you already found out that she knew Brentwood?"

Absently, Juliette drew a curl over her cheek to see if she could disguise the discoloration. "No," she said, taking her time. "No, Thomas, I had her disposed of because I could see that Kit was falling in love with her."

Sir Thomas paled considerably. "You had her killed simply because Kit fancied the wench!"

"Yes!" she hissed, turning around. "I would do away with anyone who stood between Kit and me." Her eyes narrowed as she eyed him defiantly.

"You have forgotten your promise to me already," Sir Thomas returned, his shoulders stooping with defeat. "I'll have to have you confined to your room, Juliette."

"Hah!" she sneered. "That won't keep me from Kit!"

"When Kit returns, I'm going to send him away, Juliette. I'm going to forbid him ever to return to Jamaica as long as I live."

Juliette's face reddened with fury. "You can't do that! You can't! He'll go away and I won't see him again! I'll kill you before I let you separate us!" Picking up a small cosmetic knife, she ran towards him, her hand upraised to strike at his chest.

Sir Thomas was able to twist away from the weapon, but took its point in his arm. Wincing from the pain, he bellowed for a servant, while Juliette backed away from him, searching for another weapon. Before she could do any more damage, the servant arrived and Sir Thomas directed him to hold his wife while he tied a scarf about the bleeding wound.

"Damn you, unfaithful bitch!" he ground out. "I'll have you thrown in the dungeon, and Kit, too, if he tries to effect your escape!"

"No!" she cried. "You wouldn't leave me down there! I —I couldn't stand it, Thomas, please!"

Despite her fury of a moment ago, she was quite capable of beseeching him with pathetic eyes now, and Sir

Thomas wavered. After all, how could he put his own wife in prison? Warring within himself, he nodded to the servant to release her.

"But she will remain locked in her room until I give orders to let her out!" he commanded.

44

"Kit?"

"Hmmm?"

Crimson rolled over on her side to trace patterns between the dark curls on Kit's chest. They were both naked, lying on the sand, sheltered from the eyes of the crew by a line of boulders. They had just finished swimming in the sparkling waters of the cove, to which they had returned after sailing from Barbados.

"When do you think we'll be returning to the castle?"

Kit opened one eye lazily. "*You* won't be returning at all, Crimson. Not after what you've told me about Juliette. I wouldn't trust that woman for your safety."

Crimson sighed and let that pass. "Well then, when will *you* be returning to the castle? Your father will probably be wondering where you went off to in such a hurry."

He shrugged. "Father never wonders about me, Crimson, but I suppose I'll be returning in a few days. Are you trying to tell me you're tired of me already?" He caught the hand that was pulling at his chest hair.

"Oh, no!" she objected quickly. "But I was wondering

414

about Nick Brentwood, I mean whether or not he was going to be leaving soon for England. You know that when he leaves he may be taking your father with him." She looked closely at his face to watch his reaction.

Kit got up on one elbow and looked at her. "Crimson, my father and I have never really been all that close. I mean, we don't hate each other, but we've never been overly affectionate either. If he goes to England to stand trial for treason, I would do nothing to stop it. After all, I could very well be hanged as a pirate for the same reason, in which case I'm sure my father would not lift a finger to help me."

He sighed softly and his free arm went out to bring her closer to him. "It's not my father you're worried about, is it, Crimson?"

She blushed. "I—I don't know what you mean, Kit."

"Of course you do, my sweet. You're wondering about Nick Brentwood, aren't you? Wondering why he didn't try to find you, why he fell victim to my stepmother's charms without seeing the malice that lurks beneath the surface?"

Crimson bit her lip. "All right, Kit, I admit it." She gazed at him through her lashes. "I'm afraid that Juliette might do something. I don't know exactly what. But it's you she really loves, Kit! You, and the treasure," she finished cynically.

"Whether she loves me or not hardly signifies, Crimson," Kit returned mildly. "I *know* that I don't love her, but what concerns me is whether or not you love Nick Brentwood."

"Love him! Kit, how can you ask—"

He pushed her away gently. "What if I told you, Crimson, that I truly loved you, that I wanted to marry you. Yes, I'd go that far, though I know Delia would be mad enough to flay me alive, but she'd get over it." He laughed briefly.

"Marry me, Kit?" she questioned him. "How could you expect me to be the wife of a pirate, a criminal, if you will?" She paused and looked at him. "I wouldn't want that, Kit, I'm sorry."

He shrugged. "I could hardly expect you to, but if we

went away somewhere together, Crimson, where we could start life fresh, a new land?" He reached to draw her against him once more, rolling over so that she was beneath him in the warm sand. "We could be married and go away from here, never see Port Royal again." He kissed her tenderly. "I do love you, Crimson."

"Oh, Kit—I—I don't know what to say. You make it sound simple, but there is so much more."

"Like what?" he asked her, nuzzling her gently. "Just you and me, Crimson. It is that simple."

"Kit, please, don't force me to make a decision now!"

He stopped his teasing and looked deeply into her eyes and she could see the sadness in his. "You're determined to make yourself unhappy, aren't you, my love? You think you want Nick Brentwood, you may even think you love him. But he doesn't love you like I do, Crimson! Why should you throw your love away, yearning for him when I want to make you happy?"

"Oh, Kit, it's too complicated! I don't even know what I feel!" she cried, hating to hurt him. "I've got to be honest with you, Kit. What would happen if I agreed to marry you, to go away together, and I didn't love you? It wouldn't be right, and sooner or later you'd come to hate me for lying to you."

"Crimson, I could never hate you!" he said fervently. "Believe me. I only want to love you and cherish you."

In a sudden fit of passion, he crushed her beneath him. His desire aroused, he spread her apart to make an entrance for him. Crimson clung to his shoulders and closed her eyes tightly. He thrust into her quickly, kissing her with heated lips as though to force her to love him.

Despite her silent resolve, Crimson felt her body answering his lust, felt the warmth of desire suffuse her as she returned his thrusts. God! How could she play the wanton with him and tell herself that it was truly Nick she loved! Her self-accusation tormented her even as she responded to Kit's expert mastery of her body. The culmination was bittersweet and, afterwards, she began sobbing from reaction.

416

Sated, Kit looked down and kissed the tears gently away from her cheeks.

"Tell me what you want of me, Crimson," he urged her.

"I want nothing from you, Kit," she sobbed. "Only—"

"Only this," he sighed, caressing the taut flesh beneath his. With a despairing sound, he rose from her, standing up and stretching, realizing with bitterness that his idyll with her was coming to an end.

"All right, Crimson, I'll return to my father tomorrow," he promised her suddenly. "I'll try to warn Nick. Yes, I'll even help condemn my own father," he said, shrugging his shoulders at her surprised look. "But in return, my lovely, you must promise to leave the island—with me."

"Kit, you still want me even though you know that I don't love you?" she asked, sitting up in the sand abruptly.

He nodded. "I would want you even if you hated me, Crimson. Perhaps by exacting this promise, you will hate me for a time, but I'll do everything in my power to insure that you do not regret coming with me."

She gazed at his face a long time. It was easy to see that he was being honest with her. He loved her. She was amazed at the depth of a man's love, that he could go on loving her when she did not reciprocate that love. But could she learn to love him? The memory of Nick's face rose before her eyes—the handsome, lean features, the dark blue eyes that never revealed his secrets. Could she come to forget that face?

"Kit—"

"Do you promise to leave with me?" he asked.

She lowered her head. "I promise to go with you."

He breathed a heavy sigh. "All right then, I'll return to my father's house tomorrow morning."

"When will you come back?" she asked, standing to brush away particles of sand. It kept her hands from trembling.

"The following morning," he promised.

They looked at one another for a long time. Then, Kit extended his hand for her to take.

"We'll get dressed, Crimson," he said quietly.

She took his hand and nodded.

Crimson kissed Kit good-bye and watched him as he sat in the longboat with a few of his crew as they rowed out of the cove. She waved half-heartedly, hating the disguise he must wear as the Barracuda. She knew he would go to Delia's rooms to change into Kit again and couldn't help wondering what the girl would say when he told her of his plans. Was Delia capable of taking Kit and giving him over to the authorities? Crimson hoped not, although she knew the girl would be heartsick at Kit's news. She cared for Kit—cared for him in the way that Crimson wished she could feel.

The day passed slowly, the night even more so as she tossed about restlessly in the bunk she had shared with Kit for nearly a week now. Her dreams were filled with images of Nick and Kit, the two sometimes merging into one so that she wondered if she really knew her own heart.

The next morning dawned and she had already been up an hour. She had washed carefully and donned the best dress that Delia had left for her, a pale pink muslin that would do as her wedding gown, Crimson thought ruefully. She supposed that Kit might bring back a minister with him, although she didn't even know if there was one in Port Royal. At any rate, she would soon know, she thought as she climbed up on deck.

The crew, those who had stayed aboard, were busy with their duties. Kit had given them their orders the night before his departure. He had been honest with them and had bequeathed the ship to any of them who wished to remain marauders of the high seas, once he and Crimson had been safely set on some friendly shore.

It was nearly noon before Kit's longboat was sighted and by then, Crimson was nearly ready to tear out her hair with frustration and worry. She had thought that Delia must have turned him in, but was so relieved to see Kit's form in the boat that she wept. Her own reaction startled her. Perhaps she did love him a little, or was it just anxiety to hear the news about Nick?

As he came on deck, she rushed to him, flinging her

418

arms about him tightly, regardless of the gapes of the crew. "Oh, Kit, I was so worried," she cried.

He disengaged her arms from about him and hurried her to his cabin where he closed the door firmly and turned to look at her. She could see the struggle in his face, the uncertainty.

"What is it?" she asked anxiously. "Is—is everything all right?"

He stole a look at her, then rubbed his face with his hands in perplexity. "Crimson, my father—" He took a deep breath and began again. "Juliette and my father have found out about Nick's business in Port Royal. They know he was sent to spy on them."

"Oh, no! But how—"

"How isn't important right now. They've got him locked up in the dungeons below the castle. My father has ordered him to be hanged next Saturday."

"Saturday!" Crimson thought quickly. "That's only three days away, Kit! What can we do? How can your father have him hanged? On what charge?"

"Calm down, please. My father did not see fit to confide in me. But I did talk to Juliette, through her locked door. It seems they've quarreled and he's confined her to her room. I was only able to bribe the guard to let me talk to her from the hallway." He passed a hand over his brow. "Nick's to be hanged on a trumped-up charge, of course. Trafficking goods from pirates, I believe, or something like that. Since my father is the highest authority on the island he can hang him by merely putting his name to the paper. Later on, when the new governor arrives, I'm sure he'll have some glib excuse to cover the lie. Ah, everything is so simple—for him, I'm afraid, Crimson."

"But, Kit, couldn't you talk to your father, convince him to let Nick go?" she pleaded desperately.

He shook his head. "I'm afraid the misunderstanding my father and Juliette had was over me. He, in effect, has banished me from the island while it is under his jurisdiction. Juliette threatened to run off with me and the gold. The woman is a fool!" This last was ground out with

419

angry contempt. "I don't know why my father ever married her!"

"I don't care why he married her!" Crimson cried, beside herself. "I can't stand by and let Nick be hanged! It would be monstrous!"

Kit stepped over to her and gathered her hands in his. "Remember your promise to me, Crimson, that we would leave together. It looks as though I'm in danger of being thrown into prison too, if I don't take my father at his word."

"But, Kit, an innocent man will be hanged because of a woman's greed."

"I know, I know, and the worst thing about this is, once I'm out of the way, I'm sure Juliette will come to terms with my father and she'll end up with the gold anyway. Of course she'll still be married to the old goat, but I'm sure she'll have enough lovers to satisfy her." He whistled softly. "I never realized she wanted me that much."

"And you wanted her too!" Crimson accused, angrily drawing her hands out of his grasp. "I saw you with her—more than once—looking as though you wouldn't say no to a night with her. What kept you away? Was it really your father?" she jeered.

He clasped her shoulders and shook her. "I admit she was tempting," he said bitingly, "and, yes, there were times when I would have gone to bed with her, but I had too much pride to put myself into the position where she wanted me. And then when you came—"

"Oh, Kit, I'm sorry," she said, suddenly repentant. "It's just that I'm so worried about Nick." She looked up at him beseechingly. "Can you understand how I feel?"

After a moment, he nodded grimly. "Yes, Crimson, I *can* understand."

She flushed. "We've got to get him out," she said quickly. "Please, help me get him out and then we can go away."

He shook his head violently. "No, Crimson, I'll not risk my neck to free the very man to whom I could lose you!"

"Kit, please, I'm begging you!" Crimson said, her hands clutching at his coat. "I could never love you if I knew

420

that there was a chance to save Nick and you wouldn't help him!"

"There is no chance to save him, Crimson," he said swiftly. "He's locked in the dungeon. Even if I could get the key to his cell, I'd have to go through the whole garrison just to get to the prison! It's impossible!"

"No, Kit!" Crimson interjected, her face brightening as she remembered. "When Juliette took me down in there, there was a door that was locked which led through a tunnel out to the other side of the mountain! She said the tunnel was used as an escape route, but had been partially blocked by a cave-in."

"But, if it is blocked, how could we possibly get through, assuming of course that we could even find the entrance in the mountainside?"

"We have three days. Surely you have men who have been trained as scouts. Let them search the slope."

"All right. Then if we find the entrance, what then? We'd still have to search the tunnel, perhaps even dig through part of it where the cave-in occurred. That would take more than three days, Crimson."

"Kit, we've got to try! If we could get in that way, we could take the guards by surprise, get Nick and—"

"Oh, Crimson, you are determined to try this crazy scheme, aren't you?" Kit sighed. "If I agree to the plan, I'll have to have something to offer my men for risking their lives. They won't enjoy the idea of freeing one man for all this trouble."

"Let them into the treasure room!" she cried. And then at his astounded look, "Yes, let them have the treasure! I would rather they have it than Juliette!"

"But what about the key?"

"You have gunpowder, don't you? Blow open the door!"

"My dear, that would rather take away the element of surprise," Kit smiled.

She stamped her foot. "By then, it wouldn't matter. Besides, the noise might add enough confusion to allow everyone time to get out through the tunnel!"

"I don't know if the men will buy your plan, Crimson—" Kit began.

"They must!"

"I'll talk to them tonight—"

"No, talk to them now, Kit, *now*! We can't waste any time!"

He nodded, defeated by her insistence. He held her a moment longer and kissed her. "I'm probably the biggest fool in the Carib', Crimson," he murmured against her mouth.

"*Now*, Kit," she insisted.

He released her and left the cabin.

She paced the room anxiously, awaiting his return, wondering if the men would prove greedy enough to approve the daring scheme. It took little more than an hour before Kit returned to the cabin, his face wearing an uncertain smile.

"They've approved the plan, Crimson."

"Oh, thank you, Kit!" she cried fervently. "Thank you."

She clasped her hands together and turned away from him, missing the pain that crossed his brow as he watched her joy at the news that the man she truly loved would go free.

45

The plan worked smoothly, and Crimson breathed easier once the scouts had discovered the old entrance to the escape tunnel. It had been hidden by a straggly bush, which shielded it from sight of the ocean. The men had been lucky enough to find it on the afternoon of the next day. Immediately, Kit had ordered part of the crew to take axes and shovels to the site in order to see how far along the tunnel went, before the sliding earth made it difficult to move through. When they found the place, they were to begin digging out the earth to see if it was still running on the opposite side.

Crimson insisted on going to the site with the crew and, despite Kit's initial protests, finally succeeded in getting his reluctant permission. They went to the entrance without mishap, for there was a wide ledge leading up the slope to the hole.

After cutting away the bush, candles were lit and stuck into makeshift sconces so that the men would have light as they entered the darkness. Crimson followed behind Kit at the rear of the party, holding her own lighted candle in her hand.

The tunnel went about fifty feet in before the way was blocked by earth and rocks. Crimson waited impatiently while the men looked about, seeking an alternate route, but there was none.

"We'll have to dig, sir," one of the crew shouted back to Kit.

"All right, men, you'll have to stick your candles on the sides of the tunnel and work with your axes to move those rocks first," Kit ordered. He ushered Crimson back out. "You'd best stay out here, Crimson. The heat will be pretty bad in there."

Chafing, Crimson walked about the ledge, idly gazing down the slope at the shimmering sea. She would not let her thoughts turn towards failure. They would make it through the tunnel in plenty of time to rescue Nick, she was sure of it. She trusted Kit to do it. Somehow, she knew he would not hesitate even though it meant freeing the man he considered his rival.

But she would keep her promise to Kit, she thought firmly. She had given her word to marry him, and she would. Besides, she thought wistfully, Nick had never said he loved her—he had, in fact, tried to rape her at their last meeting. Kit had really no need to worry.

The crew worked until dark, by which time the heat inside the tunnel was cooled somewhat. Crimson had hoped they would continue after a resting period, but Kit ordered them back to the base of the slope, where they had set up a makeshift camp.

"Why not continue?" she ventured tentatively.

Kit gave her a wary look. "Because they've had enough for one day," he answered her bluntly.

She was aware of his weariness, and kept her mouth shut, even though she hated to waste the entire night in sleep. Only two more days! She slept restlessly in Kit's arms. He hadn't pressured her to make love that night and she was glad of it.

The next morning, the crew was up at dawn on their way back up the slope. Crimson was about to follow with Kit, when a voice stopped them.

"Ho, there, Kit!" It was Delia, running across the beach to meet them. She arrived out of breath. "I had to find out what was going on," she said. "I had someone row me out to the cove and one of your crew told me you were here." Her brows were raised in impudent disbelief. "I hear you're going to effect some daring escape!"

Kit nodded briefly.

"It's not really true, then, is it?" Delia asked in surprise. "You're going to break into the dungeons below the castle? My dear Kit, isn't that a bit risky even for you?"

"We're going to free Nick Brentwood," Crimson put in hurriedly.

"Free—?" Delia turned to Kit. "You're insane," she said flatly.

"Please, Delia, no encouragement," Kit returned, wincing a little.

She put her hands on her hips belligerently. "You're risking your neck to free some stranger, for God's sake! Well, I'll be damned, this wench has really turned your head, hasn't she?"

"Delia, I don't need your sarcasm now," Kit responded impatiently.

424

"Kit, you can't do this! You could be killed, dammit! I won't let you do it!"

Crimson watched in dismay. She wished she could hurry Kit away from the other girl. She wanted him to return to the tunnel, to get away from the common sense that Delia was throwing at him.

"You can't stop me, Countess," he said. "I've given my word to Crimson."

"In exchange for what?" she cried. "That perfumed body? For God's sake, Kit, all women are the same in the dark. You don't need her to make your nights comfortable!"

"It's not the same, Countess. I want to marry Crimson."

Delia's jaw dropped open. "Marry her?"

For a moment Crimson thought she was going to cry, but Delia stopped the trembling of her lips with an effort. The two women looked at each other, and there was no real rancor in Delia's gaze, only a defeated bitterness that hurt more than anger.

"Well," Delia muttered bravely, "I suppose congratulations are in order, but you're not going to have much of a honeymoon if you insist on this crazy scheme."

"There's more involved, Countess," Kit explained patiently now. "The men have been promised a share of the treasure in my father's storeroom if they succeed in making it through the tunnel."

"A share of the king's treasure! Kit, how—"

"You mean my father's treasure, Countess. He had no intentions of turning over any of that wealth to the king. So why not share the loot?" His look challenged her to deny him.

Delia looked thunderstruck, but she nodded slowly. "Yes, as you say, why leave it to one man?" She rounded on Kit suddenly. "All right, darling, if you insist on this foolish feat of daring, I'll have to insist on coming with you."

"Countess, now who's being foolish? There's no reason for you—"

"I want to do it, Kit," she repeated quietly. Her eyes

425

held his for a moment, then turned to meet Crimson's gaze.

"My God, why did I have to be so blessed with such independent women!" Kit cried, throwing his his hands up in mock dismay. "All right, Countess, but don't blame me if you get your pretty head sliced off."

"If I get my head sliced off, you can be sure I'll have done some slicing of my own," she returned sourly.

The three of them turned towards the slope silently. Once at the tunnel again, Kit went inside to help the men, leaving Delia and Crimson alone for a moment. Crimson was about to follow him inside, but Delia caught her arm.

"Are you really going to marry him?" she wanted to know.

Crimson shook her arm free impatiently. "I hardly think that's your business," she returned sharply.

"Don't use that haughty tone with me," Delia said just as sharply. "If you'll kindly remember, I was the one who told Kit where you were when Captain Thornton kidnapped you. If it hadn't been for me, my dear, you would be miles away in Captain Duncan's fond embrace with no chance of rescuing your precious Nick Brentwood!"

Despite her impatience, Crimson realized that Delia was right. "I'm sorry. You're right, I owe you a lot, Delia. If there's a way that I can repay you—"

Delia laughed shakily. "Yes, I'll take Kit's life for a start."

Crimson blushed. "I promised to marry him if he would rescue Nick from hanging. I'll keep that promise."

Delia nodded. "I can respect that, but do you love him, Crimson?"

The other girl sighed. "He knows I don't love him, Delia, and he doesn't care."

"Oh, he cares all right, you can be sure of that. But he's not going to tell you he cares, for he's afraid you might just disappear and leave him with nobody but me." Delia swallowed. "God, do you realize that Kit could be killed doing this crazy thing?"

Crimson could not meet the other girl's gaze. "I *know* Nick will be killed if he doesn't do it."

"Lord," Delia groaned anxiously. "You love Nick, but yet you'd go away with Kit. Crimson, you're a bigger fool than I am for loving Kit and letting you have him."

"I'm sorry, Delia, I'm truly sorry," Crimson said. It was all she could think of to say.

"Let's just hope that Kit's not sorry when you two go off together and he finds out that you're still madly in love with another man," Delia replied soberly.

Crimson was silent. The two women went to join the men in the cave, seeking to help in any way they could.

It was nearly dark again before the obstruction was removed and the men could go further to explore the rest of the tunnel. A jubilant member returned to say that the only further obstruction was the door itself, which led to the prison chambers. It was locked from the other side, but with the help of the axes, it could be broken in in short order.

"We'll wait until dawn," Kit ordered.

Crimson would have wished to go in now, but was wise enough to remain silent and acquiesce to Kit's wishes. They all returned to the camp in order to get a good night's sleep before the attack the following morning.

Crimson had decided not to sleep with Kit, telling him that she wanted him to get his full measure of rest, but really because she was embarrassed to lie with him with Delia there. Quietly, she took her blanket and rolled up in a spot close to where Delia had chosen.

She was dozing in a light sleep, when she suddenly felt an insidious hand run up her bare leg. Thinking it was Kit, she kicked out a little, expressing her displeasure at his untimely interest. The hand insisted though and traveled to the inside of her thigh, trying to locate her womanliness.

"Kit, please!" she murmured grouchily.

The next moment, the blanket was torn off of her and a man's body was hot against hers, his mouth smashing into her lips. Crimson's eyes flew open, wondering if Kit had gone crazy, but her eyes beheld a different visage, one that seemed vaguely familiar, but in her half-sleepy state she couldn't place it.

"Ye're mine now," a voice breathed, sending streams of

427

offensive odor over her nostrils. "I told ye Jack Hawkins would have ye, wench!"

Jack Hawkins! Memory flooded back of the boy who had tried to rape her on the voyage from England, the boy who had been about to be keelhauled when the Barracuda attacked their ship, the boy who had murdered a member of the crew and escaped to the pirate ship! Oh, God, why hadn't she recognized him among the crew!

His hand was tight on her mouth as his body wiggled sexually against hers. She could feel his organ, hot and probing between her legs, and she tried to clasp her thighs together, but one of his hands reached down to stab at them painfully with dirty fingernails, forcing them open.

"I've waited for this day!" he crooned softly in her ear, his excitement almost beyond his control. "Aye, patiently I've waited for yer tender body!"

He was trying to rip her bodice to capture her breasts, but her squirming made it impossible for him to keep one hand on her mouth and her thighs spread apart. He had to use his free arm to bar it across her throat. She remembered this tactic from before as he pushed down to squeeze her breath from her. She fought the closing unconsciousness.

"Crimson?" Delia's voice, tentatively coming through the darkness. "Crimson, are you there?"

Crimson's voice was muffled by his hand and no sounds could come from her constricted throat. She flung her arms out and searched for the dagger that Kit had given her. She had never had occasion to use it, but had kept it close to where she slept, imagining using it on some crawling thing. Well, here was a crawling thing on top of her now—if she could just find it.

"Crimson?" Delia again, her voice more urgent.

Crimson heard her sounds as Delia rose from her blanket to investigate. Hawkins heard her too and he tensed against Crimson's body, his hand reaching inside his shirt for his own knife. Crimson pushed furiously against the sand, trying to warn Delia off. Her hand searched frantically for her own dagger.

"Crimson, what—"

Delia was suddenly thrown back to the ground by a whirling body, taken by surprise as she felt the man on top of her.

"Damn ye for a prying bitch!" Hawkins whispered furiously. "I'll cut yer throat and take care of the other one later!" He raised his knife and Delia closed her eyes.

Suddenly, the boy let out a curious moaning gush of air. Delia opened her eyes at the same moment he slumped on top of her, his knife driving ineffectually into the sand. Delia felt something warm drip on her outstretched arm.

"Delia! Delia, are you all right! My God!" It was Crimson, trying to push the boy's body off her. "Kit!" she cried out louder.

In a moment, several members of the crew were blinking the remains of sleep away, helping to drag the boy's body off Delia.

"Delia, thank God, you're all right!" Crimson breathed with relief when the girl got to her feet.

Kit looked from one girl to the other. "What in hell is going on here? Hawkins is dead!"

Crimson turned on him. "Yes, the horrible animal is dead, and I killed him, Kit! He—he tried to rape me on board the *Margaret*, and he tried to rape me again just a moment ago. Delia heard him and tried to help me, but he jumped on her and was about to kill her!"

"I'll be damned! I'd forgotten how the lad came to be on the ship," Kit said, frowning. "My God, are you both all right then?"

Crimson nodded. "Thanks to Delia." She smiled shyly at the other girl. "If it weren't for you—"

Delia smiled back weakly. "Don't thank me, Crimson. 'Tis I who'll be thanking you!" She looked sharply at her. "I owe you a life now."

46

Dawn came and the crew were scattered the length of the tunnel, ready to pour in through the door once it was shattered by the axes of the first five men. Crimson, Delia and Kit were in the forefront, waiting anxiously. Kit had secured the exit with six of his best men. The entire crew was well armed with swords, flintlocks and daggers. Kit himself held the gunpowder in a sack inside his shirt. He gave the signal to break open the door. . . .

Upstairs, inside the castle, Juliette was wide awake, pacing her room like a caged animal. She had ordered the guard outside her room to send for her husband. She would speak to him now.

It took several minutes for Sir Thomas to arrive. He'd hurriedly donned a pair of breeches and his dressing robe.

"What do you want, dearest?" he asked, mingling sarcasm with wariness.

She smiled her sweetest. "Thomas, you've kept me in here long enough. Kit has left by your orders. There is nothing I can do but remain here with you. My dearest, can't we start over again?" The black eyes gazed at him fondly, the red, red lips pursed slightly as though ready to kiss him.

"Start over again? How do you propose to do that after what has been said?" Sir Thomas asked her, frowning.

Juliette barely kept herself from rubbing her hands together. At least he was willing to listen! It wouldn't be hard to have him in the palm of her hand again, the bloated fool!

"I'm willing to forget what was said, if you are, Thomas," she said smoothly. "Kit was a—fascination with me, but now he's gone I'll not let myself worry about him anymore. He's simply not worth it, dearest."

"I see," Sir Thomas murmured. "The treasure is worth more than my son. You are an intelligent woman, Juliette."

She smiled again. "Thank you, Thomas. You know how I value your opinion of me."

His own smile faltered. Was she ridiculing him? "Intelligent, yes, Juliette, but your viper's tongue can still cause you trouble," he observed drily.

She lowered her eyes. "Forgive me. I admit I am still a trifle upset about what has happened between us, but I know that we can work out our problems, Thomas. What's to stop us? Brentwood will be out of the way tomorrow morning, Kit has gone and that troublesome girl is dead. There's just you and me left, my darling."

"Very true, Juliette."

She went on, coming closer to him, her hands extended in front of her to smooth his dressing robe. "You and I, we could have a comfortable life with what riches we've accumulated, Thomas. When the governor arrives, we could stay here if you like. It would be easy to find a place to keep our treasures. Or, perhaps, you would like to leave. Go back to England and live in the style suitable to your station."

"Would you like that, Juliette? Would you like to live in England?"

She sighed sensually, imagining the court, the licentious life, the eager young stallions who could, with the flick of a sword, free her permanently from her tedious husband. The Widow Gardner, eager and willing to satisfy any of those reputed libertines of Whitehall. Even the king!

"Yes, Thomas," she murmured in a rush. "I would like to live in England."

431

He rubbed his brow thoughtfully while she let her hand slip suggestively to the slight bulge in his breeches. "Perhaps, perhaps we can work something out, Juliette." He breathed more heavily now. "I can understand the feelings of a young woman your age with a handsome lad like Kit around, I suppose."

Juliette nodded, smiling up at his face while she deftly led him towards her bed. Easy enough to seduce this randy fool, she thought confidently. A few heated gasps and drawn-out moans and he would be willing to do anything she said.

She had just succeeded in pushing him down onto the bed when a sudden explosion in the bowels of the castle caused them both to jump up in alarm.

"What on God's earth was that?" Sir Thomas sputtered, rearranging his clothing hurriedly as the guard entered the room.

"Sir Thomas, there's pirates in the dungeons, sir!" the guard broke in. "The garrison's going down to defend—"

"The treasure!" Juliette wailed, interrupting.

"Pirates, here!" Sir Thomas said unbelieving. "Who would be so bold!" He hesitated only a moment. "I'm coming down!"

"I'm coming with you," Juliette said.

"For God's sake, Juliette, this isn't a court ball. Stay here where you'll be safe!" Sir Thomas ordered.

Juliette waited long enough to take her pistol from a drawer and follow him. The guards had all disappeared and she realized she was free to go where she wished. For a moment, she thought of packing her things in a trunk and fleeing to the town in order to go aboard some ship bound for England. But without the treasure! Ridiculous! She wasn't about to leave all the gold behind! Quickly, she ran down the steps to the wine cellar and then through the dark corridor. Her nose picked up the sharp smell of gunpowder as black smoke was sifting through the air.

"Thomas!" she called uncertainly, wavering at the last fork. She looked to the right and saw where the door that led to the tunnel had been smashed open. How could the pirates have known about that? Through her amazement, a sudden unwelcome thought was born. The girl had escaped death—that damned girl! Somehow, somehow Kit had found out, had rescued her and she had brought him back here for the treasure! No, not just the treasure, she realized. She had come back for her lover, for Brentwood! Damn! A blind rage pushed her forward into the passage that led to the dungeons.

In the guard room, soldiers were pouring in and the fighting was furious. Pirates leaped out from the passageway, their swords drawn, knives in their mouths. The soldiers used their pistols, but the quarters were too close to get accurate aim before someone's movement caused their arm to move away from their intended target.

Deafening yells and screams, mixing with dying moans and the shouts of the prisoners, made the place a mayhem. Crimson was backed up against one of the walls, trying to search with her eyes for the keys to the cells. If she could find them, she would let the prisoners out—all of them, as Kit had instructed her. They could use the extra help for the soldiers were still coming from the garrison and the pirates would soon be outnumbered.

Finally, Crimson's eyes lit on the iron nail upon which the ring of keys had been placed. Carefully, she began to inch her way towards it, avoiding the struggling humans that practically filled every space of the room. She wondered fleetingly where Delia had gone, but the next instant she saw her bright hair in the opposite corner of the room. She was testing swords with one of the soldiers, her wrist delicately parrying his clumsier thrusts.

Crimson took her eyes away from her to watch the combatants around her. She kept close to the wall, moving so slowly, so slowly. She must be careful or one of the soldiers might guess her plans and snatch the keys before she could reach them. She licked her dry lips and moved closer to her goal.

She had reached the wall where they were hanging, her hand was already extended to snatch them from the nail, when one of the soldiers backed into her after having wounded his immediate assailant.

"What do you think you're doing, wench?" he yelled at her.

His sword barred her from going nearer to the keys and his eyes followed her gaze. Laughing suddenly, he reached forward and took the keys from the nail.

"If it's these you wanted, you'll not get them now, bitch!" he snarled.

He was about to put them in his pocket, when one of the pirates engaged him from behind, his sword going through the soldier's shoulder. A gasp, and the keys fell from his nerveless hand on the floor, nearly at Crimson's feet. Without waiting to see if the man was dead, Crimson bent and snatched them from the ground.

Quickly, she ran to the prison cells, wondering desperately in which one Nick was kept. But she couldn't search each one first. She must throw them all open. In the last cell she opened she came face to face with Nick.

She could see the dark beard on his cheeks, the matted hair and filthy clothes, but it didn't matter. Her arms went around him joyfully and she realized she was laughing and crying at the same time.

"I've found you!" she whispered happily.

"Crimson! What's going on? How did you get here?" he wanted to know, his hands on either side of her head to raise it from his chest.

"Kit! Kit is taking the treasure. He agreed to rescue you, Nick, if I—"

"Kit? It looks more like a pirate crew out there!" he interrupted. "Have you a weapon I can use, Crimson?"

"Yes, here's my knife," she answered, shoving the weapon into his hand. "But, Nick, you don't understand, Kit *is* a pirate. He—"

"No time to explain, darling," Nick said swiftly. "You'll have to tell me when this is all over."

"But—"

Then he was gone before he had even kissed her and she was left holding emptiness. She wanted to weep, kick out, crush something in her hands. All this effort, the danger, the work to free *him*! And he didn't know, didn't appreciate! She brushed away the tears hurriedly. Well, it
434

didn't matter. She would be gone with Kit tomorrow. Let him find out then.

She went back towards the guardroom. The treasure room had already been blown open and she suspected that some of the prisoners would head for there immediately and leave Kit's crew to do most of the fighting.

There was utter mayhem in the guardroom now, and the fighting was still intense. Several pirates and soldiers lay strewn on the ground, tripping up those still fighting. Blood splashed the walls and dripped from wounds. Swords sparked against each other in the moist heat of the room. She could smell scorched hair from men who had backed into the torches in the walls. Everywhere the cries of the dying mixed with the straining grunts of the living.

She picked Nick out at the far end of the room, a sword already in his hand, probably taken from a dead man's grasp. He was fighting with a furious intent despite his days in the dungeon.

She could see Kit, quite close to her, using his sword with a skill that was instinctive in him. He had not bothered to disguise himself and she heard a hoarse cry from behind her on the steps leading up towards the garrison.

"Kit!"

Looking up, she saw Sir Thomas on the step, gazing at his son in total disbelief. The man's face seemed to shatter into a moan and he clutched his chest as he reared back. Was he having some sort of fit? she wondered.

Crimson had stepped towards the old man when a harsh laugh made her whirl around. The soldier who had tried to keep her from taking the keys was laughing cruelly at her while his sword pointed straight at her heart.

"You've succeeded in your little mission, wench, but you won't be getting any of the treasure for yourself!" he shouted.

Crimson darted sideways, just missing his sword. The soldier made to plunge again, but Kit, seeing her distress, hurriedly engaged the man. Despite his wound, the soldier proved a worthy opponent and Crimson watched fearfully as the two men fought furiously.

"Get away, Crimson," Kit puffed. "I'll meet you back at the ship. Hurry before—"

"Kit!" The woman's cry tore through the air.

Reflexively, Kit let his guard down just a moment, wondering if Delia had called to him. The soldier seeing his advantage, drove the point of his sword deep into Kit's chest. Crimson cried out, a cry that was answered by the same woman. Glancing in the direction of the scream, Crimson beheld Juliette's tortured face as she gazed, horror-struck, at Kit's sinking body.

"Oh, Kit!" Juliette cried again, but was prevented from coming to him by the press of combat.

The soldier who had wounded Kit was engaged by another pirate, and Crimson was able to bend down to him, cradling his head in her lap. His face looked pale already and, desperately, Crimson tried to staunch the flow of blood from his chest. Kit coughed, spitting up blood. At the sight, Crimson broke down and sobbed, painful sobs that racked her body.

"Kit, no! Kit, you can't die now!" she pleaded.

He coughed again, trying valiantly to speak to her, to tell her something. Crimson's tears fell unheeded down her cheeks and she bent her head closer to his lips.

"Love—you—Crimson," he barely whispered, his hand trying feebly to caress hers.

"Kit, oh, Kit! Please don't die," Crimson cried, barely able to see his face through the tears. "I love you, Kit, truly, I love you!"

He smiled, lifting the corners of his mouth with an effort. "I—knew—we could—be happy," he murmured with a sigh.

His hand fell away from hers and Crimson hugged his face to her breast, rocking him like a child. Her vision was blurred and her throat was sore from the sobs that escaped her. Kit was dead! He couldn't be dead! She held him tightly, willing the dark eyes to crinkle up at her, to stop staring at her blankly! No, he couldn't be dead!

Through a haze of tears, she looked up, sensing a presence standing above her. Juliette's figure wavered in a blur.

"He's dead because of you!" she declared painfully.

Juliette's face seemed to crumple for a moment and her cry was like that of an animal's in pain. Then, slowly, her hand raised, leveling a pistol at Crimson's head.

"He's dead because of *you*!" she accused deliberately. "I wanted to see you gone—away from him—dead! Now he's gone from me, but I'll see you dead for certain this time."

In the space of a heartbeat, Crimson held her breath and waited for a death she could not even imagine. At the same time, a whirling figure pushed her away even as the pistol went off. The figure crumpled next to Crimson. Delia's golden hair brushed against her shoulder.

Crimson turned almost as though in a trance to see Delia's face turned towards her, her mouth open in a soundless cry of pain, the wound from the pistol ball gushing blood.

Unbelievably, her mouth was moving slowly. "Owed—you—" was all she said before her breath expired in a soft hiss.

47

Crimson woke up in her old room in the castle. Incredibly, she didn't know how she had gotten there. Was she a prisoner? Memory assailed her with gruesome pictures of her friends killed in front of her very eyes. Kit was dead, the promise made between them lost through a soldier's sword point. Delia, dead because of a jealous woman's spite.

Tears threatened once more. And Nick? She had no idea whether he was dead or alive! Heartless bastard, she thought. Kit was dead because he had agreed to rescue Nick.

As though her thoughts had caused him to appear, Crimson glanced up to see Nick appear in the doorway to her room. He was freshly shaved and dressed in clean clothes. A bruise on his temple heightened the whiteness of his old scar, and she noted he limped slightly, as though from a wound in his leg.

"What do you want?" she shot out, hating him at the moment.

He looked at her, his eyes gazing deeply as though searching for her innermost thoughts. She was the first to look away.

"Crimson," he began and there was no mockery in his voice now.

"Go away!" she sobbed. "You're free now, at the expense of two people who died rescuing you, because I forced them into it!"

Nick sighed. "Crimson, I know how you must feel. Perhaps you don't think I appreciated—"

"Appreciated!" she laughed on an hysterical note. "Well, perhaps you ought to send me a thank-you note instead of calling in person. Would that make it easier for you?" she inquired contemptuously.

"Crimson, I'm sorry that Kit is dead. I know what he meant to you."

"Do you? *Do you?* He wanted to marry me, take me away someplace to start afresh. But like a fool I persuaded him to rescue you first! Rescue Nick, the man I was foolish enough to fall in love with first. And he agreed! And now he is dead!"

"Crimson, I'm sorry that he's dead, believe me. I know he saved my life," Nick said slowly, with difficulty.

"Well, at least you can go back to the king now with good news," she flung at him. "I suppose you have ordered Sir Thomas to be put in prison?"

Nick shook his head. "The king's man, Lord Malbrough, arrived only this morning and put Sir Thomas and Juliette under arrest. He'll be returning them back to England." He frowned. "If it hadn't been for Kit—and you, Crimson, Lord Malbrough would have been too late, for I would have been swinging from the gallows at dawn."

Crimson shrugged. "What of the pirates? The treasure? How did you explain all that to Lord Malbrough?"

"There was nothing to explain. The pirates attacked the castle, broke into the treasure room and stole it away. I didn't see the point in giving him the particulars. Sir Thomas had a slight seizure and has been confined to bed since last night. Juliette—"

"Ah, yes, poor Juliette," Crimson interrupted viciously. "Did you find a way to comfort her in her hour of need, Nick? I've heard you've already found it interesting in each other's arms!"

He lifted a brow in the casual sardonic gesture she knew so well. "No more interesting than you found Kit's bed, I'll warrant," he replied smoothly.

"At least Kit was man enough to satisfy me!" she flung at him bitterly, regretting her words the instant they were out as she saw the glitter in his eyes.

"Really?" he drawled dangerously. Stepping closer to the bed, his eyes seemed to pin her to the mattress. "Are you, perchance, insulting my manhood?"

"Your manhood?" she jeered. "Is raping me out in the garden considered an act of manhood? I'm afraid that is the only chance I've had to compare you with Kit, and I'm afraid I've found you sadly lacking."

"Damn you!" He flung the curse out intensely. "Do you know what it cost me to leave you alone every night on this island?"

"Yes," she returned spitefully, "I know exactly what it cost you. A few shillings for the services of a tavern whore!"

Angrily, he stormed towards her and threw back the blanket that covered her. Ripping away her nightgown in one sweep of his hand, he pounced on her, flattening her out on the mattress with the weight of his body.

439

"You've wanted this since the moment you found out I was on the island, didn't you? Didn't you!" he breathed in her ear. "You've ached for me to take you, to make love to you, but you were too damn proud to let me know. Too damn proud to come to me!"

"Me! Too proud!" she interjected, struggling to push him away. "I'll not run after any man," she declared, brushing away the memory of the night she had intended to come to him in his room. "You arrogant bastard! You think so highly of yourself it makes me sick!"

He laughed gratingly. "Words, Crimson, only words you use to deny the real need inside of you. Come on, say it, admit that you want me!" He looked down at her with a searing glance. "Or aren't you woman enough?"

She was so angry she was beginning to cry, and the thought that she was about to humble herself before him made her even angrier. "I'll admit no such thing, you blackguard! Kit was a thousand times better than you! I was a fool to insist that he save your miserable life from the gallows!"

"And why did you insist on it, Crimson?" Nick asked her insinuatingly. "Why? Crimson, I'll tell you why. Because you love me."

In her surprise, Crimson stopped struggling and looked into his eyes, eyes that were so dark blue at that moment that they could have been twin sapphires gleaming at her with some inner flame.

"I love you?" she repeated slowly, feeling heat in her cheeks.

"Yes, Crimson, you love me," he said, beginning to caress her now that she lay still beneath him.

"Well, I—" she began, trying to stir up her anger, not quite sure of the sudden turn in conversation.

"Hush," he ordered abruptly. "Let me make love to you, Crimson. Let me assuage that huge ache that I've caused in your heart."

Crimson couldn't believe he was admitting he'd done wrong. She looked up at him suspiciously, but he only smiled, slightly mocking now. She wondered if he was
440

merely playing with her. How had he known she loved him? Was it so obvious?

"How—" she began, but his mouth on hers silenced her lips.

His mouth—ah, could ever a man's mouth taste so sweet, make her own lips tingle with the sheer overwhelming mastery of his kiss? He parted her lips, capturing her tongue and exploring the inner surface of her mouth. They kissed forever, it seemed, until Crimson had completely lost herself in his subtle magic. She didn't know when he stripped off his own clothes. She only felt his nakedness against hers with a kind of wonder that was quickly superseded by a wave of hunger, of need that crashed over her awareness.

His hands were on her body, caressing her arms and shoulders, moving to her tautened breasts, teasing the stiffened tips before he replaced his hands with his mouth. She groaned softly as he kissed the delicate flesh, his hands moving ever lower until they found that place that seemed burning with a kind of inner fire. His fingers moved to assuage that fire, to build it up to a crescendo that peaked with a sudden crashing inside of her as she melted against him, panting softly.

"Nick," she moaned, clinging to him now as a drowning person clings to his lifeboat.

"Crimson, don't deny me now," he replied softly, bringing his mouth back to her lips, crushing them without hurting, sucking the life breath from her body.

Gently, he parted her legs, positioning himself between them. Crimson trembled, sensing herself on the brink of complete vulnerability. God, how she wanted him then! Her hands brushed his back while her knees arched and her feet rode high on his hips to bring him to her.

As he drove into her, she let out a gasping sigh, closing her eyes as she let her body enjoy the thing he was doing to her. He moved slowly at first, wanting to make sure that she was with him. She followed his thrusts, meeting them with her own, her hands pressing low on his back to bring him back to her each time.

Soon, the dizzying heights of sensual bliss had surrounded them both and they made love with a passion that left them both breathless. Sweat dripped from his brow and their bodies slipped against each other with maddening intimacy. Crimson squeezed her eyes shut and strained against him, even as he quickened his strokes to reach his culmination.

Suddenly, he was pounding her in his frenzy, causing her to retreat for a moment, but in the next instant, her desire burst forth and made her as eager as he. She felt as though she were whirling in some kind of intense vortex that was sucking the life from her body. In a shared moment of incredible joy, they kissed hungrily, feeling their emotions hit a peak of excitement. A white-hot explosion seemed to blossom inside of her, and Crimson sighed into him, letting her body relax.

"Nick," she whispered softly, bringing her hands up to brush at his wet hair.

He nuzzled her shoulder for a moment, where he had collapsed at the peak of their lovemaking. Then he raised himself on his elbow and eyed her, smiling weakly. His kiss was warm, gentle.

"Crimson," he began slowly, "we've both been such fools. Not only because we've denied ourselves this happiness, but because we denied our love to ourselves. Can you forgive me?"

His blue eyes looked deeply into hers, seeking the truth in those depths of smoky blue-green. Her eyes opened wide and she smiled softly up at him.

EPILOGUE:
Love in A New Land

    Crimson sat alone in the king's bed-chambers, glancing around her nervously, her hands twisting together as she awaited the man whose need she had denied before. Her eyes automatically noted the appointments of the room, recalling them from the other times she had been here.

"Crimson!"

He was here, with her, his dark features shaped into a smile that was both happy and unhappy. The black eyes gazed at her with a sense of loss as he moved towards her.

Crimson rose from her seat and curtseyed deeply, keeping her eyes on the floor in sudden overwhelming embarrassment. His hand touched her chin, bringing her face up, tilting it to the light of the candles.

"God, you are beautiful," he whispered almost reverently.

"Sire, you flatter me," she objected in proper fashion.

He continued to look at her, ignoring her remark, and his hand remained under her chin as though afraid that should he let go, he would lose the pleasure of her loveliness. Crimson trembled as the warm gaze of the king washed over her.

"I have just spoken to Nick," the king said slowly, as though realizing that saying the name would break the spell.

"Yes, sire?"

"He—wants to marry you, Crimson." The king smiled tightly. "He asks my blessing—a mere formality if I can tell by the look of him when he speaks of you. But I do appreciate the gesture."

"Sire, we would wish for your blessing," Crimson began.

He released her chin and she backed away from him a little, as though trying to escape his overpowering magnetism. He noted her reaction and, for a moment, a lingering hope showed in his eyes, but he quickly snuffed it out as she spoke softly.

"I love Nick with all my being, sire. In Jamaica, when he came so close to death, I realized that my world would be empty without him."

"He loves you very much, Crimson. You can be sure of that," the king said wistfully. "I had never thought Nick would fall victim to a woman's spell, but you have proven me wrong. But then, you are a remarkable woman, aren't you, my darling?"

She blushed and left his question unanswered.

"But I suppose you are impatient to be with him again, and resent my holding you here so long," he sighed. "Ah, Crimson, if only I could have the strength of a woman's love like yours—" He shook his head quickly and then resumed speaking more briskly. "Such is the curse of men of power," he said, almost to himself.

"Sire, with your permission, Nick and I would like to leave England, perhaps forever, and make a new home somewhere in the Americas." She looked at him beseechingly.

Charles II smiled magnanimously. "My dearest Crimson, if Nick seeks a release from his duties to me, you can be sure I have already granted it. I would not stand in the way of your new-found love, nor your wish to begin a new adventure, a new life in a new land. I would only hope that you would see fit to visit London again in the future. I —would like to see you again." The mask of king lifted for a moment and he was just a man to her, loath to see old friends leaving him.

"Sire, if it is possible, you can be sure we will return," she promised.

He sighed with something like relief. "You are both very dear to me. Always remember that."

"Yes, sire."

He fidgeted with a ring on his finger for a moment. "You will be leaving on the next ship then?"

"We have to clear up some legal matters first," she said. "But we would like to married in our new land, so you can understand our impatience to be off." Her bright smile smote him and he felt the weight of his crown with a weariness that he had never before experienced.

"I understand. If you need any help securing passage on a ship—"

"Thank you, sire. You are most kind."

Kind, he thought cynically. *Ah, if you only knew, Crimson, but my love was so little to you. . . .*

He reached over to bring her close to him, catching her hands in his. Gently, he bent down to take her lips. Crimson hesitated briefly, then her eyes closed and she accepted his kiss. The king's lips were warm, lingering, but her thoughts were on Nick and after a moment he released her.

"I give my blessing to the marriage," he said in a low voice. "Be happy, Crimson. And now—" He turned away from her. "Please leave me."

Crimson reached out to him involuntarily, sensing his inner need, but a moment later, her hand fell to her side and she curtseyed silently to his back. Quietly, she walked out of the room, glancing back once before hurrying into the anteroom where Nick waited for her impatiently.

The sails of the clipper spread with the sudden breeze, a lingering effect of the recent storm. Scattered gray clouds still blocked the sun and Crimson leaned against the ship's railing, watching the receding coast of England for what might be the last time. Beside her, Nick stood with his arm around her waist.

"Are you excited, Crimson?" he asked her softly.

She looked up at him and smiled. "Yes, Nick. I was so pleased with our wedding gift from the king."

"A tract of land in the new colonies. Only a king could be so magnanimous," he agreed, laughing. "I hope you like Charlestown, Crimson."

"I'll be happy, Nick, as long as you're with me," she sighed, leaning her head against his shoulder.

He moved his head to press his lips to the fragrant auburn locks that streamed away from her face with the lifting breeze. His arm was tight about her, his shoulder a strong bulwark on which to rest her head. She sighed with contentment. Nick heard her sigh and pressed a kiss to an unruly auburn curl.

"I love you, Crimson," he murmured tenderly. Suddenly, the sun burst from behind a cloud and a golden ray touched the curl, bringing it to a blaze against his lips. "My Crimson glory," he murmured.

Mary Stewart

"Mary Stewart is magic" is the way Anthony Boucher
puts it. Each and every one of her novels is a kind o
enchantment, a spellbinding experience that has wor
acclaim from the critics, millions of fans, and a permanen
place at the top.